A Curiosity of Consequence

A Curiosity of Consequence

Kel White

VULPINE
PRESS

Published by Vulpine Press in the United Kingdom in 2023

ISBN: 978-1-83919-515-0

www.vulpine-press.com

For my son, Quinn

Overture

With each spin of the wagon wheel, Mado's anxiety accelerated. As he rounded a bend, and the brushland opened into fields, he spotted a farmhouse to the north.

"We're takin' a turn upwards," he said over his shoulder while directing his horse, Chester, along the smaller trail towards it.

Chester had barely slowed to a trot when Mado leapt out of the wagon, rushing his short haffelin legs up to the farmhouse. He struck his knuckles against the door and passed an anxious glance back to his wife, Calarin, who lay in the wagon bed. Sweating. Panting.

The door squeaked open.

"Another knock and run, eh? If only I were quicker on my feet."

Mado turned to the speaker. An older mohra man with shaggy grey hair and a bushy beard that hung to his chest. Woven through it were pink and yellow flowers, seashells, and other trinkets. His eyes sparkled with a prankster's glee as he avoided the haffelin's desperation.

"Excuse me, sir, I need your help!"

"What's this? A disembodied voice, polite in tone but impolite in appearance? Where are you, ghostly speaker?" Calarin's pained scream from the wagon shattered the old man's smile. His bushy eyebrows rose in alarm. "Someone's hurt? Were you attacked?"

"Well, yes. But no," Mado held his hand over his neck, hiding the deep scratches that dripped blood freely onto the collar of his shirt. "That's my wife, fixin' to turn me from a husband to a father!"

1

"Little haffelin, fortunate you," the man fixed his eyes on Mado. "Your luck comes not once, but twice today. I'll fetch my medicines and other kit."

Mado returned to his wife. The old man followed behind with pillows, blankets, and candles to combat the setting sun. He talked her through it. And it was there that it happened, in the back of the family cheese wagon, on the road to Bhaile Cala.

Their daughter arrived.

The old man inspected the new-born, "Clear skin, round pupils. No fangs or quills. No sign of the tornblood at all."

The newly minted parents breathed a unified sigh of relief. The birth affliction that had worried all parents-to-be in the years following the Collision had not found their daughter. They'd been blessed with a perfectly healthy girl.

"Have you a name?"

"Yes," Mado nodded. "Kjara. Thank you, Mister…?"

"Roce. You're welcome, twice-your-luck."

Baby Kjara took a sudden deep breath and cried. It was a loud and piercing howl that drew dark spiral patterns across her skin. Radiating out from her chest, they wrapped around her arms, legs, and neck. The entire wagon shook. The candle flames flared up to ten times their size, and alien shapes flickered through the heat. A deep, droning sound vibrated the air, growing louder and louder. The wood of the wagon buckled and twisted. Kjara continued to cry and the world itself pulsed in time with her wails.

Calarin held Kjara against her chest and began to sing.

The flames died down. The wagon settled. The droning noise faded, leaving the air silent but for Calarin's calming song. Kjara's eyelids closed, and a quiet sleep took her.

Roce broke the silence, "Well…at least she isn't a tornblood."

Though he'd tried to ease the tension, the air tightened with an unanswerable question: if it wasn't the taint of the tornblood across her body, then what, by all the gods, was it?

Chapter 1

Kjara

In Bhaile Cala, Fifthmoon was market day. For Kjara Chedderheart, market day was awful. The stall work was repetitive, the customers intolerable, but the worst part was the heat. A hot day back at the family farm was not a problem. Kjara could roll up her sleeves, or strip down, because no one was around to see her skin. No one for miles. In the heat of Bhaile Cala, despite the bubbling ocean-side breeze, she suffered in sartorial sweat. She couldn't dip her feet in the harbour, she couldn't roll up her sleeves.

Because then people would see.

And they would ask questions.

The only snippets of Kjara's olive skin on show were her wide, pointed ears and round, freckled face. The rest was marked, so she kept it covered. She wore a green vest over a high-necked white linen shirt, brown flax trousers tucked into mid-calf boots, and fingerless gloves.

This morning her dad, Mado, had secured a stall close to the centre of the market square, a coveted location that ensured the greatest flow of traffic and coin. But while he pottered about in the wagon, collecting samples of cheese to display, she made herself appear as small as possible, hoping it might shrink her workload. Considering her haffelin height, all three-foot-ten of it, Kjara would have been successful if not for him.

Mado shot her a look of mild annoyance. "Stop it."

Kjara feigned ignorance, "Stop what?"

"You know what," he said, soft but stern. "Stop sulkin'. Makes it look like you don't want to be here—"

"I don't."

"And it'll put the customers off," he finished.

Her cheeks flushed in frustration.

"Here, arms out," Mado instructed.

Kjara rolled her basil-green eyes and held out her hands.

Mado stacked wheels of cheese into her arms before clambering further into the wagon. "This is good for you, you know," he said as he continued foraging. "It's character buildin'."

"It's soul-destroying," Kjara replied.

Nothing sucked the joy out of her sixteen years of life as fast as work. Perhaps Papa Roce and one of his pranksterous tales could ease the pain of her employ. And being Fifthmoon, she knew exactly where he'd be.

"Can't I go to the temple of Lyrdahl?"

"Nope."

"Just for a little bit?"

"Nope."

"Blasphemer," Kjara accused.

"Nice try," Mado flashed a broad smile that cut dimples into his cheeks. "Won't work."

Kjara groaned in defeat. Working the market often kept her from Papa's sermons, but his routine always played out the same. He would spend an hour sitting on the grass outside the temple of Lyrdahl (the idol of order) proselytising the mighty gospel of *his* god, Fyaldha (the master of mischief). His dishevelled appearance and unconventional delivery attracted both attention and disdain from the worshippers of Lyrdahl, but that was how he measured the true worth of his preaching. Not only did Fyaldha expect its followers to throw a raspberry into the face of the god of order, Fyaldha encouraged it. Or so Papa said. And he matched his love for the god of mischief with years of well-refined trickery, living always by its central doctrines.

"Where's the step ladder?" Mado jumped down from the wagon and walked over to the stall. "You did pack it, right?"

Arms piled high with produce, Kjara shrugged. The step ladder remained exactly where it needed to be, shoved in the back corner of the barn at home. And for good reason, she'd left it there on purpose.

Mado sighed, taking the cheese from her, and stacking it on the counter, "Kjara, it's important to meet the customers at eye level. If you let them look down on you, they will think that they can take advantage of you."

"Well, that works for the mohras and the faeduin," Kjara said smartly. "But then we end up looking down on other haffelins."

"That's not the…" Mado pinched the broad bridge of his nose and took a breath. Reaching into his vest, he pulled out a pocket watch. "I'll see if someone has a few harvest crates we can borrow. Should be time enough before the rush. If anyone comes make sure to—"

"Count the coin carefully," Kjara finished. "I know my numbers."

"I should hope so," Mado tidied her messy, brunette bob cut. "Remember to smile."

"Yes, Dad. I know."

"I'm trustin' you," parental pride glimmered in his eyes. "I love you."

Kjara winced in mock agony, "Go get your crates, then."

Mado strode across the market square, disappearing beneath the bustling, largely mohra, crowd. Kjara leant on the counter of their

6

stall, watching the bluster of the townsfolk. Little mohra children played run-around between the streetlamps, fisherfolk shucked oysters while farmers shook the dirt from their carrots. The local Garnisaire rolled out her latest wallpaper patterns to the appreciation of gathered nobles while the Lanthornist peddled his latest lantern-oil blends. Some burnt green, others burnt blue, though she was particularly taken by a vibrant purple. Aromas of fried fish and saltwater wafted in on the breeze from the harbour, mixing with the rich, earthy scent of freshly dug vegetables.

"It is considered courteous, haffelin girl, to respond when one is spoken to."

The harsh voice brought Kjara out of her thoughts. In front of the stall loomed a large, unpleasant woman. Make-up clumped on the folds of her swollen eyelids and smeared her jaundiced, buttery-white skin. Overstated fabric in a clash of green and pink stretched to breaking point across her body. Hanging by her hip was a chubby, sweaty boy with chocolate-stained fingers and the air of a child mistaking arrogance for confidence.

Kjara straightened up, "How can I help you, miss—"

"*Thairis* Pedigray," the woman corrected, "of the Pedigray estates and holdings. I am hosting a banquet in a few days, and I require cheese. Provide me with samples of your wares. If it is to our tastes, we shall discuss the price of a bulk discount."

"As you like, thairis," Kjara responded.

"It is not 'thairis', girl. It is *my* thairis." Pedigray scoffed. "That is the *correct* way to address one's superior. Surely, a farmer must know that, even if they know little of anything else. The samples, girl."

Pedigray snapped her fingers.

Kjara stiffened, "Kjara."

"What?"

"Kjara Chedderheart," she puffed up, "of the Chedderheart farm."

Thairis Pedigray narrowed her eyes, "Are you being deliberately facetious?"

Kjara tugged on the bottom of her vest and cleared her throat. The woman used foreign words. Or as good enough to a farmer's daughter.

"No," she answered with an uncertain shrug.

Thairis Pedigray's face burned a light shade of red, "Then do as I say and do it with alacrity. That means swiftly."

"Swiftly!" the boy echoed. "Now, now!"

Kjara swallowed her irritation, "Certainly, *my* thairis."

Preparing two samples of an ashed goat's cheese—one of their most popular—Kjara held them out on two flat sticks. The boy snatched one from her hand and shoved it into his mouth. His lips smacked together with a loud, wet slap before he whipped the stick out and tossed it to the ground.

Thairis Pedigray held the cheese up to her nose and took a long, deep sniff. She squinted her eyes in deliberation, before slapping the stick, cheese side down, on her tongue. After a few muffled grunts of embellished consideration, she opened her eyes with a facade of indifference, "How much for twenty wedges?"

"It is one silver per wedge. So, one gold and eight."

"What?" the woman's double chin jiggled with outrage. "Surely you are mistaken."

"I'm quite sure, my thairis. Twelve silver to a gold means one gold and eight."

"I know the exchange rate, child!" Thairis Pedigray huffed. "I am not innumerate. There is no discount to be had if I am to pay one gold and eight. Have you no business savvy?"

"Stupid haffelin, yes?" the boy jabbered, seeking approval from his mother.

She responded by handing him a boiled lolly. He tore the paper from it and crammed it into his mouth, gnawing and drooling. It would be so easy to decline the woman's custom. Even easier to call her out on her pettiness. But Kjara didn't.

"Twenty wedges are of no less quality than one, my thairis," Kjara stated. "And so, the price stands to reason as it is."

Thairis Pedigray snorted, "I'll not spend such outrageous coin on so bland a product. I offer you one gold or nothing."

She snapped open her purse and carelessly flung a single gold piece onto the counter. It rolled to a stop by her hand.

Bland.

A greater insult than any other. Bland, the opposite of flavour, good or bad. Kjara curled her hand into a fist to distract her growing anger, "If you are unhappy with our prices, my thairis, I can return your coin and wish you a good day."

"Fine," Thairis Pedigray grumbled, shrugging the purse off her shoulder. "But I expect free delivery. I shall *not* be fleeced of extra coin for that."

The woman dug about and threw down the remaining coin. She removed a pencil and a small, gilded book, scrawled a few notes, tore out the page and slapped it on the counter.

"Instructions, child. When and where to deliver. Assuming you can read?"

Heat prickled Kjara's neck. Squiggles and lines covered the paper. Crosses, dots, familiar shapes in unfamiliar patterns. Numbers, she knew. Writing, she did not.

"Cheese girl, you've gone silent. And quite red." Thairis Pedigray leant in, pausing for a moment, before erupting into laughter. A hideous bray that battered Kjara's ears. The little boy parroted his mother, burbling out a shrill, slimy cackle.

"Mercy me. I've been bartering with a simpleton!" Pedigray wiped a tear from her magenta eyelid. "Of course, it all makes sense now!

Shall I have my son draw you a picture instead? He's become quite competent with his crayons," her amusement lulled.

Again, she reached into her purse and tossed a handful of coins onto the counter.

"Here, you've earned it. I haven't had a decent laugh in an age. Oh, maybe you could purchase a book with it. A book on how to read!" she exploded with another burst of derisive giggling, slapping the counter with her pudgy hand.

Enough was enough. Kjara boiled over. She snatched up the coins and flung them back. They bounced off the woman's belly and fell to the ground. The laughter stopped.

"Keep it," Kjara curled her lip. "Maybe *you* could buy a salad."

Pedigray's face turned to stone, "Careful, girl. You risk losing my patronage."

"I feed pigs at the farm, not in the city," Kjara snapped. "Take your coin elsewhere."

"How…dare you!" Thairis Pedigray bellowed.

"Kjara! Wagon. Now!" Mado's voice cut through the market bustle, louder and angrier than it had ever been.

Having never heard his voice so fierce, Kjara complied, slumping against the wood in the back of the wagon with her arms crossed in seething resentment. Straining one ear, she could make out some of Mado and Thairis Pedigray's conversation. The woman's words were clear and shrill, more outrage than anything interesting. Mado nodded his head often and responded occasionally. Short words: "Yes. Yes. Of course. I understand. Certainly. Absolutely."

Kjara bit her lip at the instantly recognisable tone. It was the same tone he used when he'd spilled milk all over her mum's sewing or when he had to put down their sickly stock. Whenever guilt was felt, or apology needed. But he wasn't in the wrong. Nor was Kjara. So, no apology was needed. Unless it was from Pedigray. She clenched her jaw, wanting nothing more than justice for the woman's disrespect.

Once Mado finished speaking with Thairis Pedigray, he walked over to the wagon, his eyes glaring beneath grim, furrowed eyebrows. He crossed his arms, "Well?"

Kjara tucked her knees into her chest. "Well, what?"

"Care to explain? Or shall I presume her story is the same as yours?"

"Depends. Is she the hero or the villain?"

"She is the woman who I've just had to calm down because you threw coin at her and insulted her," Mado began. "A noble with considerable reach and influence. So, before I start shoutin' and hollerin', I want to understand your intent."

"She started it," Kjara mumbled.

"She did, eh?"

"Yes! She did. She called me a simpleton. She threw coins at me. She called our cheese *bland!*" Kjara waved her hands in frustration. "You don't believe me?"

"No...I believe you," Mado looked back into the market square as Pedigray haughtily stomped towards the honey stand. "She's a beastly woman, empty soul."

"So, what did you do about it?"

"I gave her fifty percent off her buyin's and free delivery."

"What? She gets rewarded and I get punished?" Kjara scrunched up her nose. "After what she did and what she said? How is that fair?"

"It's not about her. It's about you, your actions, your words. What *you* chose to do," Mado leant in towards her, folding his arms over the wagon edge. "And you chose to stand in front of our namesake and loudly, publicly insult a thairis in the middle of the market."

"She insulted *us!*" Kjara inflated with indignation. "Why can't I call her out on it?"

Mado smiled ruefully, "She's powerful. As powerful as gold gets you. And people with gold they've not had to work for can be very, very small. It's better to humour them, or they might find sport of makin' your life a misery."

"That's daft."

"I agree," Mado rubbed the faded scars on his neck. "But that's how the world is."

Kjara deflated, "If that's how the world is, then I want a different world."

"It's not perfect, I know," a sly grin crept over his face, "but if it makes you feel better, her punishment is worse than yours."

"What's that, then?"

"She has to go on wakin' up every day bein' her."

Kjara thought for a moment. "I guess my punishment comes a close second."

"Punishment? Kjara, this is a valuable lesson," Mado stated, before leaving her and returning to the cheese stall.

Kjara sunk into the corner of the wagon, "Valuable lesson, indeed."

Mutton, the family dog, uncurled himself from his sleep in the opposite corner. A great hulk of a thing, terrifying to look at, but as docile as a lamb. His nails clicked on the wagon floor as he wandered over and dropped his huge head in her lap.

"Hey boy, come to keep me company?"

Mutton blew air from his nose.

"Thanks, you too."

Trapped and bored, Kjara took to people watching. Mohras were such fascinating creatures, like a haffelin that'd been stretched out longways. And so concerned with wealth and appearance. A large array of ladies' fashion decorated the marketplace. Bodices and corsets, embroidered dresses, gigot sleeves and ruff collars, worn by women young and old.

"All that extra cloth," Kjara said, petting Mutton's withers. "They'd hang off me like bedsheets, I reckon. Must cost a fortune."

It was easy to credit her ensemble to a pragmatic lifestyle. Living and working on a farm, it was never wise to have loose-fitting clothes. They could catch on a fence post or a cow's horn. At least, that's what Kjara told people, for the same reason she told them she couldn't swim, so she could avoid removing her clothes in front of others. So that people wouldn't see the dark spirals that patterned her skin, the birthmarks on her and her alone. After sixteen years, her excuses were so well practised they were no different from breathing.

Across the marketplace, Thairis Pedigray's argumentative tones clashed in disagreement with one of the nulls at the Nullifidians' honey stand; an isolated commune that lived outside the city, and outside the care of the gods.

Kjara didn't recognise the null, but if autumn were a mohra he would be it. He was a younger man, nineteen or twenty, with short, straw-coloured hair parted to one side, skin like rust, and a narrow chin dotted with stubble. He wore a sleeveless saffron habit, black scapular, and a sour expression. She frowned, a new recruit perhaps, putting his faith in the faithless.

"Poor fellow," Kjara muttered. "I hope he can read, at least. Look at her, Mutton. Probably trying to sneak another discount. Why do those with the most coin have the most trouble spending it?"

The more Kjara watched Pedigray's performance of petulance, the more she longed for retribution. The woman needed humility. No, she needed to *be* humbled. A valuable lesson of her own. A prank perhaps. But for that, Kjara needed an accomplice, and she had the perfect one in mind.

She scanned the terraced front of The Eyeglass Pub, and sure enough, there he sat. Papa Roce, the pranksterous priest of Fyaldha. The town pest, known by all locals and avoided by most, lest one be found a ripe sport for his trickery. While Kjara took care in her appearance, Papa couldn't seem to care less for his. Frizzy grey hair blew around his driftwood complexion, his overgrown beard and moustache—braided with flowers, seashells, and trinkets—dripped with beer foam. He leant back in his stained brown robes, dirty bare feet propped up on a table, casually watching the markets before letting out an almighty belch and a chuckle.

Kjara glanced back to Mado, deep in the middle of his sales pitch with a potential customer and paying her no mind. She grabbed her haversack and slung it over her shoulder.

"I hereby promote you, Mutton. Keep the rats away, yer? I have a prankster to partner with," Kjara quietly vaulted over the side of the wagon and weaved through the market crowd, tracing a path to The Eyeglass.

Chapter 2

Kjara

Kjara slunk up against the wall of The Eyeglass Pub. Bending down, she grabbed a small handful of stones and tried to underarm one into Papa Roce's beer. It missed and bounced onto the floor. She held her breath and ducked down out of sight.

Her ears probed the air. No creaking wood or sliding chairs. So, Kjara tossed a second stone. This one landed true, with a light plip, and sank to the bottom of Papa's glass. She sidestepped out of view then peered back, waiting eagerly.

The first sip. Nothing. The second, also nothing.

Papa coughed a little. Then another, throatier cough. His eyes darted about, and he attempted to call for the tapster's assistance, but no noise came out. He clutched at his throat, made a retching sound, and slapped his chest. His head dropped to the table, his eyes rolled back, and his frame went limp. His glass toppled to the floor.

Kjara stood in shocked silence, staring at the unmoving old man. She shivered, scurried up on the veranda, and cautiously approached.

"Papa?" she asked, "Papa Roce? Hey?" Kjara reached out a trembling hand and lightly pushed his shoulder. Nothing. She pushed again, harder. Still nothing.

You've killed him, A wave of panic rose up in her. She stepped up on a chair to meet Papa Roce at eye level and gave his head a push. No movement.

"Oath…" Kjara muttered and slumped back in the chair.

Wait…He's old, maybe he just died of old age? Yer, of course he did. And that's what you can tell them when they ask. If you go to get help now, they'll believe you! Get up and run!

As Kjara jumped down to leave, a long rumbling wind drummed against Papa's seat, pitching up into a shrill, squeaking trumpet. She spun around to catch Papa Roce staring at her, his eyes glinting with glee. He stuck out his tongue and let the stone dribble onto the table.

"Sticks and stones, eh, half-your-luck? Could've killed me with that little prank," his smile broke with a dry cough. "By Fyaldha, I think I nearly killed myself. Oh…That's bad." He waved the air from his backside in her direction. "Here, smell."

"Papa, you…donkey!"

The old man let out a bray.

"Are you going to apologise?" she said.

"No chance. That was one of my finest!" he spread his hands out with a showman's flourish. "I call it, paint stripper!" He cocked a fuzzy eyebrow. "Are you not working the stall today?"

"I'm on break," Kjara lied. "Got Mutton to cover for me."

"Careful. The easiest way to lose your job is to let someone more qualified do it."

Kjara widened her eyes and dropped her jaw with mock hurt, "You saying a dog is a better worker than me?"

"Seems you're saying it," Papa answered, "being that you left him in charge."

Kjara winced. The old man was the best disputant she knew, even when he was wrong. But today, he was right. She needed to reset the conversation, guide him in the right direction, "How was the sermon this morning?"

"Record numbers, today. The most Fyaldha and I have ever had!"

"Really?" Kjara said, impressed. "How many?"

Papa leant in and lowered his voice, "Nine."

Kjara laughed, "Nearly double digits!"

Papa Roce swept one arm down to collect his glass. Looking into it, and seeing its contents missing, his eyebrows furrowed. "The price of a decent joke, I suppose," he said. "Another please, over here!"

"A joke? For a moment, I thought you'd shuffled off to The After-All."

"That's what you get for inspecting a body the wrong way. If you want to know for certain, you've got to put your fingers, two of them, here," he demonstrated, placing two fingers against his neck, below the jaw. "Feel that thump? That's your heart beating."

"I know what a pulse is, I just didn't want to prod an old man's corpse."

"Then thinking I was dead is your fault, that's what comes of laziness," Papa scratched himself. "Also, the dead tend to shit themselves. That's another way to tell."

"Then you must be dead too, with the smells you give off."

"No one ever appreciates my work," Papa pouted with mock sincerity, before perking up again as another beer slid in front of him. "Thanks, Ayleth, you're a peach!" he grinned, scooping the glass up in one hand and taking a characteristically loud chug. "Ah, beautiful."

"I know," Ayleth replied courteously, the natural pout of her full lips curling into a smile.

Even though Papa had complimented the drink, not the server, the opposite could have easily been true. Ayleth's appearance was a constant source of fascination, not just for Kjara, but for most patrons of The Eyeglass. Tall and thin, she had bronze skin, high cheekbones and two stiletto ears that stretched back along her head. She appeared ageless, but such was the fortune of the long-living faeduin race. And like all faeduin, Ayleth had no hair on her head. Instead, she grew soft, long feathers that hung and curled like ribbons. They were a shimmering copper tone, held back from her face by a green bandana.

As the finest tapster in the city, Kjara could easily forget Ayleth's blindness were it not for the milky white of her eyes and the speckled scars around them. She stepped away, her yellow dress sweeping back behind her as she deftly weaved through the tables. All eyes were on her as she passed, some with curiosity, others with less savoury intent. The only exception was Papa, who kept his attention firmly on the marketplace.

Kjara recognised the look but played dumb, "What are you looking for?"

An impish gleam sparkled in Papa's eye, "An opportunity for salvation."

"Oh?" Kjara said coyly. The moment had come. "Can I pick one?"

Papa squeaked a thoughtful whistle through his teeth, "Sure."

"There," Kjara pointed. "At the honey stand."

Papa followed her finger, "Oh, excellent choice. Look at that lemon-faced fid."

The word 'fid' was a common though harsh insult for the nulls, but the way he said it removed its heat. He made it feel almost playful.

"All straight-backed and rigid. Godless heathen, he caught me smiling at him earlier, you know, and spun away. That's how afraid of fun he is."

The young null's brow knitted together over sullen brown eyes as he endured the thairis' lecture. Kjara shook her head, "No, no. Not the null. The woman."

"Oh, glorious day!" Papa's eyes glimmered. "A chance to save not one, but two souls from the suffering of solemnity! We will both of us be blessed by Fyaldha for this holy work!"

Kjara beamed with anticipation, "What are you going to do?"

Papa clicked his tongue, "Watch and learn, half-your-luck. Sneaking a stone into a mug is a mug's game. But true mischief...Now, that is an art unto itself. And those two. They are the perfect canvas."

He plucked a yellow flower from his beard and looked at it appreciatively, "Ah, is there any other colour for a lemon, I ask? None better, by truth. So, by Fyaldha, let us paint!"

Papa threw a shrewd wink at her, and dropped the flower into his drink, whispering a few unknown words. Downing the contents in one unbroken swig, he wiped the beer foam from his scraggly moustache and released a powerful, extended belch toward the honey stand. It shook the table with its thunderous force. It scared the nesting birds from the roof of The Eyeglass. Kjara's jaw dropped, and she looked back at the old man with an expression halfway between disgust and admiration.

"The die is cast, my little friend," he said cryptically. "And now, we watch. We wait."

Kjara turned back, fixated on the exchange between Pedigray and the null. Waiting, hoping, as if in a trance, hypnotised by anticipation. The null handed Pedigray a second clay pot of honey.

It exploded.

A sticky torrent of gold sprayed over Pedigray and the null. A waterfall of honey, inexplicably vast in quantity. It splashed down her chest and ran into her cavernous cleavage, soaking through her dress and corset. Sharp splinters of clay pot clattered to the flagstone path. Her eyes widened in shock. The null swallowed nervously. Pedigray, now a dripping mess of incredulity and indignation, glowered at him. Her nostrils flared, and her jowls ignited.

She spewed venomous contempt at him, "You…little…shit!"

Pedigray hurled the remains of the clay pot at the null's head, honey spiralling outwards and into his eyes. He extended one hand to defend, swatting it away from his face. and straight for Pedigray's pest of a child. The broken clay pot caught the boy square in the nose. He threw his head back, bubbling up a maelstrom of snot, tears, and blood.

Pedigray fixed her eyes on the null and lunged over the counter with a primal growl. She swung her drawstring purse for his head, but he bent backwards out of its reach. Having overextended herself, Pedigray lost balance and plunged into the counter. Wood buckled and snapped as it collapsed under her weight, and stacks of honey pots flew into the air.

The null reached out, catching as many as he could, but the remainder crashed down around him and the woman. Sticky oozy puddles seeped into the cracks between the flagstones. Pedigray clambered towards him and took another swipe. He leapt back, finding another pot beneath his sandal. It rolled out from under him, and he toppled backwards. His leg kicked up and out, driving a foot straight into the woman's chins. Pedigray threw her leg back to stabilise herself but slipped in a runny puddle of honey. She grabbed one corner of the stand, but her girth outmatched its construction, and she took it with her as she fell.

Kjara stared dumbly at the mess, frozen in amazement. Pedigray lay trapped beneath a mound of broken pottery and wood. Her child still wailed uncontrollably, and everyone in the market had their eyes fixed on the turmoil.

The null helped the woman to her feet, "Are you okay, Miss—?"

"*Thairis!*" the woman bellowed. She thrust a finger at him. "Do. Not. Move…Guards. Guards!" The woman marched off through the market, a sea of onlookers following her storm of indignation. Her son hurried his plump legs after her.

Kjara couldn't help herself. A giggle turned into a fit of laughter, joyous and unbridled, at the turn of events. The null wiped the honey from his brow and headed for the harbour, glaring at her as he passed. With a nod of appreciation, Papa leant back in his chair and signalled for a fresh round of drinks. Another of the nulls hurriedly cleaned up the broken wood and busted clay pots.

Papa raised his glass, "Peer Darys, fine day!"

The null looked up from his tidying. He gave a wide, honest smile and waved back.

"Fine day, indeed, Papa!" he called back. "A beautiful sun shining day. Did you see all that hullabaloo just now? Remarkable, why I remember a few years back we had…"

Kjara tuned out Peer Darys' natter. She'd rather revel in justice well served than indulge idle gossip. Powerful Pedigray taken down a size, and better than Kjara ever could have anticipated. Not even the null's accusative glare could dull her mood. All was right, and nothing was wrong, and fairness had been restored.

Chapter 3

Kjara

Kjara enjoyed Papa's tall tales of fantastical creatures. The Nofrum, he called them. They were a delight, a perfect conduit for his wild imagination. As the Finer Gods conspired to make mohra and haffelin, he'd say in his sermons, so did Fyaldha make the Nofrum. And he spun his yarns with such conviction that sometimes Kjara almost believed them. His current story concerned the quirble, little ferret-faced creatures. He gestured wildly as he spoke, as though The Eyeglass Pub's veranda had become his new sermon site.

Haffelin elders told infants similar stories to make them go to bed, do their chores, or eat their dinner. But in those stories the creatures weren't little, they were giants. Like the greugef, which were huge lumbering creatures made entirely out of fur that sucked your hair while you slept, leaving it a mess when you woke. But her favourite folk tale was that of the draejr, a creature that Papa swore up and down didn't exist.

"Mushroom growers too, quirbles, well-practised and well-regarded amongst the Nofrum," Papa continued, waving his enthusiasm around. "Once, I saw a quirble-grown mushroom as big as a dinner plate. Bigger, by point of fact! About this much," he held his hands up to indicate the size. "And they adore butter!"

For as good as the story was, Kjara's enjoyment of it was broken by the sight of a guard approaching: a square-shouldered woman, with skin the hue of smouldering coals, and grey-streaked hair pulled tight across her scalp. Her lips ran straight and thin, as though merriment and mirth were foreign languages to her. Sharp, narrow eyebrows cut across her forehead to create an expression of perpetual annoyance.

Rather than the usual guard's uniform of a padded jacket with leather buckles up its centre, she wore a buttoned doublet of blue and white. Instead of a single-shouldered cape, finely embroidered epaulettes adorned her shoulders. A basket-hilted longsword with a tapered diamond in the pommel hung from her belt, balancing a square leather pouch on her opposite hip. But she seemed to have no interest in Kjara. Standing at the stairs leading to The Eyeglass, arms crossed, she glared at Papa.

Papa frowned at Kjara, "Is my tale of quirbles too dull?"

"No," she replied, "but it may need a retelling. It's about to be interrupted."

"Roce. A word," the woman ordered, her voice as sharp as her appearance.

Papa twitched with recognition and turned his head slowly, a sly grin spreading across his face. "Apple."

"What?"

"Apple," he scratched at his chin with his thumbnail. "You asked for a word. The word offered is "Apple". Twice now, by point of fact." The woman's tired eyes blazed a fire. "Is apple not what you were after? I can hardly blame you. I'm not much of a fan of apples myself. Would you care for a different word?"

"What about honey?" she shot back.

"Honey?" Papa frowned with false confusion. "Why honey?"

"You tell me. Why honey?"

The two looked at each other in silence, the woman tensed with mute frustration. Papa took an exaggerated chug of beer, not breaking eye contact. When she seemed at the absolute edge of her patience, he spoke.

"Because it's delicious, sweet, fun at parties. And it has healing properties," Papa burst into rhyme:

"Honey helps if your health has been struck,
You can place it on burns or on cuts,
But if horribly maimed,
Or a sword through the brain,
Then my friend you are terribly—"

The woman drummed her fingers on the pommel of her sword. Kjara shrank in her chair from the subtle threat of force, but Papa straightened up in his.

"Out of luck," he finished.

"And what happens when you spill it?" the woman tapped her foot as Papa stroked his beard in dramatic contemplation.

"Spilt honey?" Papa clicked his tongue. "Why, Captain Deonto, I have no idea what you're talking about."

Captain?! Kjara's heart skipped. She cast a worried look over to Mado. If she could slip away from the table, she could remove herself from the ensuing conflict. Captain Deonto jerked her thumb over her shoulder at the null's honey stand. Peer Darys had collected a mop and was trying with little success to clean the honey off the stonework. Kjara slipped from her chair and faded away from the conversation. Step by step, deftly avoiding the creaky planks, Kjara crept towards the edge of the veranda.

"Oh! Spilt honey, of course!" Papa leant over the table with a secretive hand to his cheek. "I saw the lemon-faced null throw honey all

24

over Thairis Pedigray. It was quite a scene. There were broken clay pots and shouting and all manner of beastly behaviour. I watched the entire thing from over here. The place I have been the whole time since my sermon concluded this morning."

Kjara dropped over the lip of the veranda and listened for any sign they'd noticed her exit.

"You don't believe me," Papa said.

"I never said that," the captain replied.

"You didn't need to say it, I can see you don't believe me. You never believe me."

"Because you always lie, Roce."

"Fine! If you don't believe me, ask my little friend here. Kjara, tell the captain what we saw!" Papa demanded, clicking his finger. "Oh, cheeky. Look, she's run off, but if you find her, I guarantee she'll verify my account of events!"

Kjara scowled, *Thanks a lot, Papa.*

"And where might I find this Kjara?"

"She's Mado's daughter."

"Chedderheart's girl?"

Kjara panicked. It was one thing to shirk her responsibilities, chase a bit of fun, but another altogether if the law became involved. That would be too much trouble. Ignorance would be her shield against accusations from the law, but useless against her father.

Kjara peered out into the market square and cursed. Captain Deonto had stepped away from the pub to speak with Peer Darys, blocking the path across the square. She'd have to take the long way around. South. Behind the pub, behind the town hall, and around from the west. She spun on her heel and ducked low, passing through the laneway between the pub and the bakehouse beside it.

The Eyeglass backed onto a thicketed knoll atop which sat the city gardens. Kjara darted along the thin dirt path that ran between them.

If she were quick, no one would notice her. Passing the backdoor, she threw a glance down the laneway between the pub and the town hall.

As she pelted along the path, Kjara sidestepped a mislaid flagstone and leant up against the back wall of the town hall. She stole another glance across the market. Mado stood by Mutton, hands on hips and face dark with frustration as he surveyed the surrounding area. Kjara swore under her breath. The logical thing would have been to identify herself and answer any questions asked of her. The truly logical thing would have been to follow Mado's instructions in the first place. To have been sensible and stayed put. But sensible was a dirty word. She drew her head back out of sight and continued sprinting.

Out of nowhere, Kjara hit an obstacle. Bouncing off it, she slid along the dirt path on her chest, arms and legs sprawled out. She grogily got to her feet and felt something grab her by the strap of her haversack. Her heart froze.

Kjara slumped her shoulders in defeat and turned to face her punishment. It wasn't Mado or Captain Deonto. The hand belonged to the lemon-faced null, who towered over her, eyes glaring.

"Gods be!" Kjara cried and tugged on her bag. His grip held strong. "Let go!"

The back door of The Eyeglass slammed open as a portly, middle-aged man in dockworker's clothes staggered out.

"Oi! What're youse doing?" he slurred through sunburnt lips. "Youse robbers or robbees? Oi! Rob'ries! Sneak thieves!"

Turning the distraction into opportunity, Kjara tugged her bag strap again and escaped the null's clutch. He reached out to grab her, but she ducked low, bolting through the drunken dockworker's legs, and slamming the back door of the Eyeglass behind her.

"Oi! Wassh out, you basserd!"

The null pursued, throwing the door open. Kjara slipped and dipped between the tables, dodging legs and elbows. She zipped underneath a table while the null, copying her step for step, rounded the bar. As he passed her, she stuck one foot out to trip him and buy herself a distraction, so she could sneak out the back door.

The null toppled forwards into a table of venturists, upsetting their drinks, meals, and temperaments. One of the men, a tall, lean and clearly seasoned fighter, hoisted the null into the air by the scruff of his habit. The man grinned, revealing a row of broken teeth, before bringing his tattooed forehead firmly down on the bridge of the null's nose. He fell back against the table, and the corner of it stabbed into his lower back.

The other men stood up and surrounded him. A voice cried out, "Bar fight!"

The Eyeglass erupted into a bedlam of fists, improvised weaponry, and cursing. The broken-toothed man swung a wild haymaker that hit the null in the ear and knocked him to the ground. At the same time, an errant glass shattered against the man's skull. He stumbled forward, clutching at his head, and tripped over the null's prone body into the table next to him. More patrons entered the fray.

The null crawled towards Kjara, "Come here, damn you!"

She scuttled further under the table. The null tried to chase, but the broken-toothed man grabbed him by the belt and ripped him back up onto his feet.

"Wahay!" the sound of Papa's glee rang out. He twirled around the edge of the room. Moving through the chaos like a dancer through a storm, he drained any half-full glass of booze he saw and lobbed them with abandon into the madness.

A flash of Ayleth's yellow dress disappeared below the bar. Plates of food clattered against the walls, bread and vegetables bounced across the floor. Splatters of sauce painted the chairs and stained the wallpaper.

The null dodged and parried, giving as good as he got. Better, even. The broken-toothed man fell to the floor, eyes closed, beside Kjara. The null followed, dropping down to meet her eye line. She whipped a fist and struck his face. He cried out in pain and grabbed his nose. Another patron tripped and fell on the null's chest.

Kjara crawled out from the table and got to her feet. Somehow, someone was hanging from the ceiling fixtures. Broken tables and chairs littered the ground, offset by the bodies that couldn't keep fighting. The railing against the stairs to the second floor splintered and tumbled to the ground as a hefty man fell into it. More glasses flew across the room.

"Enough!" a voice, full of authority, rang out and silenced the fray.

The pub went still. Improvised weapons—chair legs, glasses, plates—clattered to the floor. The patrons hung their heads, whether in shame or fear Kjara couldn't tell. In the doorway of The Eyeglass, silhouetted against the bright day behind her, stood Captain Deonto.

Jefen, The Eyeglass' proprietor, hurried over to greet her. He was a balding man with thick mutton chops, tawny skin, and dark circles under his eyes, "Captain Deonto. Praise Lyrdahl. Bury some sense into the heads of these reprobates."

"That is my intention," she stated. "Who is responsible for this?"

One of the venturists pointed straight at Kjara, "She is. She came running through and upset the whole place."

Captain Deonto eyed her, "She did? How troublesome a creature this little haffelin must be to set all of you off into such a frenzy." Kjara bit her lip as a strange indignation washed over her. "Jefen, what really happened here?"

"That fella there, the fid. He just ran in, went tumbling into a table of venturists. You know how they are. One slight table bump, and it sets them off."

He didn't just run in. Kjara's cheeks reddened.

"Very well. Null, with me," Captain Deonto pointed at Papa. "You too, Roce."

Papa pouted, "What did I do?"

She ignored him, "Jefen, tally the damages. I will return to discuss it with you."

"Oi, what about the haffelin?" the same venturist whined.

"Give it a rest, idiot," said another. "She didn't do nothing."

"Yer, what could she do?"

"Maybe she stole his butter knife!"

"To use as a sword, no doubt!" A burst of laughter.

"Oh no! Watch out, it's a haffelin! She'll corrupt us with her evil *little* ways!"

"Help lads, she is using her powers on me. I'm sorry, mate. I have to punch you. The haffelin made me do it!"

Another guffaw spread through the pub. Kjara's stomach churned. Her ears flushed with blood.

Captain Deonto silenced the crowd with a look, "Have some dignity about yourselves. The culprit is claimed. There is nothing to be gained by slandering this poor girl. Accept your responsibility for this mess. And be thankful I do not take you all in."

"I have a name!" Kjara snapped, words travelling faster than sense.

"How very good for you," the captain straightened up. "You two, let's go."

Kjara's heart thumped, and her fists curled. The disregard sent shards of resentment straight into her chest, "I did it."

"Pardon?"

"It was me, I said. I started it," the captain blinked, remaining un-convinced. Kjara's eye twitched. "It's true! That null was chasing me. I tripped him up as a distraction, so I could get away from him. Got all the venturists angry at him, so I could escape!"

"Is that so?"

Kjara nodded defiantly.

"And yet here you stand, unescaped," the captain replied. "You'll be coming with me as well, then."

Kjara deflated. Her sense caught up to her words, anger gave way to regret. Captain Deonto marched her down the stairs of The Eye-glass and across the market square. Peer Darys, eyeing the null, shook his head mournfully. A few of the wealthier-looking folk gave a cheer at seeing Papa Roce in custody. He responded by loudly proclaiming his innocence. Repeatedly. Kjara hung back behind him, trying to make her small frame even smaller. It wasn't enough.

"Kjara?" Mado's voice.

Kjara winced.

"You found her!" Mado said, running across the square. "Care to explain your whereabouts?"

Kjara dropped her eyes to her boots.

"Mado Chedderheart," the captain explained. "If you wish to speak with Kjara you will need to attend the Guardhouse this afternoon. Your daughter has been arrested."

Chapter 4

Kjara

Arrested.

Kjara sat curled up on the bunk in her holding cell. Cold brick walls. Thick iron bars. Lumpy bed. The null sat in the cell next to her. Papa opposite him, on the other side of the hallway. Captain Deonto strode down the corridor, pencil and notebook in hand, and out the far door.

Arrested.

"I'm innocent!" Papa called after her. "Innocent, I say!"

Stupid, stupid girl. Why speak up when silence would keep you free from consequence? With nowhere else to go, her anger threw itself at the sullen null.

"This is your fault, you know," she said.

The null, sitting legs crossed and eyes closed in the centre of his cell, ignored her.

"Hey, you hear me…fid?" Kjara spat the nullifidian insult out but again got no response. Kjara pouted and slumped back against the wall. "Deaf and mute. Brilliant."

Papa had put a pause on his complaining, instead searching the ground for any pebbles, rocks, and other bits. He had started to gather quite a collection, and his activity drew Kjara's curiosity, "What are you doing?"

He offered no answer. Instead, he pressed one finger to his lips and jerked his head in the null's direction. Despite her sour situation, Kjara smiled and shook her head. Even the arrest couldn't stop Papa's pranksterous personality, and it was somewhat admirable, in the way that persistence often was. Kjara adjusted her sitting position, so she could have a clearer view of the null and Papa, and waited to see what the old man had planned.

It was a little underwhelming, considering his previous work. Nothing unexpected or surprising. Just an old man piffing rocks. Kjara scoffed, "I thought throwing stones was a mug's game."

Papa shrugged, tossing another pebble across the corridor. It tinged against the metal bars of the null's cell. Papa rolled his eyes and sorted through his collection for another projectile.

Kjara clicked her thumbnail, "Why is she taking so long?"

"Probably sharpening the gallows," Papa said.

The blood rushed from her face, "That's not very comforting, you know."

"You'll be fine," Papa waved his hand dismissively. "She's not going to kill you."

"Dad might."

Ting. Another miss.

"Look, in five years this won't matter, so why make such a deal of it now?"

"Because I've never been arrested, Papa!" Kjara cried.

"Neither have I."

Clink. Closer.

"Liar."

Papa, lining up his next throw, paused, "Why don't people ever believe me?"

"You're awful calm, then," Kjara chewed her lip. "You're not afraid of punishment?"

32

"Punishment is for the guilty, I'm calm because I'm innocent. De-onto will just huff and puff like she always does. All threats and warn-ings. But she knows *she* can't do anything because *I* didn't do any-thing."

"That's not true," the null responded, snatching Papa's last pebble out of the air before it hit the ground.

"Oh, he speaks!" Papa exclaimed. "I think you should check your innocence before you go accusing other people."

"I didn't accuse you."

"Just as well. Because. Glasshouses. Throwing stones. All the rest of it."

The null pursed his lips, "I didn't do anything."

"You chased me through a pub!" Kjara said.

The null sighed, "I wanted to ask you a few questions."

"And that's how you do it?" Kjara asked. "Attacking people from behind?"

The null dropped his head, "I didn't attack you. I was trying to get your attention."

"You grabbed my bag!"

"You might have run if I didn't."

Papa scoffed, "Ah, purse snatching. The noblest pursuit!"

"Oh, would the lot of you quit your bleating?!" snapped an irri-tated voice from the cell next to Papa.

A girl of about eighteen or nineteen, with scarlet red hair to her shoulders, seashore skin and blue eyes, sat up from her bedroll. She was curved where Kjara was flat, flat where Kjara was curved. She wore a loose-fitting blouse with full bishop sleeves, and a pair of high-waisted tan breeches with fine gold buttons adorning the hips. Her feet were bare, but a set of moss coloured knee-high cavalier boots lay by her side.

"You're making enough noise to wake the dead. Ain't none of you been arrested before? Rule one. Speak soft and respect the quiet. People here might be praying...or sleeping off a hangover."

Kjara's curiosity piqued, "Is this not your first time here?"

The girl laid back against the bars, "Me? Oh no, I'm a regular."

"So, how long does it take before we can get let out?"

"Depends. Did you steal? Did you kill?" The girl pulled on her boots as she spoke. "Oh, did you set fire to anything? Or did you upset the shrug by being too independent of a thinker?"

The girl used the slang term for the guards, 'the shrug'. The term came from the single-shouldered capes the guards wore, but also because when they questioned the less savoury individuals on matters of misconduct, all they'd ever get as an answer was a shrug. It was not a term typically used by the law-abiding, meaning the girl was most definitely trouble.

Papa cleared his throat, "I didn't do anything. I'm innocent."

"Me too," The null added.

The girl raised an eyebrow, "If you're innocent, I'll eat my boots."

"It was just a little marketplace scuffle," Kjara said. "...That spread into The Eyeglass and caused a slightly larger scuffle."

The girl slapped her thigh with delight, "Ah! The worst of all then, mayhem! You'll be here for life, no doubt."

She must have seen Kjara's concern. Her voice softened.

"You'll be here a couple of days, tops. Although with The Satin Bull coming to town, it might be a tad longer. The fancy folks don't care much for us causing any ruckus while they're about. Makes the place look bad."

Kjara had heard of The Satin Bull. Most people had. It was a moniker provided to the naistinn of Cradh, Loreena Farlight, to describe the way she ruled. Soft and elegant but stern and strong. Papa and the null glanced at each other before speaking in unison.

34

"The Satin Bull is coming to town?"

"Yer," the red-haired girl replied. "But not just her. I heard the Regal-apparent Londre Tamou is coming over as well. All the way from Glainne. That's why the captain is so antsy, I reckon. She'll probably keep you lot in here until they've done their business and left. So as not to have you messing up the place and making an embarrassment of the region master."

"What business have they here?" the null asked.

"And how do you know about it?" Papa added.

The girl shrugged, "Couldn't tell you, but I reckon it's something big if it warrants the attendance of not only our naistinn but the son of our neighbour's head of state as well. Maybe The Satin Bull has finally succumbed to the idea of an heir and is ready to wed."

Papa shuddered. Kjara wondered if it was because of the idea of a wedding, or the arrival of the heads of state, or both.

"That makes no sense," the null said. "There's nothing to be gained by a union with Glainne. Cradh is already part of the Aonadh."

The girl narrowed her eyes, "What's your name?"

"Soren."

"Right. Okay, Soren," the girl straightened up, "let me explain what a joke is."

Soren pursed his lips, "I know what a joke is."

"Are you sure?" the girl turned to Papa. "He always this bad at smiling?"

Papa shrugged, "I've only known him a day."

The girl unrolled her make-shift pillow, a knee-length velvet doublet, and slid it over her shoulders, straightening the collar, "Anyway, since you've gone and disturbed my sleep, I think I might go find someplace else to nap."

She tapped her foot against the stone tiles on the floor of her cell. Finding one looser than the others, she reached down, pried it out of the way and collected a few thin, metallic tools. With her arms through the cell bars, she began working the latch. The null went to speak, but the girl silenced him and rested her ear against the lock. After a moment, a distinct clicking sound signalled her success, and she bumped the cell door open with her hip. She tossed the tools back into her hidey-hole and slid the stone back into place with her foot. Giving a curt bow, she stepped out of her cell and strolled down the corridor towards the exit.

"Where are you going?" Soren asked.

"To collect my things."

"Oi, aren't you going to let us out as well?" Papa called after her.

"You lot? No chance. You three are trouble."

And with a pull on the heavy wooden door, she disappeared.

Chapter 5

Kjara

The hours passed in relative monotony. Though Kjara's panic had dropped to a dull fuzziness in her gut, it hadn't completely disappeared, and when the door to the south swung open, it rose back up with full force. She had expected to see the captain, and true enough there she stood. But the addition of Mado sent a wave of nerves curling through Kjara's belly. She turned to Papa for reassurance, but he had passed out, softly snoring in his cell.

Mado walked up to her cell, his face painted with solemnity. Kjara scrunched herself up, avoiding eye contact as he approached. He waited there a moment, hands on hips, a key dangling from one finger. She said nothing.

He blew air from his nose, "I've been speakin' with Captain Deonto, and accordin' to the publican, the total cost of damage done at The Eyeglass today was thirty-five gold pieces."

Her throat tightened. Thirty-five gold was more than Kjara had ever even seen at once and it would take two months of solid market day trade, at least, to make that kind of coin. She tried to imagine how much it would weigh, how much space it would take up. And what she could buy with such a bounty.

Mado tapped the iron bars, bringing her attention back to him, "Bein' it was you that was responsible for it. You'll be goin' about paying it back."

Kjara tensed her jaw, "It wasn't my fault."

"Maybe not all of it, but half at least."

"But—"

"I haven't finished," Mado glared. "There's more cost been tallied up here than gold. There's also the cost of the good captain's time. And the harm you've done to our farm's reputation. And the hurt you've caused me. I gave you a job to do, Kjara," he thrust his words at her like a knife. "I trusted you. And twice you broke that trust."

"I'm sorry," Kjara mumbled. "I am. Can't we just go home? I'll do my punishment. Four weeks of dawn feeding, if I must. Eight weeks, if it'll make you happy."

Mado shook his head, "That won't do. Not with the debt you've accrued. The captain and I have already decided on a consequence for your behaviour. Bein' that you need to learn some responsibility and accountability, and I seem to be doin' a poor job of teachin' you…you'll be staying here. Workin' for the captain, until you've paid off your debt, and whatever interest she sees fit."

Shock flooded her fingertips and numbed her hands, "What?! You can't leave me here? Where will I stay? What about clothes? Food? My duties back at the farm?" Kjara threw every excuse she could muster at him, hoping to replace her punishment with something more lenient.

"The captain has kindly offered board right here in the guard-house. You'll be her ward. She says it won't be free though, you'll be workin' for your keep and your food. Between your livin' expenses and the debt, we figure it'll take about two months to pay it all back."

"You're serious…"

Mado nodded. It was a ridiculous suggestion. Two months of distance from her family. Sleeping in a guardhouse. A terrifying thought occurred. *What if this cell is my accommodation?*

"Can I at least say goodbye to Mutton before you go?" Kjara pleaded.

"Yer," Mado unlocked her cell. "And I dare say he'd have some things to say to you too."

Kjara joined Mado's side and walked towards the exit, "Mutton can't talk, Dad."

"Shows what you know."

Outside, Kjara walked down the cobbled steps of the guardhouse towards the family wagon. Mutton lounged about beneath it, chewing on a stick. Chester stood tied to the hitching post near the entrance, nose deep in the watering trough. The stall had been packed flat and strapped down in the wagon. The shade cloth hung over dense mounds of cheese.

"We didn't sell much..." Kjara said.

"Yer. Had to pack up early. Wanted to make sure I had enough time to make it here," Mado ran a hand through his curly hair. "I'll be takin' most of what's left to The Eyeglass. A quick drop off on the way home. Free of charge."

He didn't need to say why. Kjara swallowed and rubbed her forearm. More money lost, not only from lack of sales but also from compensation. The day's events had left an impact on the family. Any remaining stock would last another week, and it could still be sold. At a discount. But it needed storing until then, and she'd not be at home to help unload it.

Mutton perked up as Kjara got closer, and he ran up to her, barking a happy hello. She bent down and scratched his chin in response.

"Hey there, doggo," she said. "You're a good watchdog, aren't you?"

He snorted and rolled onto his back, pawing at her arm for attention. She obliged, rubbing his belly. With all the anxiety and confusion in her guts having subsided, her hunger resurfaced, "Dad...can we eat something before you go? I've still not had lunch."

Mado looked to the sun, "Yer, I should have enough time."

They settled into the back of the wagon, side by side, legs dangling off the edge. A spread of fruit, bread, and cheese between them.

"So," Kjara began after her stomach had been satisfied, "you're really going to leave me here? All by myself. With no one."

"I know what you're tryin' to do," Mado said, taking an apple slice. "It won't work."

Kjara chewed her lip. Regular guilt gathered no traction. It was time for advanced guilting. She unbuttoned her sleeve cuff and rolled it up, exposing the black spiral pattern on her skin. "What about this? What am I supposed to do about this?"

Mado looked at her arm, and his eyes softened. He stayed silent for a moment, a thoughtful expression on his face. "I'll be back next Fifthmoon for market. I can bring some of your personal effects if you tell me what you want. In the meantime, you'd best keep yourself clean because you'll have naught but what you keep on you until then."

"Aren't you worried someone will see?"

Mado rubbed the faded scars on his neck, "It's not about me, is it?"

It wasn't that he didn't care, Kjara could see as much on his face. But for some other reason, one that she couldn't pin down, his words made her awkward. When all other times he'd have something to say—some wisdom to impart—this time, nothing. Perhaps it was his lack of answer that did it. Kjara adjusted the strap of her haversack.

"This is a good thing," he said after a time. "Truth be truth. You've been given an opportunity."

Kjara picked a seed out of her apple slice, "I've been given a punishment, is what. As good as being put to the noose, but the noose being preferable. At least that would be a quick death."

"If it's a quick death you're chasin', keep runnin' off when you should be keepin' put," Mado replied, popping a wedge of cheese into his mouth. Kjara rolled down her sleeve and sighed. Not even the threat of exposure worked. Nothing would change his mind. Kjara had to be honest with herself. And him.

"…What if I make a mistake?"

Mado paused and took a long hard look at her. His crow's feet crinkled at the corners of his eyes, "Then fortunate you, to make a mistake. Some people never even get that far."

"A haffelin working for the guard," Kjara picked the dirt from her nails. "I'll look like a fool."

"A fool, you say?" Mado stroked his chin and took a flick knife from his pocket. "Here. Pass me an apple from Chester's bag. And a cheesecloth."

"…Why?"

"Go on, humour your old dad."

"Fine," Kjara huffed, leaning across the wagon and taking an apple from a hessian sack. Fetching the cheesecloth, Kjara passed them both to Mado. He took two small bites from the apple, leaving divots on its surface. Then he took a third bite, long ways beneath the first two, but kept the flesh attached by the skin. "What are you-?"

"Wait for it," he said, before stabbing through the centre of the cheesecloth with his knife and inserting the blade into the core of the apple. He spun around, holding his knife with one hand, the cloth draping over his forearm.

"Hello there, haffelin girl!" he spoke in a squeaky voice, shaking his arm, so the apple flesh flopped up and down like a mouth. "I hear you're the new recruit!"

"She is, indeed!" Mado answered.

"Fantastic," cried the apple, "I couldn't have *picked* a better one myself!"

Kjara groaned.

"If you want any tips," the apple said, "I have all the in-cider in-formation!"

"Apple guard," Mado chastised, "do you have to make these core-ful jokes?"

"I apple-ogize for my behaviour."

Kjara grabbed the apple and lobbed it over to their horse. "Chester. Lunch."

"Hey!"

"It was for your own good. You looked incredibly foolish."

"I did? Perfect. Let's see what happens."

They sat in silence for a few moments, Mado looking around with fearful eyes as if searching for encroaching danger. Kjara tapped her heel against the wagon but soon grew tired of the act, "Nothing is going to happen, Dad."

"Exactly," he replied. "Nothin' is going to happen. You'll be fine. You might even enjoy it."

"Maybe…" Kjara shrugged. "You know, the captain stopped the whole pub with a single word today. Everyone, they all listened to her."

"Ah," Mado nodded sagely. "That's the kind of power gold can't get you."

"What's that, then?"

"Respect."

After lunch had all been eaten and tidied away, Mado harnessed Chester and prepared to take his leave. Being that Kjara couldn't write, and neither could read, she relied on repetition until she felt confident enough he'd remember her requests; two fresh sets of clothes, a comb (the wooden one, not the bone one), her dice, and her deck of cards. She expected to have some free time, and the dice and cards were her way of occupying it. Mado was dubious but agreed to bring them all the same, assuring her that he would remember them for next Fifthmoon. As Kjara gave her farewell, a sudden strange urge welled up in her chest. Before Mado could hoist himself up onto the wagon seat, she threw her arms around him in an embrace.

"What's all this, then? Huggin' your old dad out in public?"

"I don't know. I'm just going to miss you."

Mado let out a soft chuckle and returned her affection, "Now, don't go about bein' so fretful. It'll only be two months. Less even, I'll be back in a week. What's the worst that can happen?"

But even though he projected a sense of ease with his words, his arms squeezed around her a little tighter than usual.

Chapter 6

Kjara

Kjara woke up a little nervous, a little tired, and a little stinky. It was her first day on the job and the full extent of her duties had not been explained to her. Her imagination buzzed with possibilities. Even so, the scraps of sleep she got were few and far between. If it wasn't the strange sounds of the city or the snoring guards that woke her through the night, it was the occasional complaint of Papa from the cells below.

Kjara had been assigned a bunk in the guard's quarters, much to her dismay, but Deonto had made a point of respecting her privacy. She had arranged for her to have a corner bunk and strung up sheets to separate her from the rest of the guards. Even so, she had remained fully clothed, except for her boots. The extra layers, coupled with poor ventilation, had created perfect conditions to amplify her body odour.

Food first, Kjara decided. *Then freshening up. If I can find some-where.* No noise came from behind her makeshift curtains, so she peeked through them. The bronze and orange shades of dawn light washed in through the windows. Bunks, footlockers, but no guards. *Pre-dawn start?* Kjara thought, pulling on her boots. *Not so different from the farm.*

As she approached the door to leave, it swung open. A young mohra guard stepped through, yanking his cape over his head. He walked straight past her and threw it on top of a bunk along with his

44

sword. He had short, brown hair, tan skin, and a broad-shouldered, athletic build. When he threw off his shirt, she cleared her throat.

He spun around. Brown eyes with heavy dark circles. Not attractive necessarily, but not unattractive either. Right on the cusp of handsome.

"Oh! It's you," he said.

"Hi."

The guard scratched his head, "Weren't you the haffelin in the lockup yesterday?"

"Yer. I was. Now I'm here. Under instruction from Captain Deonto."

"The captain?" he chuckled. "You're serving your sentence as a guard, then?"

"Is that funny to you?"

"A little, yer. You don't think so?"

Kjara clenched her teeth, "Because I'm a haffelin?"

"Because you're a criminal," he yawned and dropped onto the edge of his bunk.

"I'm not a criminal."

"Oh?" the guard began unlacing his boots. "Put in lock-up by mistake, eh?"

"It was a misunderstanding," Kjara lied.

"Not like the captain to make mistakes."

"It wasn't a mistake; it was a misunderstanding."

The guard smiled and extended his hand, "I'm Harwin."

Kjara returned the handshake, "Kjara."

"Nice to meet you. Now if you'll excuse me. I have a date with a mattress," he began to unbuckle his belt.

"Where's the kitchen?" Kjara asked, hoping her question would halt his undressing.

Harwin pointed, his other hand still on the waist of his trousers, "Downstairs, left-wing. Far end of the mess hall."

"Thank you," Kjara said, turning away before the sound of fabric hit the floor.

Kjara took to exploring the guardhouse as best she could and, following Harwin's directions, entered the mess hall. It was a drawn-out room, with two rows of long tables and bench seating. The far end had a serving area, with the kitchen behind it. Picking through the ample larder, she found some bread, butter and raspberry jam, and fashioned a sandwich.

Wandering through a door in the eastern wing, Kjara entered a strange long room with a sunken centre full of water. Not a huge pool by any means, but big enough to house maybe four to six people at a time. There was an anteroom to the north and one to the south, and an archway at the far side. She'd heard of bathhouses but had never been in one, and was pleased to find that, like all the other rooms, it was empty.

Kjara pushed the last crust of her sandwich into her mouth with her thumb, dusted off the crumbs from her shirt and peered into the water. To strip and soak was not an option.

Too deep. Too open.

Kjara grabbed a washcloth and a pail from the corner, filled it with water, and ducked into the southern room. Even sitting on the wooden bench against the wall, Kjara felt too exposed and decided a brief wash of the extremities would have to suffice. It would be quick and easy to roll down her sleeves if someone approached, but not so if Kjara had to throw her whole outfit back on.

Kjara peeled off her gloves and rolled up her sleeves. Unsightly black spiralling patterns covered the backs of her hands and ran the length of her arms. Kjara grimaced.

"You see them cows out there? With the black and white patterns?" she began, mimicking Mado's voice. "We call it piebald. Happens to cows, sometimes horses, birds, dogs. We figure sometimes it must happen to haffelins, too."

"So why do we hide them?" Kjara asked herself.

She answered with a word-perfect recital of a moment etched deep into her memory, "There's enough reasons for folks to find fault with one another. No point adding fuel to the fire."

Perplexed, Kjara traced one of the patterns along her forearm with her finger and sighed. They appeared darker than usual.

Maybe it's just the light in here. Kjara figured, dipping the washcloth into her bucket and scrubbing her forearms. The water was like ice on her skin, but apart from that, it was like every other puddle Kjara had encountered. It didn't wash away the patterns either. Nothing got rid of them. Not even scraping them off with a blade. No, all that caused was pain and blood. Kjara ran a thumb over an old scar near her elbow.

If you had all the power, what would you do with it?

Kjara chuckled, "That'd take the kind of power gold can't buy."

You mean like the kind of power Captain Deonto has?

Kjara rubbed the washcloth along the nape of her neck, and across her face. Undoing the top few buttons of her shirt, she scrubbed the cloth under one armpit. Footsteps echoed towards her, so she whipped her hand out and buttoned back up. She reached for her gloves but hadn't the time to put them on before a figure turned into the doorway of the anteroom.

"Fine dawn," Captain Deonto said customarily. Kjara noticed that her right eye was bruised and slightly swollen, and she had a dull red cut along the tip of her cheekbone. But she was too struck by courtesy to question why. Hurriedly, she shoved her hands under her thighs.

"Fine dawn," she answered with an awkward smile.

"I went looking for you. You weren't in your bunk."

"Yer. I thought I should get ready for the day."

Captain Deonto looked at the bucket with a raised eyebrow, "You've not used a bathhouse before?"

Kjara's cheeks prickled with heat. *What have I done wrong?* she thought, worried and self-conscious. *Did I grab the wrong cloth? Is this bucket not for water? Gods be, what if it is for peeing in? Have I washed myself with a pee bucket?!*

Kjara shook her head, "No, Captain. Truth be truth, I have not."

"Right. Come with me," Deonto ordered, gesturing with one finger.

Compounding fear swept over Kjara. If she stood up, Deonto might see her hands, if she stayed seated, she was refusing an order. Would she get in trouble for that? And if so, what would be the punishment? Kjara delayed her decision with a question, "Where are we going?"

"If you've never been to a bathhouse, you should learn how it works."

"Isn't it just a big pit with water?"

Immediately after the words left her mouth, Kjara recognised the ignorance of her question, and her heart sank. If it weren't more than just a big pit of water, there would be no need to show its inner workings.

If Deonto was amused by Kjara's lack of knowledge, she didn't show it., "No. It's not. Now come along."

Kjara stood to her feet, hands behind her back. Deonto turned and walked past the bath to the far side of the room. Kjara snatched her gloves off the bench and jammed her hands into them, keeping a careful eye on the captain.

She led Kjara through the doorway on the far side of the bathroom, and down a narrow set of stairs curling back underneath the bath. The bottom widened into a simple room with a low ceiling, not much higher than Kjara herself. Deonto had to stoop her head as they entered, but Kjara's height made it easy for her. A fireplace had been built in the wall beneath the nearside of the pool and a small stack of cut wood sat beside it. There were also several metal tools including a poker, shovel, brush, and a pair of tongs.

"This is the furnace for the bath. It heats the water. It takes some time to heat up but stays hot for quite a while."

"How does it work?" Kjara asked.

Deonto bent down and pointed through the fireplace, "Those brick pillars in there, they sit directly below the bath, and on the far side, see those little holes in the wall? They are the flues. When the fire is on, the flues help draw the heat through the pillars and under the bathwater, heating it."

The concept of using hot water for bathing was something Kjara had never considered. Washday for Kjara's family back at the farm consisted of taking a long walk down to the river with a basket of clothes. Slipping in cow manure was never a problem on the way to the river, but gods be with anyone who slipped up on the return journey.

"I didn't know bathhouses used hot water," Kjara said. "We've only ever used hot water for tea and the like. It seems a bit strange to soak someone in it."

"It is quite a ritual for some. I've heard nobles add scented oils and perfumes to the water. Gods know why, though, seems rather wasteful. We only light ours up once a week. It gives the guards a chance to soak any injuries sustained while performing their duties," Deonto explained. "Clinician Rosalind, amongst others, believes doing so greatly assists in the healing process."

"What day do you light it up?"

If it was today, Kjara might get the chance to try it.

"Firstmoon," Deonto answered.

Tomorrow, then. Not long to wait, Kjara thought but she was still too nervous to ask outright if she would be allowed to use it, "It's fascinating."

"It's not without its drawbacks. Like all machinery, it needs maintenance and upkeep. The water needs emptying and refilling. The tiles of the bath need swabbing, as does the floor of the bathhouse. The wood needs to be chopped, brought down here, and stacked. The coals from the fire need shovelling, the ash needs sweeping away. The flues need clearing. And see the blackness on the pillars? That's smoke residue. It needs to be scrubbed away, too. And the pillars need to be checked to make sure there is no degradation. If they break down, the bath could collapse, and this whole area would end up underwater."

Kjara's stomach tightened, "When does all that happen?"

"Today. Before lunch. Then you will report back to me. Welcome to the guard, young Chedderheart. You've got your list. I suggest you get started promptly."

When Captain Deonto said the chores were to be completed before lunch, Kjara had mistaken her to mean a specific time of the day. But when Kjara knocked on the door to the captain's office a few hours later, she was made aware of her error. The captain explained to her, with greater clarity, that lunch was *not* to be provided to her until *after* her assigned tasks had been completed. At that point, Kjara had only made it halfway down the list. Still, she made a vain attempt to convince the captain of a light snack to relax her hunger-knotted stomach.

She failed.

By the time Kjara had finished her work, the sun was a tiny sliver over the horizon, and she was ruined. Manual labour she could handle, but labour without respite or meal breaks pushed her to the edge of tolerance. When at last Captain Deonto came to inspect the bathhouse, she presented Kjara with yet another task, much to her surprise and more to her dismay.

"As you will be fixing yourself a meal, you may as well feed the lockups," Captain Deonto instructed. "Roce may have a simple sandwich and a glass of water. Nothing more. You may help yourself to the larder as you wish. But be advised, the costs of your meals will be tallied up and added to your debt. The more you eat, the longer you'll work. There is a leather-bound supplies ledger on the kitchen counter with a page marked for you. Be sure to document all of your takings."

Kjara scrunched up her nose. The captain gave her a sidelong look, "Is there something you wish to say?"

Kjara cleared her throat, "No."

"Then you may go."

Kjara nodded and turned to leave as Captain Deonto shuffled some papers on her desk. As she approached the door, the captain stopped her.

"One other thing," she called. Kjara's skin prickled. "You worked well today, Chedderheart."

Kjara's chest swelled with a feeling she couldn't quite explain, "...Thank you, Captain."

"I expect the same tomorrow."

Chapter 7

Kjara

If it weren't for her overwhelming hunger, Kjara might have been put off by the demanding and meticulous instruction from Captain De-onto to document her meals. But once in the kitchen, the concern evaporated. Her stomach assured her that whatever score she accrued could be worked off.

Searching through the larder, Kjara fixed a heaping plate of food. Two pieces of flatbread with savoury relish, three figs, an apple, a sprig of grapes, some quince paste, a quarter wheel of hard cheese and a tall glass of milk. For Papa, she made a tomato and cheese sandwich, with spinach leaves and butter. And a glass of water.

Kjara threw the tomato offcuts into the compost bucket beneath the kitchen, and a wicked thought sparked in her.

"Slow revenge beats no revenge," she reasoned, taking a few potato peels and stuffing them into Papa's sandwich. "Perfect."

Placing everything on a carrying tray, she stepped down from the stool she had been using to reach the bench.

"…Ugh, the paperwork."

The ledger rested open between the knives and some hanging pots, with a pencil affixed to it by a piece of thread. With some hesitancy, Kjara leant across to fetch it. The pencil untangled and tapped along the benchtop as she pulled the book closer. "So, which page is yours, then? Well, you're the most recent addition to the guardhouse. So probably the last page with scribbling on it."

Kjara took a breath and flicked through the ledger, recognising the numbers but none of the words, until she found it. There were a few scribbles on the page, and some lines drawn lengthwise to separate each sequence of symbols at the top. She turned back to an earlier entry and, matching the column symbols with numbers in it against a similar one on her page, wrote down the number "2". In the column to the left of it, she drew a crude picture of flatbread. Continuing in this pattern, she wrote down the numbers of each of her takings, alongside a drawing of the food.

Kjara closed her eyes and sighed deeply, before shutting the book, picking up the tray and heading to the cells. Harwin stood in front of the thick, mahogany doors to the lock-up.

He smiled, "How was your first day?"

"Different," Kjara replied delicately.

"Yer, I'll bet it was," Harwin chuckled. Looking at the tray in her hand, he continued, "A lot of food for one person. The old man's getting quite a feed."

"Oh, it's my lunch as well. There was more of it earlier, but I ate two figs on the way here. I was pretty hungry," Kjara said, hoping he didn't notice her blushing. "I've been cleaning the bathhouse all day."

"Oh, yer! Tomorrow's Firstmoon!" Harwin perked up. "I've got a nasty cut under my ribs I've wanted to soak all week. You'll garner favour with all the guard folk once they hear you've shined the place up. We all love a hot bath!"

Kjara smiled awkwardly, "I've never had one."

"Then you are in for a treat! There's usually a line, but I'll make sure to save you a spot. It'd be a real shame for you to miss out."

Her face went pale with fear.

"Oh, gods! I'm sorry," Harwin's face reddened. "We've got guards of all genders here, and I didn't even think. It's kind of a done thing, the one bathhouse. I haven't met many of your—I mean, I don't know what your customs are for—"

"It's fine. No harm. I am excited to try it. But maybe I'll wait until last. I don't want to skip the queue; some folks might get mad."

Harwin nodded with relief, "That's smart."

Silence.

"So, are you guarding the lockups or going on patrol?"

He deflated, "Neither. The captain has assigned me to the trove. Copying parchments."

"Sounds boring."

"It's not so bad. Some of the reports are amusing. But it can be a bit lonely."

More awkward silence.

"Here, I'll get the door for you."

"Thank you. Enjoy your books."

"I'll try," Harwin cleared his throat. "You could drop by if you like, enjoy them too."

Blood heated her ears, "Okay, sure."

Kjara stepped into the corridor that ran the length of the cells. Soren was laying down on his bunk, eyes closed and presumably asleep, or perhaps just moping. Kjara didn't care either way. Papa, however, was sat up in his cell, plaiting his hair. She called out a greeting and he whipped around, a toothy grin spreading across his face.

"At last, food! And company! It's been so dull in here! Come, tell me things, how long has it been? Weeks? Months? What has changed in the world? Oh, that smells delicious!"

Kjara smiled and shook her head at his eccentric enthusiasm before sliding him his dinner. She sat across from him, legs bent, resting her plate in her lap. He greedily bit into his sandwich, leaving a blob of butter caught in the whiskers at the corner of his mouth.

Kjara started with the flatbread, sweeping it through the relish. A few mouthfuls passed in silence before she spoke, recounting the events of her day, and the interactions she had had with Captain Deonto.

"She's a beast that one," Papa huffed, wiping tomato seeds from his beard. "Locking me up in here for no reason, whatsoever."

"You're still sticking to that story?" Kjara asked.

"Because it's the truth!" he argued. "Oi, give us a few of those grapes, would you?"

Kjara laughed, breaking off a stem and passing it to him. "Papa, you were running around like mad yesterday, downing any glass of beer you could grab, and throwing them all about. What did you think was going to happen?"

"Oh…" Papa paused in thought. "Oops."

He took another bite of his sandwich, before his nostrils flared and he spat it out. He spread the bread apart and stared incredulously at the potato peels hidden between the spinach leaves.

Kjara suppressed a grin.

"By Fyaldha…you fiend!" Papa moaned. "The only food I've had all day. Ruined by prankery most foul!"

"Consider it payback. Now we're even."

"Eh? What do you mean?"

"For yesterday," Kjara plucked another grape. "When you ratted me out to the captain."

Papa blew air from his lips, "If you are going to play with things beyond your reckoning, half-your-luck, be prepared for unpleasant consequences." Papa took another bite and smiled wide through crunching teeth. "And you'll start to relish the taste of it."

Chapter 8

Kjara

Had Kjara asked Harwin where the trove was, perhaps she'd feel less intrusive while exploring the guardhouse, but she didn't, so the feeling followed behind her like a hungry chicken. She wandered through the long corridors, passing through a door out into the training yard. A soft, white light bordered the equipment, the dummies, and the targets. Distant noises of the city winding down littered the air. Occasional footsteps and drunken laughter wafted over the guardhouse walls on the ocean breeze.

The mess hall tables glistened with a fine, wet sheen; benches perfectly aligned in two long, empty rows. The earthy aroma of baked potatoes still clung in the air. Sounds of splashing water, clinking plates and muffled conversation filtered out from the kitchen. But there was no one in sight. Kjara continued to wander. Captain Deonto's office door was closed, but a faint light flickered from beneath it. Silence.

Further along was another room Kjara hadn't explored, unopened but unlocked. As she opened the door, the musty smell of paper struck her nose. Row after row of bookshelves filled the room. Thick books, thin books, tall books, and short books. Spines of green, red, brown, and black. There seemed no real order to it.

Oil lanterns shed a dim glow near the walls, and a softer light shone from the back. A soft scratching sound with an occasional sigh grew louder as Kjara walked past the shelves toward the light. Hunched over a table at the back of the room sat Harwin. A few candles dotted the area, a stack of books piled on one side of him, sheets of paper on the other. An open book lay in the centre of the desk. The quill in his hand scratched against the parchment as he tirelessly copied each page.

"Hi again."

Harwin lifted his eyes in surprise, "Oh, hey. Come to save me from my loneliness?"

"No, I…I was exploring."

"Sneaky. You're very light on your feet."

"I'm fairly light all over," Kjara joked, referencing her size, but he didn't get it. He would have laughed if he did, surely. "What are you copying?"

"Uh, boundary dispute," he dipped his quill in ink. "Out in the eastern farmlands."

"Oh? Which farms?"

"Underbranch and Sunthistle."

Kjara chuckled shortly, "Sunthistle made the complaint, didn't he?"

"Good guess."

"I can do better than a guess," Kjara perched on the edge of the table, pointing to the book without looking at it. "Sunthistle complained that Underbranch was sneaking cattle into his far grazing paddocks. But Underbranch claimed the land was his."

"Yer, actually."

Kjara smirked, "I want to say it escalated into…manure-covered windows—No, setting a barn on fire."

Harwin read ahead in the report, "How'd you know?"

57

"It's what the Underbranch family does. The moment you stop checking every inch of your holdings, they'll try to muscle onto it. And Sunthistle is quite a protective haffelin."

"You from the farmlands, eh?"

"Born and bred."

Harwin leant back in his chair, "The farmer's life. Simple, laidback, not a care in the world. That'd be nice."

Annoyance and embarrassment struck her, "It's quite a lot of work."

"Sorry, I meant no offence," Harwin held up his hands in apology. "Which farm do you work?"

"Chedderheart. It's my family's farm."

"Oh? They make the best cheese."

Kjara crossed her legs and spun to face him, "You've tried it?"

"Once or twice," Harwin put his hand on his stomach. "Now you've made me hungry."

"You've not eaten?"

"Duties before dishes, Captain's orders. No food until I'm done."

"Said the same to me. Seems unnecessary."

"I think it's supposed to motivate us."

"I think it's foolish."

"You know, the slowest part of this job is looking back and forth. If you read this out to me, I could copy faster," Harwin suggested. "Then we could both get some food."

Kjara was torn. She wanted to help, if only to continue the conversation. But helping was impossible. And explaining why even more so.

"I've already eaten," Kjara deflected.

"I haven't."

"Then maybe you should write faster," she quipped.

"Then maybe you should stop distracting me."

"Okay…Maybe I will," Kjara dropped off the desk and walked away.

"You're leaving?"

"I'm exploring," Kjara said over her shoulder. "Don't want to distract you."

She wandered through the rows of books, occasionally pulling one off the shelves and leafing through it, "There's a lot of crimes in Bhaile Cala."

"It's not all criminal records," he clarified. "There's official documents, trade agreements, history, fiction. Pretty much anything you'd care to read about. Probably even cheesemaking techniques. You might learn something new."

"If I don't already know it, it's not worth knowing," Kjara replied. "So why is it called the trove? Isn't that for mountains of gold, stores of treasure and the like?"

"I suppose whoever named it reckons this stuff is just as valuable. There's books here going back…I don't even know how long. Some are so old they're barely readable."

"Why hasn't the captain got you copying them, then?"

"You're distracting me again."

"Sorry," Kjara grinned. She continued to browse the library. The books largely had no appeal. Long scrawling in fancy handwriting. And with few pictures to provide additional context, there was no way to even guess at their nature. But with no alternative to entertain her, she persisted.

Until it called to her.

It was an older looking book. Not much longer than a trowel. As thick as a hatchet handle with a dark purple spine and hardcover. Scuffed bindings and creased pages contained simple font. Fifteen words, none of them familiar, but somehow enticing.

Kjara opened and leafed through it. Page after page of dense blocks of text. A few illustrations, abstract in nature and completely nonsensical. Arrows pointed from the scribblings to the images, but none of them made sense. She turned page after page of illegible, monotonous and foreign words until she found a double-page spread covered with images of frightening familiarity. Dark spirals in heavy black ink curled out across the pages. Her heart stopped and her breath caught in her throat.

Illustrations of her markings.

Kjara moved beneath one of the lanterns for better lighting and leant in closer to inspect the pages. A distant, quiet hum caught in her ears. Vibrations seemed to coarse through her arms and the illustrations on the page began to shake. The ink dripped and shifted, jittering back and forth, faster and faster. Kjara let go and the book landed with a heavy thud that thundered through the room.

"You okay?" Harwin called out.

"I'm fine…I dropped a book."

"What kind of book?"

"Um…" Kjara looked at the cover. Squiggles and lines. "A small one."

"Ha-ha. Funny. I meant what's it about, its contents?"

Kjara didn't know. But she wanted to. She needed to. She couldn't ask him to read it for her. It would be humiliating. He already thought she was a simple farmer.

"Give us a look?" Harwin had left his chair and stood in front of her, hand out.

"Uh, sure."

Harwin took the book and flipped it over, "Neither Here nor There: A Speculative History on the Death of Magic. By V.S. Crane. Sounds compelling."

"Yer," Kjara said, copying his sarcasm. "A real page-turner."

"Let's have a read then," he opened the book to the first page and began reading. "Throughout history, creative endeavours have been riddled with mistakes and misgivings. But in matters of art—as with matters of heart—they are unavoidable."

Harwin looked at her.

"What?"

"Doesn't seem much about magic."

"Because it doesn't say it in the first two lines? Keep going a bit."

"Okay," Harwin shrugged. "…When one presents their creative conceptions to another, when they offer their gift, it is with a solemn understanding and grim acceptance of two things. One, the recognition that the work becomes a conversation, a question to be answered by their confidante. And two, the question the confidante hears is not always the question being asked. Thus, in their hearing lies a mistake, and in their answer, misgivings. And so it has been. Since the very first offering."

Kjara listened carefully, hanging on every word, much of which she didn't understand. But she needed him to continue. Harwin's eyes drifted further down the page.

"When a balladeer plays a song, it may be misheard…songs of apology become songs of conquest…Gods be."

"What? What is it?"

"This book," Harwin closed it and returned it to her. "It's got nothing to do with magic at all. Where'd you find it?"

"Over there," Kjara pointed.

Harwin followed her finger, "Ah, fiction section."

"Fiction…"

"Yer. Not real. Made up."

"I know," Kjara lied. Harwin's stomach growled. A chance to exit. "Go finish your work before your belly eats itself."

61

"That would be a shame, it is a nice belly," Harwin smiled. "Until tomorrow, Cheddersneak."

"I, uh. Yer, tomorrow. Good night."

The moment Harwin left her sight, Kjara slid the book under her vest and scurried back to her bunk in the dormitory. Sitting crossed legged with nothing but the moonlight to aid her, she flicked through it over, and over again. It was hard to see, but more frustrating was the inscrutable ink stains. What did they mean? What was that sound? Thoughts, more questions than answers, ran a mile a minute through her head until at last, she succumbed to sleep.

Chapter 9

Soren

The haffelin girl had gone, the old man had passed out, and Soren was left alone. His mind was a hive of hysteria. He had assaulted nobility, destroyed the Nullifidians' property, and been arrested in a drinking den. The thought of Peer Darys, the biggest blabbermouth in Bhaile Cala, churned his guts. He would be compelled to share his shameful circumstance with every Nullifidian in the commune. The rumours would be thick and fast, and the consequences even faster.

Peer Fennack once joked that if Darys got stung on the lip by a bee, he might fall silent for a few days, and they would have some peace. Soren knew better. The moment Darys could speak again, he would, at twice the speed to make up for the lost time, and worst of all, he would have another boring story to tell.

Nothing could be done to stop Darys. And since stewing over it was useless, Soren conceded to his current thoughts and focused instead on meditation. As he did, the recurrent thought of beers, meads, and ciders danced through his head. The times he least had access to alcohol were the times he most desired it.

He'd become so wrapped up in himself that Captain Deonto's approach barely registered. She had a set of keys hanging off her belt and a dark purple discolouration around her right eye. Flecks of reddened skin curled up around the cut beneath it. He blinked in confusion.

"No doubt you heard the total damage to The Eyeglass," Deonto said. "Or am I to believe you weren't eavesdropping?" Soren remained silent, avoiding eye contact. "I see you aren't in the mood for conversation. So, I'll do all the talking, Soren, and you can do all the listening." Deonto leant her wrists on the lock. "Normally, when people break the law, I have them locked up and kept so. Let them reflect on their actions. Let them consider how they might atone. But more time to sit and think won't do you a lick of good, will it? Might even do some harm. Wouldn't you agree?" Soren's mouth dried out. "I spoke with Peer Darys. About you. About when you joined the Nullifidians. And the state you were in when you first got there."

Soren prickled.

"Distraction is what you need, isn't it? Something to lose yourself in. Manual labour. Hard work. Something that leaves you too tired to think." The captain removed a folded piece of paper from her pocket. "I've lately come around to a new manner of recompense. So, rather than keep you locked up, we're going to try something different, you and me. You've put a stain on Bhaile Cala, and so you will clean it up. A few things need fixing around here. This is your to-do list." The captain held out the paper, but Soren kept his hands folded. "It's either do the work or do the time."

He still refused.

"How did you lose the hearing in your ear?"

"I don't have—"

"You favour the left ear whenever you are listening to someone. And you focus on the mouth more than the eyes when someone is talking to you."

Soren sighed as frustration gave way to despondency. He had worked so hard to go unnoticed for so long, but now it felt pointless. She'd figured it out so easily. Her scrutiny made him anxious, the way someone gets when their secrets are about to be made public. Soren assessed his posture, his facial expressions, checking for anything that might betray him further.

"Hunting accident," he lied, hoping to shut down her line of inquiry.

"What kind?"

"Does it matter?" his stomach swirled with fear and guilt. Did she already know how it happened, what he'd done? And if she did, would she take him back to Cacot for judgement? He tried to think of a way to get her to reveal what she knew without revealing anything himself. He searched around for the right question but drew a blank. She'd gotten to him, and she knew it. He could see it in her eyes. She'd found the crack in his defences.

Deonto straightened her shoulders, "I suppose it doesn't."

Soren scowled, "Then why bring it up?"

"It got you talking," Deonto waved the paper. "Are you going to do the work or do the time?"

Soren rubbed his finger with his thumb, "How do you know I won't leave if released?"

"I don't."

Conflicting emotions and thoughts crashed together. Reluctance, confusion, danger, trust. Did she trust him? Or was she testing him? The unbearable thought of blacklisting another town and starting over again made his gut fold into itself. Soren wouldn't run. He couldn't. He held out his hand and took the paper. Captain Deonto unlocked the cell and led him towards the exit.

"What about me?" called out the now-awake Papa, stopping Deonto mid-stride.

"I'm not interested in your hearing loss, old man."

"Hearing loss? my ears are as sharp as any other. I hear the crabs scuttling on the breakwall from here. I can even—" Deonto shut the door behind her, cutting him short.

"Poo."

Chapter 10

Kjara

Kjara hadn't even taken off her boots, and barely had she closed her eyes when a fresh morning probed its way into her rest. The dawn light filtered in through her makeshift curtains and a soft, pained groan tumbled from her lips. She slung her head beneath her pillow and hid away, shielding herself from encroaching responsibilities. Her charcoal-stained hands throbbed with a threat of cramps; stiff muscles pulled tight across her lower back. Everything ached. Laying in the cool dark, she held her eyes tight and nestled into the blanket.

It is too early for tomorrow. Surely, it can wait another day.

Kjara's nostrils twitched. The smell of day-old dried sweat mixed with scrubbing soaps and soot joined her in the bed. And stale bathwater. A wave of anxiety swept over her.

Gods be! The furnace!

Kjara flung herself out of the bunk, sending the book toppling to the floor. She swept it up and shoved it into her haversack, before running down the corridor. Scurrying through the bathhouse and down the stairs, she stacked a pile of kindling in the furnace, snatched the fire striker and flint, and ground the two together while cursing under her breath. A few decent sparks, but not enough for the tinder to catch.

"Come on. Come on! Light!" Kjara urged. A muttering of voices gathered in the room above and drifted down the stairs, dulled by the humming that overtook her senses. With a final swipe of flint against steel, the sparks flared up and swarmed over the tinder. A fire roared, unnaturally bright. Licks of flame sucked between the pillars and up the flues. The heat pulled sweat from her pores. She turned her head and dropped her tools, defending herself against the luminous blaze. The humming subsided.

Kjara half-opened one eye. It was a healthy fire, admirable, but a confusing one to burst so vividly from such a small spark. She sighed with relief. Taking a few extra logs and arranging them neatly over the steel grate, she tiptoed to the bottom of the stairs and cast a worried ear. The flames may have been strong, but the water still needed time to boil.

Silence. Then a splash, and another.

Laughter mixed with jovial conversation. Kjara carefully climbed the steps and peered out. A carpet of steam, rising off the water and curling into the corners of the room somewhat obscured her vision. She stared, mouth agape, eyes blinking in confusion.

A group of guards sat soaking in the bath. They hadn't noticed her, but if Kjara kept staring, they might. And if they did, they might mistake her bewildered expression for deviance. It was best to leave unnoticed. She stuck to the wall and snuck her way to the exit.

"Hey!" called a voice from the water's edge. Kjara froze. Harwin, up to his chest in the water, smiled at her. The water and steam covered everything below the waist. Thankfully.

Kjara gave an uncomfortable wave. "…Hi."

"Thank you, this is great. It feels amazing," he grinned. "Are you coming in?"

Kjara shook her head, "Later, the guards should go first."

"Oh. Shame, the first round is the hottest. It won't be as good later on."

"True," Kjara nodded in agreeance. "But I can come back in a bit and throw some more wood on."

Harwin tapped his head with one finger, "You're a thinker. How was your sleep? Get much rest?"

"It was…louder than I expected. The city stays awake a lot longer than the farmlands. And the ocean is much closer. I could hear it all night."

He nodded, "Hey, see this?"

Harwin pushed himself out of the water, revealing more of his torso. Kjara recoiled instinctively but relaxed once she understood what he was showing her, a long gash below his belly button.

"That looks pretty nasty, what happened?"

Harwin straightened his shoulders, "Patrol along the south road, near Cacot. I barely made it out with my life."

Kjara had several questions but didn't know which one to ask first, and in that moment of indecision lost the chance.

"Chedderheart," barked Captain Deonto's voice from the doorway. "With me. Now."

Harwin deflated back into the water, "Good luck."

Chapter 11

Soren

Soren's view from the roof of the guardhouse was picturesque. Its position close to the harbour gave a clear north side view of the docks, the bay, and the ocean. A faint silhouette of the Timelong Mountains stretched out beyond the city limits to the west. To the east lay the long flat fields of the farmlands that provided most of the crops to the people of Bhaile Cala. Below, the urban sprawl of buildings bordered the comings and goings of its denizens.

Declining the captain's offer of cellblock accommodation, Soren purchased a bed at The Crossed Candle. It was an establishment of ill-repute that charged by the hour. Staying an entire night accrued a significant bill, but he received neither the satisfaction offered by its employees nor the restful slumber he craved as a result.

The beaming sun overhead wore on Soren's tired eyes and settled into his skin, providing an uncomfortable but not unmanageable warmth. He reached for the water skin hanging off his hip, popped out the cork with one paint-speckled thumb and took a long healthy quaff. Painting the guardhouse was oddly therapeutic. Working up there on the roof kept him far away from any conversation.

"Peer Soren?" the distinct tone of Peer Darys' voice broke his calm.

Soren sighed and dropped his head, "Yes, Darys. I am here. What is it?"

"Hello, Soren!" Darys chirped. "Lovely day! How's the view from up there? I bet it's quite a stunner."

"Come up and see for yourself," Soren suggested. *So I can push you off.*

"I might have to take a pass on that one. I'm not much of a fan of heights. But do you think you can come down here for a moment? I have some things for you."

Soren's ears pricked up.

"What things?" he asked reluctantly.

"Well...your things, actually."

Soren cursed. Evicted, kicked out of the Nullifidians with no opportunity to explain himself first. He pressed a tightly balled fist into his forehead and took a long, deep breath. A scream crawled in his throat, threatening to escape, but he swallowed it. Anger and shame swirled in his gut, twisting it into nauseous knots of resentment. The damage was done. Tallied up and added to the long list of his poor decisions.

Soren promised Deonto he wouldn't leave town until he had worked off his debt. Every fibre of his heart pulsed with regret; it was a fool's promise. He should have spoken to Darys before he left the market. Should have said something to the haffelin girl instead of grabbing her bag. Or risked the night travel and gone back to the Nullifidian commune rather than staying at The Crossed Candle. He could have made it back before dawn and would still have kept his promise to Deonto. Should have. Could have. Would have. Thinking it wouldn't make it so.

"Leave it by the ladder."

"What?" Darys called up.

Soren bit his tongue, secured his tools, and descended. Although doing so was tedious, it would be easier to have the conversation face-to-face. Peer Darys smiled at his approach and dropped a large canvas backpack off his shoulder.

Seeing Soren's expression more morose than usual, Darys offered a small reassurance, "I know things look grim now, but they needn't stay that way."

"That's not a comfort," Soren grumbled, kneeling to pick up his belongings.

"Peer Fennack says it might not be forever. He says you need to earn your way back."

"That's not a comfort either. Did he say how?"

Darys shook his head. Soren dug through one of the two side pouches, finding only a tinderbox and a fire striker. *Perhaps it's in the other pouch.*

"Not in so many words. Mostly, it was 'when he has found his path again, if it leads to us, he may return'. What are you looking for?"

"My coin."

"Oh, I moved it into the central pocket. It's underneath your clothes and the, uh, other things."

Soren ground his teeth, "You went through my things?"

"Not with any malice. I was travelling up by myself. I didn't want bandits finding anything, so I made sure it was all well hidden in there."

Soren snorted. The five miles of road between the Nullifidian commune and the city was hardly a hotbed for bandit activity, but he couldn't be bothered to make the point. He unclasped the leather straps holding the main bag shut and pawed around inside, removing each item. Two sets of linen trousers, two shirts. A thin navy jacket and hooded cloak. A rusted mess kit, with a fork and spoon but no knife. A short-handled metal mallet, chisel, a single half-burnt torch, and a jar of oil. A feather and plug wrapped up in a dirt-stained leather strap. All that he had in the world.

72

"Settle a bet for me?" Darys asked.

"We aren't supposed to bet."

"True. But we aren't supposed to beat people up in the middle of a pub either," Darys pointed to the leather-strapped bundle of tools. "What are those things?"

"Plug and feather," Soren answered. "Used to split rocks."

"Oh. Never picked you for a miner. Didn't know you were that way inclined."

Soren ignored Darys and, feeling a familiar cloth purse at the bottom of his pack, relaxed. He poured its contents into his hand and set about counting the coin. Twenty-two silver and nine copper. His entire life savings.

Lodgings and food at the Crossed Candle would put Soren back just over one silver a day. If he was selective with his meals, he might be able to shave it back to one silver even. Less perhaps, if he could strike a long-term arrangement with the proprietor. As it stood, if nothing went wrong, if none of his clothes or things broke, he could make it to the end of the month.

"Gee, that's not much coin," Darys mused, peering into Soren's hand.

"No. It isn't," Soren grimaced and started repacking his bag.

"Well, then it's a good thing Peer Fennack was so kind to you. The coin we lost from all that spilt honey, and the busted vendor stall. I don't even want to think about how much all that would cost. I'm surprised he didn't force you to pay it back actually, now that I think about it. With the renovations and all that. I guess they'll have to wait now though. Can't make the coin without the stall. Not that you'll be making any. Or helping out with the renovations. What are you going to do next?"

Soren stood up, shoving the coin purse into his pocket, and heaved his pack over one shoulder. As he did, the shifting of weight caused a tear in the base of the bag, and all its contents spilled out over the ground.

"Look for work."

Chapter 12

Kjara

Captain Deonto ushered Kjara into her office. Strewn across the desk were stacks of paper, a pot of ink with a quill, and a few rolled-up maps. But sitting open in front of the visitor's chair was the leather-bound ledger from the kitchen. Her illustrations stared up at her. Deonto walked around to her chair, before signalling for her to sit. Kjara did so, hesitantly, sensing punishment forthcoming.

Captain Deonto pressed her index finger into the page in front of Kjara, "Can you explain this to me?"

"It's what I took from the larder. I drew the—"

"The instruction I gave to you was to write it down. Not draw pictures."

Her throat dried out, "I know...I just..."

"You chose to draw rather than following the instructions."

"No, it's..."

"Yes?"

Waves of embarrassment pushed Kjara down into her chair. She said nothing. Captain Deonto spun the book around. She took a pencil from her desk and struck a line through each of her drawings. Beneath, she wrote out all of Kjara's takings in the correct format, then closed it and slid it off to one side. She laced her fingers together.

"Why didn't you tell me you can't write?"

A hot prickle spread across the nape of Kjara's neck. She had no explanation. At least none that would be satisfactory. None that she wanted to admit.

"I don't know."

"You don't know," Deonto repeated, leaning back in her chair. "Well, that's not any kind of answer at all, is it?"

A heavy silence hung in the air as Kjara stared at her boots. The bookshelves loomed over her like towers of judgement. Deonto tapped her thumbnail.

"But you do know your numbers?"

Kjara nodded, "We use numbers for coin counting and stocks and such."

Captain Deonto's expression softened, "What about reading?"

"One or two words. We never had need of it at the farm. No one in my family can read or write, really," Kjara shrugged. "I can't think of anyone out in the farmlands who can."

Deonto crossed her arms and pressed one thumbnail into her lower lip. She looked at the pile of papers on her desk, the quills, the inks, maps, books, pencils. She glanced at the open leather-bound ledger and finally at Kjara.

"Starting immediately," Deonto instructed, "you'll no longer take meals with the others. Nor will you take them at the same time. Instead, from the first hour past dawn, you will be in this office with me. You will spend another hour here before lunch, and a further two hours before dinner. We will start with the letters you don't know. Then we will move to words and sentences. But, since you already recognise some letters, we will not be starting completely from scratch. It shouldn't be too much of a challenge for you to learn to recognise the sounds as they are written."

Kjara shuffled in her chair. More duties. Manual labour she could handle, but reading, writing, she couldn't. It would be too difficult, the risk of failure was too high, and the captain would not accept that. There would be consequences, further punishments. And worse, humiliation.

Kjara wanted to say no, to ask for alternative work, but the image of the small, purple book stopped her. The answers to her markings held captive behind the inscrutable scribbles on the faded pages of *Neither Here nor There*. No, this was more than another task, this was an opportunity. Captain Deonto was offering her a key. Kjara had to accept, no matter the captain's motivations.

"Thank you."

"That is not necessary," Captain Deonto replied. "There are several jobs I require you to complete for which reading and writing is essential. If you do not currently possess these skills, then you must be taught them if you are to be of any use."

Kjara felt foolish for responding as she did but tried her best to swallow the feeling. Captain Deonto slid open the middle drawer of her desk, collected up a few sheets of parchment and placed them in front of her. On top of this, she placed a sharpened pencil.

"We will start with C. For Cheese."

Over the next few hours, the captain demonstrated each of the twenty-four letters of the mohra alphabet, which she explained dominated the written word for the nation of Cradh and its companions. After explaining which letters, and combinations of letters, made up most of the sounds in the spoken language, she tasked Kjara with copying each letter again and again. The day melted into a routine of writing, and Kjara found herself entranced by the process. The more she copied each letter, the more she came to recognise the shapes, whether from passing street signs, hanging shop fronts or—most importantly—from the thin, purple book hidden beneath her pillow.

The captain, meanwhile, had spent some time eyeing off the region map on her wall, before sighing and switching her attention to a stack of papers on her desk. She grimaced at them, before drawing them closer. Her eyes puzzled over the pages, and she rubbed her temple with two fingers, as if willing away a throbbing pain.

Kjara's curiosity compelled her, "What are you reading?"

The captain shot a look back at Kjara, as though the question were an insult. But even if it was, she was not withholding in reply.

"Incident reports," she said. "Accounts of some recent disturbances at the mine off the southern road to Cacot."

"They seem to cause you pain."

Deonto's sharp edges seemed to soften, just for a moment, before she pursed her lips in thought, as though wondering what to share.

"Fine workers miners may be. But literate and articulate they are not. Their reports cast more shade on the matter than light. And until I find the time to investigate their claims for myself, it will remain a mystery."

"Oh. That's unfortunate," Kjara said absently. "You can't send anyone else?"

Deonto gave Kjara another stonewall look, her inscrutable brow cutting straight across her eyes. It was enough to freeze Kjara's tongue, and she probed no further on the matter. Silence returned to the room, save for the occasional scratching of pencil on paper.

"Still alive, Captain?" a voice asked from the doorway, smooth and lilting, almost musical. It broke Kjara from her concentration, and she peered over one shoulder to find its owner. Leaning against the doorframe was a wiry sienna-skinned woman with umber hair worn in an updo. Her hands were buried deep in the pockets of a slender brown and white coat with jade trim, a pair of matching spectacles completing her ensemble.

"Not sure. What time is it?" Deonto asked. "Is lunch ready?"

"Lunch is over," the woman replied, striding across the room and relaxing into the chair next to Kjara, seeming not to notice her. Kjara didn't mind. It was a simple fact that, unless they were explicitly involved in the goings-on in a room, haffelins seemed to be almost invisible to the taller races. Doubly so, if the goings-on involved adults and the haffelin in question was not.

"Oh, sorry," Deonto replied.

Kjara was surprised by the apology. It seemed uncharacteristic of the captain. In fact, the moment the woman had entered the room, the mood felt lighter. Just as before, Deonto's expression softened, and Kjara chose to remain silent, unnoticed, in order to find out why.

"You should be. It was delicious," the woman said, crossing one leg. "How's your eye?"

"It's fine. It's my head that's causing me grief."

"Serves you right," the woman quipped, before surveying the vast pile of papers on the desk and the look of defeat on the captain's face. "Need me to do anything?"

Deonto shoved the paper stack across to her, "Take these far away from me."

"Ah, the dreaded miner's reports," the woman scanned the top page, before measuring the pile with her thumb and forefinger. "It's gotten bigger. Still haven't cracked the case?"

"No," Deonto leant back in her chair and rubbed her eyes. "But it's not the forest-grown. Can't be. They've never gone after iron before. They have no use for it."

"Sfarggs, maybe?" the woman offered. "Tell the miners to leave out meat and sugar, that'll satisfy their mischief."

Deonto gave her a dissatisfied look, "The mine isn't being interfered with by make-believe creatures, Rosalind. The culprit—or culprits—are flesh and bone. Not ink and hearsay."

Kjara snuck a peek as the woman, Rosalind, casually flicked through the papers. Handwritten accounts scribbled in pencil, smudged with dirt. The stack gave off the odour of dusty air, like a dirt road on a windy day.

"Odd smells…eerie noises…I feared for my life…" Rosalind blinked with incredulity. "Gold turning into goo. Bite marks in torches? Are these statements from adults, or are they children's stories?"

"Exactly," Deonto extended her hand. "I need to investigate for myself."

Rosalind returned the papers, "Then do it. So I can get a decent night's sleep."

"I don't have the time."

The strange descriptions from the miners had an air of Nofrum familiarity to them, and it sparked an idea in Kjara's head. For who better to ask to make sense of such strange events than her elderly pranksterous friend? Kjara summoned the courage to speak.

"You could ask Papa about it."

Deonto's attention snapped back to Kjara. As did Rosalind's.

"Oh, hello," Rosalind said. "You're new. Have you been here the whole time?"

"Not the whole time, I don't think," Kjara replied. "But all of today, at least."

Rosalind smiled and let out a light, musical laugh.

"Rosalind, this is Kjara Chedderheart," Deonto explained. "Kjara, this is Clinician Rosalind. Of Rosalind's Medicary."

"And our Captain's long-suffering wife," Rosalind added, not appearing upset by the captain's omission, but amused by it. Most likely it had been Deonto's professionalism that had kept her silent on the personal connection. "A pleasure to meet you, Kara."

Kjara's ears burned at her mispronounced name, "Likewise, Miss Rosalind."

Rosalind narrowed her eyes at the pencil in Kjara's hand before looking back to the captain, "You finally took my advice and hired an assistant?"

Deonto cleared her throat, "Not exactly. Kjara claimed responsibility for a recent disruption at The Eyeglass. She is working for me to pay off the damages incurred to Jefen's establishment. Tables, chairs, glasses."

Rosalind turned back to Kjara, "So, you're not an employee, you're a conscript."

"I'm not sure I know the difference," Kjara said.

"It's easy, one jangles with coin and the other with chains," Rosalind laughed again. "You know, that's not such a bad idea, Laine, perhaps you should speak to Papa Roce. He's second-to-none when it comes to strange bumps in the night, eerie happenings and strange smells."

Deonto folded her arms, "If you're suggesting I try to solve the pain in my head with the pain in my arse, the answer is no."

"Why not?" Rosalind adjusted her glasses. "He is an expert in the Nofrum."

"He isn't," Deonto scoffed. "He's a lawless, infuriating old fart who can't tell where reality ends and his wild fantasies begin. I'll not entertain his delusions."

"He could be useful."

"He's an arse, Rosalind."

"Maybe. But the arse is an important body part, Laine," Rosalind leaned in conspiratorially to Kjara. "Maybe even the most important."

"Ridiculous," Deonto grouched.

The distant bells from the harbour rang out and the captain moved to the window, presumably to shut out the noise. But once there, she paused, letting the cool breeze wash over her. With a stretch, Kjara could almost copy the captain's sightline, and could tell she was watching moored ships bob gently in the sparkling water. Her shoulders relaxed, the salted breeze seeming to temper her growing frustration.

"I mean it," Rosalind continued, offering her wisdom to Kjara now since the captain seemed distracted. "If you don't have an arse, you can't shit. And if you can't shit, you die."

Deonto closed her eyes, "Shit."

"Exactly," Rosalind nudged Kjara. "See, she gets it."

"No, I just remembered. The region master has ordered that I have all the uniforms repaired," as Deonto spoke, her voice grew more exasperated. Rosalind uncrossed her leg and listened in silence, cheek in hand, nodding sympathetically. "But priority one," Deonto rifled for a piece of paper. "A request for another fealty audit."

Rosalind scrunched up her nose, "Again? Why?"

Deonto cast a dissatisfied smile.

"That's it?" Rosalind adjusted her glasses. "You don't know?"

Deonto cast a side eye at Kjara, giving her the impression that more would have been revealed had she not been sitting in the room. Instead, Deonto simply said, "More information will be disclosed when relevant."

"The cage of bureaucracy grows ever tighter," Rosalind scratched her lip in thought, failing to notice the captain's concern for Kjara's presence. "He wants to make sure there are no leaks in his ship."

"Correct," agitated, Deonto rearranged the papers on her desk, as though doing so might diminish the workload. "All the wheels must turn in turn."

Rosalind nodded knowingly, "Ah, of course. We must ensure all things are polished and prepared for the arrival of—" the captain shot her a silencing glare. "I mean, that everything is in tip-top condition."

"Squeaky wheels are greased," Deonto said firmly. "So that they might be *silent*."

Rosalind frowned at the captain's odd turn of phrase, mirroring Kjara's expression. But while Kjara remained in the dark on the matter, understanding seemed to dawn on Rosalind and she offered an apologetic smile.

"Suppose I'll leave you to it, then," she said as she stood up, adjusted her spectacles, and walked towards the door. "If you're looking for me, I'll be the grieving widow upstairs."

"I'm not dead yet," Deonto replied.

"Miss dinner and see for yourself," Rosalind said as she closed the door.

Kjara turned back to Deonto. The softness had vanished once again, leaving Kjara none-the-wiser for the conversation, but Deonto gave her no mind. She was too busy looking at the region map on the wall. Or perhaps it was slightly to the left of the map, at the diamond-tipped sword mounted over the fireplace.

Chapter 13

Soren

The sun brushed against the horizon, and the harbour hummed with the excitement of workers nearly at the end of their day. Livers prepared to combat the pickling they'd get from the harbourside pubs once the work was done. Soren walked beside the dockmaster, an elderly pot-bellied man with sandy blonde hair and a liver-spotted, ivory complexion, as he patrolled the piers of Bhaile Cala's harbour.

He peered over his underwire spectacles at Soren, "Can you swim?"

"No. But I can climb."

The dockmaster scratched his bulbous nose, "Climbing's all well and good, son. But what I need most right now is a fixer. Any experience working with wood by chance?"

"The Nullifidians taught me some joinery and woodturning."

The dockmaster shook his head, "No, that won't quite do you, I'm afraid. I'm talking about big things. Structural stuff, scarfing planks and the like. My shipwright's recently done himself in. Fell asleep under the rotting stern of a ship. It collapsed and…Well, anyway, I'm in the market for a new one."

"I could work on the dock."

The dockmaster clicked his tongue, "No doubt there's some muscles under that cloth, but I've got more than my share of lifters, carters, and carriers. Tell you what though, if you can swing a pickaxe, you might be in luck. Half the folks I have on the docks at the moment have come up from the mine. No one seems to want to work it."

Soren prickled at the prospect of prospecting, "Why?"

"They reckon it's haunted," the dockmaster snorted. "Bunch of scaredy cats. A couple of spirits bumping around ain't nothing to be afraid of. I fought in the Collision. If you want to know what real terror is, I can tell you." As if to punctuate his statement, the dockmaster leant up against some crates and unbuckled the strap around his knee. Removing his wooden leg, he handed it over to Soren. "Cheers, the blood flow gets a tad backed up in there sometimes," he said, giving his thigh and stump a light massage. "Makes it feel a bit tingly."

"There's no possibility of work then?"

"Look, I can see when a fella's hurting for coin. And you appear to be a fairly honest type." Soren winced at the word honest. The dockmaster didn't seem to notice. "Here's what I can do for you. There's a pub on the docks, called The Bait and Tackle. They run cards and dice most nights. And I've been known to dabble. I had a decent win a while back but have yet to collect my earnings because the person I was up against didn't come through with the goods. If you can find that individual and see to getting me the coin I am owed, I think it's only fair you see a cut of it. I know it's not what you're after, but it's all I got right now. Say ten per cent?"

The dockmaster held out his hand.

Soren held out the leg, "Deal. What do they look like?"

"Medium height. Long red hair. Wears a velvet doublet. She's there most nights she isn't locked up. I heard they grabbed her the other day, so you might have to try the guardhouse first."

Not likely. She'd slipped out of there as easily as Soren had gone in, "I might try my luck at the pub."

Soren knew The Bait and Tackle was not a fine establishment by any stretch, but the prices were reasonable, and the location was agreeable. As he passed through, fisherfolk sat around tables, exaggerating their day's catches, and trade sailors acquainted themselves with the local brews and other delicacies. The patronage was predominantly mohra, with a sprinkling of haffelin and faeduin.

Ayleth, the blind faeduin from The Eyeglass, sat with a tall glass of green juice in her hand, casually conversing with a party of venturists. A man filled the chair opposite her, his body showing all the hallmarks of the liathaum race. He loomed a full foot higher than the others, a grey-skinned mountain of muscle with arm hair thicker than a bear's fur. A strange sight to see so far north of the rock and metal mountains near the Narrow Sea.

Next to Ayleth, a tornblood of similar age lounged across two chairs. The amber in his eyes matched the orange hue of his skin. Long quill-like hair follicles had been slicked back over his head. His cross-shaped pupils occasionally flickered over the guitar at his feet. Both rare breeds, but not unexpected. The Bait and Tackle attracted many brands of outcasts, and neither bothered to disguise their abnormality.

Unable to spot the woman he was looking for, Soren stepped up to the bar to gather some information. The tapster, a thin, gangly apricot-skinned man with a weak chin and bushy moustache nodded a greeting.

"What can we get you?" he said with a surprisingly deep voice, his prominent Adam's apple bobbing up and down as he spoke. "Beer? Cider? Mead? We've got most of the good ones. And the cheap ones too. And if you think cheap is good, then we've got all the good ones."

"Tea if you have it," Soren requested. "Hot water if you don't."

The tapster raised an eyebrow, "It's not our specialty, but we can accommodate. Honey in the tea? It's local." Soren shook his head. "Anything else?"

"I'm looking for someone. I'm hoping she's here. Medium build, velvet coat, red hair."

"Ah," The tapster smiled a knowing smile, filled up a kettle and placed it over the fireplace behind him. "Looking to deal with the Mother of Cards? We hope you're feeling lucky, She's in the backroom, table four. We think there are one or two chairs left at it."

"Sorry, who?"

"The Mother of Cards. The Gambler's Bane? The Dice's folly?" the tapster offered each title with increasing incredulity. "If you haven't heard of her proper, we might suggest you pick a different table to play with. Unless of course, you're happy parting ways with all your coin tonight."

"I don't intend to play," Soren said. "I only need to speak to her."

"He doesn't drink, doesn't gamble. He's picked a fine place to be," the tapster chuckled. "Suit you, all the same, she's at table four. The door on the left. We'll have the tea brought out to you. One copper for that one."

Soren nodded his thanks and placed his coin on the counter, before walking across the room and through the door. A heavy fog of smoke clung to the ceiling, making the small room appear even smaller. It stung his eyes and bit his nostrils, but he did his best not to cough for fear of drawing unwanted attention. There were several tables, each with a different game set up, but the clientele was slim. Some only had two or three players, and they seemed to be engaged in the gambling more for the sport of it than for any monetary gain.

Except for table four. Onlookers crowded around it, providing a running commentary of the game by way of laughter and applause.

Rowdy comments and sidelong glances peppered the crowd and a few even placed bets on who would win the game they watched.

And there she was, her red hair tied back, her velvet doublet resting over her chair. She sat in direct competition with three others: a heavyset man, a broad-hipped woman with shaved black hair, and a genderless haffelin with an intricate collar of tattoos.

Soren watched them play for a few rounds, trying to figure out precisely the rules of the game and waiting for the right moment to interject. The game involved dice and cups, and the objective seemed to be correctly guessing how many dice would be unveiled and the numbers they would display. One could also win by successfully out bluffing and outbidding the other players. The players were serious and highly competitive, each having custom dice. Soren noted the red-haired woman's set, black with scarlet numbers, and a capital "S" in place of the one.

The playful and charismatic banter tossed back and forth presented an air of familiarity. But behind it ran a distinct undercurrent of tension, as though violence could erupt if someone pressed the wrong point or made an unwise decision. They studied one another's faces as each participant called and raised, and not a single eye twitched at the increasingly heavy pile of coins growing in the centre of the table.

The heavyset man folded first, declaring he had not enough coin and preferred to play it safe. The black-haired woman bowed out next, tossing her dice cup aside and draining her drink in commiseration.

It was the red-haired woman's turn to bid. She stared the tattooed haffelin dead in the eye, unblinking, the air as thick with tension as it was with smoke. Then, the tiniest flash of movement as the red-haired woman broke first to lock eyes with Soren. His heart seized up, having become so engrossed in the game he had forgotten himself. The tattooed haffelin frowned and stole a look in the same direction as zir competitor.

"Focus on the game, Sabel," ze said.

The red-haired woman, Sabel, smiled, "Two gold down. Three sixes."

"With only four dice left?" the tattooed haffelin squinted.

"I'm feeling lucky, Orpip," Sabel boasted, throwing another glance at him.

"Then I'll be feeling rich," Orpip gloated, "when you lose."

"Maybe," Sabel shrugged. "So, what's it to be, raise or fold."

"Call. You're bluffing."

Sabel nodded and revealed her dice, a six and a three. Underneath Orpip's cup, glimmering in the lantern light, a six, and a three. Ze let out a relieved laugh.

"Ah, I was close. Shame," Sabel said. "You win, Orpip."

The crowd applauded a game well played and set about clearing the table for another. She beckoned Soren over, "Hey, null. I see you are a free man. Almost didn't recognise you without the robes."

Soren scoffed. Although she had been referring to freedom from the guardhouse cells, he couldn't help but connect her statement to his recent removal from the Nullifidians. It didn't feel like freedom. Even though he had changed out of his null's attire and into street clothes before seeking employment, he still felt beholden to them.

"Not quite. I still have a debt to work off."

"Ah-ha," she replied. "Shall we deal you in? We're about to play dink."

Soren lifted a hand defensively, "I don't gamble."

"Is that part of your null code?"

Soren ignored the question, "I'm here on business for the dock-master."

Sabel laughed, "Blinny wants his money but is too lazy to come collect for himself. Well, you can tell him that he can have his money when he wins it fair-and-square."

"He seems to think he did."

"He seems to think a lot of things. And most of them are wrong. He cheated his way into that coin. And now it has been liberated from him."

Soren sighed. It was never easy prying money from the maws of sharks, "I don't know what history the two of you have. And I'm not here to listen to it. I'm only here to collect."

The tapster entered the room, handing Soren his tea, before efficiently collecting the orders of each of the other patrons. Sabel, noticing the tea, cocked her head.

"No alcohol. Is that part of your null code, too?" she queried, but Soren gave her no answer to go off. "Tell you what, null. I'll give you Blinny's supposed winnings, in full. In fact, I'll even give you a chance to double it for him. On one condition."

Soren's mind raced. Doubling the winnings for the dockmaster would be double the commission for him. He could even withhold the additional coin for himself and say nothing of it to Blinny. But what was the condition? Safer not to know.

"I don't gamble," Soren stated. "I'll take the original sum."

"Who said anything about gambling?" she smirked.

Soren's stomach churned. Speaking with strangers made him miss the solitude of the Nullifidian commune, "What do you mean? What else would I do?"

"I want you to sit and have a drink with me. And I'll double Blinny's coin for you. You know how much that'll be? Fifty gold. Square and true, from me to you."

Fifty gold was a hard number to turn away from. It could set a lot of things straight. Soren could clear his debt, purchase new personal effects, and give the rest to the Nullifidians as compensation. The commune that prohibited drinking. The commune that had rejected him.

"Just one drink?" Soren checked.

"Just one drink," Sabel replied wickedly.

Chapter 14

Papa

"Breakfast, Roce. Wake up."

Papa kept his face pressed into the flat, lumpy bedroll. He refused to address captain Deonto. Refused to acknowledge the terrible, terrible word. Breakfast. Breakfast meant morning, his mortal enemy.

Captain Deonto tapped her foot against the floor, "Do you want this or not?"

"Maybe..." Papa fluttered one bleary eye open. A metal plate with two slices of seed bread, a shallow glass of milk, and an apple lay at her feet. He smacked his lips together. "What time is it?"

"Half-dawn."

Half-dawn. A word worse than breakfast, a sight worse than daylight: the sunrise itself. Mother of pain. Destroyer of joy. The thought of it sent a shiver through his blood.

"What?!" Papa snarled. His voice bounced around the prison cell and rattled his brain. "How dare you! I refuse to be roused at such a cursed hour! Begone! Come back at noon like a normal person."

"As you like," Captain Deonto's footsteps echoed down the corridor.

Papa's hunger, more awake than he was, lunged for the food, but his pride blocked it. Instead of grabbing the bread, he took the apple and hurled it down the corridor. It smacked with a soft splat against the door near Captain Deonto's head. Spatters of juice dotted her hair. The apple bounced along the floor a few times, before rolling to a stop near his cell.

"I told you, I don't like apples," Papa grumbled, laying back down.

Deonto, stone-faced despite his reaction, returned to him. With hands on hips, she waited a moment, but Papa ignored her presence. She shrugged and leant down to collect the plate.

"Oi, that's mine."

"If you don't want it, you don't get it. And if it stays here uneaten, sure enough, the rats will know, and they'll want it. I'll bring something else at noon."

His ego wanted to refuse the meal on principle alone, but his stomach lay empty and desperate. A true dilemma. His bladder awoke and sloshed a solution through his guts. Papa smiled. The perfect way to save his pride and his breakfast.

"No, no, you can leave it. I'll eat. Wait a second."

Papa got to his feet and walked to the rusty chamber pot in the corner. He scratched his beard and hoisted his robes above the waist, baring his full naked rear to the captain. With a soft grunt, Papa began an unsteady stream of yesterday's refreshments.

The sharp ping of fluid against metal carried through the cells for a time, gradually overtaken by a watery swash as the chamber pot filled. Papa flexed his buttocks to shoot out the last few drips and wiped his hands on his robes. With a smug grin, Papa kicked the chamber pot along the floor towards Deonto. Steam from the fresh, hot urine wafted out, catching the rays of the morning sun.

"Take that with you, would you, dear?" Papa winked, before noticing her black eye. "Nice shiner, by the way. Clumsy captain, what did you run into?"

Deonto ignored his antagonism, looking instead at the chamber pot, "So much straining, and such little result."

"I am dehydrated. A lack of attendance from your guards," Papa pouted. "If I had more to give, rest assured I would."

Deonto held out her hands. Celebrating his success, Papa picked up the chamber pot and thrust it out with a flourish. Maintaining smug eye contact, he dropped it, but she pulled her hands away. The chamber pot clanged to the ground, splashing its contents up his legs and almost over his breakfast.

"By Fyaldha—my seed bread!" his nostrils caught the scent of his expulsion. "Urk, you've agitated the stink of it! Why would you do that?"

"I guess I must be clumsy," Deonto turned away.

"Where are you going?" Papa asked.

"To get you a mop."

"So, you're making *me* clean up the mess *you* made?"

Deonto sighed, "I'm too busy to play today, Roce."

"Oh, I see how it is!" Papa sulked. "Too busy to care for old Papa. Too busy looking after fancy foreign folks, more like. I'm rotting away in here, and you're off guarding gentry. Let me out already. I've done nothing wrong!"

She spun back to face him, "What did you say?"

"I said I've done nothing wrong! The same thing I said all yesterday. And yesterday night. And every other time you have come hassling me."

Papa wasn't exaggerating. He had indeed kept up his complaining all through the evening and well into the night. Until he had gotten bored and tired, and fallen asleep.

Deonto shook her head, "No, the other thing. Fancy folks?"

"You know, The Satin Bull, the Regal's son. All them lot."

Deonto narrowed her eyes, "Which Regal's son?"

Papa sat with legs outstretched and placed the plate in his lap. He dipped a slice of the seed bread into his milk and crammed it into his mouth.

"The very royal first son of Glainne. Tamou's boy, you know. Has the old bastard up on the Overbite got you run so ragged you can't tell who's coming and going no more?"

Deonto sighed, "Must all authority find the same disdain from you, Roce?"

"Firstly," Papa began, as a trickle of milk ran through his chin hairs, "that was a term of endearment. And secondly, are you much of an authority if you need me to tell you what is going on within your own walls?"

Papa dipped another chunk of bread into his milk and awaited her response. When none came, he chuckled, "Lost for words, now there's a first."

"Where did you hear this?"

Papa paused, setting his food back down on his plate. He wiped the milk from his beard with one hand, "Do you not actually know about it?"

Deonto remained silent.

Papa rolled his eyes, "By Fyaldha, you're just no fun at all today. Look, if it'll make you feel better, it's probably all a bit of rumour-mongering gone astray. All he said, she said. Blah blah. Think nothing of it. Now, can I please get out of here? It smells like pee."

Deonto looked down at the puddle leaking into the tile grooves. Spying the apple nearby, she rolled it into his cell with her foot, "You're a better throw with a glass than an apple."

"Eh? What are you...Oh," Papa dropped his arms into his lap and smiled regretfully, sucking air through his teeth. The cause of her black eye revealed as his own recklessness. "A busted eye from The Eyeglass, eh? I don't suppose 'sorry' will expedite my release?"

Deonto offered a reserved smile, "I was going to let you out after breakfast, but now you've no chance. I won't have you running around when two royals are coming to town. Get comfortable, Roce."

After she left, Papa looked up to the sky and muttered, "I suppose you think that's hilarious, don't you?"

Chapter 15

Kjara

Captain Deonto and Kjara sat in silence on opposite sides of the desk in the captain's office. It was the third day of Kjara's new employ, but the tasks, coupled with the myriad of curiosities on the surrounding shelves, made it difficult to focus. She placed another finished sheet of parchment on her pile and shook the cramp from her hand.

"What are you writing?" she asked.

"Incident report. From the business at The Eyeglass," Deonto responded, glancing across the desk at Kjara and correcting her pencil grip. "Hold it like this. You will get straighter lines."

"Like this?"

"Better," Deonto slid her a fresh sheet of paper. "Start again. From 'A'."

This alphabet has too many letters.

Kjara had no interest in incident reports. She was more curious about the books and wondered why the kitchen ledger was bound, but the captain wrote on loose paper.

"Do you always write on parchment?"

"Not always. I have a pocketbook and a pencil if I need to take notes while on patrol. Ink, however, is more permanent. And proper. When one is using a quill, it is easier and neater to write if the page is flat. The ink doesn't run as much, and there is less chance of smudging."

Kjara looked down at her pages. Many of the letters beneath her writing hand were blurred. She turned her hand over and saw a sizable grey stain on her glove from where it had been resting.

Deonto, spying her bemused expression, continued, "That will happen less as your technique improves. It might also help to remove those gloves."

Kjara feigned indifference to hide the stab of anxiety. She rubbed her hand on the thigh of her trousers and distracted the captain with another question, "So, ink is for paper, and pencils are for books?"

"I've never thought about it like that, but that is an accurate summary."

"So, shouldn't I be writing in a book?"

Deonto shot Kjara a look that made her shrink a little in her chair. After a moment's silence, she spoke. "Let's test your learning. The word I am about to write is "the". You write it on your paper and hold it up."

Kjara grabbed her previous piece of paper. Beside each example letter provided by the captain were her repeated attempts at replication. Slowly, under her breath, she sounded out each sound of the word, scanning the sheet for the correct symbol combinations. With reasonable confidence, she wrote out the word and held it up.

"Correct. Now, Eyeglass."

Eyeglass. A harder one. Kjara repeated the process, less sure of herself, and again showed her paper.

"Incorrect. The word 'eye' is different from the letter 'I'."

Kjara furrowed her brow, "That is foolish. Why would they have more than one way to write a sound?"

Deonto's lips hinted at a smile. Or perhaps it was a frown.

"The rest of the word, however, is correct. So, let's try for one more. A real challenge. The word is 'instigated'."

Kjara dropped her pencil to the desk, defeated, "I don't even know what that means."

"It means started," Deonto explained.

"Then why not use the word started?" Kjara suggested. "Seems like you're just complicating things for the sake of complicating things."

"Perhaps. But the two words aren't synonymous."

Kjara raised her eyebrows, giving the captain a pained look of disbelief.

"They aren't exactly the same," Deonto continued in simpler terms. "Instigated refers more to starting something bad."

"Oh. So, a game of cards would be started, but a fight would be instigated?"

Deonto nodded, "Correct."

Kjara contemplated the word for a moment, "Do you think when The Satin Bull comes to town, she will be starting something or instigating something?"

Deonto folded her arms at the mention of the naistinn, "You've been listening to too many of Roce's fanciful tales."

Kjara shook her head, "No, it wasn't him that said it. It was the red-haired woman locked up with us. She said it was The Satin Bull and some other man. From Glainne, I think."

Deonto tapped her finger against her arm as she mused over this new information. She stood up and fetched the sword from the mantlepiece behind her.

"I think we should get you a book," she declared.

Chapter 16

Papa

After pacing back and forth for an hour after breakfast, Papa collapsed in a fuzzy heap on the floor and began drumming on his chest. The beat became heavier and rhythmic, and he complimented it with the hum of an old, half-forgotten song. His humming grew into song, and as he tuned his ear to the acoustics of the room, he found the reverberations of his voice agreeable, even inspired.

"Step up and beat your wicked drum with mine.
There is no point in fighting for the past,
Drive out the coward if she tears your back
And if death finds you, may she find you last."

Papa bellowed the last line at the top of his lungs, beating one final forceful hit to punctuate the stanza, and set off a maelstrom of spittle and coughing. He cursed, rolled over and flung an errant glob of saliva from his throat. It splattered across the stone tiles in the cell next to him. He turned his lip, admiring the distance his phlegm had flown, then returned to lying on his back.

"The joke has worn out its welcome. Are you going to get me out?" Papa stared at the ceiling. No reply. "Fine," he grouched, sitting back up. "I'll do it the proper way."

He untwirled a seashell from his beard and held it between his hands. Holding it to his lips, he closed his eyes and mouthed a few silent words. A moment passed. Another. He opened one eye and scanned the lockup for any sign of celestial interference. Nothing. He lifted the shell to his ear and shook it, blew in it, and shook it again.

Still nothing.

Papa blew a raspberry and tossed the shell onto the stones, "No audience, no show, eh? Is that how it is? Well, let me ask you something. If I'm stuck in here, then who is going to attract the crowd?"

Ever so slowly, the stone tile that the shell had landed on rose up, on a slight angle. The shell rolled off the side, across the floor, between the bars and into the adjacent cell, coming to rest on another tile. If Papa's memory served correctly, it was the same tile that had kept secret the red-haired girl's lockpicking tools.

"Don't mind if I do," he snickered. "Glad we have an understanding."

He scrambled over to the edge of his cell and slid his arm through the bars. They were far enough apart to put his shoulder and most of his head through, but no matter how Papa shuffled his shoulders, they couldn't both fit. His fingers scraped at the corner of the stone as he grunted and strained to get his nails to leverage it. But it was useless.

Papa lay there a moment, defeated and lazy. But as the muscles in his shoulders began to cramp, he attempted to right himself. As he did, the bars bent inwards, not enough to be seen, but enough to be felt. And enough to stop him from leaving.

"Yer. Nice one. You got me," after a few moments of struggle, Papa dropped his head in frustration. "Okay. So that's how it's going to be? Fine. Guards!"

A few seconds passed before the sound of jangling steel signalled his success. Metal clinked as the lock of the door shifted out of place and the door swung open. He relaxed as leather footsteps bounced off the stones in his direction.

"What is it, Papa?" Harwin asked. "Run out of songs to sing?"

Papa groaned pathetically, "I'm stuck."

Harwin took a few steps past Papa and crouched down on his haunches, "I can see that. What were you doing?"

"I was trying to get my shell," Papa lied, pointing. "I dropped it, and it rolled over there. Help me!"

Harwin nodded, flipped through his keyring, and unlocked the empty cell beside him. He picked up the shell and placed it into Papa's hand. He blinked at Harwin's smiling face.

How could such a sharp woman as Deonto leave such a blunt mind in a position of custodianship? Let alone give it a sword to carry. Perhaps it's only ornamental.

"Oh, fantastic," Papa said. "Now that I have this shell, I can escape this prisonous torment."

Harwin's smile dropped, and fear crept over his face.

Papa rolled his eyes, "Sarcasm, boy. I'm stuck fast and going nowhere faster."

"Oh. Maybe I can help? Hang on," Harwin unlocked the door to Papa's cell.

"What a wild idea," Papa grumbled.

Harwin grabbed Papa's ankles with both hands, widening his stance and planting his feet firmly on the ground.

"1...2...3...Pull!" Harwin strained, but Papa didn't budge.

"Come on, boy. Put your back into it."

Harwin picked up his other leg and counted again. This time, as he pulled with all his strength, the metal bars loosened their hold. Unprepared for such easy success, Harwin lost his grip and tumbled backwards, tripping over the protruding stone tile. The keys flew up in an arc and landed by his face. Papa snatched them, stuffed them into his pocket, and got to his feet.

"Excellent work. Free at last."

"That's good for you. But now I'm stuck!" Harwin's torso had wedged fast between the bars on the opposite wall of the cell.

"Oh, no. Terrible. A real tragedy."

"Roce? Can you help?"

Papa answered by slamming the cell door shut. The metal lock snapped into place. He walked down the corridor and held up Harwin's key chain with a wink.

"Don't worry, maybe a shell will help get you out? It worked for me," Papa snickered, before walking away, spinning the key chain on his finger and whistling.

Chapter 17

Kjara

Kjara had never been in a bookstore before. Although she and Mado had passed by the front of Elent's Elegant Emporium often on the way to market, she had only ever seen the wares from the outside. Now, standing amongst the row after row of books, writing tools, inks, and other literary sundries, she lamented each time she had passed it by.

The owner was an exceptionally tall, thin mohra with a shaved head, chalky-white skin, a fine green collarless shirt and orange vest, and dark round ruby-tinted glasses. His voice had a husky edge to it.

"Greetings Captain, have you brought more pages for me to bind?"

"Not today. I've come to purchase a notebook," Captain Deonto answered, "and to have a little chat."

Kjara had taken her words to be code for "official guard inquiry" and kept her distance from them. Leaving one ear trained on the conversation, Kjara explored the shop, picking up book after book. She couldn't read more than a few simple words in any of them, but she could recognise all the letters.

How could one hand write so much? Her hand ached from just a few hours of work, and she had written less than a tenth of even the thinnest book there. She imagined the scribes must have wrists of iron, and fingers to match. She placed the book in her hand back on the shelf and cast a quick look over at Captain Deonto.

"Haven't seen her," Elent was saying. "Not lately."

The captain narrowed her eyes, "She hasn't come by to fence anything?"

"Nope."

"Elent," she lowered her voice. "Am I to believe The Gambler's Bane has had no winnings to vendor?"

"I don't know what to tell you," Elent adjusted his glasses. "Maybe luck has finally run out for the Mother of Cards."

"Doubtful," the captain straightened up. "When was the last time you saw her?"

Elent tapped his cheek in thought, "About a week ago. Came in with a couple of others. A larger woman and a haffelin. She sold me a silver and gold ring."

"Did she say where she got it?"

"Some passing venturist apparently. Didn't have the coin to buy in. Used the ring instead," Elent reached under the counter and held out the ring. "Worth significantly more than the bid, though."

"Poor judgement on their part."

"Maybe they were a sucker for redheads."

Kjara's ears perked up. *Redhead...*

"The haffelin," Captain Deonto opened her notebook. "Male or female?"

"Neither."

"Ah," the captain said knowingly. "What did ze look like?"

"Ze had tattoos around zir neck. Average height. Curly hair. Fancy colourful clothes."

The captain scribbled a note. "And the woman. Larger build, short black hair?"

"Yer," Elent nodded.

"Orpip and Mayji," she closed her notebook. "Thank you, Elent. You've been very helpful." The captain looked around the store. Kjara quickly switched her focus back to the shelves, her eavesdropping unnoticed. "How much for the writing book?"

"One silver and two. Do you want me to add it to your account?"

The doorbell jangled, and a haffelin entered, draped in a garish array of coloured fabrics, an intricate collar of tattoos adorned zir neck. Ze carried a pair of fine, silver candlesticks. Ze looked at her for a moment, as Kjara blinked in recognition.

"Captain. Orpip's here!"

Deonto spun around. Orpip locked eyes with her, and with the kind of sharp instinct a criminal develops over a lifetime of felonies, turned tail and bolted from the shop. Without thinking, Kjara chased Orpip, closely pursued by the captain, out into the streets. She caught sight of the edge of Orpip's colourful coat flickering down an alley and dashed toward it, slipping between pedestrians and vendors. Deonto followed, shouting an official order for Orpip to halt. But Orpip heeded none of the captain's authority.

Kjara ripped down the alleyway, leaping over crates and darting through barrels. Orpip looked over zir shoulder and heaved one of the candlesticks straight for her face. She ducked it and shot back a determined glare. Orpip hurled the second candlestick, but this time she was prepared, catching it with one hand. Orpip let out a chuckle of admiration before slipping through a thin crack between the wooden fence blocking off the alley.

"Fine catch. You should try juggling!"

Incensed by zir taunt, Kjara followed through the fence, her shirt sleeve catching and tearing on a splintered piece of wood. She was too focused on catching her quarry to care. Deonto, too large to fit through the gap, peeled off to circle the other buildings and cut Orpip off before ze made it back to the main street.

"You're a persistent one," Orpip said, before hopping up a stack of crates, scrambling up the wall and grabbing a window ledge. From there, ze pushed off and upwards to a second-story window. With practised precision, Orpip threw one leg up over the gutter and hoisted zir frame onto the tiles. Slightly out of breath, Kjara watched the acrobatic ascent and knew she couldn't copy it, but climbing up the drainpipe would take too long.

In one final show of hubris, Orpip turned back to face her, bent one leg, gave a deep, dramatic bow and blew a condescending kiss, "Orpip the Funambulist always makes a grand exit. Nice try, though."

Kjara's pulse, heightened from anger and exertion, thudded and thrummed in her ears. She threw the candlestick at zir head. It flew wide, past the arrogant acrobat and any sense of accomplishment evaporated. Orpip winked and made to disappear over the ridge, then something remarkable happened.

As if time had slowed down, the candlestick froze mid-air. It spun about and rushed forward, connecting with a solid crack across the back of Orpip's head. One foot slipped out from under zir, and ze toppled off the roof, bouncing off the stack of crates beneath and spilling out prostrate on the paved alley.

Orpip didn't move, didn't speak. Zir eyes were shut.

Kjara knelt and reached two fingers out, pressing them under Orpip's jaw. As she did, Kjara caught sight of the tear in the forearm of her shirt and, even more unsettling than Orpip's stillness, the dark markings moving beneath her skin. The patterns pulsed, growing lighter and darker as a ripple of movement gave the illusion of them travelling up her arm.

Kjara stared, utterly bewildered. She forgot about the prone performer. She forgot what she was doing. Where she was. Time and space were meaningless, or meant something so completely different that she couldn't understand them anymore. Her eyes glazed over, and as her pulse softened a deep, humming vibration shuddered through her body. From somewhere far, far away, a voice called her name. It was Captain Deonto.

"Kjara, what are you doing?"

Chapter 18

Kjara

"What have I done?" Kjara's mind raced, her eyes darting back and forth as she tried to process what had happened. Something inside her told her to run, but something else told her to stay. If Orpip was dead, actually dead, she might be seen to be at fault.

No. She was at fault. It was because of her that Orpip had fallen. She threw the candlestick. But it had missed, hadn't it? No. It had hit zir. Right in the head. But from behind, not from the direction she had thrown it. Had her markings really moved or was it the rush of the chase playing tricks with her? How much had the captain seen? Did she hear the humming? Did she feel the vibration?

What was that?

"Kjara?" the captain repeated. "What are you doing?"

Remember where you are, Kjara.

Kjara blinked and spun around, holding the torn sleeve behind her.

"Checking for a pulse. Orpip fell off the roof, and ze isn't moving," she stammered weakly. The captain moved up next to the prone body and inspected zir, pressing two fingers into zir tattooed neck. The captain nodded, satisfied.

"Pulse is there," she said and unsheathed her sword.

"What are you doing?"

The captain held the flat of the blade against Orpip's upper lip. "Checking for breathing. Sometimes it is too shallow to see the movement or even feel it with your hand. See, there?"

Kjara leant over, keeping her arm out of view. Two tiny patches of fog started to coalesce on the steel in front of Orpip's nostrils. Kjara breathed out her relief.

"Wouldn't a hand mirror be safer than a sword?"

"The less one needs to carry, the better. And if a perpetrator is merely pretending, a blade by their throat may keep them from attempting anything foolhardy. This one though," the captain said, sheathing her sword, "is out cold. For the next few hours at least," she stood back up and took the pencil and notebook from her pocket. "What happened here?"

"Ze climbed up onto the roof, then fell off," Kjara lied.

"I know Orpip. Ze is one of the finest acrobats in the city, if not a little underhanded at times. Are you sure ze just fell?" the captain inquired sceptically.

Kjara offered the most honesty she could, "I threw a candlestick at zir head, and ze lost balance."

Technically, it was the truth; just with a few key pieces of information tactically withheld. The captain scanned the area, seeing the candlestick, and judged the height of the fall.

"I see. Quick thinking."

"Thank you, Captain."

"It was also reckless. If Orpip had landed poorly, ze could have died. You would have killed someone for no greater crime than resisting arrest. If the choice is either quick thoughts with reckless outcomes, or slow thoughts with prudent ones, one should always choose the latter. Consideration is not a courtesy, Chedderheart. It can save lives."

"I understand," Kjara said, the prickle of embarrassment heating her cheeks.

"I will need to take Orpip to the Medicary. Make sure ze hasn't sustained any significant damage, and if ze hasn't, I'll have zir woken up for a few questions. You left your book behind when you ran off. Collect it from Elent and return to me."

"Right away, Captain," Kjara replied, eager to be somewhere private so she could fix her shirt and gather her thoughts. She turned to leave, but the captain stopped her.

"One last thing," the captain said, inspecting the back of Orpip's unconscious head. "The cost of Orpip's medical attention will be added to your debt."

Chapter 19

Soren

Waves lapped over one another like a gentle lullaby and licked at Soren's feet. The warmth of the sun soaked through his shirt. But the jutting rocks beneath his body felt less like a bed and more like a bane. A sharp toe dug into his ribs, followed by a croaky chuckle and a greeting.

"Fine dawn, Lemon-face!" the chuckle said.

Soren's eyes flickered open, and he squinted a moment before throwing up one hand to defend against the painful, piercing sun. The outline of Papa Roce silhouetted against the light cut a frightening shape, and Soren's gut swirled his last meal as a threat.

"Oh, I know that face well," Papa said, biting into a skewer of fried fish. His other hand held a long, thin jar of what Soren assumed was white wine. "You've been visited by the muugiflu, haven't you?"

Soren scrunched up his face, "Muugiflu? What are you talking about?"

"The muugiflu. The little creatures that find you when you've had too much to drink. They beat you about the head, void their bowels in your mouth and steal your coin pouch," Papa dropped onto his rear beside him, dangling his legs in the water. "You've never heard of the muugiflu?"

Soren sat up, propping himself against one of the large stones at the foot of the break wall, and shook his head. The sudden motion forced a pickaxe of pain through his skull, and he winced. He peeled his tongue off the roof of his mouth and ran it about his teeth and gums, trying to lubricate his words.

"No. I haven't."

"Well, you have now. Here, the only known remedy," Papa shoved a fish skewer under Soren's nose. "Muugiflu hate fish. Eat. It'll help to stop them from stomping around in your noggin. Might drive them out completely if you're quick enough on the chew."

Soren recoiled from the smell of it, pushed it away from his face, and shot a pained expression at him. Refusing to accept his refusal, Papa continued to argue the point.

"Eat, you stubborn ox. I can barely survive your sour face at the best of times, and right now it is so dismal I fear it might kill me. I would smack the grump out of you with force if I could. Eat. You will feel better, believe me. Or, if you prefer, drink," Papa jiggled the jar. Definitely wine, the smell of it turned Soren's stomach. "Make your choice Lemon-face. Or I will leave you to your misery and have both for myself."

Soren didn't have the energy for argument, so he chose the skewer. Reaching out with a shaky hand, he drew the stick to his mouth, bit down, and chewed with the speed of a snail.

"By Fyaldha, you've done a number on yourself. You're too busted even to argue. How did you get into such a state?"

Soren closed his eyes and fought hard against passing out, retracing the previous twenty-four hours for a solid memory to catch. There were flashes of the dockmaster, The Bait and Tackle, the woman with red hair. Conversations about currency. A tall glass of beer. There it was. The culprit. He took another nibble of Papa's offering, before rolling his bloodshot eyes around to meet the old man.

113

"I was painting the guardhouse. Then I went looking for more work. I ran into the red-haired woman from the cellblock. We spoke about something…Wait!" he pawed through his pockets trying to find the coin purse he'd taken with him to The Bait and Tackle. Finding it offered him no comfort, for he found it had been drained dry.

Soren curled his lip in frustration before throwing it into the water with a curse. It was all starting to come back to him. The agreement he had made with Sabel and the fight that came of it. Cold waves of nausea shuddered through his body. Soren had kept his end of the bargain, but the empty coin purse indicated that she had not. How could he have been so careless and thoughtless? He should've known better than to expect Sabel to honour any dingy deal made in the back room of a pub.

Just one drink, I said. Idiot.

Over the next few minutes, Soren explained the circumstances of the previous day to Papa. By the end of it, his fish nearly finished, he felt a little less bleary. Admitting Papa was right would only fuel his arrogance, so he kept silent on the matter. Papa, on the other hand, did not.

"See, most people will swear by fried eggs or coffee. Or both. But that is a fool's mistake. Muugiflu love the grease, and a breakfast of that nature simply sends them tunnelling down your gullet to rest in your belly. You can feel them sloshing about in there, and when the fat congeals their feet get stuck. And then you get stuck with a muugiflu gut," Papa lectured, sipping his wine between sentences.

"Roce, does your rear end ever envy your mouth?"

"Why should it?"

"Because you speak more dung than you defecate," Soren shot, healthy enough now to be ornery.

Papa chuckled, "Perhaps. But you look me straight and say you don't feel a little better off after heeding the advice of kind old Papa."

"Kind…" Soren sighed. "You're a menace."

"I'm a delight!" Papa retorted, indignantly.

"How?"

"How?!" Papa made a wounded face. "All I ever do is give people a reason to smile. Get them to stop taking everything so seriously. And you mark my words, one day I'll succeed with you too."

"Perhaps, but on that day, I may well be dead."

"Now that's grim," Papa softened. "Is that what you were doing last night, then? Trying to drink your way to the After-all?"

"No," Soren squeezed his eyes. "But I've got no coin, no work, and no home."

"You won't find any of that in a bottle, null."

Soren scratched his ear, "I'm not a null anymore."

"Because you've no roof to hide under?" Papa scoffed. "Being in a commune makes a man a fid no more than swimming in the ocean makes a man a fish. The best part of disbelief is that it's a solo sport. Feel free to feel faithless!"

"It's not a lack of faith, Roce. It's faith in something real, each other, ourselves. Not a group of sky sitters," Soren rubbed the kink from his neck. "I mean, I've heard stories of the Collision. You must have lived them, how can you put faith in the gods after that?"

"Surviving the Collision, null, is precisely why I do," Papa shook off his sincerity. "And as for no coin and no work: there's plenty of fish in the sea. Why not be a fisher? Or work the docks? You've got some muscle on you."

"I tried. The dockmaster said he had no need for crate shifters. Said he was full up with miners taking all the jobs."

"Miners should learn to mine their own business," Papa twiddled with an errant strand of beard hair. "Why are they working here and not down a hole?"

115

"Reckon the mine is haunted. Strange smells, odd noises, missing tools."

Papa tapped his chin, "That doesn't sound like a haunting to me. Sounds more like some kind of prank being prunk, perhaps. So, not the forest-grown. More likely to be…" excitement spread across his face. "Oh, you cheeky little bastard! I'm coming for you. Ready or not!"

Papa rose to his feet, tossing the wine jug into the sand, and stormed up the sandy beach towards the docks.

"Where are you going?" Soren asked.

"The mine, of course! Never too old to venture someplace new!"

As the old man waded up the shoreline, Soren sighed in defeat. If the mine was haunted, or even if it weren't, the old man wouldn't stand a chance. Papa didn't have the correct equipment, nor any expertise in navigating underground as far as he could tell.

He swore under his breath, taking stock of his options. One: try to talk Papa out of his fixation, two: let him go alone, or three: guide him through the mine. The first option was no option at all, and his guilt couldn't permit the possibility of Papa perishing somewhere down a mineshaft.

"Wait, Roce. Wait up," Soren bounded to his feet, the sudden motion agitating his gut and his head. "You can't go down there by yourself."

Papa turned around, "Oh? And you're going to stop me?"

"No," Soren responded, regretting his decision even as he made it. He knelt down and scooped up Papa's discarded wine jar. "I am going to help you."

Chapter 20

Kjara

Kjara had seen a roll of cloth in Elent's Elegant Emporium. With a little persuasion and mild pleading, she convinced Elent to add it to the captain's account. He must have found her quite odd. As she spoke with him, she stood at a three-quarter angle, as though she were a stage actor addressing an audience, with one arm behind her back.

Kjara didn't much mind if he thought her odd though, so long as he didn't notice her markings. Taking her writing book and complementary pencil, she wrapped the cloth around her arm like a bandage, covering the tear, and left the store. She received an odd look from the captain upon meeting back up with her, but no questions were parsed as they continued to Rosalind's Medicary.

Orpip lay unconscious on a chest-high green table in the back room of the medicary while Kjara stood further back, avoiding the bright sunlight reflected into the room by ceiling-mounted mirrors. Cupboards lined the walls, painted white with green accents to match. The scents of calming soap and burning incense on Rosalind's desk twirled in the air. Rosalind leant over Orpip, inspecting zir injury.

"That is one cracker of an egg. How did it happen?"

"Ze fell off a roof," Deonto replied. When Rosalind looked at her confused, Deonto clarified, "Kjara threw a candlestick at zir head and ze fell off a roof."

Rosalind raised her eyebrows, though in concern or approval Kjara couldn't tell. She combed Orpip's hair back into place with her fingers.

"Ah. Well, I can put a cold stone compress on the head to reduce the swelling, wrap the ankle and clean the cuts. But Orpip is going to be out for a while. A few hours, I expect."

Kjara breathed a silent sigh of relief. As long as Orpip remained unconscious, her account of events would remain unchallenged. And with any hope, the time might scramble Orpip's version of events somewhat. Hopefully.

She shook her head.

That's kind of a grim hope, Kjara.

Rosalind opened a low cupboard against the far wall and removed some cotton gauze, scissors, a clay pot, a handful of dried leaves and a mortar and pestle. Throwing the leaves into the mortar, she unstoppered the clay pot, shook a handful of grey pebbles in, and poured a dash of water over them. As the ingredients crushed and mixed under the pestle, cold vapours emanated from the mortar.

"Cut me off some strips, would you?" she asked Kjara, gesturing to the gauze.

Kjara did so, passing them over to Rosalind who spread the now-gelatinous mush across them and wrapped Orpip's head, securing them with pins. Deonto seemed less pleased by Rosalind's diagnosis.

"Can we get zir awake any quicker?" she asked. "I have some questions I need to ask zir."

Kjara swallowed hard.

"Actually, yer. I have just the thing, freshly delivered," Rosalind beamed with excitement. "It is...uh, over here? I think. I really need to organise my supplies."

She searched through her desk drawers and let out a grunt of frustration. Moving from cupboard to cupboard, she continued to search while Kjara scanned the papers strewn across Rosalind's desk.

"Your desk looks a lot like the captain's," she said.

"Can't heal the world without paperwork," Rosalind quipped. "Ah, here it is."

She held up a small glass jar of toe-shaped magenta berries. Each one had a green line around their middle. She placed two of them into a small soapstone diffuser.

"How long will that take?" Kjara asked, a little more nervously than she would have liked. But her demeanour went unnoticed.

"A few minutes, maybe," Rosalind lit a candle and placed it beneath the diffuser. "Or longer, I've not tried it before."

Deonto sat down at Rosalind's desk, "So, we wait."

Rosalind leaned against a cupboard, "We could. Or...we could have lunch? Is she feeding you, young conscript?"

Kjara blushed a little, "Yer. I mean, I make it myself. And I need to record my takings, but I'm allowed as much food as I like. It just gets added to my debt."

Rosalind gave Deonto a disapproving look, "Really, Laine?"

Deonto didn't answer.

"C'mon, it's time for lunch. Laine, you're in charge of making the tea, at the very least. Tea, Kjara?"

"Yes, please," Kjara replied with a smile. Rosalind had said her name correctly this time.

Rosalind headed back to the front room of her medicary, flipped the sign hanging in her window from "open" to "closed" and locked the door. Stepping back behind the front counter, she bent down to collect plates and glasses.

"How did you go with the mine, Laine? Did you ask Roce for help?"

"It didn't come up," Deonto said, stuffing kindling into a cast-iron wood burner and placing a kettle on the stovetop. "We had other things to discuss."

"You got into an argument."

"We exchanged opinions," Deonto replied, taking a knife from the top drawer, and a tomato from the wicker basket on the counter. "His were different to mine."

"How so?"

"He thinks that "old bastard" is a term of endearment."

Rosalind unsheathed a loaf of stone-baked bread from its paper cradle, "You called him an old bastard?"

"No," Deonto paused, halfway through slicing a tomato. "That's what he called the region master."

Rosalind looked to Kjara with a glinting eye, "Well, if anyone would know…"

Kjara stifled a chuckle. It seemed not the wisest choice to pick a side.

"That's not the point," Deonto stepped over to the window planter and snapped off a handful of basil leaves. "He should follow proper etiquette."

Rosalind laughed.

"What?"

"I just think it's funny how similar you and Roce are."

Deonto scowled, "How, by the moons, is he anything like me?"

"Neither of you can stomach authority."

Deonto chewed her cheek, "At least I respect it."

"Hardly a week goes by without some delinquent laying insults on you," Rosalind said, taking the basil leaves from her hand and sprinkling them over slices of bread. "What makes Roce different?"

"His sense of superiority."

Deonto dragged a set of waiting chairs from the front of the room over to the counter and collapsed into one. She gestured for Kjara to sit in the other. Rosalind slid them both sandwiches. Thick, soft bread lightly spread with butter. Piled high with crisp vegetables, hard cheese, and spiced relish. Kjara's stomach growled with anticipation.

"Plenty of people act superior," Rosalind said, sweeping up half of her sandwich. "Especially when they have no reason to."

"I know. But I feel like, in this instance, he might," the whistling kettle interrupted Deonto's first bite. She walked over and lifted it off the flame. "He knows about our impending guest," she explained, preparing the tea. "Including some details that I was not briefed about."

Rosalind passed a hesitant look to Kjara, no doubt recalling Deonto's prior concern for confidentiality. Deonto waved it away.

"It's fine," she said, handing out the teas. "Kjara knows what is going on. More than me, I feel, and at least as much as Roce."

Kjara smiled with as much conviction as she had knowledge of the situation. Which was not a lot. The captain had put more faith in Kjara's understanding than she should have.

Rosalind leant against the counter, cupping her mug with both hands, "You don't think he was lying?"

Deonto shook her head, "Too specific."

"So, the ship has sprung a leak."

"And I don't know where to plug it," Deonto continued, sitting back down. "But apparently, more than just Naistinn Farlight, the Regal-apparent Londre Tamou of Glainne will also be joining her. Which I was not briefed about. I don't know when they're expected. Or why they're invited but the other leaders in the Aonadh aren't."

Kjara had heard of the Aonadh. It was spoken about to various degrees of pleasure by the older patrons of The Eyeglass Pub. Papa had also mentioned it once or twice, explaining to Kjara that it was an agreement between several neighbouring nations, including Cradh and Glainne, made in the wake of the Collision. An alliance of sorts, to protect against any future invasion. So why were they gathering in Northern Cradh? Did they suspect another Collision? Or were they planning to break the agreement? Was it preparation for war? Kjara's mouth dried out, and she sipped her tea in silence. The steam wafted over her nose and brow, calming her.

Rosalind looked over the rim of her mug, "If you want answers, start asking questions. And not to me, Laine. You know to whom."

Deonto scoffed, mouth half full of sandwich, "The quickest way to lose your job is to start asking questions."

Rosalind let out a patient sigh and lay her hand softly on Deonto's forearm.

"There is such a thing as too much respect for authority," she said, giving a little squeeze. "Maybe you need to rattle the cage a bit."

"Hello?" called a weak voice from the back room. Deonto dropped her sandwich and dusted the crumbs from her shirt. She stood up, strode through the hallway, and filled the door, one hand on her sword.

Orpip groaned, "Gods be…Arrested?"

"Not yet," Deonto replied, before casting a look down the hallway and stepping out of view, closing the door behind her.

Kjara nibbled absently at her sandwich for a moment, running back over the conversation. Peeling one crust from the bread she asked, "Do you really think the captain is like Papa?"

"Absolutely."

"I don't see it," Kjara said. "She keeps the law intact, but he seems only to want to break it."

Rosalind chuckled, "Those two have known each other a long time. And truth be truth, I think she rather enjoys their cat-and-mouse chase. He challenges her. It keeps her on her toes, keeps her wit sharp. Gets her out of the office. Away from all the paperwork."

"She doesn't really like that, does she?"

"Oh yer. It is a frequent clash in our conversations. If it were up to her, she'd still be a venturist. No restraints, regulations. And importantly, no paperwork. But I say no. She's worked hard for our safety. I'll not let her give that up."

"The captain used to be a venturist? What happened?"

"The Collision," Rosalind said sombrely. "She leant her sword to the frontline and got paid for it in scars."

Kjara imagined Deonto cutting a swath through an onslaught of enemies. Muddied hair, surrounded by smoke and fire, soot-streaked face. Then bloodied from battle, perhaps having caught an arrow, and being taken into a medical tent.

"Is that how you two met?" she asked. "Did you have to patch her up?"

"I didn't serve on the frontline," Rosalind sipped her tea. "No, all of her injuries were managed by Papa Roce. Though it was just Alba Roce, back then."

"Papa served too?"

Rosalind nodded. "They volunteered together."

Kjara blinked in astonishment, "I can't imagine that either."

"When folks care enough, they'll do almost anything."

The door down the hall swung open and Deonto marched out, heading for the front door. As she grasped the handle, she looked over her shoulder.

"Kjara, return to the guardhouse. I may be some time, so practice your words until I return."

"Hang about," Rosalind said. "Where are you off to?"

"The Overbite," came Deonto's short reply as the door shut behind her.

Kjara frowned. The Overbite was a long cliff running the northern edge of the coastline a few miles west of town. She had been assured the view from the top was stunning, capturing views of the Tohl-Mor Bay and the circle sea, but she failed to see its relevance. She turned to Rosalind for guidance.

"Why the Overbite?" she asked.

Rosalind licked a tomato seed from her lip, "Because there is a manor up on that cliff. And it happens to be the home for our dear region master. Looks like she's going to start asking some questions. Good for her," she sighed. "Though I wish she'd finished her lunch first."

Chapter 21

Kjara

The trip back to the guardhouse took Kjara through the trade quarter where she caught sight of Papa and Soren. Their signature outlooks appeared in strong contrast, Papa babbled on about some insignificant topic while Soren kept his expression blank and his eyes forward. She crossed the street to meet them as they were about to enter Minter's General Goods. Papa noticed Kjara approach first, and he waved a cheerful hand at her.

"Well, well, half-your-luck. What's this? Are you free and unchaperoned? Or is the cross arm of the law lurking about?" he asked, casting a cautious eye about the street.

"Interesting you say free, Papa. I should ask you the same thing. How is it you aren't in lockup?"

Papa shrugged, "Early release for good behaviour."

Kjara ignored his response for the moment, turning instead to Soren's irritating face, "And what are you doing with him?"

Soren made to respond, but Papa interjected, "We're going mining!"

"Is that so? And did Soren invite you, or did he sneak up and grab you?"

Soren looked sheepish. Papa slapped his hand on the null's shoulder, "Do you want to come with us? It'll be fun."

Kjara scrunched up her nose, "Go underground with this creep? No chance!"

"Oh, come now, don't be so rude. I know you've bad blood. But it's a two-mile walk out of town. You can reconcile your differences on the way."

"Reconcile? This *stranger* got me arrested!" her voice raised a few eyebrows from passers-by.

"He got me arrested too; I don't mind."

"You've probably been arrested plenty of times!"

"Maybe," Papa leant against the Minter's window. "What's the big deal?"

"The big deal is I haven't. And now I'm stuck scrubbing floors and writing letters—"

"I'm sorry," Soren mumbled, interrupting the conversation. "I should have thought it through, called out to you first or something. But you were running so fast and I just...reacted. I didn't think. I'm not great at talking to people, I make a lot of mistakes."

His admission softened Kjara. The man standing before her looked so humble, so awkward. Not at all like the aggressive, violent, and dangerous image she had built up in her mind.

"I see," she said carefully, not quite ready to forgive. "Well, you would probably do well thinking a bit more first. One should choose slow thoughts with prudent outcomes over quick thoughts with reckless ones."

Papa blew a raspberry, "Who told you that nonsense?"

Soren nodded at Kjara, "I'll try to remember that."

Kjara's irritation eased, "Why did you try and grab me?"

"I saw you sitting with Roce. I wanted to know how he did it. The honeypot prank. I thought you might have known the answer."

"Me?" Papa cried. "I didn't do anything. Fyaldha did it."

Soren remained unconvinced, "What a childish way to avoid responsibility."

"The gods can't give you powers, no matter how much you pray," Papa stuck his little finger in his ear and shook it. "Could you imagine if they did? What a terrible business model that would be. Now, we've all said our apologies and all the rest, are you coming to the mine with us, Kjara?"

"That's not an apology," Kjara said.

Papa threw his head back with an overly dramatic groan, but Kjara didn't budge.

"I'm sorry Fyaldha pulled a trick on you," he said, and after seeing Soren's stone-faced and unimpressed expression groaned again. "I'm sorry I *asked* Fyaldha to pull a trick on you. There, can we go to the mine now?"

"I have to stay here and work off my debt," Kjara explained.

Papa blew a long, dismissive raspberry and opened the door to the Minter's General, "If you ask me, clearing out ghoulies from the mine so it can be operational again falls well and truly under the category of community service. Besides, when we catch what is in the mine, we'll be so rich Deonto will be working for us!"

Soren and Kjara looked at each other, sharing a moment of confusion.

"Look, if you are so worried, tell Deonto I kidnapped you or something," he added, seeing her reluctance. "And Soren can say he chased after us to rescue you. I'll look like a villain, but if it stops you two moping about and agree to come along, I am prepared to fall on that sword."

Kjara considered Papa's proposition. Not the kidnapping idea, that was foolish. But if she could return to the captain with proof the mine was safe for operation, it would be an ideal result for everyone involved. It would go a long way towards repaying her debt and might even make up for her fumbled attempt at catching Orpip.

Deciding the outcome of the excursion was a prudent one, and as such would be approved of by the captain, Kjara agreed.

"Okay, I'll come along. But I need to be back at the guardhouse before dark. What is it we're trying to catch?"

Kjara stared at Papa in disbelief as they approached the entrance to the mine. It had taken roughly an hour to walk the two miles south along the road to Cacot. For the entire travel, Soren and Kjara had pestered Papa to explain himself, and for the entire travel, he insisted he would explain when they got there.

Now, as Kjara peered into the dark mouth of the mine, she started to regret every step of the journey. It was clear why he had refused so vehemently to tell her earlier. If she'd known about the ridiculous reason Papa had to explain the mine's disturbance, she would have stayed back in the city.

"A chezplou," Kjara stared cynically at Papa. "Truth be truth, Papa, a chezplou?"

"You can't be serious," Soren added.

"Of course, I'm serious," Papa huffed. "You don't believe me?"

"That's not a real thing."

"Oh, really?" Papa asked. "I suppose you think ylfes aren't real either."

"I've seen ylfes," Soren countered. "I've never seen a chezplou."

"So that's how it is. If you haven't seen them, they aren't real. Kjara, have you ever seen an ylfe?" Kjara shook her head. "I guess ylfes aren't real then, are they, Soren?" Papa argued flippantly, his eyes carefully scanning for movement from inside the mine. "Here, pass me the milk and saucer."

Soren passed Papa the jug of milk and the shallow bowl he'd explicitly requested back at Minter's General. He had been so stubborn and loud in his demands, the proprietor threatened to expel him from the store.

Papa complained again when it came time to pay, and Kjara pointed out that if he wanted to go so badly, it was only right that he financed the expedition. Disgruntled, he agreed but insisted Soren carry the supplies: Fifty feet of hempen rope, ten torches, a jar of oil, a crowbar, a half-dozen pitons and a replacement backpack for it all.

The old man set off running across the dirt, skipping over the mine cart tracks, and landed inside the edge of the mine drift. He laid the saucer down on one of the rails and poured a few quarts of milk into it. Stoppering the glass jug, he plucked a clover from his beard and placed it daintily in the centre of the milk. Then he ran back, gesturing for Kjara and Soren to hide down behind one of the abandoned mine carts that littered the area. Papa slipped down next to Kjara, behind one cart, while Soren and the backpack slumped behind another.

Soren watched as Papa peered up over the edge, "Chezplous aren't cats, you know."

"Thought you said they weren't real," Papa shot back.

"They aren't."

Papa blew a raspberry, "Next you'll tell me sfarggs aren't real."

Hands folded over the side of the cart, he narrowed his eyes and craned his neck forward, calling for silence again. He peeled one index finger out to direct her eye.

"Something's moving," he whispered harshly. "Coming out of the tunnel. Look. Careful."

Kjara poked her head up next to him, scanning the tunnel for movement, and gasped. A faint shape shuffled about in the darkness. Soren, ever dubious, noticed her response and peered out from behind the side of his cart. For a moment, his mouth opened in astonishment, but as the creature scurried out of the darkness and began lapping up the milk, he let out a loud scoff.

The noise scared the creature, and it ran off, up the side of the hill and into a distant tree.

Papa grimaced, "Bloody cat." However, he did not look disheartened. "Looks like we're going in," he said. "Prepare us a torch, lemon face!"

Papa strode over to the start of the drift, picking up the saucer and sipping from it while he investigated the timber supports inside the mine mouth. Kjara sidled up beside him, watching curiously but saying nothing. Meanwhile, Soren took a torch from his back, dipped the tip of it in the jar of oil and removed the fire striker and flint from his pocket. He lit the torch and moved forward, but then stopped.

"Maybe I should stay here," Soren said. His face held reluctance, an undercurrent of fear, but he gave no reasoning for his suggestion.

Papa shrugged, walked over to Soren, and snatched the torch from his hand, "Suit yourself. More reward for us."

"Papa, we can't go in without him," Kjara said. "We'll get lost. He's the only one with experience. And he has all of the equipment."

Papa rolled his eyes and grabbed Soren's arm, "Come on then, donkey. You can have an extra portion of the loot."

Chapter 22

Kjara

Half an hour had passed since Kjara entered the mine. She had used her writing book to draw a simple map as they explored. Soren led the way, while Papa filled the air by expositing the folklore behind chezplous. His lecture included which stories were true, which were false, and which were deliberately spread to confuse the first two.

"A chezplou," Papa began, "is about one foot tall, and three feet long, if you account for the tail. Which you should, because the whole thing altogether is about 85% tail. That's what it hangs its treasure purses on, you see. It's got stumpy little legs and you'd swear a third of the body which isn't tail is mouth. Big round eyes like upside-down teacups, and a tuft of thick hair like coiled rope on its head."

When he ran out of authority on one creature, he moved on to the next mythical beast in his seemingly unending roster. Each of the Nofrum creatures Papa spoke about seemed to be small in some way. Kjara wondered if maybe the stories had grown out of history before haffelins and mohras knew of each other.

"They like to balance upside down on the tip of their tail," Papa explained, moving onto the subject of chezplou pastimes. "Then they spin around like a whirligig, juggling their treasures—usually coins, or other misplaced trinkets—with their feet. Can't find your keys? Chezplou. Can't find your trowel? Chezplou."

Soren shook his head sceptically, "By the moons, Roce, what's next? Draejrs?"

Kjara smiled. Her favourite folk story, the draejr. She recalled the stories told by her aunt Gerde when she was a child, piecing together an image in her mind. A body somewhere between a cat and a horse but covered in scales and fur. Claws instead of hooves, head and wings textured with feathers, two tails. And gigantic. Some said as big as a house, some said bigger.

Papa chuckled, "No such thing."

"Finally, we agree on something."

"It's simple logic," Papa continued. "Draejrs are huge creatures, right? Consider how much food they would need to live. Where is it coming from? How do they manage to eat their fill without being spotted?"

"So, what you're saying is, they aren't real because you've never seen them."

"No. What I'm saying is, there is no way they could go unnoticed. By anyone. Quirbles, muugiflu, chezplous, sfarggs. Small. Quiet. Sneaky. Draejrs? Wings, antlers, and big!" Papa flapped his arms. "Not very inconspicuous. I've never seen one, and I've never met anyone else who'd seen one. Besides, even if they were real, they'd all be gone by now."

"Why?" Soren asked.

"Big creatures. Big threat. If ever they existed, they would have been hunted to extinction long before you or I had even drawn breath."

"I heard they love metal," Kjara said. "Folks say it's what they eat. They have a furnace for a heart, and bellows for lungs. So, they sleep in water to keep cool. They'll eat swords, arrowheads, cutlery…minecart tracks. So, if you've lost your coin, it could have been a draejr."

"How do they get your coins?" Soren asked.

Kjara winked, "Friends in small places. They make minions of the little ones."

"Wouldn't want to make one sick," Papa joked. "Imagine what they'd spew."

"Slag," Soren replied.

"Hold your tongue, null," Papa pointed to a patch of tunnel mushrooms. "They're getting more regular. We'll be getting close to the chezplou's lair, I'd wager."

"I thought grey moss was the tell-tale sign of chezplou hide-outs," Soren said.

"That is one of the myths, Lemon-face. Weren't you listening?" Papa rapped him on the head as punishment. "Wait. Look, there."

Papa pointed to a mine shaft a few feet in front of them, surrounded by a wooden barricade. A pile of gold coins by the edge of the hole glinted in the torchlight. Soren stepped forward, but Papa grabbed his arm.

"Don't touch. If you do, he'll know we're here. And he'll run. We need to go down the shaft. Get the rope out."

Soren unspooled the rope and tied one end around one of the support beams in the tunnel. He gave a few hard yanks, to ensure the knot held, then threw the other end down the shaft. Papa, excited by the prospect of finding the chezplou, reached for it, but Soren held him back.

"I'm the heaviest. I'll go first."

Papa grumbled in agreement and stepped away. Soren took the rope and artfully abseiled down the shaft into the darkness.

"All clear," he called back up.

"I'll go next," Papa said. "You drop the torch down when I've hit the dirt. Then you'll be able to see where you're going."

Papa handed the torch to Kjara and began climbing down the rope, hand over hand, until he finally passed below her field of view. She stood there listening for the signal, but a strange sensation washed over her. Something was watching her. A sound, the scratching of dirt and rock, trickled from somewhere in one of the adjoining tunnels. And another sound. It was familiar, like a breeze rustling through wheat. She listened intently.

It was breathing.

Dry, rasping breath. And it was getting closer.

In a moment of panic, Kjara stepped back from the source of the sound and onto the pile of gold. Her foot squished into it and whipped out from under her. The barricade had been built for mohras, and as she staggered backward, it became painfully apparent they were not made for haffelins.

Kjara's small frame slipped under it completely, and she tumbled into the shaft. The torch flew from her hand and clattered to the ground by the rope, still burning. Her stomach lurched with a sickening rising feeling as she plummeted into the darkness of the mineshaft.

I'm going to die!

No, you aren't. There is a rope here. Grab it. There's plenty of time. Grab the rope.

The voice in Kjara's head urged her to reach out, so that is what she did. Her body lightened; her descent relaxed. And everything froze. The rasping breath disappeared, leaving nothing but the blood pounding in her eardrums. She reached out blindly and there it was. The rope. In her hand. And it wasn't moving. Or rather, her hand wasn't moving. It wasn't sliding down the rope as it should naturally do. And there it was again. The humming, the vibration, louder and louder. It rolled her up in it. And it became her, somehow.

"All clear," Papa's voice echoed up the tunnel. "You there?"

Gravity took hold again, and Kjara slid down ten or so feet before she clutched the rope with both hands and stopped her descent.

"Yer. I'm coming down."

"Torch first, yer?"

Kjara swore under her breath. She would have to climb back up and get it. But if she did, would the breathing thing still be up there?

"Yer. Just a second," she took a deep, calming breath, and jammed her feet into the rock wall of the shaft, preparing for her descent. As she did, the rope slackened, and once again, she was in free fall.

As Kjara hit the ground, the air exploded from her lungs. Tens of tiny sharp rocks caught her landing and punctured her skin. The rope fell after her, coiling messily over her body as she lay winded, gasping for breath, Soren held out another torch, casting light over her crumpled body. Papa rushed to her aid.

"Can't. Breathe. Am I dying?" her voice wheezed through strained breaths.

"No, no. You've just had the wind knocked out of you," Papa clarified. "Try to relax. Curl up into a ball if you can. It'll stop your muscle spasms." Kjara did so and found it helpful. "I'm going to see if you've broken anything. Arms first. I'll have to roll up your sleeve."

"No!" Kjara cried, pulling away before wincing with another surge of pain.

"It's okay. Soren's not looking. He won't see them," Papa whispered, countering the fear in her eyes with genuine care in his voice. Kjara nodded and let him inspect her.

"Is she okay?" Soren asked, scanning the area.

"Huh…Well now, that's odd," Papa squinted. "Soren, bring the light closer."

Kjara furrowed her brow, but Papa smiled a rare, calming smile that told her it was okay. Soren held the light out a little closer. Papa reached out and placed his thumb on her left cheek, pulling her eyelid down to get a better look at her eye. He repeated this with the right eye before glancing back up the mine shaft.

"How is your vision, Kjara?" Papa asked. "You've burst a few blood vessels in your right eye, unusual with a fall, but not impossible. Can you think clearly? Can you see okay?"

Kjara nodded, with a slight wince.

"Good. Rest awhile. Get your breath back. When you're ready, tell us what happened."

The moment Kjara could breathe and move again, she performed a quick self-examination, to ensure none of her clothing had ripped. There were a few minor tears, but nothing big enough to draw attention to her skin. And in the dark, it was even less likely Soren would notice.

At this rate, I'll be naked before Fifthmoon. Clothes all torn to pieces, Kjara thought, looking down at her damaged sleeve. Continuing to inspect herself, she discovered strange, sticky goo pressed into the tread of her boot. A mush of pink, orange, and green.

"Gross."

"She okay?" Soren asked, looking over his shoulder.

"A few cuts, a few bruises. But I don't think anything is broken," Papa answered.

"What about that eye thing?" Soren knelt to inspect a series of strange scratches on the wall. They were about four feet from the ground and about an inch deep, running six or seven feet long. "Is that something to worry about?"

Papa shook his head, "A bit of blood. Few scrapes and scuffs. She'll be right. What about you?"

"I'm fine," Soren said. He stood up and turned to face Papa. "I think we should leave, Roce. This was a stupid idea. Someone is going to get hurt."

"Someone already has," Papa said. "You said the line was safe."

Soren's fist clenched by his side. He stared down Papa's accusatory glower, "It was."

"Not anymore," Papa replied dryly. "Now it's on the ground."

"Kjara, what happened to the rope?"

"I heard a noise up there," Kjara said. "I turned around and slipped in something. And I dropped the torch. It must have burnt through the rope."

"What did you slip in?" Papa asked.

Kjara held out her foot, pointing to the multicoloured goo, "This? At first, I thought it was the gold pile we saw. But it was squishy."

Papa's brow furrowed, and his expression darkened, "Oh, dear."

"Rope wasn't burnt," Soren added, inspecting the end of the rope. "It's been cut. Clean through."

"…Oh, dear."

From above, there echoed a clinking of wood against rock, and the torch Kjara had dropped clattered to the ground near her feet. She picked it up, puzzled.

"The rag's been snapped off," she said, holding up the stick.

Papa shook his head, "No, not snapped. Bitten."

"What?" asked Soren and Kjara in unison.

"It's not a chezplou in this mine. We need to leave. Now!"

Above them, echoing down the shaft, the same dry breathing came, twisting itself into horrid laughter.

Chapter 23

⊚

Kjara

The encroaching smell of tobacco smoke, the retching cackle, and the crunching sound of nails digging into dirt tightened Kjara's throat with concern. Papa leapt into action. Motioning for Soren to grab the backpack, Papa lunged over it, helping Kjara to her feet, and pointed to the closest mine tunnel.

"This way. Quick!" he urged, hurtling through the narrow passage, followed by Soren with Kjara—due to her height and injuries—bringing up the rear. The scratching and smoke grew louder and closer, and as she ran, Kjara threw a quick look backward. In the fading torchlight, she caught a brief glimpse of the pursuer as it crawled out of the shaft. Gnarled hand. Long fingers. Frayed Rope. Dangling patchwork cloth.

Onward she rushed, ducking under beams and outcropping rocks, twisting and winding through the tunnels. Small veins of iron and other minerals glinted in the torchlight. Shadows bounced frantically along the cold tunnel walls as the flame flickered in time with Soren's steps.

The heavy, icy air caught in Kjara's throat and pricked at her lungs. The cuts, bruises, and scratches on her legs filled with salty sweat and screamed for respite, but she could not give it. Papa had ordered they run like their lives depended on it, and she was not one to argue against staying alive. Approaching a fork in the tunnels, Papa hurled a rock down one tunnel before darting down the other one.

Kjara's heart battered against her rib cage, "Why?"

"Wishful thinking!" Papa called back, ducking beneath another sharp outcrop of rock.

"Can't you do something?" Soren asked.

"Like what?" Papa demanded.

"I don't know. Call on your god?"

"Don't you ever listen, Soren? I'm a Fyaldha convert. We're being chased by a native! In the hierarchy of worship, I am severely out-ranked!"

Around another corner they turned, the musty smell of dirt and stone thick enough to choke on.

"Can you ask, at least?"

"Fine! But only to prove a point!" Papa grouched. "Brazen Fyaldha! Oh, Hoaxing Archer! Let loose your malapert quarrel unto—"

A crunching thud, pained curse and body collapsing echoed down the tunnel ahead of Kjara. She stopped. Soren stopped. The sputtering, crackling torchlight threw shifting shadows across the ground. No sound of the pursuer. No sound of Papa.

Did it get him? Did it sneak around us? Take another pass and cut us off?

"Papa?" Kjara whispered into the darkness. "Are you there?"

"...Yep," he groaned. "I think so."

Soren adjusted the backpack and inched forward. Kjara followed. Papa was lying on the ground, nursing a head wound that pulsed blood from his temple, which pooled in his beard. Kjara knelt by his side.

"What happened?"

"Tripped. My sandal went sidelong, and I smacked my head on a rock," Papa glanced skyward. "Nice one."

He attempted to stand but winced in pain as he put pressure on his foot.

"You've rolled your ankle."

"Thank you, Soren. I hadn't noticed," Papa spat. "Here endeth the lesson, Lemon-face. Never pray and retreat at the same time. Back-pack."

Soren passed the torch to Kjara and slid the pack to the ground. Papa rustled through it, finding a roll of bandages, and wrapped his ankle.

What was that?

Smouldering tobacco and scratching stone filled the tunnel behind Kjara. She checked over her shoulder. Past the previous bend, at the edge of the torchlight, it crept into view. First billowed smoke, then a long thin pipe probed out from the darkness. A flash of red patchwork and curling out from beneath it, grey-blue fingers moving snake-like along the ground.

One hand. A second. A third.

Then a face, whiskered and gaunt, with an upturned nose and stretched, flat lips, half-shadowed by a tall, brown hat. Its eyes sparkled from the shadows and it grinned, its teeth somehow luminescent. Two hands dug their sharp nails into the stone wall, sending a shrieking scratch down the tunnel. It rushed for Kjara, scrambling and giggling awfully.

The creature launched itself into the air and tackled her to the ground. The torch clattered against the stones. She squirmed, trying to escape the unnatural thing, but it was too strong. And it had too many hands, too many grips to shake. For the second time in as many hours, Kjara thought she was going to die.

Thunk.

Metal belted against flesh. A crowbar collapsed the creature's snout, sending it flying backward with a spray of blood. Kjara shielded her face with one hand, but the viscous mess splattered across her. She curled her nose up in disgust while Soren helped her to her feet.

"You okay?"

Kjara wiped her face with her sleeve and nodded.

Soren approached the creature, shining the torchlight over it. Lying splayed out, it wasn't much larger than Kjara. A strange mix of pink, green and yellow fluid dribbled from its crushed-in face. The red patchwork belonged to a coat. And the frayed rope she had seen earlier was its tail. It had five appendages, two arms on the right side, one arm on the left, two legs, with each limb ending in a hand. Its face was bordered with tufts of spindly grey hair.

"What is this thing?" Soren asked. "Roce? You still with us?"

"Fiedrig," came Papa's reply from the shadow's edge.

"Fiedrig?" Kjara repeated.

"They're a dark trickster. They like playing gruesome pranks."

"Like cutting the rope?"

"Didn't seem like a prank," Soren said.

"I did say gruesome. These aren't fun and fancy, these Nofrum are vicious," Papa sniffed. "Grab it and let's go."

"Why?"

"Proof, null. Evidence for Captain can't-take-a-joke," Papa waved his hands sarcastically. "We solved the mystery of the mine. Hooray for us."

"What about the gold?" Kjara asked.

Papa scoffed, "Fiedrigs don't hoard gold. Lemon-face, pour the rest of that milk over it, would you?"

"What? Why?"

"So it doesn't dissolve away, obviously. Unless you want to lose our hard-won trophy and return to the captain with nothing more than dusty lungs."

Soren, looking confused, poured the remaining milk over the creature's mangled form to Papa's approval.

"That should do it. C'mon, let's leave."

"Can you walk?" Kjara asked.

Papa crawled to his feet and tentatively tested his ankle, "Well, I won't be cartwheeling out of here. It'll be slow going, but yer. And give us a torch as well. I think we need a bit more light down here."

Soren slung the pack over one shoulder, and the Fiedrig over the other. Its fluids mixed with the milk and dribbled out of its face down his back. Kjara collected up her torch, lit another for Papa, and led the way back to the mineshaft, but upon reaching it, discovered the rope was gone.

"Fiedrig probably ate it," Papa said.

"If we're lucky we might find a ramp back up to the next level," Soren said. "If we can get back up, the map should make it easy to find the way out. Which way, Kjara?"

Kjara opened her writing book, "That way, I think."

As they continued, the mine tunnels began to change, becoming less deliberate and more organic. A soft, distant sound pricked at her ears, "What's that?"

"Sounds like the wind," Papa answered. "We must be close to the surface."

Kjara wasn't so sure but didn't want to confuse the matter. Soren and Papa seemed to know what they were doing, and she was in no position to argue. However, when at last she found the source of the sound, she wished she had been. The path widened into a large limestone cavern. The ceiling was beyond the reach of the torchlight, but a few tips of dripstone hung down out of the blackness. Rocks glistened, appearing wet, but were dry to the touch. A narrow inky black river cut across the path. Running water pattered against the rocks. It wasn't the wind Papa was chasing, it was an underground stream.

Papa sat against a rock, "Poo."

Soren hung his head, "We're never getting out of here."

"Ugh. Such pessimism," Papa elevated his swollen ankle.

"We're lost, Roce," Soren slumped against the cavern wall, letting the fiedrig flop to the ground. "We're lost, and we're trapped, and we're going to die."

The torchlight caught something metallic in the rocks by the river. Kjara crept down the stones to investigate. A single, metal button. She picked it up: hard, cold to the touch, real. She held up the torch. Across the water, more buttons trailed off into the dark.

"There's buttons down here. Metal buttons," Kjara pointed. "Look."

"Ah-ha!" Papa cried out. "Our path to freedom."

"Because we've found buttons?"

"Of course! Where there are buttons, there is civilisation. C'mon!" Papa said, before hobbling down to Kjara, hitching up his robes and wading across the stream.

She took a few steps back and attempted to leap across but landed shy of the far bank, up to her knees in the water. Soren shook his head, walked a few feet along the river's edge to a narrow stone crossing, and stepped nimbly from rock to rock over to the other side.

Moving further into the cavern, the combined torchlight lit up a huge anchor, some iron wheel spokes, sections of a bent and rusted fence, and a collection of rebar poles. A few swords of various designs lay on wooden shields stripped of their metal facades. Littered all over the cavern floor were smaller metal items, a few coins, some rings, more buttons. Kjara was so focused on the floor that Papa's gleeful cry startled her.

A golden mountain of coin stood in front of him. Arranged loosely in a pile taller than any two of them combined and spread out across the entirety of the cavern floor. More riches than any Kjara could have imagined. Enough to pay their collective debt one thousand times over.

"By Fyaldha," Papa muttered in awe. "Have you ever seen so much coin? If this doesn't set a smile on you, Lemon-face, I don't know what will."

He swept up a handful and let it trickle through his fingers.

"That's a lot of gold," Soren replied.

"You're damned right, it's a lot of gold!" Papa fell back into the pile, making angels with his arms and grinning wildly.

"That doesn't look comfortable. Or easy."

"It's not!" Papa laughed. "But maybe I'll just pay for a massage to fix it when we get back to the city. Open up the bag, null."

Soren crunched up through the strewn gold and dropped the backpack and the fiedrig. If he was still morose about their circumstances, he had stopped showing it. Opening the largest pouch of the pack, Papa and Soren began tossing equipment to free up as much room as possible.

"Not too much, you'll rip it," Soren chided.

"Not enough, and we'll have to come back!" Papa said eagerly.

More curious than excited, Kjara circled the mountain of gold. Her boots squelched across the ground as she passed a large rock pool on the far side. Several glow-worms wiggled on the cavern wall behind it. She pushed her torch into the pile, bent down, counted out thirty-five gold pieces, and stacked them in a lazy pyramid.

So, this is what thirty-five gold looks like, Kjara thought, before lifting the flap of her haversack and scooping in the coins. Giving the mountainous treasure a second glance, Kjara took an additional ten pieces and a silver ring with fine engravings, as gifts for her parents. It might not be much of an apology, but she hoped it would soften their disappointment in her.

Kjara stood back up, collected the torch, and took two steps before the noise of water rippling and dripping drew her focus. Brow furrowed, she turned around. When she saw it, her mouth fell open.

Unfurling its huge body from the water, a creature unlike anything in existence revealed itself. Cat-like eyes pierced from beneath a pair of antlers. Scales ornamented its lower jaw while feathers framed its face like a mane, running back over its head to meet the fur on its upper body. A sharp clap cracked through the cavern as it shook the water from its wings and folded them over its back. One claw lifted from the water and crushed into the golden carpet of coins as it lowered its head to meet Kjara's eye. In a quivering breath just above a whisper, Kjara did the only thing she could think of.

"H-hello…My name is Kjara."

"Hello…Kjara," it responded, the hot air of its breath sweeping over her face as its lips parted, revealing two rows of pointed teeth. "My name is Azmariliz."

Kjara hadn't expected a response, she hadn't thought that far.

"Are you going to eat me?" she asked.

"…Are you going to eat *me*?" Azmariliz countered.

"I don't think I could eat you if I tried."

Azmariliz paused a moment. "I think that I could eat you if I tried."

Kjara's face drained of colour, "I would much rather you didn't."

A smooth, hearty chuckle bubbled out of its maw. "It's impolite, I should think, to bite one's guests. But I suppose it's also impolite to not offer the guest a bite to eat. Had I known of your arrival, I would have prepared something for you."

"Thank you. It is a kind consideration."

"It is in my nature."

Kjara looked the creature over, "…Are you what I think you are?"

"I am exactly what I am," Azmariliz cocked its head. "And what are you, little thing?"

145

"A haffelin."

"A little haffelin," Azmariliz murmured. "Are you sure?"

Something about the way Azmariliz posed the question, the way it looked at her, made Kjara immediately self-conscious. Exposed, perhaps, or vulnerable? But not threatened. She wasn't afraid, she just felt...seen, in a way she never had before.

"Quite sure. I have been one all of my life."

"Then you should know exactly what you are."

This last response plunged deep into her mind. The creature spoke so strangely. Was it merely agreeing with her claim, or was it hinting at something else? Something she didn't know, but that she should know. She made to question it, but Papa bounded around the edge of the golden mountain with a pair of round-cut rubies over his eyes.

"Kjara, look. Look at me! Guess who I am! I'm Captain Angry-Eyes!"

"Oh, I have another visitor?" Azmariliz gasped. "Wonderful."

Papa lowered the rubies from his eyes in response to the deep rumbling voice. At the sight of Azmariliz, Papa recoiled, slipping over a goblet into the hoard of gold.

"We are three, by point of fact," Kjara said. "Soren, come here!"

Soren stepped around to the pool, backpack in one hand and a fresh torch in the other. Seeing the creature, his face drained white. He upended the bag to pour the stolen coin back onto the pile.

Azmariliz smiled, "There is plenty here to spare. You would not take it if you did not need it. Take what you can carry, it will not bother me; it's barely a snack."

"That is kind of you," Kjara said.

"Yes, it is!" Papa agreed, scrambling back to his feet and heaping handfuls of gold into the bag.

"This is Papa Roce. And that is Soren."

"This is not your Captain Angry-Eyes?" Azmariliz inspected Soren's dour expression.

"He is more gloomy than angry," Papa clarified. "Angry-eyes is our Captain Deonto."

"She runs the guards where we are from," Kjara explained and, pre-empting Azmariliz's question, added, "Bhaile Cala. North, by the ocean."

Azmariliz blossomed with understanding, "How fortuitous you should be here today."

"Fortuitous?"

"Yes, you're being here is unexpected. Unforeseen," Azmariliz paused. It inspected each one of them from head to foot. "I know of this Bhaile Cala. And of the malevolence that seeks to destroy it. I worried, I wondered, how could I prevent it? But now, you are here. It is fate. Fate has sent you to me."

Kjara exchanged glances with Papa and Soren. Azmariliz leant in closer, a solemn fear in its eyes.

"Listen, and listen well, two-footed ones. I will show you the way out of this stony mountainside. I will leave out more coin for your coffers if you wish it so. But you *must* do this one thing I ask of you…"

Kjara's skin prickled, "What is it?"

"The naistinn of your country is in terrible danger. There is a plot on her life. When she reaches Bhaile Cala, they intend to have her killed. And it will spread a great tragedy across these lands. It *must not* come to pass. You must warn her."

"They? They who?" Soren asked.

Its eyes darkened with gloom, "Alas, I know not who. my visions are not so precise."

"Visions?" Kjara repeated.

"I am a soothsayer of sorts. Though my apparitions are rare, they are never wrong."

"Hang on," Papa said." If you are saying such sooths, why not say them direct?"

"I cannot make myself known to your kind," Azmariliz lifted itself out of the water, revealing deep scars across its lower chest. "The civilised can be very much the opposite when brought to fear."

Kjara softened at the sight of the slashes in its skin. A body marked against its will. Living in solitude, hiding its secret. Somehow relatable, familiar. She stood to her full height.

"We will help, however we can."

Azmariliz hummed in approval, "Excellent. You are a noble soul, little…"

It paused, its eyes narrowed in thought.

"Haffelin," Kjara finished.

"Haffelin. Of course."

Chapter 24

Kjara

Kjara left the mountains through the mouth of the underground river, the warm sun against her face provided a pleasantly jarring shift in temperature. Pollen floating on the breeze tickled her nose and water bugs buzzed around her wide, pointed ears.

"So, what will you do with your coin, Kjara?" Papa asked. "Are you going to pay off your debt?"

Kjara smiled but said nothing.

"That's the right choice," he continued, neglecting her silence. "You must be happy knowing you'll soon be out from under the thumb of Captain No-fun. Free and unburdened! That's the only way to be!" he beamed with excitement. "Maybe I'll open a shop. No. I'll commission a statue. A great big statue in honour of Fyaldha, and park it right in the greenery opposite the temple of Lyrdahl. And I'll pay a balladeer to play whenever those pomps are worshipping. How about you, Lemon-face?"

"I'm going to settle my obligation to the captain, repay the Nullifidians," Soren said. "Anything left I'll use to purchase fresh belongings."

"All problems solved with gold, eh? First, a bribe to save your time, and then a bribe to save your soul."

"If that's what it takes."

Kjara frowned. The prospect of being unshackled from her debt didn't feel as liberating as it seemed for the others. The captain was a hard woman, to be sure, but in their short time together, Kjara had developed a fondness for her. Also, and though she wouldn't admit it aloud, she had started to enjoy the reading and writing lessons. The thought of finding out what was written in all of Elent's books enticed her. All the books in the captain's office too. And the trove. A history of Bhaile Cala, all its comings and goings.

Kjara's curiosity had always been bound by the knowledge of others, and their tolerance for her questioning. Reading, though, bypassed that: no one could tell her "that was enough questions for now". And then there was the book she had taken. The one still in her haversack. The markings on her skin, the humming, the vibrations, the strange occurrences, that book could explain it all.

"How are we going to warn the naistinn?" Kjara asked once her thoughts had run dry. "How do we get her to believe us?"

Papa, having dropped behind to search the underbrush for a make-shift walking stick, offered an answer, "We'll just say it straight. Keep it simple."

"Simple," Soren repeated dubiously. "A future-reading draejr warned us about a discreation plot against the naistinn. Because it had a vision. And we'll just tell her how exactly?"

"Okay, Lemon-face. What do you suggest?"

"We don't say anything," Soren swatted a fly from his face. "This isn't our problem."

Kjara stopped walking and turned to face Soren, "We have to say something, we gave our word that we would help."

"She's right," Papa called out, testing the durability of a stick by leaning on it. Satisfied, he limped back to Soren. "We did agree to help. By warning 'her'. And I have just the 'her' to warn. We'll tell the captain, she's the supposed authority and protector of the people."

"You think she'll believe us?" Kjara asked.

"Doesn't matter. We're under no obligation to be accepted as truth-speakers. What she does with the information is up to her."

"And if she is a part of the plot?" Soren asked.

Papa shrugged, "Then we've told her nothing she doesn't already know."

"Yer, we have. We've told her that we know."

"Calm down, she's not a part of it," Papa said, waving away Soren's paranoia. "No one that uptight can also be that duplicitous. She is a pain, but we can trust her if no one else."

"What if you're wrong? And she arrests us? Or worse."

Something worse. Something worse like what? Something cruel? Something violent? Kjara's mind flashed back to the scars on Azmariliz's chest.

"We can't mention Azmariliz," she said. "If anyone finds out there is a draejr in the mountains, just imagine what they might do."

"And what it might do to us," Soren added. "If we give away its secret."

"Fine," Papa grunted, throwing one hand up in defeat. "We'll leave out the part about the draejr. We'll say we overheard some people plotting in the pub. Is that acceptable?"

Kjara nodded. It may not have been the whole truth, but it would be enough to satisfy the agreement. Reaching the outskirts of Bhaile Cala, Papa suggested finding somewhere quiet and secluded to hide the gold. That much coin would be noticeable walking around the city and would draw the wrong kind of attention.

Papa knew of an old watchtower a few hundred feet west of the road in the thicketed bushlands at the base of the Timelong Mountains. It was used during the Collision but had since fallen into disrepair, and Papa assured Kjara that no one ever went there.

"We should take just enough to clear our debt at first," Papa suggested. "And return later, taking small quantities at a time, so as not to arouse suspicion from our spending."

He hid their coin beneath the floorboards and covered the damaged wood planks with an abandoned storage chest. All told, Soren's bag contained three hundred and twenty-seven gold pieces. One hundred and eight gold apiece, with the extra coins going to Soren for carrying everything.

Returning to the guardhouse, Harwin greeted Kjara warmly, but his positive demeanour darkened on Papa's approach.

"A fine set you got on you, coming back here," he said, glaring at the old man. "Or have you recognised the error of your ways and returned to apologise and finish your sentence?"

"Muzzle your barking, pup," Papa said dismissively. "We've business with the captain that will serve my sentence for me. And then some. Step aside."

"No. That was a cruel trick you pulled on me. I'm stuck copying papers every hour after lunch now. And door duty for the rest. It's the cruellest punishment, boredom."

"Fine. Here. The best apology I can provide," Papa replied, holding out five gold.

Harwin stood resolute. Papa groaned and waved a frustrated gesture at his companions.

Kjara intervened. "Harwin, if you let us see the captain, we will see to it you're put back on active patrol."

"That is kind of you, Kjara. But I doubt you'll have much sway with her."

"I beg to differ, Harwin. We've something she'll very much want to see. Soren?"

Soren stepped forward, unwrapping the cloak he had bundled around the fiedrig. Harwin took one look and curled his face up in confused disgust as one of the spindly grey arms flopped out. Papa used the moment to barge past him towards the captain's office. He shoved open the door with a dramatic entrance hand outstretched triumphantly.

"The Liberators of the Lode have returned," he proclaimed as Soren and Kjara joined him. "Victorious in their pursuit of the prankly perpetrators that have plagued our city so!"

Captain Deonto looked up from her desk with surprise that immediately dissolved into hostility. She wasn't alone. Sitting across from her was an older man. Partway through his fifth decade perhaps. A bald head with a ring of short-cropped greying hair. Heavyset and broad-shouldered, with extra weight around his waist. The physique of a seasoned soldier turned sophisticate. He wore a fine, fur-lined cloak over a high-collared silken doublet with delicate embroidery.

He turned to face the door, revealing an impeccable full moustache that curled into perfect points over russet cheeks. Thick bushy eyebrows raised in surprise and delight at the sight of their intruder. A slow, broad smile stretched his lips, crinkling the corners of his eyes.

"Hello, Alba," his voice resonated with a warm, rich tone of authority and compassion. It was the voice of a man well versed in conversation and accustomed to being heard. "You're looking well."

"I could say the same," Papa replied coldly. "Fine trousers."

Captain Deonto got to her feet and bowed her head, "I apologise, my thairis, for the intrusion. Harwin, remove Roce immediately!"

Papa leant down to Kjara and gleefully whispered, "I think we've interrupted something important."

"With whom are you speaking?" the man asked. "Have you other surprise visitors in the corridor?"

"Ignore them my thairis," Captain Deonto strode across her office. "Out, Roce. Now."

"Fine. We'll leave!" Papa waved his arms dramatically, before adding, "I can see you're busy…We'll show you later."

At this, Deonto's visitor tilted his head, "One moment, Laine. Alba has caught my interest. I would like to see what he has to offer us. If there are others in the corridor, invite them in."

Deonto, her concern visible, nodded her head and ushered Kjara, Soren, and the stinking lump beneath Soren's cloak into her office. Papa gestured for Soren to put the bundle on Deonto's desk, so he did, dropping it with a loud thud.

"A feast for the senses!" Papa claimed as Soren peeled back the cloak to reveal its secret. "Behold, the mine monster!"

Deonto's visitor gasped before letting out a deep laugh.

Deonto glared, "Roce, what are we looking at?"

"Fiedrig," Deonto's visitor answered. "They're dark tricksters. Lucky you caught it; their pranks can be quite fatal."

Captain Deonto gave her visitor a curious look, but if she had more to say she kept it to herself.

"This pesky little powrie is what's kept your miners so scared of digging. But now it is dead, and the mine may re-open," Papa added with a flourish. "You're welcome. 'Community service' completed. 'Debt to society' repaid."

"If that is the case, Roce. There is a level of gratitude you are owed. Consider your original punishment pardoned," the captain stated. "And you Soren, I expect you wish this act to clear your debt as well?"

Soren shook his head and placed a pouch of gold on the corner of her desk, "The coin is what I owed. The coin is what I will pay." Captain Deonto cast a cynical eye at him. "A lucky hand at The Bait and Tackle," he lied.

"What about you, Chedderheart? Do you have any convenient coin to disclose?"

Kjara straightened her shoulders and cleared her throat, "Captain, my debt was to be paid in time. And that is how I shall pay it."

Deonto raised one razor-thin eyebrow, before nodding decisively. Her visitor, who had been focussed on the fiedrig now fixed his attention squarely on Kjara. He half-cocked his head, as if in recognition, before leaning back to Deonto.

"Is this her?"

"It is."

Kjara's imagination inflated with fear. The captain and this man had been talking about her. But what had been said? Had the captain seen more of the incident with Orpip than she had let on? Had she seen the candlestick move? The man exuded wealth and class. The way he had inspected the fiedrig made it clear he was interested in things of an extraordinary nature. Was he a collector of the strange and exotic? Had the captain seen Kjara's markings? Had she told him of them?

The man extended one hand, marked with faded scars and adorned with several jewelled rings, "My name is Thairis Geov Brast, it is nice to meet you, Kara."

Kjara was unsure if she should correct him. Thairis Pedigray had gotten very angry when Kjara had corrected her.

"It's 'Kjara', my thairis," Captain Deonto said.

An odd heat surged in Kjara's gut, a feeling somewhere close to pride, despite her having done nothing to earn it. For whatever reason, the captain felt it *mattered* that Brast got it right; enough to correct him. Which meant it mattered to the captain. It meant that *she* mattered to the captain.

"Oh, my apologies," Brast said. "It is nice to meet you... Kjara."

"Likewise, my thairis?" Kjara took his hand.

Thairis Brast chuckled and shook it, "That is correct."

"Thank you. I'm afraid I don't know what is proper. I did meet a thairis recently, but it left me more confused than informed."

Thairis Brast smiled again, the sharp blue of his eyes catching the window sunlight, "I didn't know what was proper either before I found out. I think that's true for most things though. If one is to know something, one must first know they don't know. Would you agree?"

Although his logic was confusing and cryptic, Kjara understood the thairis, "I believe so, yer."

"Well, this has been fun," Papa interjected. "Nice seeing you Geov. A pleasure as always Captain. Time to go, Soren. Let's leave these fine folks to their frippery."

Soren narrowed one eye in confusion, "Roce, what about telling the captain—"

"Yes, Soren! I know we spoke about asking for a reward," Papa bellowed, drowning out Soren's voice. "But let's not be greedy. Freedom is more than enough, don't you agree? Let us leave right now and enjoy ours!"

Captain Deonto stepped into Papa's path, "One moment, Roce. While I have determined your original punishment settled, there is a further list of charges laid against you for which you must still atone."

Papa scoffed, "What charges?"

"You deceived and struck another one of my guards," she began. "Escaped the lockup, absconded with my ward without permission and put her in significant danger. You made a mockery of our system of law, Roce, and will be placed back into lockup to serve a further twenty-four days. Minimum. Harwin, shackles."

"What? A whole month?!" Papa cried, incensed. "Geov, c'mon! This is ridiculous!"

Thairis Brast shrugged as Harwin took Papa by the arm and led him from the room, "The law is the law. You'll not find me arguing with her."

"This is an outrage! Justice most corrupt!"

Once Papa was out of earshot, Thairis Brast turned to Captain Deonto. "Laine. Is it possible to reduce his sentence?"

"My Thairis, are you sure? Letting him wander freely, considering current events—"

"Yes. I am sure. It is not a worry to me. Can we make it…twenty-four hours? I would like to have these three over for lunch tomorrow," Thairis Brast turned to Kjara. "I'm interested to hear your story. If you'll accept my invitation, of course."

In stunned silence, Kjara nodded her agreement.

"Excellent! Then I shall see you anon! Captain Deonto knows the way. Bring the fiedrig with you if you don't mind," he beamed, getting up to leave. Oh, and Laine, do take Kjara shopping for fresh clothes. Ionesco should have something appropriate. And a bath, too."

When he left, Kjara turned to the captain, "Captain, what is Thairis Brast the thairis of?"

Deonto raised an eyebrow, "That was the region master of Northern Cradh, Kjara. And I think you have his attention."

Chapter 25

Papa

"Is this because I made you look foolish?" Papa asked as Harwin led him through the halls of the Guardhouse. "You know that wasn't personal. I was just bored in there."

Harwin said nothing.

"How *did* you get out of those bars? Oil or butter?"

Still nothing.

"I see. Silent treatment. You've been spending too much time with the captain. Her steely morosity must be rubbing off on you. You need a good laugh to cheer you up."

Harwin dropped his head, stopped, and turned around, "You put Kjara in danger, Roce. Taking her down into the mine like that. It was irresponsible. Thoughtless."

"Ah, so that's your problem. Look, I've known that girl since the moment she was born, pup. Helped her with it, by point of fact," Papa waved a finger at Harwin, his shackle chains jangling on his wrists. "She isn't as defenceless as you think she is."

Harwin sighed, "That's not my point."

"Then what's the problem?"

"You, Roce. You and your disregard. You don't care about anything or anyone else. It's you and your pranks, and that's it. Come on," Harwin turned and continued walking.

Papa shuffled along behind him, "You know, you should come to one of my sermons, then you'd understand how wrong you are."

"Not interested."

"C'mon. Be shown the healing power of merriment."

"I'll pass," Harwin opened the large, mahogany door that led into the cell block.

The familiar grey brick walls and iron bars pulled the heat from the room, leaving behind an unwelcoming chill in the air.

"Ah, lovely. my home away from home!"

Harwin walked down the corridor, stopping in front of Papa's previous cell. But Papa had a devious plan, "Praise Fyaldha, you worried me for a moment."

"What?"

"I thought you were throwing me in *that* cell," Papa pointed to the adjacent cell. The cell that had previously been occupied by the red-haired girl and the hidden lockpicking tools. "I was terrified."

"Why?"

"The view is terrible. It's the worst one in the entire lockup. But this one," Papa pointed to the first cell. "This one has the best. That's why I always request it."

"Really?"

"Yer," Papa said confidently. The plan was working, Harwin was hooked. "So, open it up, and in shall I go."

"No. Not today," Harwin took Papa by his robe collar, unlocked the adjacent cell, and shoved him into it.

Papa spun around as the bars slammed in his face. The plan succeeded. Hook, line, sinker. It just needed one last push. Something to ensure Harwin's departure.

Holding up his shackled wrists, Papa asked, "Do I get these off at least?"

"No chance. Don't worry, you can still enjoy the view."

"Oh, a joke! Not bad for a first try. But you need to work on your delivery, see you—" Papa stiffened and held out a wary hand. "Wait...Do you hear that?"

Harwin frowned, "Like that's going to work."

"Shh...Listen. There's something here, I can feel it in my gut," Papa scanned the dark corners of the room. "I think something followed us from the mine."

Harwin followed Papa's gaze, placing one hand defensively on the grip of his sword. Ever the seasoned performer, Papa held back his smile and committed entirely to the bit, enjoying his audience's confusion.

"It's a fiedrig!" Papa hissed. "I can smell its smoke!"

"I can't smell anything," Harwin sniffed repeatedly, probing the air. His expression dropped in disgust. "Gods be, what in the...Roce, that's revolting!"

Papa let out a hearty belly laugh, his shaggy beard wiggled on his chin, "I got you again. Admit it, I got you good!"

"Okay, I'll admit it. You got me. That was pretty funny."

"Yes! See? I told you a good laugh would set you right again."

"Want to know what else is funny?"

"Absolutely."

"This," Harwin pulled the key from the lock and left the room.

"Oh, yes. Very good!" Papa moaned dramatically as Harwin walked away. Once satisfied Harwin was out of earshot, he chuckled, "Ah, the naivety of youth. Right, time to get out of here."

He tapped his foot along the stones of the cell floor, searching for the red-head's tools. When he found the loose stone, he let out a smirk of satisfaction, before dropping to his knees and prying it up with his fingers. He rolled the stone away and smugly reached into the hole.

Empty.

Papa blinked in disbelief and stared at the hole for a good long minute before smiling.

"Damn it. He was right. That is funny. Cheeky pup," he looked to the ceiling. "Did you catch that one?"

No response.

"You'll never believe what I saw today," Papa said, as he settled into his bunk. "Unless you were watching. Were you? I'll just assume you weren't. Must have been busy doing something else. Maybe you were baking a pie. Are you ready? Really ready?"

His voice dropped to a whisper.

"A draejr. Can you believe that? An actual, factual draejr. And you told me they weren't real. Shows what you know!" he laughed and slapped his knee. "So, the joke's on you I guess," he said as his smile disappeared. "For once."

Chapter 26

Soren

Shortly after the meeting with Thairis Brast, Soren left Kjara and Papa and travelled to The Eyeglass Pub. Mid-afternoon had left the bar light on for clientele, but the quiet only compounded Soren's discomfort. It was as if his involvement in the bar brawl had been the primary reason for the sparse patronage. The damage had been cleared away, leaving the main space much more open. Fewer chairs, fewer tables, fewer places to hide. A temporary banister had been affixed to the stairs. Made of simple, unfinished wood, it contrasted heavily against the finely varnished steps. He took a long intake of breath.

As he walked up to the bar, Jefen scoffed, "What do you want?"

"To set things right," Soren rubbed his stubbled chin. "I want to apologise."

Jefen snorted, "All well and good null, but words alone don't absolve one's actions."

"I know," Soren replied, setting a pouch of coins onto the countertop. Jefen swept it up, maintaining a cold glare. He shook it by his ear and his icy expression melted away.

"Well, well," he said with a broad smile. "This is an apology I can understand. It is accepted. What can I get you? An ale to wash down my amnesty, perhaps?"

Soren's stomach turned at the thought of it. Instead, he ordered a pot of sweet tea and the pub's special of the day, a chargrilled vegetable stack in white cheese sauce. Taking a seat in the back corner, away from the busier section of the main floor, he sat in silent contemplation. He observed the casual activities of the patrons, but most of his attention was devoted to watching Ayleth.

The otherworldly appearance of her faeduin heredity hypnotised him. The sharp yet delicate angles of her face, her large white eyes. He wondered what colour they used to be, and he wondered what had happened to her.

"Something the matter?" she asked gently, placing a pot of tea and a cup in front of him. At such a close distance, the faded scar tissue around her eyelids drew his attention and muted his response.

Soren sniffed. "No."

"Well, that's a lie," Ayleth replied. "I can tell when a person's hurting. It's coming off you like a stink. Do you want to talk about it?"

"No."

She tittered, "Well, that's a lie too."

She was right, of course. Soren did want to talk about it. He wanted to talk about everything. He wanted to tell her about the day's trip to the mine, about what he saw, what he met. The way her presence enticed him to speak the truth was hard to fight. It was almost supernatural. He'd heard the faeduin had no word for 'dishonesty', no word for 'lie'. Maybe there was something to it. Was it possible for a culture to radiate openness, to draw honesty out of others like a well draws water?

Soren wanted to tell her how he had felt the mine tunnels closing in on him. How the cold, musty smell of the air had made his heart pound and his palms sweat. How his mind had buzzed with panic as he descended into the darkness. How his memory had attacked him.

Soren wanted to tell her what it was like seeing Kjara lying scuffed up, dirty and bloodied on the stones at the bottom of the mine shaft. He wanted to release the wave of anger and guilt that surged through him when Roce accused him of endangering them with his poor rope tying. He wanted to explain why it hurt so much. He wanted to tell her about the last time he was in a mine as well, but he didn't.

"You're right," Soren said after a time. "It is a lie. But I don't know how else to say it."

"Mostly, I say it true," she suggested. "One truth is just one truth, no matter the outcome. One lie is never just one lie."

"That's admirable. I wish I could do the same."

"So why don't you?"

"It's hard."

"Lying isn't?"

"Lying is easy."

"Why is that?"

"I've had plenty of practice."

"Well, then. There's the fix," Ayleth poured some tea into his cup. "You just need practice. You can start with me if you like, tell me one truth."

Soren's throat collapsed, dried out and tightened with fear. As much as he wanted to share his story with Ayleth, to unload the guilt and angst scraping at his brain, he couldn't. If he told her the truth—if he told anyone the truth—it could only end in one of two ways: imprisonment, or death.

"I'll pass, thanks."

"I don't know what black dog is chewing on you," she continued. "But if I leave you alone at this table, it might eat you up completely. And then where would I be? I'd have to settle *your* bill with *my* wages."

Soren laughed bitterly, despite himself.

It brought a smile to her face, "Okay, how about this? I'll show you how it's done. Ask me anything."

"Anything?"

"Anything."

Soren took a deep breath, "How did you lose your sight?"

"Ah," Ayleth nodded with recognition and sat down across from him. Sitting straight-backed and open, she answered. "I got into a fight. With someone I cared about deeply. Someone who could be extremely jealous."

"An abusive relationship?"

"Of sorts," she replied.

"What was the fight about?"

"I saw something I wasn't supposed to see," Ayleth explained. "And I refused to stay silent. When I brought the matter up, things got a little heated."

"That's the truth?"

"Every word."

Soren stirred his tea, swallowed, placed his spoon on the table and began, "I...I'm scared."

An unexpected fist of emotion hammered his chest and left a sucking sensation in its wake. He fell silent.

"That's a good start. Why?"

"I've...made mistakes. I've made a lot of mistakes, and I've made a really, really big one. I'm scared of it. It terrifies me."

"Why?"

"I don't know."

"Are you sure it's the mistakes that scare you, then?"

Kjara Chedderheart and Papa Roce flashed across Soren's thoughts. The Nullifidians allowed him to join their commune, but with Kjara and Papa, it felt different. More than mere toleration.

"No," he answered after some thought. "I'm scared I'll get caught. I'm scared that the people around me think I am a decent person when I'm not. I'm scared they'll find out I'm lying to them. And then…then I really will have nothing."

"I understand," Ayleth responded. Warmth shone from her as she spoke. "But I wonder. If they don't find out, and you keep lying to them, how is that any different? Don't try to carry it by yourself is all I'm saying. Whatever you're feeling," she continued. "It's always too heavy for one person. Nothing wrong with feeling it, but everything wrong with hiding it. You can share it with me, you can share it with them. Just, don't let it eat you, okay?"

Soren fought back the swell prickling in his eyes, "I'll try."

"Good," she said. "This world's too big to go it alone."

Chapter 27

Kjara

On the walk to the trade quarter with Captain Deonto, Kjara's mind wrestled with Papa's abrupt change to the plan. So sudden, so seemingly pointless. It was *his* plan, why change it?

"Ionesco is one of the most reputable clothiers in the city," the captain explained. "His use of clashing colours is too garish for my tastes, but the nobles keep him in high demand. Driven to out-peacock one another, no doubt."

What was his reasoning? Kjara's brow tightened her expression into something akin to an absent scowl. *He didn't even warn us first. Or consult us.*

"He operates the Needle and Thread. No doubt you've seen it," the captain continued. Noticing Kjara's expression, she added, "You're distracted. What is on your mind?"

"Huh?…Oh," Kjara reached for the quickest lie she could find. "I was just wondering how long Harwin will be on door duty."

"I see," the captain's lip twitched. "And why has Harwin taken your interest?"

Kjara's cheeks prickled at the sound of his name. The way the captain said it gave it more weight than usual, as if implying something extra. But what? And why?

She pushed the suspicion from her mind and shrugged, "We offered to have his sentence reduced if he let us pass. I want to keep my promise, that's all."

"That's all," the captain repeated.

Kjara's ears heated, "He prefers active patrol over door duty. And he seems good at it, I don't see why he shouldn't be working to his strengths."

"Harwin is an able enough guard, for someone so young," the captain nodded a greeting to the folks she passed. "But there is more to protection than carrying a sword and wearing a seal. One must also be taught to think carefully. To be critical and objective in one's dealings with others. One must be resolute against the woebegone eye of the guileful offender. There are far more malevolent tricksters and liars in the world than Roce. There are those who will use your empathy to deceive you, those who will use your compassion to conquer you. Some may even use your ignorance to kill you.

"Harwin isn't copying accounts of criminal incidents because they require writing. It is because they require reading. So he can learn from them. Harwin wants to help people. But he must learn to distinguish between those who need his benevolence and those who will abuse it. Those who will use him to get what they want."

"Like Papa," Kjara suggested.

"Yes," the captain replied, "or you."

A hot pulse detonated in Kjara's chest and bristled through her body. The prickly pang of accusation.

"I didn't do anything."

"Remind me, what did you offer Harwin to let you past his post?"

Kjara's eyes dropped to the ground, full of shame and recognition. Intent on trying to help him, she hadn't thought anything of it at the time.

"When you promise something you cannot guarantee, it isn't kindness," the captain explained. "It's deceit. When your words and your actions misalign, people will stop listening to you when you speak."

Kjara nodded and travelled the rest of the way in silence.

Chapter 28

———— ◉ ————

Kjara

The sheer selection of material on display boggled Kjara's mind. Swatches of coloured cloth hung from oak beams and thick rolls of fabric formed long corridors. Assorted designs hung off racks with some prominently presented on simple wooden mannequins. Thairis Pedigray, her usual prumpity self, pawed through the offerings, taking no notice of her entry. A terrible thought dawned on Kjara: if she were to be outfitted with fresh attire, would she have to try it on first?

Kjara's eyes darted across the walls, searching for a fitting room or an alcove of privacy. Anything that would hide her—and her markings—from Deonto, the clothier, or any other onlooker. Unable to find one, Kjara's heart sank.

Ionesco approached, focused on the captain but not Kjara. He was a short man with narrow shoulders and a round belly that matched his equally round head. His hair was completely shaved, his eyebrows neatly groomed, perfectly symmetrical above his arrowhead nose. He wore black from head to toe, which let the white measuring string hanging around his neck pop like a priest's stole. On one shoulder, affixed to his top, was a lavender pin cushion.

"Captain Deonto, it is a pleasure to see you, though surprising. I hope that this is for avocation and not arrest?" Ionesco spoke with quiet reservation, soft and deliberate, as though his throat were made of silk and he feared he might tear it. "Are you finally ready for a fitting to match your frame, perhaps?"

"It is indeed for a fitting, Ionesco. But not for me, rather for her," Captain Deonto responded, gesturing to Kjara.

Ionesco frowned in disappointment, before passing a look over her. Anxiety tugged on her tongue. Dirt and blood stained her shirt and vest, tears in her trousers, scuffed muddied boots. Aware of how unpleasant she must look, Kjara shifted uncomfortably but remained silent.

"A farmer, are you? Or a miner, maybe? You seem to have taken a tumble young haffelin," Ionesco turned to Captain Deonto. "This girl is a mess. She'll not be able to try anything on today. Off the rack is out of the question."

Kjara breathed a silent sigh of relief.

"Bespoke will be fine if you have the time to do it. We need some presentable clothes for her. And we need them made fast."

Ionesco raised an eyebrow, "How fast?"

"By tomorrow morning."

"Expensive. Can you afford my time?"

"I am not the one purchasing it. This order is for Thairis Brast's account, as he is the one who has requested her presentability."

"I see," Ionesco said, performing quick calculations on his fingertips. "Let us pick out some fabric and discuss style. Is it to be trousers or dresses?"

They both looked to Kjara for an answer.

"…Trousers."

"A fine choice. For trousers, I have some footwear to match."

He led her to the counter where he retrieved a large book of patterns, styles, and colour palettes. Kjara flicked through it, amazed at the staggering range of designs. Eventually, she selected a high-necked powder blue shirt and a pair of pleated butterscotch trousers. Over this, she added a three-quarter length burgundy doublet with golden embroidery. Ionesco described the shirt as a loose-fitted sleeve, so she requested a set of elbow-length gloves to match.

Finally, Ionesco presented Kjara with mid-calf folded boots in either tan or black. She chose black. Ionesco suggested silk for the gloves and shirt, brocade for the doublet, and a rich velvet for the trousers. Leaving it to the expert's opinion, she agreed.

"Wonderful," he said. "It's a recent import that I've been dying to use."

Ionesco took Kjara's measurements, with such speed and precision it left her overwhelmed. When questioned about the subject of alterations, should her clothing not sit right, Ionesco shot the captain a fiery glare.

"Only amateurs measure incorrectly, Captain," he declared with pride. "If the clothes do not fit tomorrow, it will be because the haffelin girl has changed her shape overnight. Do you intend to change your body, Kjara?"

Kjara's markings flashed across her thoughts. If only it were so simple.

"No."

"Then these clothes will fit."

Once the business concluded and the two prepared to leave, Kjara spotted a cloak in the corner of the shop, hung up on a dressmaker's dummy. It was patterned in dark green with gold trim, a hood and a golden clasp fashioned into two hands folded over one another.

"Might I take that cloak as well?" Kjara gestured.

"Of course, dear girl," Ionesco approved. "A sharp design to complete your ensemble. I'll even offer it at a discount."

"Why is that?" Kjara asked.

"Oh, do not fret. The quality is exceptional. But I've been having trouble selling it. Most of the nobility are too...robust for such a slight accessory," Ionesco cast a glance at Thairis Pedigray. "It's too short for them. And too narrow."

For Kjara, it was the perfect length.

Once the captain and Kjara returned to the guardhouse, she spent the rest of half-eve practising her writing. She requested the opportunity to improve her handwriting by copying pages from the shelves of incident reports. There were various accounts from citizens, including a few names that, once Deonto had pronounced them for her, Kjara recognised. Not all the handwriting met the same high quality as the captain's; some of it was so illegible she had to concede defeat and skip them entirely.

After finishing her writing, Kjara prepared dinner for both herself and Papa, a ritual fast becoming common practice. She slid over a steaming bowl of soup with buttery, crusty bread, and sat cross-legged on the other side of the cell. Papa slurped down the soup and burped approvingly.

"Why did you change the plan?" Kjara asked, stirring her soup with her bread.

"Eh?"

"You stopped Soren from mentioning anything."

"Ah. I know that man, Geov Brast. I've known him for a long time," he said, waggling a finger at her and sending splatters of broth from his spoon to the floor. "And I can tell you the singular thing about him that towers above all else. He is possessed by a horrible compulsion to achieve. I wouldn't be surprised if he was the one planning the whole arrangement. Bump off the naistinn so he can take her place."

Kjara tore her bread in two, "So, should I go tell the captain now?"

"No, she'll go straight to him. And if Brast is behind it and finds out that we know…" Papa lowered his voice. "We need to be careful.

We can't go about willy-nilly telling anyone. The only ones we can trust are each other."

"And Soren."

Papa considered her comment for a moment, "I'm not sure. He is a quiet one. And quiet ones are dangerous, too. They think too much and say too little. It's unnatural."

"So, what do we do?"

"I say, you bust me out of here. We hole up somewhere south of the city, along the road, maybe the old watchtower, and we wait for the naistinn's procession. Then...we chase her down and warn her. Tell her there's a plot against her. If we save her from the carver's blade..." Papa grinned with glee. "Riches. Fame. A shrine to Fyaldha in every town between here and the Narrow Sea. We'll be set for life, and beyond, to the After-all!"

Kjara chewed on her soup-dipped toast. Papa intercepting the naistinn's visit conjured mayhem best left to the imagination.

"I've been invited to join Brast for lunch tomorrow."

"What? Have you?"

"Yer. But not just me. All three of us. Soren and you, both."

Papa sniggered, "I'll not have much to eat. My arms are too short to reach his table from here."

"Longer than your sentence, though. You're only to serve twenty-four hours. Out by highsun tomorrow, Thairis Brast has ordered it."

"Fyaldha bless that kind, kind man," Papa said, popping a chunk of boiled potato into his mouth.

Kjara squinted in confusion, "So now you trust him?"

"Not even slightly," Papa scoffed. "Kindness is a cloak the cunning wear to cheat the gullible."

Although Papa's flippancy amused her, the cause of Kjara's smile was recognition. Papa's opinions on kindness mirrored the captain's with surprising similarity.

"We should use this lunch to gather information," Kjara decided. "We need to determine if Thairis Brast is someone we can trust. If he is, we will need his help."

"And if he isn't?"

Kjara took a deep breath, "Then I guess we bust you out and sit in a watchtower for the next week."

"It's not as fun when you say it."

Was Thairis Brast behind the discreation, or wasn't he? And if not him, then who? The questions rattled about in her head as Kjara travelled down to the bathhouse later that night. With approval from the captain she'd lit the furnace before dinner, reasoning that once Papa and Kjara finished, the water would be hot enough.

Cautious of being seen, Kjara relied on the light from the twin moons to guide her, instead of a lantern or candle. It cascaded through the high-set windows, giving the room an appearance of the ghostly and other-worldly. The steam from the water's surface wisped and licked the air, catching the moonlight in its fingers.

The far side of the pool would give her the most warning if someone approached. Removing her clothes, Kjara placed them deliberately in a pile on the stonework, gloves on top. She took a deep breath and dipped one toe into the water. The heat soaked into her skin, sending a shiver up her leg and through her body. Hot water for bathing still seemed such a novelty, and a snort of instinctual amusement shot from her nose. The sound resonated around the room as a reminder of how exposed she was.

Kjara placed one foot on the step just below the surface before sliding into the water. Her skin bristled as the warmth of the water pulled the cold from her body. Another instinctive shiver swept through her bones. She drew her head beneath the surface and paused a moment, suspended in the warm water. The weight of it pulled on her hair.

It's like floating in a fire.

175

As she resurfaced and leant against the side of the pool, Kjara raised her hand above the water's edge. Steam appeared to rise out of her skin. She wiggled her fingers, allowing each of the hazy trails to ripple in their own pattern.

You are the fire.

The markings on her hand and arm seemed to flare up just slightly as if they too were catching the moonlight. A trick of the light, Kjara reasoned, turning her eyes to the windows. As she did, she caught the silhouette of a figure crawling in from outside and a flash of red in the moonlight.

What was that? Another fiedrig, chasing you down to avenge its kin?

Kjara made to push off and swim across the pool, but the sound of leather footsteps stopped her. A second intruder. Kjara paused, uncertain, and listened. Two voices spoke in hushed whispers, their exact words getting lost in the distance.

A female voice, "Are you sure…safe place?"

"It's…moon," a male voice responded. The voice belonged to the boots. "No one will…around. It's safe. Trust me."

I know those voices.

"Did you remember to bring…?"

"Straight to busin…no small talk first? Starting to…you don'…me," a feminine laugh. "Relax, I'm just…with you…course I…here."

Coins passing hands jingled a metal clink through the bathhouse. Kjara's heart thumped hot recognition through her. The red-haired girl from lockup.

"Keep…down," the male voice, Harwin's voice, hissed. "These walls echo, some…might…you."

Strange, new anger flared up in her chest, compounded by confusion. Kjara wanted to leave, to be as far from them as she could. If she snuck down into the furnace room, they wouldn't discover her. Moving slowly, carefully, she crept out of the water. Every inch felt a mile as she paused to let the water drip off her in silence. She gathered her clothes and tip-toed across the room towards the stairs.

The dim light made it difficult to judge the height of the first step and Kjara overestimated, throwing off her balance tumbling down the stairs. When she finally stopped at the bottom, the voices called out after her.

"Someone there? Show yourself."

Kjara gathered up her piled clothes, desperately trying to cover herself. The voices grew closer and closer. Kjara silently pleaded with the two black leather boots that were halfway down the stairs and getting nearer. Panic overtook reason, and she froze, half-dressed in the middle of the furnace room. The fire cast a bright light all around her. Harwin's face appeared from behind the low ceiling. He looked to the left, to the right, and straight at her.

Her breath stopped; her blood froze.

He could see her. She knew it. He could see her markings. He could see everything she hadn't covered. But she couldn't move, she couldn't speak or explain herself. Terror and shame gripped her like concrete. His brow furrowed in confusion before finally he turned away.

"No one down here," he said. "Maybe it was rats or something?"

"Big rats," came a hushed reply. "You coming back up?"

"One second. The fire is still going."

"So? Leave it going. I haven't had a hot bath in an age!"

Harwin smiled, shook his head, and left.

Alone once more, Kjara breathed a heavy sigh of relief. Waiting in silence for what seemed an age before she was sure they had finished and gone. She snuck back to her bunk, her stomach twisted into knots, and her mind ablaze with questions. *What have I been witness to?*

Why were Harwin and the red-haired girl meeting? Kjara stared at the ceiling above her bunk and covered her face with a pillow. *Was she taking advantage of his kindness?*

The thought set her body on fire with that same, odd anger. Having exhausted herself with unanswerable questions and fallen asleep, dawn was too near for answers to matter.

Chapter 29

Kjara

A warm, noonday sun shone down as Kjara trekked up the hillside to Thairis Brast's manor. The trees on either side of the road swayed slightly, caught in the breeze coming from the bay. Her nervousness made her hands sweaty, likewise the heat for her armpits, but thankfully the fabric was so well fashioned that none of it showed through. She didn't want to be a sodden mess when she arrived.

The captain had briefed Kjara on the finer points of etiquette, but she heard none of it. Her body ached with exhaustion. Worn, darkened eyelids hung over dry bloodshot eyes. Each blink brought with it a feeling like standing too close to smoke.

The thoughts that had plagued Kjara's previous night had passed, giving way to more salient ones.

We spoke about testing Brast. But how? How am I supposed to know whether he is behind it or not? She sighed internally. *Papa, this plan is fine in premise, but the execution leaves much to be desired.*

"Kjara, what do you think of the null's fresh-shaven face?" Papa asked, interrupting the captain. "It makes him look closer to twelve than twenty, wouldn't you say?"

"Huh?" Kjara snapped out of her thoughts. Soren had purchased a shave and a haircut. He had also treated himself to a new outfit, a simple yet fashionable linen shirt and trousers, and dark grey boots. "Yer. Maybe."

"At least I made an effort," Soren replied, quiet yet accusative.

"I made an effort!" Papa cried. The distant echo of squawking sea birds punctuated his offence. "I washed body, clothes and beard. And look, fresh flowers!"

"Roce, when you were released this morning to prepare for lunch," Deonto stated, "it was with the explicit instruction to attend the public bathhouse and have your clothes cleaned."

"I cleaned!"

Soren scoffed, "Splashing in the bay and drying out on a rock doesn't count."

Kjara smiled at the irony. By refusing the captain's instruction, he wound up with extra duties. The captain had said Papa may be excused for his appearance if they explained it away with labour. He had protested, claiming his twisted ankle would slow them down. In response, the captain gave him a wheelbarrow and moved the departure time forward.

Papa gestured to the flopping corpse of the fiedrig, bouncing in time with the wheel, "It's too hot. Can someone else push this for a bit?"

Soren shook his head, "No chance."

"Captain?" Papa asked, wobbling one of its blue-tipped fingers at her. Her stony gaze pulled a sigh from his lips, and he dropped the fiedrig's arm. "Figures. It would be too much to ask those of the law to be useful. I suppose you are worried about your fancy fabric too."

She ignored him.

The captain's attire gave Kjara much to admire. She wore a fine brocade doublet of blue and silver over charcoal grey trousers with blue trim. With no armaments, no sword, and no notebook, she appeared slimmer but no less intimidating. If anything, she seemed more so. The lighter cloth accentuated her lean, muscular physique. The shorter sleeves exposed several battle scars on her forearms. Wearing her hair down was a nice look, too, it made her appear slightly less murdery.

Rounding the final bend in the road, the tree line opened, revealing the largest house Kjara had ever seen. Bordered by an ornate stone wall, the brick-faced building of two stories stretched out across the hilltop. It had a pitched roof of dark amber tiles, and five gables across the front of the uppermost level. Green vines snaked up the walls, and various vegetation grew from the windows and balconies. The captain strode up to the entrance built into the wall and rapped her fist sharply against the gate.

"Who're you?" asked a dreary voice.

"Captain Laine Deonto, and guests. We're expected."

"Right you are."

The gate folded back, permitting the group entry. A young man, slightly older than Soren, with a mop of chestnut hair, pale complexion, and a short chin beard greeted them with a curt wave. He held a book in his other hand.

"The thairis said to head around the back. Near the orchard."

"Understood. Follow along," the captain instructed.

His book caught Kjara's interest.

"What is in the book?" she asked.

The young man straightened with excitement and opened it to show her. There were pictures of birds, quite expertly drawn, with scribblings of writing by each one.

"Not much to do here, most days. Unless there's visitors. So mostly, I just draw what I see. These are a bunch of birds. But here, also..." he said, flicking through the book, "some trees. And little critters. Here! A rabbit. I'm particularly proud of this one."

Kjara was impressed, "And the writing?"

"Oh, I like to imagine the whistling bird noises as little conversations they're having. And so, I jot them down beside them."

"You are quite the artist…"

"Name's Garyn."

"Thank you for sharing your work with me, Garyn," Kjara said, before hurrying off, as she had fallen behind the rest of the group.

The four walked around the side of the manor, as Kjara marvelled at the pristine grounds, the abundance of flowers, garden beds, trees, and hedges. To the right of the house sat a stable, and in it, a well-appointed stagecoach and a half-dozen horses in the process of feeding. Passing into the rear yard, Kjara admired the immaculate orchard running from the far side of the land to the wall.

Set up in a central position on the lawn sat a long oaken table with carved legs. Laid out on it was a dazzling array of bread, cheese, wine, fruits (some of which Kjara had never seen before), jams, relishes, and fresh-cut vegetables. More significant than the table or its contents, however, were the three people sat around it. One of whom Kjara recognised as Thairis Brast, but not the others. One had distinctly faeduin features, while the other was mohra. Both female and staggering in their attire. Thairis Brast leapt to his feet.

"Welcome, welcome! It is wonderful to see you. And looking so fabulous. Come, join us. There is plenty of food," he said, ushering them over to the table. "May I introduce Soren, Captain Laine Deonto, Alba Roce—"

"Father Alba Roce," interrupted Papa. "Ordained of the church of Fyaldha."

"Father Alba Roce," Thairis Brast corrected. "And this is Kjara Chedderheart."

"Pleased to meet you," the faeduin woman said. She wore her feathers, a two-tone of orange and brown, back over her head in a single braid. Bronze skin, curved cheekbones, a fine jawline, and a thin chin. Long stiletto ears. Ageless. Her eyes were entirely blue, with no discernible white or pupil, as was the norm for faeduin. She dressed in a tight fit surcoat and matching gown, both sleeveless, black with an orange stripe running down the centre.

"Kjara, this is Nine Mirrors. Personal counsel and advisory to the naistinn," Thairis Brast explained before gesturing to the mohra woman. "Finally, may I introduce—"

"Loreena Farlight," finished the younger woman. "Naistinn of Cradh. It is a pleasure to meet you, Kjara."

She was young, not much older than Kjara by her estimate, but carried herself with grace, elegance, and dignity. She had fine white hair, worn down past her shoulders and kept from her face by a silver circlet inset with a white opal. Her dark rounded lips and deep brown eyes stood out against her snowy skin. She wore a gown of a similar cut to the faeduin woman, but with hanging sleeves and no surcoat, coloured burgundy on black with golden trim, and made of silk.

The naistinn held her hand out to Kjara.

Shit.

Kjara froze, "Hello."

If awkwardness had any weight, it would have crushed the table and buried it deep in the dirt. The naistinn smiled, withdrew her hand, and turned to speak with Thairis Brast. Her exact words fell behind the sound of blood thumping in Kjara's ears. Papa mirrored her expression, a cross between astonishment and confusion. The presence of royalty at the table had not been a consideration and put the plans into disarray.

"What do we do now?" Papa whispered.

"You're asking me?" Kjara whispered back.

"Please, sit," Thairis Brast insisted. Observing her discomfort, he filled Kjara's glass with wine. "Eat. Drink. Be merry. You are my honoured guests. I did not invite you to be wooden planks; be at ease."

"Perfect," Papa swept up a carafe of wine and a glass.

"Thank you, my thairis?" Kjara said. Uncertainty and anxiety rushed through her veins. Lunch with a thairis was strange enough, but being sat across from their country's ruler was a concept so far removed from reality it bordered on the insane.

Thairis Brast tutted, "There is no need to stand on ceremony here. Hungry bellies do not recognise rank, so nor shall we. At this table, you may call me Geov. Eat something, I insist. It will make you feel better."

Kjara nodded and snapped a sprig of grapes from the platter nearest her. She couldn't keep up. In one moment, mohras expected to be addressed formally, but in the next, they preferred casual. Things would be a lot easier if people would stick to one name only and use it for all engagements. She opted for silence until addressed again, to keep things simple.

Papa, never one to hide behind manners, took the lull in the conversation to steer it in his direction, "Alright, no one else is asking. What are we doing here, Geov?"

Brast popped a piece of cheese into his mouth, "Loreena and I have similar interests. We are both fascinated by the Nofrum. When I saw you yesterday, showing off your fiedrig, I simply had to have you over to share your story with us!"

"I'm very pleased to finally meet you, Alba," Loreena added, turning her attention from the fiedrig to the bearded old man.

Papa raised a sceptical eyebrow, "Finally?"

"Geov used to tell me all sorts of stories when I was a child. Your name showed up in more than a few of them."

Papa scoffed, "As a hero or as a villain?"

"Neither, for the most part. You always came across as a knowledgeable and respectable man."

"Is that so? How lovely it is to be recognised as such," he said, casting a smug glance at Captain Deonto.

"What brings you to Bhaile Cala…?" Kjara trailed off, unsure how to address the naistinn.

Farlight noticed her hesitance and smiled, "Loreena is fine for now. I'm here on holiday. And to visit old friends. I quite enjoy the seaside, but I don't see it enough. It's nice up here. Surrounded by nature; away from the city."

Papa snickered.

"Roce…" Deonto scolded.

"What?" he grumbled, lathering some bread with relish. "How can work be so horrendous for a ruler that they must escape it?"

"What is it like?" Kjara inquired. "Being a naistinn?"

"A lot different from the inside than from the outside I'd imagine. I've never known anything else, though, so it's hard to explain by comparison. Truth be truth, ever since mother got too sick to rule and I was given the responsibility, I felt like I've not done much. Mostly, it's been old men with coin or land, or both, telling me what I should be doing. Without Nine Mirror's counsel, I'd likely go mad."

"Kjara's family made the cheese on our platters today, Loreena," Brast said.

Loreena's face beamed with recognition, "Chedderheart…of course! My head is so vague of late, Kjara, my apologies for not connecting that sooner. There's not a single opportunity that Geov does not mention your family's cheese. He brings wheels of it whenever he visits mother and me. They sit beside his stories as the thing I most enjoy about his company."

The flattery fluttered in Kjara's chest. High praise for her family's work not only from the region master but the naistinn as well. This was why he has taken an interest in her. Because of her family's cheese, her family name. Not because of her markings. Not because of her…her what, exactly? Her cheeks flushed red with heat as embarrassment overtook her pride.

"Thank you," she said, disguising her awkwardness with a smile. "That is a very kind thing for you to say."

"Perhaps we could visit the farm, Loreena," Brast suggested. "Would that be possible, Kjara?"

"Really?" Kjara swallowed. "Would you want to?"

"Of course! I wouldn't suggest it otherwise. One should always follow through on what they say. Actions and words are all we have, and we should be mindful to keep them aligned."

Kjara smiled again and snuck a look at Captain Deonto. Thairis Brast's sentiments sounded strikingly familiar.

"If that is what you would like to do," Kjara said, straightening in her chair, "we would happily host you."

"Wonderful! Here, try this one with some relish," Brast suggested, cutting Kjara a wedge of cheese. "It's homemade, from the orchard behind you. I think you'll find they pair quite nicely."

Kjara took a bite of the cheese, bread and relish, and savoured it. "You made this?"

He nodded, "A pastime of mine. I love to cook. I find it relaxes me."

"Amazing," Kjara took another bite. "You should bring some with you when you visit us."

"I reckon I shall."

Kjara swallowed her bite and tried to hide her shock. She hadn't expected him to take her up on the suggestion.

Aided by the wine at the table, the atmosphere relaxed into easy conversation. Papa, with input from Soren and Kjara, led the story of the investigation into the mine and the fiedrig. Everyone ate, drank, shared stories and jokes, and revelled in one another's company. As the afternoon progressed, musical instruments appeared to accompany the washing ocean waves. Loreena proved herself adept at the violin and Nine Mirrors at the gaothib, a faeduin wind instrument akin to a flute. Thairis Brast and Papa regaled everyone with a jaunty, tongue-in-cheek song from their respective youths, encouraging everyone to clap along and join in on the refrain.

A soldier set for battle spent time polishing his kit,
Then overslept, the foolish boy, and so he had missed it.
When finally, he got there, he found every man was dead,
The captains came to see the boy, and this is what they said.

Your skill must be impeccable, your bravery so strong,
To keep you from the battle now would be to do you wrong.
Invaders are approaching and we want you in the lead,
So, take a company of men and make the bastards bleed.

Up you go again my friend, up you go again,
Until you reach the top dear boy, until you reach the end.

The boy he marched his company into a deadly fray,
But fell he from his riding horse and missed another day.
Everyone had died again on both sides of the fight,
The general saw the boy alive and smiled with delight.

He took a fancy medal and he pinned it to his chest,
"There's no way you could be alive unless you were the best.
You are the perfect man for this, just look at what you've done,
You'll oversee the captains now until the war is won."

Up you go again my friend, up you go again,
Until you reach the top dear boy, until you reach the end.

The general left the camp and as he dusted off his coat,
The enemy discovered him and opened up his throat.
The soldier missed it all for he was too pleased with himself,
And now he is the general because there's no one else.

Up you go again my friend, up you go again,
Until you reach the top dear boy, until you reach the end.
Up you go again my friend, up you go again,
Until you reach the top dear boy, until you reach your end.

The performance confused Kjara. To see Papa singing a song that held such clear disdain for authority made complete sense. But to hear the same words from the region master, and in front of the naistinn, she wasn't sure how to respond. Yet as the song continued and everyone else fell into laughter, Kjara relaxed and joined in.

"That's quite a tall tale," she said, as the song concluded. "Imagine being promoted for incompetence."

"Tale?" Papa gasped. "It's not a story, it's history. Inked in honour of our glorious Geov Brast."

Kjara's smile dropped, "Is that true? I'm so sorry—"

"Relax, Kjara. Alba is just pulling another prank," Brast filled his wine glass. "Although I do envy that soldier's story at times."

"Why?"

"He survived a war without spilling any blood."

Kjara nodded. The more time she spent at the table, the less she could believe that Thairis Brast might be untrustworthy. But a thought sent a pulse of paranoia through her, *What if you're wrong?*

Kjara shook it from her head, cut another slice of cheese, and poured herself another glass of wine.

Chapter 30

Kjara

As the sun dipped into the horizon, everyone continued swapping stories and songs. The strangeness of the situation disappeared entirely. Each of them hailed from such different places, classes, vocations, and races, but none of it seemed to matter. Conversation travelled through subjects of politics and art, philosophy and ribaldry, and even more besides. Kjara contributed when she could, but most of it flew over her head. Still, she absorbed every word.

"It's because the people of Dasaigh are heavily focussed on community, you see," Thairis Brast explained as the discussion shifted to culture. "They believe all people are connected, that's why they never say 'I', only 'we'. They don't consider 'self' in the way we do."

"I met a man recently who did that," Soren mentioned. "I thought he was just speaking on behalf of his establishment."

"No doubt he was a Dasaigh refugee. An older one I'd wager. It's a language pattern the younger ones don't seem to use as much."

"Do they still speak that way in Dasaigh, though?" Kjara asked.

A discomforting quiet settled over the table.

"Dasaigh doesn't exist anymore, Kjara," Nine Mirrors answered. "The entire country was abandoned in the Collision."

"The only people to survive are those who now live in Northern Cradh," Loreena continued. "Geov was instrumental in organising aid

189

for those who had lost everything. He helped them settle here when they crossed the border."

"We did what we could," Brast responded. "Before the Collisade was raised."

"You're being modest. You saved an entire culture from extinction," Loreena chided gently, before turning back to her. "It was in recognition of his work for the Dasaigh refugees that mother entrusted him with the position of region master."

"Amongst other things," Papa added cheekily. "Isn't that right, Fiend-Choker?"

"The sword was the fiend choker, Alba. I merely swung it," Brast said with rehearsed conviction.

"What is the Collisade?" Kjara asked.

"It's a wall. Two hundred feet high, around the entire country of Dasaigh," Nine Mirrors explained. "...Of what used to be Dasaigh."

"By the moons..." Soren muttered. "How did they manage that?"

"Ah, my favourite trick of all, calibration," Brast's moustache curled up over a wily smile. He gestured to Nine Mirrors. "You're better at explaining it than me, would you mind?"

Nine Mirrors nodded and placed her glass on the table, "Calibration is a particular skill practised by faeduin and some mohras. In the simplest terms, it allows one to manipulate the various properties of an object. One may use it to increase the density of a wooden branch, making it hard enough to crack rocks. One could soften a cloth enough to pass a hand through it like it was water, or—as was the case for the Collisade—enlarge the size of stones."

Soren scratched his ear, "Sounds like another Nofrum story."

"I can assure you it's not," Nine Mirrors said. "But it is a difficult pursuit to master. It requires years of study, training, and natural aptitude, so it's not a common practice. One needs to know what one is doing."

"Go on," Brast leant his hand against his cheek, casting an excited, expectant look at Nine Mirrors. "Share a little taste with the table."

"…Okay," Nine Mirrors nodded thoughtfully. "Okay, I remember one. One moment."

Brast, eyes beaming like a child's, adjusted his seat towards Nine Mirrors. The rest of the table followed suit.

"You're going to love this," he whispered to Kjara.

Nine Mirrors cleared the plates, cutlery, and wine glass from in front of her, and placed a splayed hand on the wood. Slowing her breath and closing her eyes, she let out a soft cooing sound, cycling through various timbres and intonations. Kjara watched in amazement as her fingertips, then her entire hand began to slip through the timber as though it had become butter. When it had passed through to the wrist, she dragged it back out again.

As she freed her hand, everyone erupted into adulation and applause, calling for another demonstration. An uncontainable grin plastered Kjara's face, and as she exchanged a glance with Soren, it grew even larger in response to his. Seeing him visibly happy was a striking contrast to his demeanour when she first met him. Hopefully, it wasn't the food or alcohol but the company that held up his spirits.

Nine Mirrors excused herself, and after a moment returned with a small book in her hand. "It's been a while. I can't remember some of the praxes offhand," she said, flipping through its pages. "Here we go. This might be entertaining."

Nine Mirrors placed the book open on the table, and Kjara stole a peek. Rows of lines and dots covered the page, peppered with illustrations and handwriting. *Perhaps it is how you write down the cooing sound,* Kjara thought, puzzling her way through it all. The notation and imagery alone didn't make much sense at all, even with the accompanying written explanation. Most of the words were too complicated for her to comprehend, but she still appreciated the handwriting.

Nine Mirrors picked up her wine glass, emptied it, and repeated the process of the humming, adding a few gestures. It shrank into her hand and disappeared. Nine Mirrors presented the glass, now tiny, to the group. They applauded, and she reversed the process, placing it back on the table. Thairis Brast refilled it.

"Thank you," she said and took a sip. But as she did, blood dribbled down the stem.

"You've cut yourself," Kjara said.

"Oh. I *am* out of practice," Nine Mirrors replied, inspecting her hand. "It's not a cut. It's distortion. A common side effect for getting the resonance slightly off. Some blood has passed through my skin. See?"

Nine Mirrors held open her palm and wiped the blood away. Her skin underneath was undamaged.

"It's why you need to know what you're doing. When I was studying, one of my fellow students pushed his hand into an anvil and got it stuck. When they finally removed it, he was two fingers shy of when he started."

"If his hand was in the anvil, couldn't they have just pulled the whole thing back out?" Kjara asked. "Softened the metal up, or whatever?"

"That is exactly what the Master Calibrists did. But his fingers had already separated from his hand inside the anvil. And they'd…dissolved. No separation between the iron and the flesh."

"Losing two fingers…that's terrifying," Soren said.

Nine Mirrors shook her head and held up her index finger and thumb.

"Three fingers. It wasn't his first mistake. He'd previously tried to make a gold ring from a coin and…" Nine Mirrors pinched her thumb and forefinger together. "Cut clean off. It fell into a river, and a crippler fish ate it. As I said, you need to be very careful using calibration."

Kjara wiggled her fingers.

All still there.

Nine Mirrors continued, "That's not even the worst distortion story I've heard. Terrible things can happen when one doesn't understand the functions of calibration."

"What are they?" Kjara asked.

"They are the essential laws by which Calibration operates. One: catalyst. You need starting material; you cannot create something from nothing. That would defy nature in an impossible way. Two: constraint. There is a limitation on how much you can adjust the material. If you push too far, things start to distort. Three: conduction. You need to transmit your intentions through the object. That usually requires the right vocal resonance and pattern, and physical contact or at least proximity."

Kjara nodded, "That's all?"

Nine Mirrors laughed, "There's more, it is an incredibly complex system, but in the simplest terms, yes. I suppose that is all."

"And the humming? What's that about?" Soren asked.

"Ah! I can explain this one!" Brast said, interjecting. "If you don't mind?"

Nine Mirrors smiled, "Of course."

"Wonderful! Okay, so, imagine a balladeer who plays his songs loud and fast. Imagine another balladeer who plays the same songs softly and slowly. Now, imagine a balladeer who plays her song soft and slow at first, but no one in the audience is interested. She can tell people want something to dance to, so she picks up the tempo for the second verse. The song remains the same, even though she changed it. With me so far?" Soren nodded. "Good! See, every object in existence has its own 'song', which they're always humming. This chair, the table. Your shirt. Even you, me, everyone here. If you can tune yourself into it, if you know the song, you can play it how you want to play it."

Nine Mirrors raised her eyebrows, "A poetic analogy, but it captures the concept of calibration quite well."

"So, distortion is what happens if you play the wrong note?" Kjara suggested, mulling over the analogy.

Nine Mirrors tapped a long, slender finger on the table in thought, "Yes, I suppose so. A sour note, a dropped beat, playing out of tune. Some other balladeer's error."

The humming and the vibrations. It all sounded frightfully familiar. Kjara chewed her lower lip, "Could you stop an object with it? Change the direction of something mid-air?"

Captain Deonto cast Kjara a curious glance.

Nine Mirrors ran a finger along her eyebrow, "In theory. If one used the air as the catalyst and conductor, yes. Technically you wouldn't be stopping the object, you would be manipulating the air around it. But it would be incredibly difficult. I can't think of any calibrists that could achieve that. Or if they did, they'd likely be bedridden for days after the fact. Longer even. Most wouldn't even try; the air is far too dangerous as a catalyst."

"Why?"

"The risk of distortion is simply too high. Air is always moving. Pulled along by the wind. To build on Geov's analogy, the air is a song that is always changing key, which makes staying in harmony with it nearly impossible. And it's everywhere. Including your lungs. Make a mistake, and all the air inside you might harden like stone. And if it distorts…"

Kjara shuddered, finishing the outcome in her head. Calibration was dangerous. Very dangerous. Too dangerous.

She needed to know more.

Night had truly set in when the lunch drew to a close. Thairis Brast undertook the tidying up himself. When Kjara questioned him on why he hadn't servants to do it, he defended his choice: "If I can't look after myself, I can't look after the region."

Kjara also let him know that next market day she would tell Mado of Brast's intention to visit. Farewells passed back and forth from all those still in attendance. Captain Deonto had excused herself earlier, explaining she had 'important business', but she'd left in such a positive mood that she allowed Kjara the night off.

Papa, Soren, and Kjara exited the gatehouse, farewelling Garyn the gatekeeper, and began the way down the hill towards town. Papa was in high spirits, having imbibed a substantial amount of wine, and sang a refrain from his previous song. Soren, the most relaxed Kjara had seen him, joined in, trying to match Papa's ever-shifting key. And Kjara too was in a positive mood, her mind churning through alcohol and curiosity. It had been such a pleasant and elucidating evening that she had almost forgotten the draejr's warning. But once out of sight of the manor, the thought returned.

"Papa…Papa! We need to debrief."

"Eh?" Papa swayed slightly but used his makeshift walking stick for balance. "Oh!"

"So?" Kjara waited expectantly. "What do we make of him? Innocent or not?"

Soren's posture stiffened, "Him? Him who?"

"Papa stopped you yesterday because he suspects Thairis Brast as the conspirator," Kjara explained. "He didn't want to risk Brast finding out that we knew of the plot."

"We had to give him the third degree," Papa slurred. "Find out where his allegiance lies. Or if it is he, himself...who lies."

"So, you think this plot is Brast's?" Soren asked.

Papa belched a response in the affirmative.

"I'm not so sure," Kjara said.

"You should be. He's trouble!" Papa rubbed his beard. "He's treacherous. He slipped something in my drink. Look at how I'm walking!"

"He didn't slip anything into your drink, you're staggering because you slipped twice as much into your belly as anyone else," Soren accused. "And you have a twisted ankle."

"Slander! Have at thee!" Papa swung his walking stick outwards in a wide arc. Soren dipped back and kicked it from Papa's hand. It clattered to the dirt, and Papa groaned, hopping over to collect it.

"Stop it," Kjara frowned. "This is serious. Stay focussed." She swam through her drunken thoughts in search of a solution, "Wait...The naistinn was right in front of us, why don't we just go back now and tell her? There's no guards, and we outnumber Brast if things get rough."

"Oh, blah," Papa snorted. "That man is a fighter. Born and bred, baptized in battle. He'd crush us. I'm too old, you're too young, and he's too...sour."

"I can handle myself," Soren said.

"What if this whole thing is a trick?" Papa remained unconvinced. "Azmariliz getting back at us because we disrupted its sleep and invaded its lair!"

"If we tell her and it amounts to nothing, isn't it better than not telling her, and it amounting to something awful?" Soren reasoned.

Kjara baited Papa by turning around and heading back to the manor, "He's just scared, Soren, let's go without him."

Soren followed.

"Hey. Hey! Wait up," Papa called out, hobbling after them. Kjara suppressed a grin. A simple tactic but highly effective. As Kjara approached the gatehouse, a squeaking metallic sound caught in the night breeze grew louder. Soren stepped up to the gate and pushed. It swung lazily open. Garyn the gatekeeper was missing, nothing there but his book.

"That's...a little worrying," Soren mumbled.

Chapter 31

———— ◉ ————

Kjara

The twin moons were waning and this, coupled with the cloud cover, made it a particularly dark night. Kjara led the way, flanked by Papa and Soren, to the front door of Brast's manor. Muffled voices, rich with jovial conversation, bubbled down the corridor to the left.

"They're in the study," Papa said. "That way."

Kjara had time enough to peer down the corridor before a scream ripped through the manor. Then a slamming sound of wood on wood. The study door swung open, bathing the corridor in warm firelight, as Brast and some unknown figure hurtled out into the corridor.

Their silver-lined silhouettes fought and struggled with one another, but Brast managed to heave his boot into the stranger's gut, knocking it back into the study. He followed after it with a furious grunt.

Kjara ran down the corridor and stopped in the doorway of the study. Books and spilt tea covered the floor. Loreena Farlight cowered behind Brast's desk while Brast and the stranger squared off in the middle of the room. Black leather armour kept the stranger's body a mystery. A bandana and hood concealed its face, a bandolier of throwing knives clung to its chest, and its fist gripped a long dagger. Kjara knew well enough what it was: a carver, someone paid to end the lives of others.

Kjara froze.

The dagger pierced the air and tore into Brast's belly. He grabbed his gut and backpeddled into the wall. The carver lunged after him with another slice, but he sidestepped and made a grab for the blade. It ducked, spun around, and slipped back up through Brast's guard.

Another stab.

Brast grunted and Loreena screamed. The carver pushed him up against the bookshelf and books and sundry toppled to the floor. Brast swung a fist, but it was dodged and stabbed again.

The carver stabbed again. Brast threw out a hand to defend his gut, catching the dagger through his forearm. He cursed and drove a heavy foot into its knee which twisted with a sharp, cracking sound and knocked the carver down. Brast ripped the dagger from his arm and raised it for an attack, but the carver buried a throwing knife into his shoulder and he dropped the dagger. It clattered to the ground, but as the carver reached out for it, a boot heel crushed its hand into the floor. Brast was angry, fierce. But bleeding. Dying.

Brast roared and stomped his boot again. Two heavy thuds into the carver's rib cage. Anticipating the third stomp, it rolled out of the way and getting to its feet, grabbed for another knife to throw. Brast seized a book and hurled it. The carver dodged and aimed its throwing knife at his face.

A blur of movement caught in the corner of Kjara's eye.

Soren had rushed the carver, grabbed its arm, and twisted it up before Kjara knew what was happening. The knife dropped from its hand and wedged into the floor.

The carver spun around, attempting to break Soren's grip but caught another blow across the cheek followed by a second into the chest. It took in a pained gasp, as though struggling to breathe. As if the wind escaping its lungs threatened to collapse them. It shook its head and blocked a third strike before stepping back, guard up, poised and ready to strike.

Soren advanced, but the carver loosed another blade and he staggered back, the knife lodged into his shoulder. The carver drove his foot into Soren's shin, knocking him off balance, then laid a kick into his cheek to roll him onto his back.

The carver stomped at the knife in Soren's shoulder, hitting once, maybe twice, but Kjara couldn't focus through the blood and the blur. Soren grabbed its foot and wrestled it to the ground. He scrambled on top of it, slamming his fist into its face.

The carver snatched for the knife in Soren's shoulder, grabbing it and pushing. Soren screamed and tried to bat its hand away, and in doing so gave the carver a chance to wiggle free. It spun on its heel and rushed for the open door, side-stepping Brast and scooping up its dagger as it did. Kjara steeled herself but the carver barrelled through her, sending her scooting along the corridor.

Kjara recognised Papa's voice, but not his words, the blood pumping through her ears muffling them. It wasn't until she reached the back veranda that she even realised she was chasing after the carver. And by then, it just seemed right to continue.

Kjara shouted something at the black-clad thing sprinting through the orchard, something she couldn't recognise, but her haffelin stride couldn't keep up, even with the carver's broken breaths. It stopped at the manor wall, the tall stone brick face blocking its escape.

"Stop!" Kjara shouted.

The carver looked back at her before leaping up and grabbing the edge of the wall. As it heaved itself up, Kjara reached the base. Sweating and breathless, she grabbed at the carver's foot. But it was too fast, or she was too slow.

From deep in the base of her skull, she heard the droning, humming thrum. It shivered through her body, set her spiral markings prickling, and as she put her hand on the wall, a rippling wave shimmered outwards. The stonework atop the wall liquified and the carver's feet started sinking in.

Suddenly, Kjara's cheek exploded with pain, and she grabbed at it. The deep droning notes silenced, overtaken by the blanketed silence of the night, the distant waves breaking below the cliff, and her own panting. She felt blood bubble up and drip down her face, and she realised the carver had thrown a dagger and sliced her chin.

She looked back up, but the carver was gone, leaving nothing but footprints atop the half-melted wall.

Chapter 32

Kjara

Kjara's stomach turned as her lunch threatened its escape.

"Geov, by all the gods and all the booze would you lie the hell down?!" Papa ordered. Brast squirmed on the floor of his study. Blood pooled around him, soaking into the carpet.

"I'm fine!" Brast declared, attempting to sit up.

"That's the fighter's fire talking, you horse's arse!" Papa said. "If you want to die, do it when I'm not around. Raise your damned arm. And stop moving!"

Brast glared at Papa with the anger of a wounded animal. But it was never wise to argue with a clinician. He begrudgingly raised his arm.

"Kjara, help him hold it up. It'll prevent blood loss."

Kjara did so, above the wrist to keep her glove clean of blood. Her mouth dried out.

Why can I smell iron?

Papa peeled Brast's shirt up.

"By Fyaldha…" he placed his nose close to the three puncture wounds and pushed gently around the area. "Good news, old mate. It doesn't smell like it's punctured your bowels. So, less chance of infection. All the fancy food keeping you fat may have saved your life."

"Go hang, Alba," Brast spluttered.

"Still pretty deep though. A decent gush coming out of you. Loreena, you know this place well enough, go fetch me some sheets. Linen preferred. I hope you haven't gone too fancy on us, 'my thairis'. Silk won't fix this mess."

Loreena rushed off, returning with a fine lavender-coloured linen sheet and Nine Mirrors behind her.

The faeduin's eyes widened in shock, "What happened?"

"Ah, good. Perfect. Come here and sort this out," Papa said, pointing to the dribbling slash in Brast's gut.

"What? How?"

"Use your cali-blah blah."

"I can't do that. I don't—"

"Brilliant," Papa rolled his eyes. "Loreena, hand that sheet to Kjara and take over holding up Geov's arm. Kjara, you are going to tear it into strips and—lavender, really?"

"Can't I have a favourite flower?" Brast hacked up a noise, half laughter, half cough.

Kjara swapped out with Loreena and started tearing the sheets into strips. Candlelight flickered disorientating shadows on the wall. She shivered and averted her eyes. Her stomach flipped again.

"Kjara, you're going to bind up his punctured arm," Papa explained. "I'll work his guts. Geov. Vinegar? Yellow root? Needle and thread?"

Brast nodded, "In the kitchen, the middle shelf of the dry store. And there's some needlework in the bottom drawer of my desk."

"Nine Mirrors—"

She nodded and turned on her heel.

"A bowl too," Papa called after her. "And a saucepan! Loreena, keep his arm up. Kjara, wrap it. Good, just like that."

Geov winced as Kjara tied off the linen around his arm.

"Sorry," she said.

203

"It's fine."

Papa ran strips around Brast's midsection, pulling tight to stem the blood flow.

"It'll hold for now. But we'll need to stitch them up quick. Keep as much blood on the inside—"

"Where it's supposed to be," Brast finished.

"Ah, he still remembers."

Nine Mirrors returned and passed Papa the needle and thread.

"This is going to hurt," he said.

"No wine to dull the pain?" Brast asked.

"I think you've had enough today, don't you?" Papa retorted. "Speaking of, my hands might be a bit shaky, so lay very still."

"Should I send for a clothier instead?" Brast quipped.

"It's your fault for having such a well-stocked cellar. Okay. Not very sharp, but...here we go."

Papa peeled back the linen strips, and set about knitting Brast's wounds closed one by one, as Brast did his best to stay still. He winced with every needle prick, breathing short and sharp as the needle dug through the skin and pulled it tight.

It looks like a tiny leather bootlace, Kjara thought, with a queasy shudder. Her lunch floated to the top of her stomach on red wine and relish. It tickled the back of her neck.

"Kjara, heat the water over the fire. Mix up a broth of water, wine, and vinegar. Nine Mirrors, mash the yellow root into a paste."

"Okay, got it."

Grabbing the saucepan, Kjara followed Papa's instructions and handed the steaming broth back to him. He poured it over Brast's stomach, rinsing off the wounds. Brast swore. As the blood and water mixed, it looked more like wine than anything else. After that, Papa applied the yellow root paste liberally over the stitches and rewrapped them with the linen.

Like wine and mustard and—Stop it. Focus elsewhere. Kjara swallowed and looked away.

"Gods be…It's worse than I remember," Brast complained.

"Quit bellyaching, it's just an aching belly," Papa snapped. "We're finished here. Stay lying, Brast."

"My turn, then?" came Soren's voice from the doorway. Blood dirtied his shirt and trousers, sweat dripped off his chin. The colour drained from Kjara's face, and her breath thinned.

"By Fyaldha…you look grim. Okay, Kjara," Papa stopped his instruction. "We've got a green one. Nine Mirrors, take Kjara out into the hall."

"I'm fine," Kjara lied. Her lunch disrespectfully disagreed.

"Pig's arse. Go!" he demanded.

Nine Mirrors took her by the shoulder and led her from the room. The moment Kjara was out of sight, she doubled over in pain. A swamp of half-digested cheese, bread, wine, and fruit expelled itself from her mouth and splashed onto the carpet.

"Gods be…" her throat burned with stomach acid; her mouth tasted of bile.

Nine Mirrors rubbed her back, "Let it out, child. It's fine."

"It's okay, I'm okay…"

"Good news!" Papa's voice drifted down the corridor. "No signs of intestinal rupture, Soren!"

Another heave of chunks lurched out of Kjara's mouth. Her eyes welled up with tears and her nostrils burned. Her stomach swirled and swirled, "I think some came out of my nose!"

"I'll get you some water," Nine Mirrors said, standing up.

"I got some on my shoes…"

Kjara leant against the wall and dropped to the floor. Wiping her mouth, she blew an errant chunk from her nostril. Nine Mirrors returned, handed her a glass of water and a wash bucket, and sat beside her.

"I don't know what happened," Kjara began, after a few sips of water. "It's just a bit of blood."

"It is just a bit of blood," Nine Mirrors replied. "And a bit too much wine from lunch. Not the best combination."

"I live on a farm. I see blood all the time," Kjara laughed. "Birthing livestock. I mean, that can get pretty messy."

"The blood of death runs darker than the blood of birth."

"You don't think they'll die, do you?"

"No. They'll live."

Kjara rubbed her arm. Nine Mirrors spoke so plainly about death, it disturbed her. She needed to change the topic. Sat in the corridor beside a calibrist, her mind wandered back to lunch, to the way Nine Mirrors pushed her hand through the table, the way she shrank the glass.

"Was it hard learning calibration?"

"Yes. It was. Extremely so. It hurt my head. It drained my energy. I wanted to quit almost every day of study."

"So why didn't you?"

"It was my duty to learn it."

"Your duty?"

"Yes. For my country. To help keep it safe."

"You helped build the Collisade, didn't you?"

She nodded.

"What was that like?"

"Hard. For everyone involved. It took six months to erect. A hundred stonemasons bringing in materials daily. Dozens of highly skilled calibrists from every part of the Aonadh, working dawn through dusk," Nine Mirrors paused. "Not all who worked on it survived to see its completion."

"Folks died?"

Nine Mirrors nodded solemnly, "Yes. But that is what it means to do one's duty. Sacrifice, giving up something of yourself for others. Even if it hurts to do so. Even if it kills you. All of us have only one life. Whether it is a short one or a long one, death is the only destination. And if you choose to give your life to save your home, your people, then it is a worthy life you have lived."

She turned her head and stared back into the study.

Kjara followed her gaze, "You believe that? You would die for your country?"

"Cradh is my home. I would do anything to protect it."

Chapter 33

Soren

Soren lay on the floor of Thairis Brast's study, listening to Papa's snores and everyone else's quiet breathing. Frustrated and unable to sleep, he got up and paced about the manor. He retraced the path of the carver, over and again, hoping to find a clue. But all that did was aggravate his injuries. He knew that come dawn, the fighter's fire would have drained from his blood, and he'd be useless.

Something out of place near the rear entry drew Soren's eye. Splatters of blood patterned the carpet nearby, but this wasn't blood. He knelt for a closer inspection and his nostrils flared in recognition and anger. A black die with scarlet numbers, and a capital "S" in place of the one. He pulled on his boots and tiptoed down the corridor to the rear entry. He opened the door to leave, but a voice from behind caught him.

"Where are you going?"

Soren froze. He had hoped to be out and back by morning before anyone had awoken and discovered he had gone. Instead of answering, he deflected.

"Kjara, what are you doing awake?"

"Couldn't sleep. I heard a noise and came to investigate. Where are you going? You should be resting."

Soren sighed, "I'm going to investigate something as well."

"Investigate what?" she asked. "Investigate what, Soren?"

Anger flared in his chest, "Forget it. I'm still a bit drunk, just need some air. Go back to sleep."

"Are you going to vomit? Papa said if you did it was a sign you—"

"I'm not going to," Soren strained to calm his voice, "...vomit. It's fine."

"Are you sure?"

"Yes," he insisted. "Do you not trust me?"

"Of course, I trust you."

Not the answer he expected, "What?"

"I said, I trust you," Kjara took a step closer.

Soren swallowed hard, fighting off the prickling anxiety which sucked the air from his lungs and dried out his mouth. That urge again, the desire to be honest, hampered by a fear that crushed his windpipe.

"Why?"

"You saved me from the fiedrig. You wanted to help Papa get through the mine. You defended Brast and chased after a trained carver, Soren. So, I know I can trust you," she said, taking another step closer. "Do you trust me?"

"Of course."

"So...Why are you lying to me?"

Lying. The word, sharp and aggressive, burrowed under Soren's skin and knotted his muscles. He swallowed again, avoiding eye contact.

"I'm not..."

Speak the truth, Soren. Kjara is offering you kindness, friendship. Don't do what you always do. Don't. Run. Away.

He inhaled slowly, "I found something. It connects Sabel, the red-haired girl from lockup, to the manor."

"So, what? You were going to go after her?"

"I…Maybe…Yes, I don't know."

"You think she was the carver? And in your state, you're going to, what, confront her? She nearly killed you tonight."

"If it was her, she won't have any fight left," Soren's hand found the door handle. "Besides, if she is at The Bait and Tackle, I won't be alone. There'll be people there, it's public. It's safe."

"Okay," Kjara said. "Then I'm coming with you."

"No chance, it's far too dangerous."

"You just said it was safe, Soren. Or are you lying again?"

Soren sighed deeply. He couldn't be responsible for something bad happening to her. But he couldn't see a way to keep her away.

"Okay fine, you can come along. But the moment it looks like even a hint of danger—"

"I can handle myself."

Soren looked at Kjara, her determined face. For a moment, he almost believed her.

Unanswered questions incited Soren's stride as he travelled with Kjara to The Bait and Tackle. How did Sabel know about the naistinn's arrival? What was her die doing at Thairis Brast's manor? If Sabel wasn't the carver, there was no guarantee of answers, and if she was, he might not make it out alive. His fists were the only protection he had, and his dominant arm was carved up four inches through his shoulder; he'd been beaten half to death. It was reckless, it was stupid, and it was keeping perfectly in character. Right down to endangering his companions.

Kjara had snuck one of Thairis Brast's coats—one of his least colourful—to hide Soren's bloody, ripped clothes. But as he passed through the city streets, no one was around to notice his condition. The Bait and Tackle, on the other hand, bustled with patrons, all too busy to pay him any mind. Ayleth sat in a booth, chatting with that tornblood and liathaum again. Both were bruised and bandaged but were otherwise jovial. They leant back in their chairs, talking, drinking and laughing.

"This place seems less than reputable," Kjara said.

"The place is fine enough. The patrons…not so much."

The tapster grinned and waved.

"Ah, he is back," he announced. "We are surprised to see you. We thought you'd be dead, the way you drank last time. We see you've taken a bit of a knockabout as well. Another tea? Or would you like something with a little more personality?"

"Is Sabel here?"

"Not on tap, no," the tapster chuckled, but Soren didn't care for the joke. "But, uh, yer, she's in the back room. The back, backroom, we think. We trust you'll recall the way."

Soren nodded, but as he went to walk away, the tapster stopped him.

"Oh, wait. On the house," he said, placing a tall glass of beer on the counter. "We appreciate your efforts."

Soren accepted the drink, but the moment the tapster shifted his attention away, he left it on a table. Kjara, trailing behind him, snuck it into her hand. He passed through a door towards the back of the pub and into a small room, a gaming room. A few familiar faces were there, including Orpip, who spotted Kjara straight away.

"You! Cheeky little shit!" ze said, dropping zir cards and moving to strike Kjara with zir hand. She startled, the ale from her glass unleashing itself over Orpip's face.

211

"Sorry…" Kjara stepped behind Soren. Orpip looked up and immediately backed down from the sight.

"My mistake. I didn't realise."

"How is your head?" Kjara asked.

"Sore," Orpip replied shortly. "Ankle, too."

"Sorry," she offered. "Again."

"Some bad blood there?" Soren asked as he passed out of earshot and towards the far end of the room.

"Maybe a little," she rubbed her neck. "What about you? Ze seemed to change tune right fast when ze saw you. Why's that?"

Soren pursed his lips, "I have no idea."

Another door stood at the back of the room, dark and easy to miss. Soren opened the door and passed through, closely followed by Kjara. He stepped into a poorly lit circular auditorium. In front of him, about fifteen feet deep, was a large circular pit. Around it curled chest-high metal barriers to prevent people from falling in. It was dingy, not well populated, and the familiar scarlet hair and long velvet coat stood out against the drab attire of the others.

"Sabel Hane, the gambler's bane," Soren muttered. "There she is."

The dark purple bruise around her left eye and swollen red cheek on the opposite side were highly suspicious. Soren glanced behind Sabel to ensure clear access to the exit. As they approached, Sabel grinned enthusiastically at him, but it quickly turned to an expression of concern.

"There he is!" Sabel stopped rocking on her chair. "By the moons, you've pulled up rather unpleasant. What's going on there? I thought you didn't get hit. Didn't look like you got hit," she said. "Nice haircut, though. Very handsome."

Soren pressed his teeth together, "Why did you do it?"

"Because it makes me money?" she responded quizzically. "Because it's fun. Are you feeling okay?"

Her avoidance boiled the alcohol in Soren's blood.

He slammed his fist on the table, "Explain yourself."

"Hey! We talked about this. You agreed to this."

Kjara turned to Soren, confused, "Soren...what is she talking about?"

"Oh, hello. Didn't see you there. You look a bit different outside of a lockup, don't you? And out of farmer's clothes, too. She scrubs up quite nicely, doesn't she, Soren?"

"That's enough."

"There is a lot of unjustified hostility here. Can someone please catch me up? Kjara looks as confused as I feel. So, let's stop...punching tables, and talk like civilised folk."

Soren's nostrils flared, "You nearly killed me."

"That was consensual," Sabel squinted at him. "You knew that, right?"

"You tried to kill the region master," Soren accused.

Sabel reeled back, utterly baffled, "What?! Who...Why—What?!"

She was either lying to cover her tracks, or she genuinely didn't know. Regardless, her avoidant attitude proved more than Soren could bear. His fist tightened by his side, preparing for a less polite interrogation. Kjara put her hand on his forearm, settling him down.

"Sabel, what happened the last time you saw Soren?"

"Ah! A question I can answer," Sabel waved her index finger in the air. "Two nights ago, I think. Soren came in here, chasing money I owed Blinny. Money, I might add, I did not owe Blinny, being that he was a dirty liar, cheat, and scoundrel. I agreed to transact his coin on one proviso: that Soren have a drink with me. Which he did. But one led to another, and before you know it, we were back here posting up bets. He kept going on about how fantastic a fighter he was, so we signed up for a two-v-two. Him and me against a liathaum and a tornblood. I didn't fare so well," she said, gesturing to her face, "but they couldn't land a blow on Soren. Or so I thought. Looks like I might have been mistaken, given your current state."

"So, you weren't at the region master's manor tonight?"

"Not tonight, no."

"Wait," Kjara took a seat opposite Sabel. "What do you mean by that?"

Sabel shrugged, "Nothing."

Soren tossed her dice on the table.

She groaned, "Curse it! Fine. Sit down at least, would you, you're making me uncomfortable."

Soren sat down, and as he did, his coat split open, revealing the long bloodstain running up his shirt to his shoulder. Sabel raised one disturbed eyebrow.

"We'll circle back around to that," she said, pointing to the mess. "Okay, look. Let's be clear. I wasn't there to steal anything. I might be a Game Shark and a fisticuff enthusiast, but I'm not a thief...anymore. And I'm not a carver. So, if anything's gone missing from the old man's home, it wasn't me."

"We never mentioned anything about thievery," Soren said. "Guilty conscience?"

"Prior experience. I've been accused of thieving before. I figure you're going to ask me if I stole anything, so I am laying everything out on the table now. I didn't steal anything from Thairis Brast, and I didn't try to kill him. I work for him."

Soren blinked, "Come again?"

"I said I work for him."

"What work do you do for him?" Soren asked.

"Mostly, I keep an ear out. Let him know what I hear."

"You're a spy?"

Kjara scoffed, "She's a snitch."

"I'm a citizen, thank you. A concerned citizen who cares for my city."

"You're a criminal," Soren corrected.

"Speak for yourself."

Soren ground his teeth.

"How does someone with your skillset end up working for a thairis?" Kjara asked.

"All you need to do is be in the right place at the right time," Sabel answered.

"He caught you stealing from his house," Soren guessed. "And he offered you a deal."

Sabel gave a sly grin.

"You're lying," Kjara said. "Thairis Brast wouldn't hire criminals. He's a good man."

"I agree. He is a good man," Sabel replied. "He looks after his people. And that's what we are. His people. And we're his before we are the law's."

"What information do you give him?" Soren asked.

"There are things that operate by the natural laws of the world. And there are things that don't. Thairis Brast has a particular fondness for the latter. Sometimes I hear people talking, passing venturists and the like. About strange, eerie happenings out amongst the forest-grown, past the boundaries of the civilised."

"That's all?"

"That's all. If Brast finds the tales curious enough, he might pay me a little extra to go investigate for him. It's dangerous out there, beyond the pale. But the coin keeps me well protected." Sabel's gaze trailed off with an expression between fear and elation. "Look. I don't want you having wasted your time coming down here, so, tell you what I'll do. I'll keep an ear out. And if I hear of any beat-down carvers, I'll share the information with you. Discount, since we're mates."

Soren stiffened, "We didn't say anything about the carver being injured."

"Educated guess, null. You didn't get slashed up painting a roof. And if it got that close to you, I'll hazard you gave as good as you got. Don't worry, I won't say nothing to no one," she looked at Kjara. "I'm not a snitch."

Satisfied, Soren said his thanks and made to leave. As he did, Sabel stopped him with the loud clunk of metal on the table.

"Before you go," she said. "Take this, would you?"

"What is it?"

"Fifty gold. Like I promised."

Chapter 34

Kjara

Kjara helped Nine Mirrors organise breakfast, and as she brought it into the guest bedroom, she heard Loreena and Papa deep in conversation. Brast remained in no state to eat, passing in and out, but the others needed food. If not for their stomachs, then for their morale. Food settled all fears.

"What are we talking about?" she asked, handing out plates of scrambled eggs, fried tomato, shredded potato, and sliced fruit.

"We are trying to organise a plan. Moving forward," Loreena began. "I would like to send for guards to provide some additional protection, but Papa isn't so certain."

Papa scooped a spoonful of eggs into his mouth, "I think you should leave town. Wherever the carver came from, it's running back there. And then it'll be coming back here to finish the job."

"That's why we need protection, so they can't get to Brast."

"Brast wasn't the target. You were the target."

"We don't know that."

"Yes, we do!" Papa argued.

"How?" Loreena countered.

Papa floundered, "Well…because you are the naistinn!"

"So, if she was the target, your suggestion to keep her safe is to send her away?" Nine Mirrors asked. "On the open road where there will be no protection?"

"It'll keep *us* safe," Papa replied. "We can't trust the guards. We don't know who's in on it. If we end up with six men in here, and they're all on the take, that's it. Lights out. All of us. No witnesses."

"If you are worried about being attacked, then why don't you leave?" Nine Mirrors suggested pointedly.

"Brast needs supervision. *Qualified* medical supervision."

"I'm not leaving either," Loreena added. "Not until Brast is safe and healthy again."

"That could be months," Nine Mirrors said. "You have duties back at the capital."

"Hang the duties," Loreena spat.

"Loreena, not to be callous, but Cradh is more important than one man."

"Not this man. I am not leaving."

While the tension and argument grew, Kjara listened and formulated a plan, "If the whole town guard was in on it, even if it was just a few of them, they'd be here by now to finish the job. We can trust them. We need to trust them."

"And if it was one of the guards?" Loreena asked.

"If it was only one of the guards, they'd be missing their duties. Or they'd look beat-down. We could ask Captain Deonto if anyone didn't make it to their shift," Kjara suggested. As she did, her mind flashed back to Harwin and Sabel in the bathhouse, and doubt filled her thoughts.

"Okay, so who is going?" Papa asked.

"I'll go," Kjara offered. "She'll believe me."

"And if she doesn't?" Nine Mirrors demanded.

"Here," Loreena slipped Brast's signet ring off and handed it to Kjara. "She'll believe this."

"Are you sure, Kjara?" Papa's brow creased with worry. "If you're wrong, and you ask the wrong guard for help…"

"I'll be fine. And who else are we going to send? You? We already know the captain wants you dead," Kjara joked, trying to lighten the mood. But inside, she was afraid.

Kjara travelled down the hill, along the narrow road that cut through the thicketed forest. A thousand trees to hide behind. Not for her. For it. The black-clad thing that drove daggers like nails into her friends and could do so to her if it wanted.

You're not a target. You aren't in danger; you don't know anything. There is no reason for it to take you.

Her eyes darted constantly from the ground in front of her, to the tree line, and down the road. Each time she looked down she saw the reddish stain patterning her left trouser cuff.

The blood of a thairis on the trouser leg of a farm girl. It wasn't like the blood she'd seen on the farm. She'd seen blood on new-born calves, blood on poorly sheared sheep. She'd seen rabbits punctured with the metal teeth of a jaw trap but never a man punctured with a blade. Her thoughts kept her so distracted that when Kjara arrived at the city gates and a voice spoke to her, she shrieked in fright.

"Sorry there. Didn't mean to scare you," the voice apologised. "Oh, it's you."

By the gates stood one of the town's guards, looking as calm as Kjara felt terrified.

"Kjara, right?"

"Yes."

"You're in a lot of trouble."

Panic spiked Kjara's chest, "What?"

219

"You've got mud on your new duds. On the hem, there," he said, pointing. "The captain doesn't take kindly to stains. I'd be giving them a thorough scrub if I were you."

"Oh...Thank you."

"Happy to help," he said as Kjara passed him and entered the city proper.

The streets bustled with traffic and customers. Vendor stalls, squished end-to-end, forming wide corridors over the cobbled stone and grass of the market square. Kjara adjusted the strap of her haversack and continued in the direction of the guardhouse. As she passed by The Eyeglass Pub, a voice called out her name. She turned around, spotting a figure darting through the crowds towards her, shorter than the rest: a haffelin.

Is it Orpip? Is Orpip part of the plot and coming to silence me?

Her eyes focused, and her heart rate dropped. She recognised the familiar face, the messy crop of hair and crow's feet.

"Dad?"

"Hey, hey there, daughter of mine, and how do you be? Gods be, hardly recognise you with these fancy clothes. But then, your mum's always had better eyes than these. She could spot you a mile away, in the dark. 'Look, there's Kjara,' she said. 'Go grab her quick!' and I'll not be one to argue."

"Mum's here?" Kjara asked, eyes darting through the crowd. She was being watched, she knew it. The carver was out there somewhere in the crowd, and it had seen her parents.

What if it thinks you're telling them what happened and decides to silence them the moment you leave?

"Yer, she's come to help with the market, seein' as you've got the guard duties. And to see you as well. Come on."

"I'm sort of busy—"

"Too busy for family? Nonsense. Come now!" he said, taking Kjara's hand and dragging her back to the cheese stall. "Calarin, I've caught her!"

As they approached, Kjara's mother, Calarin, leapt from behind the counter and flung her arms wide for a crushing hug.

"It's so good to see you, my girl! Let's have a look at you. Oh, such fine clothes. I thought you said we had to bring some, Mado? You didn't say she was gettin' new outfits. Are they feedin' you well enough? You seem a bit pale. How's things here in the city? Tell us everythin'. Spare no details!"

"I'm afraid, Mum, some details may need to be spared," Kjara said.

"Oh, secrets she has!" Calarin joked.

Mado heaped a bundle of clothes on the counter, "Here you go. Dice, cards. Comb. The wooden one, not the bone one. And two fresh sets of clothes...Although lookin' at you now, I feel a bit foolish handin' them over."

"They're fine, Dad. I do need them. And I will wear them."

"So why the dapper duds then?" Calarin asked. "Oh look, you've already grubbed them up. Here, is that wine? Some salt and vinegar will pull it out. Serves you right for drinkin'."

"I haven't been drinking..." Kjara lied. She wasn't quite sure how to explain she had been sharing wine with the region master and the naistinn the night before.

"Not what I've heard. Your Dad told me you got arrested in a pub."

"For brawlin', Calarin, not drinkin'," Mado corrected.

"Well, they're as much the same now, aren't they?" she shot back. Turning to Kjara she asked, "So tell us, what's news?"

Disorientated, Kjara didn't know how to begin, or where to begin, or even what to say. A horrible hot flash of her parent's carved up like Thairis Brast cut across her mind's eye. Her stomach tightened.

"What?"

"I said, tell us about your week. What has the captain got you doin'?"

The captain. Kjara had to go see the captain.

"Cleaning. I had to clean the bathhouse. I learnt how they heat the water."

You made the water hot, remember? The tunnel of flames?

"Oh! Did they let you try a hot bath? Your dad and I used to come into the city when we were younger and—"

"Calarin, she doesn't need to know that," Mado deflected. "Go on, Kjara."

Her head swam. *What had that voice said?*

"I've had to feed the lockups. I've…"

You set a fire with your fingers.

"Kjara?"

"Sorry. I've, um…I've been learning to read. And write."

And the candlestick. You did that too. Are you going to tell them about it? You should.

"They've got you workin' overtime," Calarin smiled. "You'll have to teach me a few words or letters when you get home."

When you get home? Where is home, exactly? Kjara's chest tightened, squeezing the air from her lungs. Her eyes burned with fatigue. *What was it saying?*

"Have the other guards been treatin' you okay? I know how tall folks can be a bit stand-offish," Mado asked.

Kjara swallowed hard and nodded. *Are you going to tell them he couldn't see you? He looked right at you, you know. Why didn't he see you?*

"Yer…They're being nice…They are—What? What did you say?"

That sound again. The humming. The vibration, pulsing and pounding. Kjara's skull rattled, her skin prickled. Her bones shook.

222

Everything felt so far away and yet, everything was right there. What? How? The humming soaked up all sound, all questions, all reason. What was that? A voice calling her name from outside. Somewhere. Distant and distorted. Calling her back...

Her lungs burned, her vision blurred, her heart thumped.

And Kjara collapsed.

Chapter 35

Kjara

Kjara's eyes fluttered open. An unfamiliar white ceiling looked down on her. To her left, window curtains billowed in the breeze, to the right stood a wooden door, framed by faded wallpaper, and below her was a bed with soft, linen sheets. Sounds murmured outside. The familiar, muffled voices of Calarin, Mado, and the captain.

Self-conscious fear hit her, and Kjara bolted upright to check if she was dressed. She breathed a sigh of relief at the sight of her new clothes and took to checking the room again. Simple décor, well organised. A chest of draws and a cupboard on the far wall. A huge bed. Bigger than her bunk, larger than she'd ever been in. A mohra's bed.

"Think, Kjara. What do you remember?"

To the left of the bed, stood a side table, with a pitcher of water on it, and her haversack beside it. She reached down and grabbed her bag, hoping to jog her memory. Thairis Brast's signet ring. *The captain! I was supposed to get the captain.*

"Hello?" Kjara called out. An excited snuffling bark let out from the foot of the bed. Mutton leapt up and nuzzled her face. She smiled and scruffed his ears with both hands.

"Hello, boy. Yer. It's good to see you too."

The door opened, and Mado entered, joined by Calarin and the captain. Seeing her awake, concerned relief shone from their faces.

224

"Kjara, gods be. You're okay!" Mado said, scrambling onto the bed and sitting crossed legged next to her. Calarin followed. The two of them looked at her in silence for a moment, uncertain. Kjara looked at her parents, and to Captain Deonto, who shared the same expression of concern on her face. Mutton let out a disgruntled whine, before settling down by her feet.

"You are okay, aren't you?" Calarin said.

"Yer, I'm okay. What happened?"

"We were in the market. You started gettin' confused and askin' all kinds of questions. Then you fell through the market stall," Calarin explained.

Kjara narrowed her eyes, trying to remember, but shook her head, "I don't recall anything. I must've hit my head. Where am I?"

"My quarters," Captain Deonto answered.

"We called for a guard when you passed out," Mado continued. "They brought us here. Said she might know what to do."

"What time is it?"

"Just past high-sun," Calarin said.

Another fear rocked her head, "What day?"

"Fifthmoon. You've only been out for a few hours."

"Anyone in?" called a voice from the corridor.

"In here. Thank you," the captain replied. "I've sent for Clinician Rosalind to check you over."

Rosalind entered the room, and once provided with an account of events, completed a routine examination. Kjara's pulse, eyes, tongue. Reflexes.

"Good news. Everything seems to be okay," she said, sunlight glinting off her spectacles. "You've got a bit of blood in your right eye from a popped vessel, but that appears to be all. Probably from the fall. Judging by the description, I'd say you've suffered from a panic attack. Quite normal, particularly in times of significant stress or change. Has there been anything in your life that's causing you anxiety? Any changes in your life?"

Where to begin? Kjara thought.

"She spent this past week workin' in the city, away from home. Might that do it?" Calarin suggested. "It's a very different place here than at the farm."

"Quite likely. A significant change in environment or workload could trigger it. I suggest you take things carefully for the next few days. Reduce the workload," the clinician cast a knowing eye at the captain. "And drink plenty of water. I would also suggest tea," she added as she packed up her things.

"Thank you, Clinician."

"My pleasure, Captain," Rosalind nodded with a sly smile as she left the room.

"It's my fault," Mado said. "I arranged this for you. I should have thought it through better. It was foolish of me."

"Dad, no, it's fine. I am enjoying my duties."

Her duties. At mention of the word, Kjara's mission flooded back to her.

"Captain," she said, holding out Brast's signet ring. "I need to pass on a message. Thairis Brast has requested your attendance at the manor. And as many of your guards as you can spare."

A look of understanding dawned on the captain's face, and behind it, a hint of fear.

"I understand. I will go immediately. Stay here, rest. Calarin, Mado, I will send someone to assist you with whatever you need. I will be back before nightfall. Be safe."

Before either of Kjara's parents had the chance to speak, Captain Deonto spun on her heel and marched out of the room, the door shutting behind her. Mado and Calarin turned back to Kjara, mouths open in tandem, eyes seeking answers.

226

"Care to share?" Calarin asked.

Kjara feigned nonchalance, "Nothing important."

"Nothing important," Mado repeated. "Runnin' messages for the region master is nothing important?"

Kjara swallowed, passing a look from one to the other, seeing the care and concern in their eyes. The events of the past week rippled and fell over each other in her mind. The fear, the confusion, the incredulity of everything she had witnessed. Everything she had done. So much had happened that she could scarcely keep up or keep track of it. And through it all, she'd been so far from home she hadn't thought about it. But now, here it was staring at her, and all the emotions she had kept in check had nowhere to go but out.

Calarin swept one hand around Kjara faster than her tears could hit the sheets. Cooing softly, cradling Kjara's head on her chest, she softly rocked her back and forth. Mado slid up on the other side and wrapped his arms around them both. Mutton whimpered and dropped his big furry head onto Kjara's knee. Together they sat—a tiny family in a giant bed—saying nothing but filling the air with comfort and reassurance.

Kjara spent the next hour catching her parents up on the past week's events. There were tactical pieces of information she left out, such as Azmariliz, and the humming incidents, but she told everything else as truth. Guilt chastised her for keeping secrets, but her parents could only take in so much at any one time. As it was, she had to repeat some details at Calarin's request, but whether it was due to Kjara's fast, young brain or Calarin's slow, old brain remained undetermined.

Kjara presented the ring from the mine to Calarin, ten gold to Mado, and her apology to them both. Mado took a liking to the ring and offered to buy it from Calarin for ten gold. Their exchange quickly escalated into a fiery negotiation of chores and favours. The way her parents interacted was always a peculiar and cringe-worthy sight.

"Thairis Brast is a big fan of our cheese," Kjara said, to move the conversation away from their odd behaviour. "And so is the naistinn. They want to visit the farm."

"Perhaps we should use that gold to buy some presentable clothes," Calarin suggested after calming herself, "if we're to have nobility visitin'."

"I do know the name of an excellent clothier," Kjara remarked. "Though it may be some time before Thairis Brast makes his visit."

"All the better," Calarin chirped. "Things done well are done better with time."

Conversation turned to life on the farm, with Mado and Calarin settling in to catch Kjara up on what she had missed. It was predictably ordinary, of course, but she didn't mind. With all that had happened over the past week, a touch of the ordinary was just what she needed.

Later in the afternoon, Harwin popped in to see what, if anything, Kjara needed. Being the game enthusiasts they were, Mado and Calarin convinced him to join them for a few rounds of cards. When he finally left, Calarin turned to Mado.

"He's quite a handsome lad," she said, "for a mohra."

Mado turned up his nose in mock disgust, "No fear. They're all too gangly, those lot."

"What do you think, Kjara?"

Her cheeks flushed, "I hadn't noticed."

"He seems to be quite fond of you," Calarin continued. "If you take my meanin'."

"Mum…" Kjara squirmed. "Don't be odd."

"What? It's not entirely uncommon for mohras and haffelins to go together, you know. Take your uncle Tuloh, he married a mohra."

Kjara cast a silent plea to Mado. He shrugged. What could be done?

"Their house is quite strange to visit, though," Calarin continued. "There's steps around the edges of almost every room. To offset the height difference, you see. And they have a step ladder in the kitchen, so he can reach the higher shelves," she cast daggers at Mado. "And it means he has no excuse to avoid doin' the dishes."

Mado bristled and hopped down from the bed with a deflection, "The sun's awful low, dear. We should probably get back and pack up the stall."

Calarin smiled at Kjara, "How convenient, eh?"

Although her mother was being sarcastic, Kjara agreed. The conversation was becoming uncomfortable and she was glad for an excuse to end it.

"I can guarantee we've sold less today," Mado remarked. "Darys might know how to start a sale, but never how to finish it. Gods be, that man can talk."

"Yer. Let's be off, I suppose," Calarin replied. "Are you comin' home with us, Kjara?"

Kjara's eyes prickled at the mention of home: all the safety, the routine, even the chores. All the things she had missed the past week. But if she returned, she would be leaving other things behind. She cast a glance at her haversack, at the distinct rectangular outlines stacked within. Her writing book and the other one, the one with the spiral illustrations. The one that held the answers to her questions. She shook her head.

"No. I gave my word to Captain Deonto to serve out the full two months."

"Are you sure? Considerin' recent events, and your health—"

"I am sure."

"Righto," Mado said after a moment of silence. "Let's be off then."

"Can I help?" Kjara asked, tossing back the sheets. "I feel bad for breaking the stall."

"You didn't break the stall," Calarin objected.

"But you said I fell through it."

"Yes, Kjara. You did. You fell *through* the market stall," Mado stressed. "Straight through it. Like it wasn't there. You passed out and..." Mado made a toppling gesture. "Didn't she?"

Calarin nodded, "But don't worry, nobody saw."

Kjara frowned at how relaxed her parents seemed to be with the event. But then, they were relaxed about almost everything.

"How is that not a bothersome thing to you?" she asked.

"I suppose it is a little unusual," Calarin said after a thought. "It's been quite a while since you've done it."

"What?" Kjara's nose crinkled. "Have I done that before?"

"Oh yer, all the time when you were a little girl. When you'd get angry, you'd run off through a wall and sulk somewhere. Or hide beneath the floor. Took ages sometimes to coax you back out again. Didn't it, Mado?"

Mado nodded, "Yer. You could be quite stubborn when you were younger. But some things don't change much, do they?"

"I think I would remember something so unusual as running through walls."

"When does a child know somethin' is unusual?" Calarin shrugged. "Only when someone tells them so. You grew out of it with no need for sayin' so on our part. So, there'd be no need to remember it as strange."

Kjara sat back against the pillow. *If mum is convinced it isn't a big deal, maybe it isn't? And if she's convinced no one has seen, then that's okay too. You'll figure this out.*

But Calarin was wrong. Someone *had* seen. Someone dangerous.

Chapter 36

───────⊚───────

Papa

Papa sat up from redressing Geov's wounds and stretched out his old bones. The early evening sun washed through the window, covering Geov, his bed, and Loreena in a sharp red and golden glow. Papa scratched his beard.

"So, are you two going to tell me what's really going on? Or are you going to continue to treat me a fool?"

Loreena pushed a strand of hair out of her face, the previous night's events having ruffled her elegant appearance, "I'm not sure I take your meaning, Papa."

Papa blew annoyance from his nose, "What are you doing up here?"

Loreena dabbed Geov's forehead with a washcloth, "I told you, I'm here on holiday—"

"Holiday, my foot. If you're on holiday, I'll eat my boots."

"You don't wear boots, Alba," Geov chuckled.

"My point exactly. You're not here for a holiday. You've got something planned. Something big. The others might have been too panicked last night to notice the maps in your study. But not me."

Loreena looked at Geov for guidance. He pulled on his moustache and gestured approvingly, but she still seemed reluctant.

Papa clicked his tongue, "It'd be foolish of me to spend half the night patching up the injuries of a discreation I paid for. I think it's safe to say I didn't bankroll your butchering."

"Loreena," Geov said, "he'll know soon enough either way. What's the difference between then and now?"

Loreena took a deep breath, "Alba, the title of the naistinn is not something I have earned. It is something harnessed to me from birth, a weight to which I have been made accountable. The virtue of leadership measured by blood and birth is not an ideal to which I subscribe. But—"

Papa rolled his eyes with aggravated boredom, "This isn't a public address, young naistinn. Speak direct."

"We intend to give Northern Cradh its independence," Loreena said. "It will become a nation in its own right, beholden to none."

Papa laughed, "You're making Geov a naistinn?!"

Loreena frowned, "Geov has proven himself through deeds as a leader. He has done amazing work for the people of Northern Cradh. He has worked tirelessly to ensure the safety of its people, including those whom we accepted as our citizens in the wake of the Collision. Under his guidance, the region has prospered beyond our imaginings. Geov is an excellent and noble leader—"

"Blaaaahh!" Papa threw back his head to expel the noise until Loreena gave up talking. "So where does Londre Tamou fit into this plan, then?"

"We need a representative of Glainne to act as a signatory. For us to be recognised and accepted as an official member of the Aonadh," Geov explained.

"Half of Cradh handed over to Geov Brast," Papa stroked his beard. "No wonder someone wants you dead. Question is, which somebody?"

Of all the potential conspirators, one name drew his attention the most.

"There is, of course, the conveniently absent Londre Tamou."

"You think he ordered the discreation?" Loreena asked.

Papa shrugged, "I'd ask him myself but…" he gestured around the empty bedroom, "he's not here."

"If that's the case," Geov muttered, "we'll need to tread carefully moving forward."

When Captain Deonto and her guards arrived, Papa excused himself to redress Soren's wounds. Papa found him out by the orchard, shuffling along next to the tomato vines.

"We spoke about this, Lemon-face," he glowered at the young null. "You're supposed to be resting."

"I needed some fresh air."

"Then open a window," Papa scolded. "The more you wander about, the longer you will take to heal. And as wonderful as it is to see the captain and all her guards, I'd much rather have your fists fighting fit than rely on the limp arm of the law."

Soren scratched his ear, "Why is that?"

"Traditionally, one says thank you when complimented," Papa scowled at Soren, waiting for a response. When none came, he answered the question. "You knocked that carver good, last night. It was impressive."

"Oh."

"I get the feeling they didn't teach that at the commune."

Soren avoided eye contact.

"No matter. I don't care where you learnt it. Just glad you did, elsewise we'd probably all be stabbed to the After-all. Oh, speaking of, I have uncovered the motive behind last night's nastiness."

Papa set about sharing the information shared with him by Geov and Loreena.

Soren listened attentively and then shook his head, "Can't be Tamou."

"What? Why?"

Soren leant against a post, "Doesn't make sense."

"How? Brast skewered, Loreena next on the list, but no sign of Tamou anywhere. And he was the only other person who knew about this whole deal, near as I can tell. Except maybe your mate."

"My mate?"

"Yer, the red-haired girl. Sabel?"

Soren cleared his throat. Papa had touched a nerve.

"Think about it," Soren said. "What does Tamou stand to gain from the discreation?"

"Ah, see. The problem with power is the more you have, the more you want. Happens to all of us, and royalty in particular," Papa plucked a tomato from the vine and munched on it. "I wouldn't be surprised if Glainne saw this as an opportunity to expand their borders."

"Then why be absent? That casts more suspicion on them, not less."

Papa stopped chewing, "Now there's a troubling point. If it isn't Glainne, then it's set up to look like Glainne."

"What if it was Brast?" Soren suggested. "With Farlight dead and no heir, he could feasibly make a claim for the throne."

"I don't know, he's in a pretty bad state. More pin cushion than person."

Soren shrugged, "Scars look good when they're from acts of heroism."

Papa cocked an eyebrow, "You're suggesting Brast took a blade in the belly just to cover his tracks? That's risky. He could have died."

"Could have. Didn't."

Papa curled his lip and stared at Soren. After a time, his surprise turned into a smile and he let out a chuckle that became a loud bellyful laugh. The comment was so delightfully cynical, the idea so absurd. To think that a man seeking power would risk his own destruction. And even more hilarious, it was hard to refute.

Chapter 37

Kjara

Kjara returned to the wagon to help her parents pack up. By Calarin's order, Harwin had joined them. His strength and size made the process considerably easier, much to Mado's delight. Kjara's mind had calmed considerably, and she no longer felt the threat of attack. Rather, she started to feel foolish for thinking it was possible in the first place: the carver's targets were Brast and Farlight. She was merely a haffelin girl, in the wrong place at the wrong time, hardly worth any consideration, let alone the carver's ire.

"Are you sure you want to stay?" Calarin asked, folding up the step ladder. "I'm sure the captain will understand if you need some time—"

"Mum, I'll be fine. Stop looking so worried."

"If anything happens," Harwin added, passing by with the stall table on one shoulder, "I'll take her straight to Clinician Rosalind's Medicary."

"Oh, you're a good lad, aren't you?" Calarin said.

"I'll say," Mado added, elbowing her. "Look at that, one-handed and all!"

Kjara heaved an exasperated sigh, "Nothing is going to happen!"

"I know, I just worry is all," Calarin stroked Kjara's cheek. "You're so special."

Embarrassed, Kjara turned away only to find Harwin staring back at her, "Not a word."

Harwin held up his hands defensively but said nothing.

Once the wagon was packed and farewells said, there was nothing to do but return to the guardhouse. Harwin however, offered an alternative, a quick patrol by the harbour and a bite to eat.

"Fresh air will do you good," he suggested. "That's what my mum always says."

"That's what everyone's mum says," Kjara deflected.

However, in the battle between her senses and her stomach, the latter won, so she agreed to the walk. Most of the dockworkers had finished for the day, and apart from the occasional fisherfolk on the break wall, the harbour was empty. The bustle of the day had fizzled along with the setting of the sun. Harwin and Kjara purchased some fried potatoes from The Plump Fin, and Harwin suggested they should head out along the break wall.

"Sure," Kjara said.

But really, what she wanted was to ask Harwin about Sabel and why he was meeting her in the bathhouse. If she asked him directly, she'd know for sure that he had seen her and was pretending not to. Or he might ask why she was taking a bath in the dark. Or he might ask about her skin. She couldn't ask direct, that would arouse too many questions that she wasn't prepared to answer.

"Harwin, how many times has that red-haired girl escaped lockup?"

"Red-haired..." Harwin's brow furrowed. "Oh, Sabel? That's a strange question. What makes you ask?"

"It's just when you saw she'd escaped—"

"Harwin! A word if you may!" a voice interrupted.

"Hang on. What's the matter, Blinny?" Harwin called out, seeing the dockmaster hobbling his way along the dock with speed, a ledger under his arm.

"Unexpected arrival. Not on the charter," he huffed, pointing to the small vessel passing through the break wall. "It might be trouble. Come with, would you?"

Kjara's heart sank, the conversation had been cut short just as she had mustered up the courage to ask him. If she brought it up again, it would seem even stranger.

Harwin adjusted the sword hanging from his hip, "Better to have it and not need it than need it and not have it, I suppose. Come on, then."

The ship was a double-masted caravel that ran about seventy-five feet from bow to stern. It appeared equipped for defence but showed no signs of any recent attack. As it approached, Kjara could make out a few figures scurrying about on the deck, readying the craft for its berth. Closer still, and she caught an eyeful of something, someone, standing on the pier-side edge, glinting in the setting sunlight.

The crew seemed to give no care where they docked and made straight for the closest available pier. The dockmaster hurried over to meet them as they threw down the gangplank.

"Hang about!" he cried. "You can't moor wherever you like! Who's captaining this ship?"

A fat, balding man with a sleeveless shirt and a hooked nose leaned over the railing, resting on one sunburnt arm.

"Don't get yourself all in a tizz mate. We're not staying long, a quick drop off," he said, flicking a thumb at the armoured figure striding down the gangplank. "Then we're on our way to Highstock Bay,"

The figure was the tallest girl Kjara had ever seen. Ebony hair pulled back over her head. Eyes that were brown to the point of black, and skin that cut two distinct tones right down the centre of her face.

The left side was a fleshy tan, the right side a charcoal grey. Kjara put her at eighteen or nineteen, but her hard-set features—a prominent brow and angular jawline—made her seem older.

She wore a steel breastplate over a blue-accented scale mail shirt that hung to her knee. The armour hinted at an athlete's body, a powerful body, muscular and strong. Hard leather bracers wrapped both her wrists, with a pattern carved into them, a leaf inset with a stylised wave. She held a silvered, two-pronged trident in one hand and had a heater shield strapped to her backpack. It was covered with the same seal, in blue and green colouring.

"Righto lads, off we trot. Pack it up!" the captain called, and with begrudging moans, the crew set about preparing the ship to leave.

"Surely not!" cried one of the sailors, a thin, round-shouldered man with an equally thin beard. "There's nothing to be gained from going now that can't be gained at dawn tomorrow. Can't we stay here?"

"Time is what we'll gain, Barnt! And money's what we'll save. I know the thoughts knockin' in your noggin."

"If the dockmaster can spare the mooring, I can spare the coin," the tall girl said, her voice heavy with an accent. "For harbour and pubs both."

"You are too kind, too kind indeed!" Barnt cried.

"Indeed!" piped another crewman. "A saint of saints!"

"A saint of sailors!" cried a third, followed by hearty laughter from the crew.

The tall girl turned to the dockmaster, "Have you space enough for this ship?"

"Well hang on a minute, you can't just sail in here unannounced and expect—"

The tall girl plucked a heavy pouch of coin from her hip and dropped it onto Blinny's open ledger.

"Yer," he said. "We should have some room."

"A little extra in there. For the trouble they'll no doubt cause you," she said with a warm smile, "and to point me to the nearest pub."

"For that price, I'll point you to the best pub. You'll not want the nearest one," Blinny replied. "The Eyeglass has room, food and board. It's not far through the city."

"We can show you the way," Harwin interjected.

"How kind of you," the tall girl bowed slightly. "Thank you again, gentle friends," she called back to the ship, throwing another pouch of coin onto the deck. "Enjoy! Don't drink it all at once."

She walked up to Harwin and extended her hand, "Zyela River-mane, Treun in the service of Lydona."

"Lydona," Kjara repeated. "Where's that?"

"It's the capital of Glainne," Harwin whispered.

"Oh," Kjara hid her embarrassment.

"Harwin Gelsin," Harwin met Zyela's grip. "Guard of Bhaile Cala."

"Kjara Chedderheart, guard of Bhaile Cala," Kjara added, not wanting to be left out.

Zyela rose an eyebrow, "You're a guard?"

Kjara's cheeks burned, but before she could reply Harwin spoke, "Lydona, that's a fair travel. What brings you here?"

Zyela straightened, "I'm here to deliver a message to your region master."

A message for Thairis Brast from Glainne. It sounded official. But official was a problem. Official messages usually meant secrecy and restricted access. Still, one couldn't hurt to try.

"Harwin and I were about to eat dinner. Would you like to join us?"

"Yes!" Zyela beamed. "I am starved. I've had nothing to eat but long-haul rations since I left Lydona."

With Harwin leading the way, the three travelled through the town towards The Eyeglass Pub. Passing by the Needle and Thread, Kjara caught an unsavoury sight. Thairis Pedigray. She bashed her ham hock of a fist against the door, hollering uncontrollably.

"Ionesco, you hack! Open up! You said Fifthmoon. And Fifthmoon is fast disappearing."

Harwin groaned and hid behind Zyela.

"I apologise, Thairis Pedigray," Ionesco's voice drifted out, maintaining its silky softness despite the urgency in it. "I had a high priority order to fulfil before I could start on yours!"

"Unacceptable! I demand satisfaction!" she bellowed. "You!"

Kjara's heart skipped as the Thairis Pedigray jutted one sausage finger in her direction. However, it was Harwin that she targeted with her tyranny.

"Fine eve, Thairis Pedigray," Harwin stammered.

"You. Here. Now," she barked. "Sort this out."

"Actually, my thairis, I—"

"Today, boy!"

"Gods be…Please excuse me," Harwin said to Zyela. "This may take some time. I'll catch up with you at The Eyeglass, Kjara. A pleasure to meet you Zyela, enjoy your stay in Bhaile Cala."

As he left, Kjara held in a sigh. So close she'd been to getting answers, but just as easily, they walked away with him.

Zyela and Kjara entered The Eyeglass, surprisingly quiet for a Fifthmoon eve. Ayleth met them, sat them, and took their drink orders before zigzagging through the tables to the bar.

Zyela watched her go before turning back to Kjara, "Was that faeduin woman…blind?"

Kjara nodded.

"She does a fine job of moving like she isn't."

"She's been working here a long time," Kjara took off her haversack and placed it beside her. "Jefen, the owner, makes a point to never move the tables around. She has the floor plan memorised in her head, I think."

"How different."

Ayleth returned with the drinks, cider for Kjara and hard tea for Zyela, and rattled off the house specials. Grilled vegetables on mashed pumpkin. Cheese and mushroom pastry. Potato and eggplant galette.

"Do you have anything with beef?" Zyela asked, clearly not taken by the selection, but remaining polite.

"We have fish. Salmon, crippler fish and tuna."

"I'd like the salmon, thank you."

"I'll take the galette, please," Kjara said. Once Ayleth had gone, she asked, "What is beef?"

"It's meat. From cows. Do you not have cows in Cradh?"

Kjara was horrified, "Of course we do, but we don't eat them!"

"What about chicken, or lamb?" Zyela corrected herself. "Sheep. Lamb is meat from sheep."

Kjara shook her head, "Lamb is baby sheep. Besides, if we ate cows, chickens or sheep, we'd have nothing to harvest our milk, eggs or wool from. It seems rather silly, eating our livelihoods."

"What about pigs? Surely, you'd eat the wild ones at least."

"No, we use pigs to hunt truffles. And the wild ones we leave well alone."

"How different," Zyela said. "So, no meat at all?"

"Not apart from fish, or anything else they pull up from the sea."

Zyela deflated, "Shame. I was hoping for a steak. That's also cow."

Kjara laughed, "Why do you have so many words for cow?"

"I don't know. I'd never really thought about it. We just do."

"Fascinating," Kjara took out her book and pencil. "How do you spell those words, then?"

Zyela laughed and spelt them out. Kjara carefully copied them into her book.

"I've never met a haffelin as interested in words as you, Hara," Zyela said, casting her eye over Kjara's page.

"It's Kjara. But don't worry. Everyone gets it wrong."

Chapter 38

Kjara

Kjara and Zyela spent close to an hour discussing the differences between Glainne and Cradh. She fascinated Kjara: her appearance, mannerisms, accent, choice of food. Kjara did her best to write down the strange and foreign words she used, becoming so involved in the conversation that she'd forgotten about Harwin. Towards the end of the second hour, dinners eaten and cake ordered, Kjara broached the subject of Zyela's missive.

"You mentioned you had a message for the region master?" Kjara asked, cider and courage sloshing in her stomach.

Zyela smiled a careful smile, "Kjara, I appreciate your company, but those are words I cannot share with you. Strict instructions have I been given: none may see it but Brast."

Kjara slumped back in her chair, but remembering the signet ring Loreena had given her, leaned forward with renewed resolve. The curiosity had become too much.

"What about his personal advisory?" Kjara whispered, slipping the signet ring onto her thumb and placing her gloved hand on the table.

Zyela narrowed her eyes at the ring. Coupled with her outfit, it must have been enough to convince her. She leant forward and lowered her voice.

"Not here. It's too public. I'll purchase a room for the night, and we will excuse ourselves."

Zyela settled the tab, much to Kjara's surprise. They stayed a while longer, finished their cake and headed upstairs into Zyela's room. Once inside, she locked the door, placed the key on the dresser, and turned to her, face darkened with disappointment.

"Okay, you've had your fun. Now hand me the ring."

Heat flared up Kjara's neck, "What do you mean? I told you—"

"Look, you seem nice enough," Zyela said, leaning against the door. "But it's time to come clean, haffelin. I don't know where you got that ring but if you hand it over now, I can look the other way. And we can forget this completely."

Kjara frowned.

"Thairis Brast gave me this ring," she said, committing to the lie. "Because I am his advisory."

"Okay," Zyela dropped her pack to the ground and opened it, retrieving a scroll case. She held it out to her. "This is the message, here."

Kjara took the scroll case, unrolled the paper, and her heart sank. Nothing but scribbles. Kjara scanned the writing, the confusion and fear in her eyes shone through.

Zyela watched her closely, "It's terrible, isn't it?"

"Y…yer. It is," Kjara lied.

"Read it aloud," Zyela instructed.

"What?" Kjara froze. Unease pulsed through her body.

"Read it aloud," Zyela ordered. Kjara swallowed hard but said nothing. Her glare burrowed into her. "If you are the thairis's counsel, surely you can read?"

Kjara shook her head.

"How different. An advisory who can't read. An advisory who has the writing of an infant and doesn't recognise the seal of Glainne on sight." Zyela stood up to her full height, towering over Kjara. Clad in metal and draped in accusation, she was the very image of intimidation, "Would you care to explain how that happens? Or would you like to admit your lie, and hand over the ring?"

Kjara didn't answer. She couldn't, fear held her tongue. She dropped the scroll and bolted, darting around Zyela and towards the door, grabbing the door handle. But it was locked.

"There's no way out, Kjara. You might as well give up."

Kjara took a desperate glance at the window behind Zyela. Zyela followed her gaze and smirked. Kjara scrambled between her legs and under the bed. Zyela seized her foot and wrenched her arm back but held up only a boot. Kjara clambered to her feet towards the window. Zyela slammed her heel against the edge of the bed, sending it scratching along the floor.

"I said, give up!"

Kjara rolled up onto the bed as it crashed into the wall behind her. Blood rushed into her ears. Throbbing. No. Humming. There it was again, that sound. Her skin rippled, her eyes vibrated. Zyela stood guarding the door, anticipating her next move.

Kjara put one hand out as a sign of submission. "Okay. Okay, I give up. You can have the ring."

Zyela straightened up, lowering her guard, "Smart girl."

As Zyela stepped forward, Kjara leapt past her, making a lunge for the key on the dresser.

"No, you don't."

Kjara gasped as the impact of Zyela's hand on her chest propelled her backwards. Kjara flew through the air, bounced off the bed, into the wall and out the other side. *This isn't right,* she thought, catching the blurred light of the moons and the stars before she clattered onto the roof of the stable attached to The Eyeglass. Too confused to slow her descent, Kjara rolled off the side, landing with a heavy thud on the ground below.

The window above her slid open, and Zyela's head appeared through it momentarily, before disappearing back inside. She was too big and her armour too bulky for her to fit through. Or maybe she didn't want to risk the jump. Both options seemed reasonable.

Run...run! No time for breathing! Breathe later!

The direction didn't matter. Only distance. Kjara ran, hobbling along with one bootless foot into the dark forested park area behind The Eyeglass. She dove into a shrub, the twigs and branches scratching her skin and poking holes in her clothes. And there she waited. She waited for what seemed like a lifetime. Trying to steady her breath and stay as quiet as possible.

Footsteps, metal clanking against metal. The noises grew closer, sending Kjara's blood pumping hard with each thud before they trailed off into the darkness. Nerves shot, she mustered the courage to leave her hiding spot and snuck through the shadowed streets towards the guardhouse. The streets were eerily quiet at night. And with only the waning twin moons for light, each building looked foreign and unfamiliar. The flagstones dug hard into her bare foot and slowed her progress. Her right eye itched. Her tongue clung to the roof of her mouth, dried out from the fighter's fire.

What was written on the missive? What was so important? Or was it all some kind of lie? A ruse, to flush out would-be carvers and conspirators? Kjara had been reckless, stupid. Too trusting of others. Captain Deonto's words echoed in her head as her feet hit the flagstones: 'There are people who will use your ignorance to kill you'.

Was that what had happened? Had Kjara offered her ignorance too freely, trusted too easily? Was Zyela really from Glainne? Was she the black-clad thing, or an accomplice maybe? Sent to clean up the witnesses? And where was Harwin? The image in the bathhouse flashed across her mind again and with it another flare of hot twisting anger.

As Kjara walked along the flagstones, she didn't notice the extra echo in her footsteps. But she felt the hand that grabbed her shoulder. Kjara screamed. It didn't matter. No one heard.

"Kjara, calm down. It's only me, did you not hear me calling you?"

Kjara focused on the voice in front of her, half-silhouetted in the moonlight. Long red hair. Velvet doublet. Bruised face. Sabel.

"You scared me half to death," Kjara scolded.

"Apologies," Sabel tilted her head and pointed to her face. "What happened there? Someone give you a knock on the nose?"

Kjara sniffed blood and wiped it away with her sleeve, "No. I...tripped."

Sabel looked Kjara up and down, stopping at her missing shoe and the dried blood on the hem of her trousers, "The flagstones can be dangerous at night. Very uneven. You should be careful where you walk."

"Thanks," Kjara replied shortly.

Sabel's presence put fire in Kjara's blood. It wasn't annoyance specifically, but something close to it. The redhead hadn't done anything horrid, quite the opposite. Nothing but politeness. Maybe that was the problem.

"I was looking for Harwin," Sabel said. "Don't suppose you've seen him about?"

There it was again, that strange anger flooding over her senses. What business did she have with Harwin? Why did she care where he was? Kjara shook her head.

"Damn. I was hoping you'd seen him," she looked up and down the street, then back to her. "Are you heading back to the guardhouse?

If you do see him, can you tell him I'm looking for him? They aren't too fond of me over there."

Kjara nodded.

"Thanks, Kjara. I'll be at The Bait and Tackle. If you can send him my way, I'd appreciate it," Sabel smiled kindly. Even with a black eye and a bruised cheek, her face was better put together than Kjara's.

"...Sure."

Sabel walked away, her long straight legs striding elegantly across the flagstones. Kjara swallowed and took a deep breath. She wasn't going to do a damn thing for Sabel until she knew what Sabel wanted.

"Why are you looking for him?"

Sabel stopped and turned back with another irritating smile, "Secret business."

Another non-answer. Fury rose in Kjara's guts, "Is it about another bathhouse meeting?"

Sabel's expression dropped, "What are you talking about?"

Kjara's heart fluttered with brief regret, but words once said cannot be unsaid, so she stood her ground, "I saw you the other night. In the bathhouse."

"It was you I heard there," Sabel stepped towards her. "Of course. No wonder he said it was no one." Kjara's cheeks burned. Sabel's voice dropped to a quiet plea. "You can't tell anyone. I was never there. I was never with Harwin. Promise you won't say anything."

Their closeness bothered Kjara. It made her stomach knot. She didn't owe Sabel anything. Kjara hardly even knew her. Sabel had no right to ask for such a significant request.

"No. I won't promise that. You are a criminal, Sabel. I won't give my word to a criminal."

Sabel stared for a time. "How could you be so..."

"What? Foolish?" Kjara offered cynically. "Naive, perhaps?"

"Cruel."

Kjara blinked, "Cruel?"

"Yer, cruel," Sabel said with more conviction. "Cruel and selfish."

Kjara threw out a hollow laugh, "That's rich! I'm not the one stealing, gambling, and fighting. I'm not the one using people to get what I want! But yes, it's me who's the cruel and selfish one."

"I'm not using anyone for anything," Sabel argued.

"Of course not!" Kjara shot. "It's just a lucky coincidence that Harwin is a guard. The fact it makes it easier for you to escape lockup has nothing to do with your interest in him!"

A tense silence clung to the night air. Sabel was the first to break it, straightening up to her full height with a long sigh. The darkness hid the hurt on her face, but not in her voice.

"You aren't nearly as smart as you think you are, Kjara Chedderheart. And if you want to go calling me a criminal, it would do you well to remember where we first met."

Sabel waited for a reply, but Kjara said nothing. What could she say? A familiar sinking feeling pulled on her guts as she watched Sabel walk away.

She's right, you know. You should go after her, say sorry.

Why? You did nothing wrong. She should apologise to you.

The battle between her stubbornness and her humility absorbed her complete attention. Until a leather-clad hand clamped over her mouth and brought her back to the moment. Another wrapped around her torso, pinning her arms to her sides. Quiet, sudden, strong.

Struggling wouldn't save her. Neither would screaming. No one could hear the muffled voice that strained through her teeth and soaked into the leather. Kjara heard though, the soft cooing sound of the black-clad thing that had its arms around her. The thing that held her tightly and dragged her further away from the dim light of the open street.

"If you follow my instructions, you will not be harmed," it said. A man's voice, gruff and blunt. Kjara knew who he was, what he was. She knew he'd come to kill her.

Kjara took the back of her boot heel and dragged it down the shin of the carver. He snarled in pain and loosened his grasp, just enough for her to escape. She lurched forward out of his grip, but his hand stretched out and caught her by the cloak. The collar dug into her neck and her eyes watered in agony. Gravity shifted as she was yanked backwards, losing her footing. The ground cracked into her back and a wooden plank drove into her spine. She tried to struggle, but the hold was strong.

"Help! Someone, help!" Kjara screamed before a heavy hand clamped down on her mouth. Kjara twisted and bent, banging her body against the stonework path. The grip held tighter. He forced a knee into her chest and a knife to her throat.

"Listen to me," he growled. "Do not resist. You are still alive. And you can stay that way. I do not wish you dead. If I did…"

Cold steel pressed flat against her neck. Kjara's eyes flared with acknowledgement.

"Now listen carefully—" the carver's voice cut off as a thick wooden plank splintered across the side of his head. He fell to the ground and Sabel stood behind him.

She dropped the plank, "Kjara, run!"

Kjara scrambled to her feet and bolted down the alleyway, with Sabel hot on her heels. A hot pain bit into her leg. Cloth tore and skin punctured. A flash of metal glinted in the moonlight. Kjara tumbled to the ground, a dagger sticking out of her thigh. Sabel stopped running and dropped down to help her up. Two more blades shot through the air, one finding purchase in Sabel's arm. Swift and certain, she ripped it out and returned it to the carver with a grunt. It dug into his leather armour, but he seemed unaffected.

"Can you get up?" Sabel asked. "Can you move?"

Kjara nodded through gritted teeth.

"C'mon. Let's go, quick—"

Sabel's head snapped back as the carver grabbed her hair and ripped her away from Kjara. She fought back, swinging a wild elbow into his jaw. She planted her feet and raised her fists, interposing herself between her and him. Kjara scrambled to her feet, but the moment she put weight on her leg, a sharp pain shot through it. Hot wetness stuck her trousers to her skin. Shallow breaths tore at her throat and Kjara fell back down.

"Move," growled the carver.

Sabel glared, "No."

"I don't want to kill you."

"Then leave."

The carver launched a fist into Sabel's stomach, and she doubled over. He followed up with a downward blow directed at her temple. Sabel threw up a forearm to defend against it and countered with a dropped shoulder, leading into a tackle. Pinning him to the ground, she aimed a punch for his face, landing two solid hits before he caught her hand. He twisted her arm and struck her ear, sending her off balance. Rolling to his feet, he bashed her into the wall and pressed his forearm against her neck.

"I said I don't want to kill you, but you aren't making it easy."

"I know!" Sabel gloated. With a confident grin, Sabel pointed towards the ground. The carver cocked his head, the throwing knife sticking out of his stomach. He sighed.

"You need to throw harder," he mocked, before pulling the dagger out, spinning it around and slicing it deep across Sabel's midsection.

She drove her foot into his shin and followed with two swift strikes into his ribs. He screamed like a wounded animal. She'd found a weak spot. She swung for a third, but the carver dodged and landed a strategic jab into her chest. Dropping to her knees, Sabel gasped for air as tears welled in her eyes.

"Stay down, girl, and that little nick won't kill you."

"Cheap...shot..." she stammered, grabbing the wooden plank from the ground and swinging it at the carver's calf.

He stepped back to avoid the swipe. Sabel launched her shoulder up towards his chest. He sidestepped and caught her foot against his own. She stumbled forward and steadied herself against the far wall. The carver swept up behind her and drove her skull into the bricks with his hand. A stomach-churning crack echoed down the alley followed by a dead thud, as Sabel collapsed to the ground, unmoving.

Kjara weakly held up her hands as the carver approached, but he grabbed her wrist and tripped her over.

"If you struggle, your heart will beat harder, and you will bleed out," the carver growled. "I do not wish you dead. Do you understand?"

Kjara did not respond. She stared at Sabel's lifeless body. *She could be alive. I should check for a pulse. I should go over there and check for a pulse. Get up, walk over and check. She is probably fine. Sabel is fine. She has to be.* A light slap across her cheek forced her attention back to the carver.

"I said, do you understand?"

Kjara nodded slowly, hot tears prickling at the corners of her eyes. Her body relaxed. No resistance. Kjara did not want it to happen again, to feel metal tear through her skin and grind against her bones. The carver grabbed her wrists and yanked them behind her body. Ropes bound them together.

Cloth jammed into her mouth and pinched her ears as it drew tight against her head.

"Don't want you screaming again."

The carver wrapped a bandage tight around her leg before dragging her to her feet. Blood throbbed above and below the wrapping.

Kjara closed her eyes and steadied her breathing. She tried to tune back into the vibrations, searching for the humming sound that swallowed her up. It didn't come. Holding her breath, she focused her thoughts on silence and calm. Nothing. She focussed on her skin, the sensation of being in her body, the movement of the cloth around her, the points of pressure. Her aching leg. Her heaving lungs.

Nothing.

Kjara stared up at the twin moons as the carver wrapped a cloth around her eyes, replacing her sight with a foggy blackness.

"Don't want you seeing either. Let's go."

Kjara continued staring up. The light of the twin moons was no more than a speckling of pinpricks through the blindfold. Her heels dragged along the ground before her legs began to step on their own accord. The carver in front of her directed her movements, further and further away from the quiet city streets of Bhaile Cala. The sound of night creatures stirring in trees tried to drown out the wrenching crack that echoed on a loop in her mind. Bats flew across the sky. Leaves rustled in the cold air. The soft ambience of the city grew smaller, the night darkened around her.

Crack.

Thud.

Kjara stared up at the twin moons.

And kept walking.

Chapter 39

Soren

The moons overhead cast a soft light over the silhouette of Thairis Brast's manor, giving its edges an ominous silver glow. Despite Papa's advice, Soren refused to remain inside. Instead, he maintained a loose patrol around the boundary walls of Brast's manor, avoiding eye contact with the guards posted up at regular intervals. To those he passed, he may have seemed over-zealous, but the truth was being indoors in bed made him feel useless. And it bolstered the unhealthy frequency of his thoughts.

Chief among them was a conflicted response to his situation. Had he done the right thing? His aching shoulder would suggest no. Had he kept his distance from the carver he'd be all the healthier for it. Had he acted quickly enough? Brast's injuries would also suggest no. Had he been swifter to decision, not just in the heat of the moment but earlier—seconds earlier—in the conversation with Roce, they'd have been in Brast's study before the carver. It could have been enough to stop its attack, long enough to inform the captain and get the guards.

But the heavier question, the one that burned across his skull, why did he try to intervene at all? It was out of character, unexpected, but he wasn't prepared to entertain any possible answers. He couldn't, not in his current state.

As Soren passed by the gates, his gut twitched with a warning. A low squeak in the road behind the lock signalled an unexpected presence. His fists clenched and fighter's fire shot through his feet. The gates rattled under a heavy, pounding fist and a voice, urgent in tone, bellowed, "Hey! Hey! Who is guarding the gate?"

Soren's jaw tightened.

The dewy night grass crunched under his boots as he stepped up to the viewing window. Carefully, he slid it open. The voice belonged to a dark-haired guard who stood at the gate, his shirt heavy with sweat and chest heaving for breath.

"Gods and fortune!" he said. "I need Roce! Urgently!"

Papa Roce, a strange request. Soren narrowed his eyes. Beside the guard stood a haffelin with neck tattoos, Orpip the Funambulist. The two shared worried expressions and, on closer inspection, bloodied shirts. Behind them sat a pushcart with a prone figure lying in it. Recognising the red hair and green coat, Soren's stomach lurched.

He began to open the gate when a nearby guard, a thickset man with a black beard and bald head, called out, "Hey! What do you think you're doing?"

"I—" Soren began.

"Tormeth?" called the dark-haired guard. "It's Harwin, let me in! I need Roce."

Tormeth peered through the viewing window then gestured for Soren to open it, enough for the cart to pass, and ushered them in.

"Her head is beat bad," Harwin said, as Soren helped him push the cart. "And there's a long slash in her belly. We tried to patch her up, but…"

"Second floor. First door on the left," Soren said as they reached the front of the manor.

"Harwin, you go," Tormeth dropped a hand on Orpip's shoulder. "Orpip, you stay."

"Go hang, Tormeth!" Orpip snapped. "I had nothing to do with this!"

"We'll see," Tormeth answered.

Harwin had scooped up Sabel's legs. Ignoring the brewing conflict between Tormeth and Orpip, he turned to Soren instead, "Hey, you. Help me?"

"Yer. Sure."

Soren swept his arms under Sabel's and together they carried her upstairs to where Papa was resting. They placed her on the nearest bed and Roce began his inspection of her injuries. From below, drifting up through the window, came the voices of Captain Deonto and Orpip. Soren leant up against the window, watching Roce while listening to the interrogation outside.

"I had nothing to do with it, for starters," Orpip explained. "And it wasn't from fighting pits, neither. Sabel and I had a gaming night planned at The Bait and Tackle. But she didn't show. That's how I knew something was up. I asked about town and heard she'd been seen with Kjara near The Eyeglass. But there was no sign of either one. So, I kept poking around. Found her in a back alley. Broken wood and blood everywhere."

"Was there any sign of Kjara?" Deonto asked.

"No, none."

Sabel's velvet coat had been shredded, strips of it wrapped around her torso, upper arm, and head. Roce peeled back the cloth that bound her stomach. Harwin looked on nervously and grimaced as Roce tugged on a few errant threads that had stuck to her skin with dried blood. Soren wondered if his wounds had looked as much of a mess as hers, and as he did, a niggling thought tickled the back of his mind. Not yet big enough for words. Just a feeling, like a nose about to sneeze.

"If this keeps up," Papa continued more to himself than anyone else, "Bhaile Cala will have two medicaries. Rosalind's in the city proper, and Brast's up here. Stuffed to the brim it is with damaged denizens."

After a few more moments of tentative inspection, Deonto strode into the room. Harwin shrank somewhat at the sight of her, as if he expected trouble, and looked to his feet. Soren clicked his tongue. The guard had more to say than he felt comfortable saying, Soren decided.

"What news, Roce?" Deonto asked.

"The good news is the slice to her belly isn't very deep," Papa announced. "Bad news is her skull might be cracked. No telling how scrambled her egg'll be until she wakes up," Papa tossed the bloodied strips of jacket into a pile on the dresser. "And I don't know when that'll be either."

"But she'll live?" Harwin asked hopefully.

Papa nodded. "Yer."

Soren let out a quiet sigh of relief and frowned at himself. He hadn't realised how much Sabel's wellbeing mattered to him. It didn't make sense to worry about her. She was a stranger, a scrapper and a low-rate criminal. But then, if she was a criminal for picking a few fights and rolling a few dice, what did that make him for what he had done?

"I hope she's not too attached to her hairstyle," Papa turned to Soren with mock glibness. "You'll have to shave the side of it so I can stitch her skin together."

On seeing Soren's expression, Papa changed his tone, "Best not to worry, Lemon-face. It'll be no help. Your lady friend here is a tricky one, and Fyaldha prefers the shifty, tricksy ones to stick around. She'll have a headache, and she won't be doing much else for a while. But she'll be okay."

Deonto turned to face Harwin, and he seemed to shrink under her eye.

"Explain to me, Harwin," she said, "why you brought Sabel here instead of taking her to Clinician Rosalind."

Harwin took a deep breath, "Captain…Rosalind wasn't there."

Soren nodded to himself. This was what Harwin had wanted to hide.

"Explain yourself."

"We already went there," Harwin said, fiddling with his shirt sleeve. "She wasn't around. No one was. The whole place was locked up. I banged on the door, hollered up a storm and all. Nothing."

Concern briefly cracked Deonto stern expression, and she took a long breath through her nose, "Orpip found Sabel after asking about town. Ze said she was seen near The Eyeglass with Kjara. She was supposed to be resting at the guardhouse, under instructions from Rosalind. And you were supposed to be looking after her."

"I know. But she said she was feeling better, and so…we just went for a walk. Fresh air, you know? We went to the harbour. But Dockmaster Blinny needed my help with an unexpected ship, dropping off a Treun of Glainne, a woman named Zyela Rivermane."

Soren's ear itched. Treuns were Glainne's emissary-soldiers. They were experts in diplomacy and combat but had no preference either way in their approach. Was she sent as a safety measure? A back-up in case the carver failed? Sure, the ship may have claimed to be from Glainne, but it could have easily been moored just past the headlands. Waiting. That would explain why the ship had not been announced, not part of the dockmaster's papers.

"We were taking her to The Eyeglass," Harwin continued. "But then Thairis Pedigray spotted me and…" he took an exasperated breath. "Anyway, I'd planned to meet up with them, but by the time I'd got done with Pedigray, it was sundown, and drinking time for the fisherfolk. I had to go to The Bait and Tackle to sort out the sailors who'd set themselves to drinking up a brawl. And by the time I'd finished with all the paperwork—"

Deonto pursed her lips, "Harwin, where is Kjara?"

"...I don't know."

Laine swore.

While Harwin was telling his story, Papa had been emptying Sabel's pockets, laying out each item next to her on the bed. A set of dice, a deck of cards, a coin pouch. A key with a rabbit's foot hanging from it, and a pocketknife too small for defence.

"Roce," Soren asked. "What are you doing?"

Roce jangled the coin pouch before spilling it out. At least a dozen silver coins and three gold, "Looking for our assailant's motivation. And being she had a pocket full of pretties, I dare say it wasn't a mugging. Hang on, what's this?"

Roce rolled her hand over, pointing out a series of black spots across her grazed, red knuckles. Soren leant in for a better look and the niggling sensation in the back of his head clicked into place.

"That's paint," he said. His stomach twisted up and the niggling grew words. "Flecks of black paint. Like from black leather armour. Same kind as from the black-clad bastard that carved me up."

Roce frowned, "That's a bit of a long bow to draw, Lemon-face. Why would the carver go after Red, here?"

"He wouldn't," Soren replied. "But he might go for Kjara. They were together, Orpip said. And she chased after it last night. New orders from the Treun of Glainne. Maybe Kjara saw its face. Maybe it's silencing witnesses."

"Silencing?" Papa frowned. "That's a grim way to say it."

Soren rubbed the knuckles on one hand with his thumb, "I gave the carver a good strike to the chest, Roce. Could have easily cracked a rib." He looked to Harwin. "A distinct injury: the kind you'd remember treating."

Deonto stiffened, her eyes darted back and forth in thought.

"Lyrdahl save me," she seethed. "Soren. With me. Now."

Deonto led him into a large bedroom illuminated by soft candlelight and housing Brast in its bed. Sat either side of him were Naistinn Farlight and her advisory. Farlight and Brast were engaged in a game of cards, while the faeduin woman read from a book. As they entered, Brast looked up.

"Laine, is everything okay? Tormeth explained the situation to us."

"Dire news, my thairis," she replied.

"Is Sabel...?" he asked, as if unwilling to finish his thought.

"The carver has taken Kjara," Soren replied, "at the very least."

Brast curled his brow, "What?"

Standing slightly behind the captain, Soren could see her hands clasped behind her back. They trembled just slightly, and it sent a hot pulse of nerves up his spine. He wondered if it was anger she withheld, but when she spoke again the quiver in her voice clarified it. She was afraid.

"My thairis," she said. "We believe the carver came for Kjara, but Sabel fought it off. Unsuccessfully. It would appear to be covering its tracks. Silencing anyone who has seen it or could identify it."

Brast stared into the middle distance for a moment, stroking his moustache in contemplation. "I will not have an innocent girl killed for getting tangled up in something beyond her standing. Take as many guards as you can spare to scour the forest. If the carver has taken her, it is likely it would hide her there."

Deonto faltered, and in her moment of hesitation, Soren took over.

"Rosalind may also be in danger," he said. "If the carver went to her for medical aid after the attack."

After you injured it, came a voice from Soren's head.

Brast's eyes widened, "I see. Laine, have Harwin lead the search party. You return to the city and look for Rosalind. If Sabel's condition is steady enough, take Alba with you. You may need him. But I hope by all the gods you find your Rosalind in good health."

"Thank you, my thairis," Deonto said with a bow, before leaving.

Soren scratched his ear as he stood awkwardly in the doorway.

Brast eyed him suspiciously, "That's an expression of eager exposition. You have more to say, young null, haven't you?"

"Harwin mentioned a visitor from Glainne," he said. "A Treun named Zyela Rivermane. She's staying at The Eyeglass, at least that's where he sent her."

Nine Mirrors had closed her book and was listening intently to the conversation.

Brast stiffened. "That arrival can't be a coincidence. She may be responsible for the new direction the carver is taking. I shall send some guards to The Eyeglass to collect this Zyela. At least four. If a Treun is in the mood to put up a fight, they'll need the numbers."

"May I suggest something?" Nine Mirrors said. "If Glainne is not responsible for the attack, they might take the act of aggression unfavourably. We should continue to act with diplomacy. It would be wise to send me to meet Zyela. Not an armed escort."

"Are you sure?" Loreena gripped her forearm. "It could be dangerous."

"We need to know her intentions, and we are more likely to get them with words than with weapons," Nine Mirrors explained. "If she has no issue being recognised as an emissary of Glainne I do not think she is a threat at this point."

Brast considered the suggestion. "Very well. Let that be the plan. Go immediately. We should not keep our visitor waiting."

"As you wish, my thairis," Nine Mirrors said.

"Nine Mirrors," Loreena added, "ensure you are well presented. And be careful."

"Of course, your majesty. I will represent Cradh with impeccable dignity," Nine Mirrors bowed and left the room.

"You've done well, Soren," Brast said. "Thank you."

"My thairis," Soren replied with a bow, before leaving the room.

Out in the hallway, Soren nearly ran into Deonto, Harwin and Papa as they marched towards the manor foyer. His stomach shook with worry and agitation. He needed to help.

"Wait," he said. "I'm coming too."

Papa had a chunk of crusty bread dipped in relish in one hand, and left splatters of it behind him as he walked. He spun around with such speed, a good glob of it hit the hallway wall. "Oh no, Lemon-face. You're staying here."

Soren frowned, "Why?"

"Because I'm fast running out of bandages," Roce said, pointing at Soren's injury. "And I'll not be patching you up if you try to tangle with your devils again. Assuming there'd be anything left of you to patch up."

"But I can help."

"Oh?" Roce threw a quick poke into Soren's shoulder.

He winced and clutched at it, "That was a cheap shot."

"That was a gentle reminder," Papa countered. "The black-clad bastard will do a lot worse than a bit of a tickle."

"I'm not running from a fight."

"You'd rather run towards a beating?" Roce argued.

"We don't have time for this," snapped Deonto.

"Someone needs to be here if Sabel wakes up," Harwin added. "Soren, I need you to look after her. Can you do that?"

Harwin's eyes shone with concern and sincerity. It wasn't a flippant request. It wasn't something to placate Soren or fool him into staying. Harwin meant it. He trusted Soren to care for her. Soren's gut swirled and through clenched teeth, he nodded tersely.

"Yer. Okay."

Chapter 40

Soren

Soren plucked errant threads from his bandages, trying to ignore the frustration of his inactivity. His injuries kept him from joining the search for Kjara, as did his promise to Harwin. The room was quiet without Papa, and with no one around to drown his thoughts with conversation, Soren found it harder and harder to be alone.

Sabel groaned and groggily opened her eyes, Soren sat up straight and adjusted himself in his chair. The noise caught her attention, and she rolled her bandaged head to face him. Wincing, she wet her lips and stared for a moment, processing the sight.

"Hey, you."

Soren offered a restrained smile, "Hey."

"You're not Harwin," she said, looking him up and down.

"No," Soren scratched his ear. "He left a while ago."

"Oh," Sabel closed her eyes. "Where'd he go?"

"He went looking for Kjara."

She snickered, "Figures. Could you draw the curtains?"

"Sure," Soren moved to the window. "He asked me to keep an eye on you."

"Is that right?" Sabel scanned his face. "Which eye?"

"Huh?"

"Forget it. Bad joke," she pointed limply to the bandages around her head. "Still a bit scrambled. And thirsty."

Soren filled her glass and passed it to her, "Do you remember what happened?"

"Yer, bits," Sabel took the glass and tipped her head back, draining it completely before handing it to him. "I got into an argument. I think I lost."

They continued to talk until the sun dipped into the ocean. Sabel rambled from topic to topic: her gambling exploits, her venturism, her love of the sea. Soren mostly stayed silent but attentive. Talking seemed to do her good, and although occasional waves of pain—sometimes hers, sometimes his—punctuated their conversation, she didn't seem to mind. Not even when she needed to stop altogether and throw up.

She had no filter, no propriety, nor shame. In every way, she was the most honest girl Soren had ever met. He offered to give her some space so she could rest, but she opposed the idea. When he returned from refilling the pitcher of water, she asked, "So, what's next for you, null?"

Soren rubbed his cheek, "Not sure."

"Trying to make amends with the Nullifidians?" she took a sip of water. "Or branch off into something new?"

Soren shrugged.

Her face lit up, "Come work with me."

"I've got no interest in gambling, nor pit fighting."

"They're not jobs, they're hobbies. Venturism, Soren," she rubbed her fingers together like she was counting coin. "Haven't you been paying attention?"

Soren scrunched his face in mild disgust.

"C'mon, be my expedition partner, it's a noble line of work," she placed her glass on the dresser. "It's profitable, it's outdoors, and it's fulfilling. More so than being a Nullifidian: making honey and seeking solace in nothingness. Besides, the forest-grown don't care much for me poking around. I could use the backup."

She leant forward.

"You know how to handle yourself...and your hands," she adopted a tone of temptation. "There is a whole lot of unexplored world out there. We'd be good together."

Heat pulsed in his chest. How could he say no?

"Okay. Deal."

Sabel held out her hand and Soren shook it.

"So, you'll need lodgings, since you ain't going back to the honey drippers," Sabel rifled through her things and tossed something to him. "Here, the key to my room at The Bait and Tackle."

Soren looked at the key, "You live at the pub?"

"Of course. Best way to gather information. There's more gossip there than booze."

"Won't that be weird?" Soren asked.

Sabel cocked her head in confusion, "Eh?"

"Sharing a bed, I mean. When you've got—"

She recoiled with exaggerated disgust. "I'm offering to share my room, Soren, not my bed..."

Soren blushed. Stupid question, stupid assumption.

"For now, at least," she added, casting a wicked smile over the rim of her glass.

Soren swallowed heavily and looked away. He thought again of the commune. No one there spoke to him as she did, but then, no one spoke much to him at all.

She giggled, "So, are you moving in?"

Soren wrapped his fingers around the key. This felt right, this was the correct choice. A new home. He smiled, "Sure."

"Good," she replied. "I'm glad I didn't have to twist your arm. That is a fight I would not win...unless I played dirty."

"And even then, your chances would be slim."

Sabel laughed. It sent tingles down his spine, shivers of warmth.

"Exactly. And that's what I like about you, null. You're like me. Honest, straight to the point."

Soren stayed silent. To speak would have been to lie to her.

Chapter 41

————— ◎ —————

Papa

Rosalind's Medicary was as Harwin had described; the door was closed. The window shutters drawn. No sign of a struggle, no broken glass or splintered wood. No sign of anyone. They were simply gone. Papa stroked his beard, knocking out a few errant flowers. The whole situation stank from earth to cloud.

Deonto pushed on the door. Finding it locked, she swore sharply. Despite himself, Papa snickered.

"What?" Deonto snarled.

"Nothing."

Deonto slid a short dagger from her boot and wedged it between the door frame and the door. Striking the pommel with her fist, she drove the blade between the jamb and the striker plate, and with a click, the door swung open.

It was quiet. Cold. A long pillar of sunlight stretched through the front room, cutting through the dark. Deonto spun the dagger in her hand, gripping it blade down, and stepped in.

Papa peered in after her, "Nothing seems out of place."

"Shh."

Deonto took another step forward. The door to the backroom hung open. She gestured for Papa to stay back as she inched her way through the room. But not to be told, he followed her after a few steps.

His ears scanned for any sounds of movement, life. Nothing. A half-chewed sweet bun sat on a countertop next to a cold pot of tea.

"Waste not," he whispered to himself, before he picked it up and absently bit into it.

Deonto glared, "What are you doing?"

"It's just a bun," he replied.

"Wait outside."

"It's cold out," he replied.

With a muted grunt of frustration, Deonto stepped down the hall-way and sidled up to the doorway of the back room. After blowing out a long, slow breath, she stepped in. Papa heard her knife clattering to the floor followed by a worried cry.

"Alba! Alba! Come here!"

Normally, he would have called her out on her contradictory commands, but she called him Alba, not Roce. Her voice held an urgency all too familiar to him, so he rushed to the doorway as a sinking, swirling sensation spun his guts.

Broken glass, furniture and tossed papers littered the floor. And in the middle of the room, a prone body laid unnaturally on the ground. A tall woman with dark skin.

And blood. Dark and sticky drops spattered over the floor.

Fear gripped his throat.

Dropping to her knees, Deonto cradled Rosalind's head in her lap.

"No...no, no, no," she searched desperately for signs of life, touching her skin, pressing her fingers to her neck. "Alba, she's not breathing. No pulse! Alba?!"

"I'm here," Papa said from the doorway. "I'm here."

He crossed the room and knelt beside her, placing his fingers on Rosalind's neck. He turned to face her with a rare sincerity in his eyes. Deonto closed her eyes and buried her face into Rosalind's chest.

Gasps of breath, muffled by the fabric, escaped her lips. Papa placed one hand tentatively on her back to comfort her.

Papa's eyes pricked with wetness, his nose tingled, and he sniffed. A few short sniffs, probing sniffs, followed by a long, analytical one. Something was off. Not an off smell, but the absence of one.

"She hasn't shit herself," he said.

Deonto frowned through watery eyes, "What?"

"She hasn't shit herself," he repeated, as though Deonto should have understood the first time. "Open her eyes."

Deonto wiped her face with her sleeve and peeled back Rosalind's eyelids.

Hope fluttered in Papa's chest, and he let out a victorious laugh, "She's not dead!"

"How can you tell?"

"Open the other one. Watch the pupil."

Deonto did as she was told, and the pupil contracted.

"That! There!" Papa pointed. "That movement? Means she's alive. Barely. But barely is great. It's better than not." He checked her pulse again. "By Fyaldha, that's weak. No wonder we missed it."

Deonto's brow creased her forehead, "But the blood?"

"What? This?" Papa bent down and dabbed a spot. "It's not blood. It's ink. See? Broken glass vials of ink. The whole place has been turned upside down. She must have put up a fight."

Deonto calmed herself and took a second look. An investigator's look. There were no signs of injury to Rosalind. Papa could see the wheels turning in her head, connecting the dots.

"This wasn't part of the attack," she declared. "This happened after. She was looking for something."

Papa stood up and scanned the room. Cupboard doors law askew, boxes of medicines, jars and vials had been sprawled out across the tables. He clicked his tongue.

"She was looking for a remedy," he suggested, and began digging through Rosalind's wares for the same. "Because she's been poisoned."

"By what?"

"Parsaralis."

When Deonto didn't react, Papa simplified his response.

"Graveroot. Its leaves are poisonous. When ingested, it gives the appearance of death. It must have been slipped into her tea. By Fyaldha, there is no organisation to this organisation at all!"

Deonto spied an empty cup beneath a chair, "Is it fatal?"

"Not in small doses, no. Too much though…" he searched Rosalind's desk. "Well, that's what too much means, doesn't it?"

"Will she be okay? Can you help her?"

"Yer. I'd wager what I need is around here. Somewhere," Papa said.

Standing in the centre of the room, he plucked a flower from his beard. Whispering a few words to it, he spun it from his fingertips and followed its path around the room. "When I administer it, she'll be stable, but she won't be walking for a while. Or talking. But I think that was probably the point, wasn't it?"

Deonto placed an affectionate hand on Rosalind's before standing up and gripping her sword pommel, "Was this dosage intended to incapacitate her or kill her?"

"I can't be sure, but judging by how weak her vital signs are…well, you know."

The flower slipped beneath a cupboard in the corner of the room. Papa groaned before lying flat on the ground and feeling around beneath it. Finding a glass vial, he smiled, pulled it out, and checked its contents. Inside were long plant stems that looked just like ferrets' tails on sticks. He gave it a celebratory shake before unstoppering it and dumping some into a nearby mortar.

"Hmm," he tongued a tooth in thought before putting the rest of the plant in. "Better to use more than less for this, I think. Oh, and here's the kicker, though you're not going to like it."

Deonto's brow curled, "Go on."

"Graveroot is most readily found in Glainne."

Chapter 42

Kjara

As the blindfold was removed, and Kjara's eyes adjusted to the dark, recognition skipped a quiet flicker of hope through her chest. She was in the abandoned watchtower. *Maybe my friends will find me. Maybe they will retrace all the places we have been together when they realise that I am missing. Or when they need more gold.*

The carver relaxed on his haunches in front of her, his dagger clutched in one hand, staring at her. His eyes were strange, one pupil cross-shaped, but the shadows hid the colour. She tried to move, but her hands and feet were bound, the gag still in her mouth.

"Can you see?" he asked.

Kjara nodded.

"Good," he removed the gag. "You're going to help me with something."

"Don't hurt me," Kjara pleaded. "If you want gold, I have none, but there is a hidden space under the floor. Beneath the chest. There is coin enough in there. If you take it and leave, I won't say anything to anyone."

"I have no interest in your coin," the man unbuckled his leather armour and lifted his shirt, revealing a large dark patch across his chest. "You see this? Your friend kicks like a mule. Broke my rib. You fix it, and you live. And then you can run back home little haffelin. You can

275

even tell them I am here if you like. But when they come looking, they won't find me."

He wanted her to scream, so Kjara didn't. She wouldn't give him any excuse to hurt her again. Her leg throbbed. "I don't know what you want me to do."

The man took her hand and undid the ropes, "Calibrate. Repair my ribs."

Confusion and alarm tightened Kjara's throat. Not even Nine Mirrors could do that, let alone a haffelin farm girl. The man moved around to her side and sat down on his feet.

"I can't—"

"Don't lie, haffelin."

Kjara looked around for some way of escape. Not too far from the stairs, not too far from a window either. Still had her haversack, it had a cheese knife in it. Probably not much use in a fight, but she wasn't that far from the city. She could run.

"Stand me up," she said.

"No."

"I can't do it sitting down."

The man paused a moment in thought then got to his feet. He grabbed Kjara by the shirt and lifted her up. She swayed a bit, her legs too close together to balance properly. Once she had found her footing, she took a deep breath.

"Okay. I'm ready."

The man stood, holding his dagger near her face. Kjara lifted one open hand in front of his chest. She closed her eyes, took another breath, and thrust her head into his ribs, the full weight of her body behind the blow. He bellowed in pain and crumpled in half, wheezing and gasping for air. She hit the ground and rolled, scooping up his dagger and running it through the ropes around her ankles. The man coughed and swore.

"Gods and piss!" he snarled. "You shit!"

Kjara moved for the stairs, but he cut her off. She brandished the dagger in front of her, but he seemed unfazed. He advanced and she backed up, finding herself pressed against the wall by the window.

Kjara leapt through it and regret swallowed her heart. The ground was far away. Too far. With a sudden jerk, she stopped, suspended in the air. But there was no hum, no vibrations.

"That's a fatal drop, haffelin girl," the carver growled. "Don't act so foolish."

Kjara looked up. Hanging out of the window above her was the man holding onto the strap of her haversack.

"I'll take my chances!" she said, wriggling out of the strap and dropping a stark thirty feet to the ground.

Kjara rolled in the grass and dirt, choking on her breath. Luck must have a limit, and if she hadn't used up all of hers, then she must be close. Still, she had little time for fact or fortune, only time to run. And run she did, as fast as her haffelin legs could heave.

Ducking branches, dodging thickets, jumping stones, Kjara sprinted until her legs screamed, and her lungs burst. Sweat stung her eyes, and her cheeks burned fiery hot, but she kept moving. She ran until her body gave out. The dagger incision on her leg wept blood, her knees buckled, and she collapsed. Looking about her, the night forest showed no signs of thinning, and a terrible dread overtook her. The city wall was nowhere, and she was hopelessly, hopelessly lost.

Dark clouds rumbled a threat of rain and muted the moonlight. Kjara sat up against a tree and adjusted the bandage around her thigh. Alien sounds floated through the leaves: scratching, creaking, feeding. Papa's tall tales swirled in her mind. Not of the playful trickster Nofrum, no. The dark Nofrum. The terrible night-born things that fed and frightened in the dark. They had been harmless, playful stories for her until she had seen the fiedrig. Now they didn't feel so harmless.

Another memory surfaced; the story told by her parents. The story of her birth. They were broken down on the side of the road and they were attacked, they told her, by vile forest-grown creatures called ylfes. That had always been a Nofrum story too, until now. The beady red eyes glowing in the dark thickets in front of her told her one thing.

All the stories were true.

Ylfes were scurrying through the darkened thickets, and now they hunted her.

The grass crunched and twigs cracked under a swift-footed charge. An explosion of squat brown-green creatures, long of limb but short of torso, erupted from the dark. Dangling pointed ears flapped behind their shoulders as they ran. Flared tails wiped hungrily back and forth in their wake. Maniacal fang-filled mouths cut their faces in two, as though someone had struck their heads sideways with an axe and stuffed broken glass into the wound.

They moved hungrily between the trees in her direction. Their wet sniffs and salivating tongues dribbled through the air. Kjara dropped to her belly, shuffled back down a slight incline, underneath a rotted log, and screwed up into a tight ball. Their footsteps pattered on the grass carpet. Soft, crunchy, and closer. Another wet sniff and a low, knowing growl. She brought the dagger up under her chin, staring over the ridge, waiting for something to reveal itself.

A grotesque stretched face with sharp eyes, and rancid skin slid into view. Kjara thrust the dagger upwards into the eye of the creature. It threw back its head and howled in pain, and a bubbling, hideous laughter filled the air behind it. She sprung from her hiding spot and further down the embankment. The creatures shrieked and pointed, careening after her. Her foot caught a root, which flung her body to the ground, tumbling and bouncing through the grass. A volley of arrows sprayed over her head. She scrambled to her feet, taking cover behind a tree, as more arrows rocketed past her. Clutching the dagger to her chest, she waited—every muscle tightened with anticipation—for something to find her. Blood pounded in her ears.

One of the things rushed up to the side of the tree, its snarling and giggling tearing into her ears. Kjara closed her eyes and took a deep breath before lunging out and sinking the blade into its belly. It gurgled and scratched at her arm. Its long nails tore through her shirt and into her skin. Kjara ducked back behind the tree, hiding from another hail of arrows. Fighter's fire thumped through her chest. The creature fell to the ground beside her, arrows peppering its back. A floppy tongue lolled from its fuchsia lips, creating an expression of grotesque mockery.

Kjara grimaced and peered out from the other side of the tree, counting seven of the creatures, including the one in front of her. Behind them, a taller shape—the black-clad carver—moved up to the furthest one. A slash of air, a spurt of blood, the ylfe coughed a wet splutter and collapsed to the ground. The others hadn't noticed the man and kept advancing towards her. Two knives soared through the air. One went wide, but the other landed true, digging into the skull of another ylfe. Four left. They had noticed now and whipped around, firing their arrows at the man. Three hits. He didn't seem to care. Taking advantage of the distraction, Kjara ran behind another tree. The man slashed and slit. Another down.

One of the ylfes charged at him, ducked between his legs, and jammed an arrow into his thigh. He grunted in pain. The creature crawled up his back and bit into his neck. The man tried to reach up and pull it off but it let out a growl and clutched his ribs. With jagged teeth digging into his neck, he ran at the nearest tree, crushing the creature against it. It coughed and opened its mouth. The man shoved a knife through its neck, pinning it to the trunk.

The last remaining ylfe spun around and launched itself into the wilderness, babbling as it ran. Lining up a shot, the man pitched a final knife into the darkness. No impact, no grunt of pain. A miss. He swore and sat on a log, inspecting the arrows in his chest.

"Haffelin. I know you're still here. Come out."

Silence.

"Damn it, girl. There's more around. Do you want them to find you alone or with me?"

Kjara stepped out, holding the dagger in defence.

"Gods be...I told you, I'm not killing you. Though I feel well within my right to do so at this point," he winced as he tugged the arrow from his leg. "Cheeky shit."

"Why aren't you dead?" Kjara asked as he twisted the arrows from his chest.

"Ylfe-made arrows aren't the finest. They didn't pierce my leathers." He swore as he tugged on the last one. It didn't budge as easily. "*Most* of them didn't pierce my leathers. Are you going to get that?"

Kjara's eyes narrowed in confusion as he pointed, but when she looked down at her shoulder, they widened in shock. Protruding from it, about a foot of slender wood. Her joints locked up with panic.

"What do I do?"

The man stood up, hobbled over and wrenched it from her body, tossing it away.

"There. Put some pressure on it," he said, limping up the embankment. "I'll be right back. Don't go anywhere."

"Why doesn't it hurt?" Kjara called out.

"That's the fighter's fire in your blood. Once it wears off, you'll feel it."

Kjara nodded and, pressing her hand to her shoulder, glanced at the nearest corpse. The ylfe wore a dirty leather wrap about its waist, with ritualistic scars across its chest patterned to copy the stars in the night sky. Patches of dried brown mud flaked away, revealing some of its chartreuse yellow skin. The creatures didn't look as fierce dead, but

280

they did look as ugly. Perhaps more so as death made their faces sag unnaturally.

The man returned, his pack in one hand, "I have some gauze in here. We'll patch you first. Take off your shirt."

Kjara froze.

"Fine. I'll go first."

The man stood up and undid his trousers. Kjara looked away, equal parts frightened and uncomfortable. But curiosity got the better of her, and she soon turned back around. He set about cleaning the wound with water, applying yellow root paste and wrapping the leg with a bandage. A crack of lightning briefly lit up the tree line, followed by thunder. A storm was approaching.

"Your turn," he said. "Hurry up, before the rain sets in."

Kjara vehemently shook her head.

"I can clean and dress it properly, or you can continue being a coward. But if it becomes infected, that's on you."

"What about my leg?" Kjara glared. "That's on you."

"That won't get infected. I keep my tools clean. And sharp. They aren't some forest creature's toothpick."

"I'll take my chances," Kjara said.

"Suit yourself," he shrugged. "But ylfes often coat their arrows in shit."

"You're lying."

"I guess we'll find out."

The man limped past her, collecting up his throwing knives. Another crack of lightning split the sky, and heavy rain fell over them. He packed up his bag and slung it over his shoulder.

"Let's go."

"I'm not going with you."

The carver sucked his tooth. The downpour matted his hood against his head. His breath, turning to fog, clung about his face. He looked around the forest and back to her, before moving past her to-wards the embankment.

Kjara stepped in front of him, "Where are you going?"

"I'm getting out of the rain. Move."

"No."

The man jabbed a finger into her shoulder and she winced.

In her moment of pain, he shoved her aside, "Hurts now, doesn't it?"

Kjara pushed the dripping hair from her eyes. She looked at the dead things in front of her, at the darkness past them, into the lashings of rain and the fog of her breath.

"Wait for me."

Kjara hurried up the embankment behind him but kept as much distance as she could. The rain had already soaked deep into the earth, and her foot slipped out on a loose tussock. She squished into the muddy grass and slid a few feet south, her cloak catching on a rotten stump and digging into her neck again. Her shoulder throbbed and her leg stung. She swore and the man chuckled.

After travelling not more than five minutes, the carver found a small rock cave in the side of a hill. A few large stones obscured its mouth, a fringe of tree roots framed the edge. He inspected it from the outside, then threw his bag inside and climbed in after it. Metal clinked against stone.

"This will do. In."

Kjara peered in but could see nothing, "Aren't we going to the watchtower?"

"There's no moonlight. It's raining. I've no idea where we are or how to get back to where we were."

Kjara ran a hand through her soaked hair and shook her wrist. This would have to do until dawn, or at least until the rain stopped. The cave was not much more than ten feet deep, with an uneven floor of rocks and dirt. The man threw his pack into the far corner and removed a torch and fire striker. Casting the flame around the room, the man took a second, careful inspection, illuminating a small stone shelf against one wall too small for him, but just right for Kjara. An old, charred campfire sat near the entrance. Some dried wood remained stacked against one wall. Hopefully, the previous occupant had no intention of returning. The man set about starting the fire. Smoke billowed up and formed a cloudy haze in the cave before pouring outwards past the tree roots. With the fire now lit and burning steadily, he peeled off his hood, revealing his face.

At first, Kjara thought it may have been a trick of the firelight, but once her eyes acclimated, her initial thought proved correct. The man's skin was a light shade of orange. He had an older face, not as old as Papa, but a bit older than Soren. Clean-shaven. Minor scars. Some bruising around his eye and cheek. His eyes were amber with one cross-shaped pupil. Fine white quills lay flat across his head, layered through medium length auburn hair.

"You're tornblood."

"Yer."

Tornblood, the birth affliction that plagued all potential parents in the wake of the Collision. The stories told by townsfolk were all much the same, babies born mangled up, too defective to survive.

"I heard most don't live past childhood," she said. "I've only seen one or two, and never one this close before."

The man chuckled cynically, "Fortunate you."

"I heard your kind couldn't be harmed."

"You heard wrong," the man licked his tooth. "Faster healers, perhaps. That's all."

He removed his shirt and placed it by the leather armour on a nearby rock. A tattoo of a chain ran down his right arm, but halfway down its length it had been broken in two. He had a trail of short

283

barb-like spines running down his spine. Rummaging through his pack, he removed a second pair of trousers and a simple shirt: farmer's clothes.

"What are you doing?"

"I'm wet. It's unpleasant."

Kjara turned away as he finished undressing and dried himself by the fire. She wiggled the toes of her bootless sock and wrung out the rainwater from her cloak as best she could. Shivering, she stared out into the rainfall.

"You have a lot in your pack. It seems very useful."

"Always."

"It was smart to grab it before you chased after me."

"Yer."

A short silence followed. "Did you grab mine?"

"Why would I grab yours?"

Another short silence. The man, now dry, had redressed himself in his farmer's clothes. He took out a pouch of almonds and threw one into his mouth. Kjara's stomach growled as she thought of the jar of dried apricots in her haversack. She shuffled to the fire, watching the man eat as he stared vacantly into the flames. He paused, one almond near his lips, and without looking at her, lowered it.

"What?"

"Nothing."

"This is my food."

"I know."

"If you wanted to eat, you should have brought your own food."

Her cheeks reddened, "I have my own food."

"Where?"

"In my bag."

The man gave another mirthless chuckle. More silence, broken by the horrid stuttering roar of some forest-grown thing thundering

284

through the trees. Kjara gasped. The man took a fine string with three bells from his pocket and began inspecting the walls of the cave. He dug two small holes into the ground by the entrance and stuck two sticks into them. Then, he wound the string around each stick and ran it back into the cave. He returned to his pack, took out some rope and moved across to her.

"Hey, wait—"

"Don't want you running off."

The man grabbed her wrist. Kjara tried to struggle free, but he placed a knee into her chest and leant his full weight on it. He bound her hands together and did the same to her feet. She squirmed about, but the ropes held strong.

"What is your plan, here?"

"I keep you around until you fix my ribs. Then I let you go."

Kjara sighed, "You might as well let me go now. I can't do what you want me to do."

"Keep telling yourself that, and you may be right. Or tell yourself the opposite and have that be the truth." The man lay down by the fire, making his armour his pillow, and closed his eyes. "You're on first watch. Wake me in two hours."

About an hour into her watch, Kjara's hunger outmatched her sense. She inched her way quietly across the cave into the far corner, eyeing off the man's pack. Whispering a few times to see if he had woken up but receiving no response, she determined it was safe, and unbuckled one of the side pockets. Moving at a snail's pace, she felt around for his almond pouch. A relieved smile crossed Kjara's face, and she delicately lifted it out. As she did, the ropes around her wrists caught on something that fell out onto the cave floor.

Food first, curiosity second.

Kjara popped a handful of almonds into her mouth, but they crunched so loud she feared she would wake the man. When she had eaten as many as she could get away with, she returned the pouch and collected the fallen object. It was a piece of parchment, folded flat with a broken wax seal the shape of a leaf inset with a stylised wave. The man shifted in his sleep, and she froze. Waited. Waited some more, but there was no further movement from him. Unfolding the parchment, Kjara ran her eyes across it, a few unfamiliar words, but a few familiar names: "Geov Brast" and "Loreena Farlight".

It was the contract for the discreation.

It was disturbing to read, if not for its intention and subject matter then for the plain and straightforward language it employed. But most disturbing of all, Kjara recognised the handwriting. She'd seen it before, in the handwritten notes of a calibration journal.

It belonged to Nine Mirrors.

"Gods be..."

Nine Mirrors had ordered the discreation. The faeduin calibrist and advisory to Naistinn Loreena Farlight was a traitor to Cradh. Kjara's stomach twisted, and a hot sense of dread drilled through her heart. The man shifted again in his sleep. She hurriedly slid the letter into the pack and shuffled back to her post. Staring out into the rain for the longest time, considering the knowledge she now had, only one thing mattered.

I've got to warn them.

How? asked another voice in her head. *You're out here, and they're up there.*

Kjara shivered and tucked herself in behind the rocks. *They'll come looking for me when they realise I've gone missing.*

Do you think they'll come and help you? The voice laughed and pushed a sinister thought to the front of her mind. An image of Sabel, lying prone on the ground. The brick wall stained with blood that shimmered in the moonlight. The nauseating crack that punctuated the outcome for anyone who tried to help Kjara Chedderheart. Guilt swelled in her throat, forming a hard lump that made it painful to swallow.

She tried to help you, the voice taunted. *The only person who knows what happened to you. Someone whom you couldn't even offer the courtesy of your confidence. And look at what happened. You are all alone out here. No one is coming to save you. Because someone like you is not worth saving, Kjara the Cruel. Kjara the Selfish...*

Kjara pulled her knees up into her chest and buried her head in her arms as best she could. The rope restraints made it difficult to move. A hot sting clawed at the corners of her eyes.

How long do you think you have? the voice asked. *How long until he stops asking you to fix him? How long until he realises how useless you are? Do you think anyone can save you from that? You're a liability.*

A quiet sob cut through the silence, muffled by the pointless finery of her shirt sleeve. Another one. And another. Over and again, until her eyes were puffy, and her nose ran with snot. Until nothing remained in her body but pain and fatigue and misery.

The warmth of the fire and the sound of the rain enticed Kjara to rest. Just for a moment. It was overwhelming, impossible to resist. She couldn't fight it; she had no fight left. She closed her eyes and slumped against the cave wall.

Chapter 43

Kjara

Kjara awoke to a heavy boot in her gut and the smell of old smoke. The rain had stopped, and the early dawn birds had started chirping. She looked up and saw the black-clad man dressed in his farmer's clothes. Too slow to react, he drove his heel into her again. Harder. She grimaced in pain.

"Next one's for your shoulder, kid. Get up."

Kjara scrambled up to sitting, holding out her hands, "Okay, okay. Please don't kick me."

"Did you see it?"

Kjara's heart sank. She cast a look towards the man's pack. It wasn't there. She glanced at the alarm system he had set up the previous night, it was still intact. Back to his face, his nostrils flared in anger.

"What?"

"Did you see what took my pack?"

"No," Kjara's heart started to beat a little calmer. "I fell asleep."

"Gods and piss!" he fumed, clambering out of the cave.

"Where are you going?"

"To find my things."

Kjara reached for a reason to stop him, "What happens if you don't come back? What if the forest-grown kill you?"

"If I die, I die," he said bluntly. "And you can wear the blame because you didn't keep watch."

"But what happens to me?"

"Maybe you'll die too. Should have stayed awake."

Kjara could stay, try to wiggle free. But then she'd be stranded in the wilderness with no weapons, no direction, no protection, and only one shoe. If she stayed and something found her bound in the cave, she'd be dead within minutes.

"Take me with you."

The man knelt and peered back into the cave.

"Okay," he said, scratching his cheek, "fix my ribs first."

Kjara's shoulders slumped, and she stared at her sock, "I can't. I don't know how."

"Guess you're staying here then."

The man stood up and left.

Kjara lay against the cold stones of the cave wall listening for the man's return. She had given up hope when finally, footsteps approached. It was a mixed feeling, seeing his face. On the one hand, it was his fault she was stuck out here. On the other, without him around, she would never see home.

The absence of his backpack surprised her, "You didn't find it?"

The man tensed his jaw, "You're coming with me."

"What? Why?"

"Up you get."

He stepped into the cave and unbound her feet. Taking the rope from her hands like a lead, he pulled her towards the exit.

"Where are we going?"

"To get my backpack."

The heavy rainfall made the ground soft underfoot, and Kjara struggled not to slip. The carver led her through the forest along the edge of a river glen. Her curiosity begged to break the silence. So many questions, but which to ask the black-clad man first?

"Do you have a name?"

Nothing.

"I've been calling you the black-clad thing. But you are no longer black-clad, nor a thing. So, it seems pointless to call you that now."

Again, no reply.

"My name is Kjara."

"I know."

"If you know my name, why can't I know yours?"

"You would do well to be less curious," he stepped over a fallen branch. "It might get you killed."

"If I am to be killed, I should at least know the name of my killer," Kjara asserted, hopping over the same branch. Her cloak caught on a smaller twig, and she shrugged her shoulders to pull it loose.

The man stopped and turned to face her, "You think I am going to kill you?"

"I don't know what you're going to do," Kjara admitted.

"I told you. I'm not going to kill you," he continued walking. "Unless you give me a reason to."

"What reason might that be?"

"Asking too many questions is a good start."

"I'll stop asking if you answer."

The man sighed, "Harijvar. It's Harijvar. No more questions."

He stopped abruptly by a tree in the middle of a small clearing. Just past it, the ground dropped off into a cliff face. Kjara peered over the edge. A long way down. She looked around for a sign of the thief's movements.

The trunk of the tree, the tallest around, was scarred with fresh scratch marks. Harijvar stepped away from it and looked upwards, shielding his eyes from the sun. He pointed.

"There."

Kjara followed his finger, on the highest branch was his backpack, nestled like a baby in a cradle.

"I am going to boost you up; climb to the top and get my backpack. Here, onto my shoulders."

"How?" Kjara asked, holding out her bound hands.

Harijvar whipped his head around with a growl but deflated when he saw her bindings. He took the rope, tied it around her ankle and untied it from her hands. He held up the other end and wrapped it around his forearm.

"Try to run, and I pull on this. Got it?"

Harijvar stood next to the tree and Kjara climbed up onto his shoulders. Stretching to reach the lowest branch, she heaved herself up and moved steadily, branch to branch. When at last she reached the highest point, she looked out around her. From her vantage, she had a clear view of the Timelong Mountains, the road, the city wall, and the northern ocean. When she squinted, she could almost make out Thairis Brast's manor up on the edge of the Overbite.

Kjara inched along the branch towards Harijvar's backpack. A strange cluster of twigs sat in front of it. As she approached, it unfurled itself to reveal a thin, stringy bi-pedal creature with fine green and brown fur. It had a long, pointed face like a ferret, and autumn leaves grew from its back like a cape. It had long bark-covered fingers and kept flat stones strapped to its feet like shoes. Its dark beady eyes blinked at her before its face blossomed into a grin.

"You have found me!" it chuckled, its voice a babbling brook. "You see much better when you are awake."

Kjara gripped the branch tighter, "What do you mean?"

"When you were sleeping, you hardly noticed me at all."

"Not surprising. You do blend well into the forest."

"Even so, you have spotted me all the same."

291

Kjara shook her head in disbelief, "You were hiding right by the things you stole."

"Of course I was," the creature jiggled at the hips. "If I had been elsewhere, there'd be no point in taking the things. You would have nowhere to look."

"What are you?"

"What I am. I am a quirble, of course."

It crept along the branch and fiddled with her shirt sleeve.

"You have an interesting coat," it said with a giggle. "What are you?"

"I'm a...haffelin..." her voice trailed off, lost in the memory of a similar conversation.

"I can see that with my peepy blinkers," it said, bobbing its head. "But what are you?"

"I'm...Kjara?"

"Are you sure?"

Kjara curled her lip, "I've given you two answers now, and both are unsatisfactory."

"No," the quirble cocked its head. "Both answers aren't answers."

"What's taking so long?" called Harijvar from below.

"It's stuck!" Kjara lied, before lowering her voice. "Quirble, I need that backpack."

"Why?"

"Well..." Kjara tried to formulate an answer using the creature's logic. "Because you can't take it from me if I don't have it. And if you don't have it, I can't come looking for you."

"An answer of sense-making. You can have the big pouch if you play to hide with me."

"Yes, I'll play with you."

"Goodly good! I'll go over here and start counting, it's your turn to hide."

The little creature cartwheeled along the branch past her and scrambled around to the far side of the tree. It squeezed its eyes tight.

"I'll start counting over here."

Kjara inched further out and grabbed the bag. Clutching it tight to her chest, she crawled back, catching glimpses of Harijvar through the dense foliage. The letter…if she stole it, she could show it to Thairis Brast as evidence. And maybe save everyone. She quickly snatched it out and jammed it into her pocket.

"What is that tree bark in your pouch?" the quirble queried.

"Shh. No peeking."

A strange rumbling noise filtered through the trees.

"Hurry up," Harijvar called out. "Something is nearby. Not ylfes. Something big."

"What is that sound?" Kjara asked the quirble.

"Oh, that is a luurg. But you are safey up here. Luurgs can't climb."

"Is it dangerous?"

"Oh, no. Quite safe. It will eat your down-ground friend, and it will leave."

The quirble spun around and closed its eyes, counting. A loud stuttering roar thundered through the air and stirred the leaves. The ground shook as the sound of heavy galloping hooves pounded the forest floor. Kjara's face paled as a harsh tug on her foot threw her off balance and sent her tumbling down from branch to branch. She hit the ground with a heavy thud as the bag slammed into the dirt next to her face.

"Why did you—?" Kjara began but stopped short.

Harijvar lay sprawled out across the clearing, rope in hand. Over him stood a horrific creature. It had thick forearms and a chest like a gorilla with patchy brown and grey skin, and hoofs on all four of its appendages. Its face was flat and covered in dense bone plating, as were its shoulders and hips.

Kjara screamed, and the luurg turned its head. It roared again, its mouth splitting open in three, and levelled its head for her chest. She froze up as it charged, but the rope pulled on her foot again, and she slid along the grass out of its way.

"Grab my bag!" Harijvar shouted. The luurg skidded to a stop and spun around, lining up another charge at Harijvar. He dodged to the right, but the creature's shoulder clipped him and sent him bouncing along the forest floor. It bellowed out another roar and stomped a hoof into his chest, pinning him to the ground and forcing a scream of agony from his lungs.

Kjara looked over the cliff edge then rifled through Harijvar's backpack for something she could use. She found one of his throwing knives and hurled it at the creature with a primal shout. It bounced off the thing's leathery hide but did get its attention.

It spun around and lined up for a charge. Kjara stepped back against the edge of the cliff and readied herself. The creature barrelled towards her, and at the last minute, she dropped flat on her belly, her tiny frame passing easily between its legs. The luurg, too heavy and lumberous to stop itself, careened over the edge of the cliff and hurtled down to the rocky riverside below. A sickening thud and silence signalled her success. Kjara got to her feet and stared over the cliffside at the broken heap of muscle splattered over the ground.

Harijvar, bloodied, beaten, and breathing painfully, limped his way over to join her.

"What, by the gods' design, was that thing?"

"I am told it is a luurg."

"And who told you that?"

"A quirble."

Harijvar's face scrunched in confusion, "You have some weird shit around here."

"What kinds of creatures do they have in Glainne?"

Harijvar's expression darkened, "What did you say?"

"Nothing," her heart skipped. "Never mind."

"No. Why did you mention Glainne?" Harijvar's face darkened. "You went through my things. You saw the letter, didn't you?"

"I didn't mean to. I was hungry. The letter just sort of fell out."

"And you read it."

"Only a little, I can't read so great."

"You read enough, though, didn't you?" Harijvar stood up and rubbed his forehead, quiet for the longest time. A clash of emotions churned across his face. Confusion, anger, sadness. Unexpected in the gaze of a professional killer. "Gods and piss, kid…I was starting to like you."

Kjara opened her mouth to ask him what he meant, but before she could speak, a swift shove to her chest knocked her off balance. The world around her slowed to a crawl, the ground beneath her disappeared. She fell backward clutching at nothing but air, as Harijvar and the cliff edge moved further and further away.

Chapter 44

―――――◎―――――

Kjara

Kjara's body throbbed with pain, her blurred vision clouded under a blinding sun. Running water caught in her hair. And staring back at her was the rear end of the splattered luurg. Laying on her side, limbs sprawled out, she blinked a few times and wiped the sweat from her brow. Thick and tacky to the touch, it stuck her palm to her skin. So not sweat, blood. She tried to stand, but the moment she moved her leg a sharp pain swept across it, and she cried out. Her shin was bent at an unnatural angle, and the fabric had a slight tear in it.

I've ripped my trousers, Kjara thought, still half-dazed. She dragged herself to a sitting position and leant against a rock. Every movement sent shocks of pain coursing through her leg. Cursing, she untied the rope from her ankle and tore her trouser leg up to the knee. The flesh around her shin ballooned out, bright red.

Kjara looked up, shielding her eyes from the sun directly overhead. Splatters of blood and a long, torn shred of green fabric decorated the rocks jutting out from the cliff face and caught her eye.

"Dashed against the rocks along the way. Caught by the cloak. Bounced off the luurg maybe?" Kjara said, looking at the dead thing lying on the sharp stones by the river, its limbs twisted and bent, unmoving. She swallowed and attempted to push herself up to standing again. Her leg could not take her weight, and another sharp pain rock-eted through her bones.

"Okay…definitely broken."

Kjara slumped against the rock, scanning back through her memory. There was a fight, she climbed a tree, fetched a bag. Someone else was there. The black-clad thing…Harijvar. She had said something to him…What was it?

"The letter marked from Glainne," Kjara closed her eyes and clenched her teeth. She cursed her curiosity and spat the stupidity from her mouth like rotten fruit. "Foolish. Foolish. Fool!"

Why did you have to read the letter? Why did you have to mention Glainne? The voice crawled back into her thoughts, spiteful and goad-ing. *You are going to die out here. No one will find you. You can't walk. Crawl all you like, but how far do you think you will get? The sun will go down, and the night things will come out. They will find the luurg and they will find you. A feast for ylfes with haffelin for dessert.* Kjara hung her head and closed her eyes. A heavy sensation pressed onto her neck as something crawled onto it.

"Found you!" the quirble squeaked. "Oh yuck. Head mess."

It shuffled around on her shoulders and pushed its face into her cheek. Kjara opened her eyes and stared mournfully at it, too disheart-ened to push it away.

"You were very easy to find. You hardly hid at all. Now it is your turn to find me again!" The quirble darted across the stream into the brushland west of the river. After a moment, it popped its head back up. "You're peeking! And you're not counting! You are bad at this!"

"I'm not playing" Kjara muttered. "Go away."

The quirble scurried back over to her, "You said you would play to hide with me. Oh, yes, you did."

"Just…leave me alone. Okay?" Kjara said. "I can't play. I can't even walk!" The quirble tilted its head and peered at the red lump on her shin. "Oh, you have given yourself a hurt. You are true. You cannot play if you cannot move."

"I don't want to play! I…" hot needles pricked at her eyes. "I want to go home."

"Well, if you want to go home, start by wanting your leg to be fixed."

"I *do* want it fixed!" Kjara spat.

"Not seeming to want enough, though," the quirble shrugged. "You should want harder."

Clamouring laughter burbled from the bushes beyond the stream. A tight lump formed in her throat. Kjara swallowed, but it didn't go away.

The quirble's ears tucked down against its head, "You should want faster, too. Unless you also want being food meat for ylfes. I don't want to. I will hide now!"

It scrambled up to the cliff face and curled up on a jutting rock, giving the strict appearance of a tiny shrub. The stuttering roar of the luurg must have drawn the ylfes' attention. Either that or the smell. Kjara dragged herself over to it, laying down on the far side of its corpse, away from sight. Beads of nervous sweat peppered her forehead as she clenched her fist and held her breath.

The quirble peeked its nose out at her, "No point to hide like that. You smell like blood and scared."

"What other choice do I have?" Kjara snapped.

"Your legs are big. Why don't you run?"

"I can't run, I told you. my leg is broken!"

"Then fix it," the quirble suggested plainly.

Kjara rubbed her lips and sucked in air through her nose. As stupid as it felt, she had nothing to lose by trying, no one was there for her to feel foolish. She placed her hand against the swollen lump and focused her breathing. Nothing. She removed her gloves and tried again, skin to skin directly. Still nothing. She narrowed her eyes and started humming tunelessly.

"What are you doing?" the quirble asked.

"I'm trying to fix it," Kjara hissed.

"Oh, I will help!"

The quirble leapt from its hiding place and scurried over. It placed its hands on Kjara's leg.

"Insides is pointing wrongly. Here. This helps!" it said, before driving its full weight down onto Kjara's shin, attempting to realign the fracture. Sharp splinters of bone tore through her muscles and scraped against one another. She screamed. Her eyes watered. Her head spun and nausea twisted through her body.

But then, numbness. A soft vibration shook Kjara's core, the humming sound dulled the forest noise. The running water, the wind in the trees, the heat from the sun, all of it melted away as she disappeared from herself. Inky dark curled at the edges of her vision. Breathing steadily through her teeth, she reached out and placed her hand on her shin. Then through it. Her fingers passed into her leg. A horrible thought flashed across her mind. The student who lost his fingers in the anvil. What if she lost her hand?

No. Focus. Let that moment leave your mind and come back to this one. Right here. Right now. Feel this moment.

Kjara's fingers touched something hard. They wrapped around the bone as it started adjusting, realigning itself with its broken half. The fractures repaired, the marrow knitted together. Muscles reshaped and swelling contracted. She pulled her hand back, counting five fingers, nails and all, intact. Her leg looked as it had before the fall. The markings on it pulsed and shuddered. Dark flecks clouded her vision. Warmth ran down her cheek.

Blood.

Distortion.

Kjara blinked and pushed her foot against a rock. No pain.

"Gods be…"

"Ha, see! Easy fixing when you try wanting harder," the quirble said proudly. But chittering laughter bounced across the water and interrupted its celebration.

"Eepsies! Hiding time!" the quirble squeaked. "You should go flat-wise. I'll be going upwardly. Run, Run! Make fast!" The quirble bounced away and scurried up the cliff face and out of view. "Come back to playing soon, though, yes?"

"Wait, how did you—" Kjara called out, but a volley of spears and arrows crashing around her set her feet into action. A cluster of ylfes scampered from the brush on the far side of the river.

Kjara turned and fled, more spears and arrows pelting into the sandy riverbank as she ran. She threw a look over her shoulder, but the ylfes seemed more interested in inspecting the hulking luurg corpse than chasing her. They swarmed around it, dancing horridly and belting their heads together. Not taking any chances, she continued to run as fast as she could, until her lungs stuck to her ribs and the air cut her throat, and the pain forced her to stop.

Still, Kjara kept going, following the river to the northern shoreline of the Tohl-Mor Bay. Her tattered clothes were stained with dry mud, dirt, and grass. Her hair matted with blood; her bootless foot raw from running on sharp stones. She kept moving, letting hot salty tears of determination cut channels through the filth on her face. She didn't care for herself, only for the safety of her friends. The letter in her pocket, the knowledge in her mind. The road to Thairis Brast's manor crossed the river not far from the ocean and she needed to get there. To let them know what she had discovered. Before Nine Mirrors did something irreparable.

Chapter 45

Kjara

The sun hung low in the sky, and a cool wind blew in over the ocean as Kjara approached the manor, dishevelled, weary, and determined. She beat her knuckles on the gates and wiped her brow. No response. She grabbed the handle and pulled it. The gate swung open with no sign of Garyn on the other side. No book. It was all too familiar.

Kjara stepped through the gates and along the path towards the front entrance. No guards around the grounds, none at the door. She turned the knob and stepped inside. The entry hall was silent. She approached Brast's study, books still littered the floor, blood still stained the carpet. It was almost exactly as she had left it when Harijvar had attacked.

Harijvar.

The thought of his name shot a hot bolt up the nape of Kjara's neck. She curled her lip and continued, catching scents of boiling pumpkin wafting through the corridors. She peered into the kitchen. A pot of soup rested on the stove, a fresh cut loaf of bread sat on the counter. So, someone was home. But where?

A silhouetted figure with long stiletto ears moved in the larder, gathering ingredients. Kjara held her breath and inched away from the door. She travelled down one of the halls towards the back courtyard. On the other side of the tall bay windows adorning the rear of the house, sat at the large oak table, were Naistinn Farlight and Thairis Brast. It had been moved onto the wooden decking at the back door.

Thairis Brast noticed her approach first.

"Kjara!" his face lit up with a smile, but it quickly dimmed on seeing her state. "Gods be…What has happened to you? Here, come. Have some tea."

He lifted a cup from the platter in front of him and splashed in a drop from the steaming pot. He handed it to her as she slumped into the nearest chair.

"Thank you…" Kjara mumbled, drawing the cup to her lips. She tilted her head. Her boot sat on the table not far from Thairis Brast.

Brast took the boot and placed it in front of her, "Yours, I believe."

Kjara nodded dumbly, "Yer, I…lost it. How do you have it? Where is everyone? Where are the guards?"

"They're out looking for you," Naistinn Farlight said. "Soren and Sabel are resting upstairs, sleeping off their injuries, by point of fact. Everyone else is back in town."

Kjara's stomach tingled at the mention of Sabel, but she ignored it. There were more important matters at hand.

"You aren't safe here. No one is safe."

"It's okay, Kjara," Thairis Brast offered a comforting smile. "Everyone is safe. The carver has been captured. Locked away in the guardhouse, awaiting sentence. Captain Deonto and Harwin are following up on information we'd obtained on your whereabouts. I should send Garyn to fetch them, being that you have found your way back to us."

Kjara shook her head. Was it too much time in the sun? Not enough food? Nothing made sense.

"No. That's not right," she said. "He's not been caught. He can't have been."

"You're overtired, Kjara" Naistinn Farlight said. "Stressed from these past days. I understand, it's been a trying time for all of us. But the carver has been caught. Captain Deonto put her in the lockup herself."

"I must say. It was a bold move. Masquerading as an emissary of Glainne," Thairis Brast said, stroking his moustache. "They should have her talking soon. And we'll know who sent her. I have some serious words to say to that person."

"That person…" Kjara echoed.

Nine Mirrors. Nine Mirrors was that person. A terrible sinking feeling dragged through her guts. Her eyes widened. Her tongue stuck in her mouth, too afraid to ask the question because she already knew the answer.

She cleared her throat and forced it out, "Who told you all of this?"

Nine Mirrors did.

"Nine Mirrors did," Naistinn Farlight explained. "She was distraught that you had been taken. When they took Zyela in for questioning, she revealed you had been put in a wheat silo east of here. That is where they have gone."

"It was quite a fight we were told," Thairis Brast continued. "I have to admit I am impressed you managed to escape losing no more than your shoe. Some of the other guards were not so lucky. But it's okay. Alba is tending to them."

"She's lying to you," Kjara said. "All of it. It's all lies."

Thairis Brast's brow furrowed, "Lying?"

"I've known Nine Mirrors all my life, Kjara," Naistinn Farlight sat her tea down on the table. "She has always been loyal to me and my family."

Kjara straightened in her chair, "The carver is a man. Not a woman. I know he is. He kidnapped me and took me to the forest. Not a wheat silo. Nine Mirrors wants you both dead. The carver is working for her."

A stunned silence hung in the air as Thairis Brast and Naistinn Farlight processed Kjara's claim.

"That's quite a tale," announced a voice from behind her. Nine Mirrors, holding a long platter with three bowls of soup and toasted bread, stepped up to the table and placed it down. "Dinner is ready, everyone. Apologies, Kjara. I didn't realise you would be joining us. I've not served any for you." Nine Mirrors took a seat opposite her and passed out the bowls. "You can have mine if you like. You look terribly hungry."

Kjara pushed it away, staring daggers at the faeduin woman.

"I see..." Nine Mirrors said. "Perhaps you've been spending too much time with Father Roce. Or perhaps it is just my sense of humour because I do not find this prank amusing. I find it rather in bad taste."

"I have proof."

Nine Mirrors stiffened. Fear flickered behind her blue eyes, hidden behind her fake smile. But she couldn't hide from the truth.

"Proof?"

"A letter stamped with the seal of Glainne," confidence lifted Kjara's voice. "Found on the carver's personal items—"

"That confirms Glainne is the party responsible," Nine Mirrors placed her hand on the table.

"Written in your handwriting," Kjara finished.

Confess.

"And you have this letter?" Thairis Brast asked.

"I do," Kjara said, reaching into her pocket, but her hand found nothing.

The letter had vanished. *The quirble. It must have stolen it from me. To keep me playing its silly game.* Kjara's hand trembled, and her mouth dried out. Her eyes remained locked on Nine Mirrors, but their ferocity faded. She had overplayed her hand to the most dangerous woman she'd ever met and convinced no one of her duplicity. Her one shot. And she'd missed.

"Kjara Chedderheart," Nine Mirrors began. "You are a bright girl, but you are too eager to flaunt your knowledge. I'm afraid, innocent child, that you have become tangled up in something beyond your standing. And it has gotten you killed."

Nine Mirrors spread her fingers across the table, and the timber warped, restraining Kjara, Farlight, and Brast.

"Nine Mirrors, what are you doing?" Naistinn Farlight demanded. "Stop this at once."

Nine Mirrors scoffed, "I tried to stop this, Loreena. But you didn't listen to me. I counselled you against your wild ideas, time and time again. But you refused to heed my warnings."

"Nine Mirrors, listen—"

"No. You listen. You are not fit to rule my country. Neither of you are," Nine Mirrors reached into her pocket and held out a glimmering metal object. With a hum, it enlarged in her hand. A polished trident, six feet in length. "Fortunately, Glainne has sent me a solution more elegant than I had originally planned. The instrument of my country's salvation. Regrettably, Zyela will die for giving me this gift. As will all of you."

Loreena's eyes quivered in panic, "Nine Mirrors, please do not do this. This is not how you protect Cradh. You will send us to war with Glainne."

*War...*Images of Kjara's home overtook her. The farm, the river, her room. Calarin, her warmth and easy smile. Chester. Mutton.

Who falls first when they march on Bhaile Cala, Kjara?

The image of Papa Roce, his potbelly, his flower-stuffed beard.

He saved Thairis Brast. Tended to his wounds. Will that effort be wasted?

"It would be better to have a country united by war than torn apart by weakness," Nine Mirrors growled. "But when I present my people the head of Zyela Rivermane and negotiate a peace with Glainne, they will understand that I should be the one who leads."

"That's what this is about?" Loreena's eyes darted about in confusion and torment.

Nine Mirrors glared, a mix of anger and pain, "I am sick of counselling you against poor decisions, only to be ignored. Sick of watching you choose your interests over that of the nation. I am sick of fighting with you, Loreena. Farewell, my stubborn young friend."

The image of Soren and his dour expression. How quickly she'd misjudged him, but in the days she'd spent with him, he'd proven himself not foe but friend.

He slew the fiedrig, he fought the carver. Will he be forced to fight again, to bleed out on some battlefield?

"Nine Mirrors, you monster! I will see you hanged for this!" Thairis Brast bellowed, fighting against the warped wood that bound him to his chair. Nine Mirrors turned, smiling at his attempts.

The image of Captain Deonto and her razor eyebrows.

She could have let you serve your sentence in a cell. But she didn't. She offered you a key, she gave up her time to teach you.

The image of Harwin, his upbeat attitude, his belly scar.

How many scars do you get fighting a war?

"Be silent, you wretched old man," Nine Mirrors spat. "Be patient. You will be the last I take. Kjara, you do not need to see this. I will spare you the sight of their deaths by taking you first."

"Nine Mirrors, stop!" Loreena pleaded. "Please don't do this!"

"Quiet," Nine Mirrors ordered, swinging the trident around with a heavy crack against Loreena's temple. The white opal fell from her crown and rolled off the table. Nine Mirrors spun and faced Kjara.

She barely noticed, too fixated on the dented circlet crown pressing into Loreena's temple, on the blood trickling from it.

The image of Sabel, her sly eyes, red hair, and stupid, pretty face.

She tried to help you, tried to save you. With no promise of compensation.

A turmoil of emotions bubbled in Kjara's gut. Another image. Her father, Mado, his messy crop of hair and his terrible jokes, fashioning a ridiculous puppet from an apple and a cheesecloth.

Aren't you worried?

It doesn't matter. It's not about me, is it?

Kjara swallowed. Her eyes itched a threat of tears.

Are you going to let this happen?

A numbness overtook Kjara. Something pulled her out of her body, away from it. Somewhere far, far away. And yet she stayed connected to it. Her vision started to blur, the ringing in her ears shifting into a deep humming. It vibrated down through her fingers and toes and radiated out, shaking her form.

Her eye twitched. A hum resonated in her skull. She kicked her foot up into the table and struck with a pulse that shattered the gnarled wood into pieces around her. Nine Mirrors lunged forward with the trident, but Kjara dropped to the floor. The metal prongs dug into the high-backed chair. Fighter's fire blasted blood through Kjara's eardrums as Nine Mirrors whipped around and drove the trident for her haffelin heart. Kjara rolled to one side and got to her feet, sniffing blood from her nose.

Nine Mirrors scowled and dropped to one knee, spreading her fingers out on the deck. The floorboards beneath Kjara twisted and stretched curling themselves around her feet. Her heart pounded. Her brain hummed.

"Be still, girl. You have no idea what you are doing. You will destroy yourself."

"Maybe…" Kjara clenched her jaw with determination. "But it's not about me."

Kjara ripped her foot from her shoe and stomped it into the ground with an explosion of wooden splinters. Her eye spat crimson tears, and she lunged forward, driving her palms into the edge of the table. The table rippled, splintering into pieces around Loreena and Brast. Nine Mirrors hummed and attempted to reshape the wood, blood prickling from her cheeks. Kjara smashed it again, the markings on her body flashing brightly on impact.

"Loreena. Run!" Brast yelled, taking a running tackle at Nine Mirrors. His shoulder slammed into her sternum, and she tumbled back, dropping the trident. Brast pinned Nine Mirrors to the ground, and she slammed a knee into his gut. A red stain formed on his shirt, but he refused to relent.

"No!" Nine Mirrors growled, as Loreena ran for the door to the manor. She reached out and grabbed the trident. The handle elongated in a flash, extending the prongs across the deck to thrust violently into Loreena's back. Her arms and legs went limp, and her head dropped to her chest.

A curdling, sorrowful scream tore its way out of Brast's lungs as Nine Mirrors retracted the trident with a wet, stomach-churning squelch. Loreena fell with a heavy thud, her gown soaking with blood.

Then, silence.

Dead silence.

A thick blanket of shock covered Kjara with a sickening paralysis. It clung to the air. To her skin, her clothes. Everything was muted, distant. Everything was somewhere else. It wasn't happening.

Not here. Not now.

Kjara turned her head, her vision trailing behind her movements. Brast laid on the ground, reaching out to Loreena. He crawled towards her, streaking the deck with blood and tears. He didn't see it coming.

Didn't feel a thing. Nine Mirrors rose behind him, aiming the trident for his head.

She drove it through his skull. Straight through it. Like it wasn't even there.

Confused, Nine Mirrors struck again. Nothing. Not a scratch. Not a sound. She glared at Kjara. Kjara glared back. Splayed out on the deck, blood and tears spilling down her face—focused and fierce—Kjara glowered, matching her gaze. The faeduin's blue eyes stretched out in terror, panic pooling tears at their edges.

What is that sound? Do you hear it?

She's gasping. Why is she gasping?

What are you doing, Kjara?

Nine Mirrors fell to her knees, dropping the trident and clutching at her neck. Her eyelids fluttered sluggishly before falling shut. Her body collapsed.

Kjara...that's enough. Stop. Now. She's not a threat anymore. If you keep going, she'll die. That's not what you want. Go and see to Loreena.

Kjara shook her head, a thick cloud obscuring her thoughts. She staggered to Loreena's body and rolled it over. So much blood. From somewhere deep and distant, Brast's voice called her name. She lifted one hand to silence him. It was a foolish idea. A dangerous idea. But it was prudent.

Kjara placed her hands over Loreena's chest. Blood stained her fingers and stuck them to the gown. She focused her eyes, deepened her breathing. The hum rose, cacophonous in her eardrums. The edges of her vision darkened. Vibrations pulled her out of herself. The cloth on her skin, the surrounding air, ground, weight, and time itself distorted. Kjara could no longer tell where she ended, and everything else began. Sweat stung her eyes, but it was a distant irritation; it belonged to someone else. Her face reddened. Her body shook. The veins in her temples flared and burst. The capillaries in her eyes ruptured. But still, she focused; still, she sang out. The markings on her arms radiated a heat that scorched her clothes, leaving a singed shadow of their patterns. The pain was a distant memory, not something she could even understand now.

Connection. Pure connection to everything.

No distinction, no separation.

Kjara didn't feel her skin tearing. Kjara didn't feel the blood pouring from her eye. She didn't feel the breaching or the rupturing or the collapse. She couldn't tell when everything went black. She couldn't feel her body hit the floor. She couldn't feel the hands that shook her shoulders. She couldn't hear her name being called.

Kjara wasn't there for any of it.

Kjara was gone.

Chapter 46

The worlds that overlapped gave birth to yours,
An unexpected side effect they got.
An accident by those who build it all,
Though purpose lacking, faulty it is not.
All things were made with predetermined zeal,
Except for this, you are completely free.
And just imagine how it makes us feel,
We're burdened with intentionality.
If struggling for meaning gives you pain,
Remember, you can choose what you will be.
You are a beautiful new accident,
With freedom, we could never hope to see.

The possibilities you do not lack,
Composers took them from you, take them back.

Chapter 47

Kjara

Another unfamiliar ceiling. Kjara lay on cool silken sheets, a soft mattress. A slight breeze came in from an open window. And pain. Her leg hurt, her shoulder hurt, her everything hurt. She sat up and took in her surroundings. Everything looked off, somehow. Flatter.

A large wardrobe with ornately carved patterns and a central full-length mirror stood against the wall by the window. Kjara swung her legs out of bed, dangling them a foot or so off the carpet. Clean white bandages wrapped around her right shin. All the scratches from the fall had been cleaned and the larger ones dressed.

A pair of soft, wool-lined shoes sat neatly on the floor by her feet. Kjara dropped down uneasily, having difficulty judging the distance. A blue linen shirt hung down past her knees. She held out her arms, smiling at the sleeves drooping down over her hands, like a hollowed-out pair of snouts. She moved her arms around and smiled briefly. A mohra's shirt, hanging off her like bedsheets. She tried on the shoes, but they were too big for her and made it impossible to walk. It was a kind gesture, whoever had left them, but sadly useless.

Kjara walked across the floor, the carpet cold under her feet, and stood in front of the mirror. Her hair had been cleaned, no mud, no blood. Tiny cuts and abrasions covered her face. Bandages wrapped around her head and over her right eye.

That's why everything looks weird, Kjara thought.

Kjara unbuttoned the top of her shirt and slid it down over her shoulder. The arrow wound had been dressed as well. As she readjusted the shirt, her mind struggled to recall events but found only worry.

Gods be. I don't remember anything.

A wave of anxiety and confusion passed over her, transforming into a low hum in her ears. She pushed it down and shook her head, then walked over to the bay windows on the east wall. An orchard. And beyond the wall behind it, a vast blue blanket stretching to the horizon. Brast's manor.

The smell of salt and water carried into the room on the breeze and rustled the curtains. Kjara leant on her elbows against the window frame. Another odour captured her attention and her stomach gurgled violently in her guts. Fried eggs, potatoes, burning butter, mushrooms, and garlic. How long had it been since she'd eaten? By her recollection, her last meal was…potato and eggplant galette…No, almonds. A handful of almonds.

Any rest Kjara had gotten from the sleep was offset by the hunger that clawed at her insides. The kind of hunger that made one forget oneself. She moved towards the door but, hearing footsteps from the other side, spun and dove under the bed. The door opened, and a pair of legs wearing soft-shoes strode into the room. Warm breakfast smells wafted in and filled the air.

"Kjara, are you awake?" asked a deep, warm voice. The voice of a man well versed in conversation and accustomed to being heard. Feet stepped over to the side of the bed. Wood rubbed against wood as a carrying tray slid onto the side dresser. Metal cutlery tinged together. "Kjara?"

"I'm down here," Kjara replied sheepishly.

Brast's bald head and fine moustache dropped below the frame of the bed and into view. A warm smile spread across his face.

"If you prefer, you can take your breakfast down there, but it will make it hard to talk to you. If you feel up for conversation?"

Aware of how childish Kjara must look cowering under the bed, she nodded sheepishly. She crawled back out, and up into the sheets. Brast collected a chair from the corner of the room and sat down opposite, picking up one of the plates of food from the tray. Kjara grabbed the other. Saliva drowned her tongue as she drove a fork into one of the mushrooms.

No point hiding anymore, Kjara thought, looking at the markings on the back of her hand.

"A word of caution. Don't eat too fast. Heavy injury can upset the stomach. Here, drink some tea first. To settle yourself," he said, pouring her a cup from the pot. "Ginger and lemon."

"Home-grown?" Kjara asked, lowering her fork.

"Of course."

Kjara tried to follow Brast's advice to eat slowly but made it through two mouthfuls before she picked her pace up. Brast smiled knowingly but let her continue in silence. He placed his plate on the bed and stood up, walked to the cupboard and collected something. She was too focused on her meal to waste valuable chewing time on questions.

The first few mouthfuls of food hit Kjara's stomach with no resistance, but her face turned a sickly pale after mouthful number four. Her body disrespectfully refused her offerings and shot them straight back up her gullet. Brast held out a bucket as, head throbbing and swirling, she emptied her breakfast into it.

"That is a cruel joke, body," she moaned. "Begging me to feed you and changing your mind so horridly."

Brast chuckled, "Yes. It is. Tea?"

Kjara resigned herself to drinking the tea with one hand and popping slices of mushroom into her mouth with the other. She sat in silence for a time, before Brast spoke again.

"What do you remember?"

"Not much. My head hurts."

Brast nodded sympathetically, "I'm not surprised."

"Everything looks weird."

Brast's smiled faded, "I'd imagine it does."

"What happened?"

Brast rubbed his chin, "You saved us, Kjara. You discovered Nine Mirrors' duplicity. You came here to warn us. She took your gesture...unfavourably. She intended to kill us, Loreena, me, you. And you stopped her."

"I did?"

"Yes. I mean...I helped. A little," Brast said, attempting to lighten the mood. "Popped a few stitches for my trouble. Much to Alba's frustration."

"I stopped her...How?"

"That is the same question I have."

Silence.

"Where is she now?"

"Lockup. Bound and gagged. She's proven herself rather slippery. I had Soren fetch Captain Deonto after the attack. She's under close watch. We have guards posted up there and here, in case the carver tries again. Or attempts to free her. Any of the guards we can spare we have combing the forest, the coast, anywhere the carver might be hiding. It won't take long for him to learn of Nine Mirrors' capture. Once he finds out his benefactor has been imprisoned and won't be paying out his contract, he'll turn to the wind as well. I'd like to catch him before that happens. But I'm not holding my breath."

Kjara groaned and buried her head in her hands.

"What is it?"

"I had my writing book in my haversack," her eyebrows folded into forlorn waves. "And another book I borrowed from The Trove. They were in my haversack and now they're gone."

"You took a book from the trove?"

"Yes. *Neither Here nor There.*"

"By V.S. Crane," Brast said. "A very interesting read, that one."

"You've read it?"

"It's a personal favourite of mine," Brast glanced at the markings on her hands. "I dare say you'll find it as interesting as I did."

Kjara subtly tucked her hands under the bedsheets, "The old watchtower southwest of Bhaile Cala. That's where the carver took me, and where I lost my haversack."

"Ah. A smart place to hide," Thairis Brast stroked his moustache. "Maybe we'll get lucky. I'll send someone to investigate. Might even find your books."

"What's going to happen to Nine Mirrors?"

"Life imprisonment at best, execution at worst," Brast shrugged. "I would counsel Loreena to choose the former, but she is in quite a state right now and may want for the latter."

"Execution…" Kjara swallowed uncomfortably. "I didn't think the naistinn would be like that."

"She's not. But betrayal is a heavy pain. And when tempered with anger, it can crush all compassion," Brast smiled wearily. "She needs time to process everything. I'll make sure she gets it. No one is above mistakes when they act faster than they think."

"Even you?"

"Especially me. I was too quick to trust Nine Mirrors, and not think for myself. She did such a thorough job of weaving her lies that I suspected an emissary of Glainne to be responsible for all of these events. She's okay by the way. Zyela. We found her out in the stables.

Tied up and hidden in the back of Loreena's stagecoach. Nine Mirrors fancied herself a better naistinn and planned to pin the discreation on Zyela, then use her execution to stop a war between Cradh and Glainne, thereby gaining the love of the people."

"I think I remember that."

"Good. Hopefully, your mind is undamaged, and your memory starts to return. We were worried. Weren't sure if you'd make it back to us," Brast leant back in his chair, crossing his fingers over his portly stomach. "Zyela told me about what happened, by the way."

"You mean the fact that she attacked me?"

"Not quite the same story as you tell it then. No, she told me to watch out for the haffelin impostor who passed through walls like they were water. She told me about your little lie, as well. You claimed to work for me. Told her you were my advisory."

Her cheeks flushed red, "I'm sorry...I just—I wanted to know."

"You just wanted to know...I understand that urge quite well," Thairis Brast tapped his thumbs together in thought. "Is that something you would be interested in?"

"What do you mean? Knowing?"

"Working for me," Thairis Brast clarified. "Is that something you would want to do?"

Overwhelming emotions churned Kjara's chest. She didn't know how to advise a Thairis or anything about politics. But on the other hand, it would be good practice. She'd need to read about histories, laws. And Brast's study held an abundance of books. There may be other things in there as well, important things. After all, he was a man of curious, obscure tastes.

"Geov...Thairis Brast, I would be honoured."

"Excellent," Brast smiled. "With my injuries, it will be difficult to keep my garden manicured and cared for. It will be helpful to have some assistance from a proven farmhand."

Kjara's heart sank. A gardening job, that was what he was offering. The disappointment was written on her face.

"What's the matter?"

Not wanting to appear ungrateful, Kjara took the first lie she could think of, "I would need to ask my parents. They might say no."

Brast nodded, "You have a point. We should speak with them first. Once everything has settled down here, we will go visit. I did promise Loreena I would take her to your farm. It will be a nice change of pace from being housebound," Brast stood up and cleared the breakfast plates. He picked up the tray and headed to the door. "You just rest up for now. If you need anything, I won't be far."

"Thank you."

"Oh, one other thing," he said, producing a small book. "A bit of light reading for you while you are resting."

He placed it on the bed by her side and left the room. Kjara picked it up, flicked through a few pages. Nine Mirrors' calibration journal. Her vision was still too unfocused to read anything. The distant hum started again, blocking her ears. Kjara tried yawning, but it didn't work. A strong gust of wind slammed the window shut. She threw off the sheets and moved towards it, passing by the mirror in the wardrobe. She paused, looking at her reflection. Something was off. Under her bandages.

Kjara leant in and peeled back the bandage over her right eye. Confused, she raised one hand to her right cheek and pulled balled-up cotton from the socket.

Sacrifice... The memory of Kjara's conversation with Nine Mirrors replayed in her thoughts. *That is what it means to do one's duty, giving up something of yourself for others. Cradh is my home. I would do anything to protect it.* For what seemed like the longest time, Kjara stared at her reflection. Gazing into the dark hollow space below her right eyebrow. And when at last she finally processed what she saw, she laughed.

It was a long, uncontrollable laugh that filled the room with forlorn air. And Kjara buried her face in her hand, the giggling gasps becoming whimpers of grief.

Chapter 48

―――――⊚―――――

Kjara

Assigned by Captain Deonto, Harwin and the other guards swept the forest for any sign of the black-clad carver. They didn't succeed. Brast concluded that he must have gone to ground or given up, and no longer considered him a threat. Harwin did, however, find Kjara's haversack, and returned it to her with an extra gift inside: a fine leather eyepatch, designed by Ionesco, very expensive and ornate. Too expensive for just Harwin alone to afford.

"Sabel paid for most of it," he told her.

Kjara tilted her head, confused, "Why?"

"It's her way of apologising, I guess."

Kjara held the eye patch in her hands, running her thumb over the fine stitching, and avoiding eye contact, "That's foolish. None of this was her fault."

"I agree. But she doesn't feel the same. She regrets walking away that night. After your argument. Reckons if she had stayed with you, or talked it out, you might not have been grabbed."

"Thank you...both of you," Kjara said with a solemn, earnest smile.

"You're welcome," Harwin smiled back, and Kjara waited in that silent moment for as long as they both could bear. Words that could have been said remained unsaid, questions unanswered, until eventually, Harwin spoke.

"I should be off. The captain has me paired up with Treun Rivermane. She asked for some help in tracking down the missing messengers."

Stay.

"Or what's left of them."

"Yer," Harwin nodded grimly, "but she's duty-bound to return their bodies to Glainne for a proper burial. And I'm happy to assist."

"Does that mean you're back on patrol permanently?"

"Sure does," Harwin beamed. "The captain's been in a positive mood ever since Rosalind woke back up. So, I'll not rock the boat."

"That's good," Kjara slumped. "Papa says I have to stay resting. It'll be a while before I can even do light duties."

"Light duties? After this, you're still paying off your debt?"

"I promised to pay off my debt with time, and that's what I intend to do," Kjara explained. "After that, I'll start working for Brast. As long as my parents agree."

"Well, I'll try to have enough fun out there for both of us," he smirked. "Perhaps I'll drop by with some paperwork you can write out for me."

"How kind of you," Kjara shot back.

Just stay. You don't need to go.

"That's me, to a tee!" Harwin replied cheekily. "Rest well, Cheddersneak."

Harwin stood up and stepped through the door, closing it softly behind him. But the sound of it could have been an earthquake, compared to the silence he left behind. Kjara sighed and stared at the ceiling before placing her eye patch on the dresser and sliding two books from her haversack. Putting her writing journal aside, she opened up

Neither Here nor There and read aloud, her quiet voice tripping over the inky words.

Chapter 49

Papa

The next few days carried an alert but relaxed atmosphere. For most, life returned to normal, or as close as it could get. Papa had temporarily—and reluctantly—taken over Rosalind's Medicary duties. Although she struggled to walk and talk, he assured her it would be temporary. With enough rest and rehabilitation, she would be back to her regular self again.

The first opportunity he could, Papa struck out for The Eyeglass. He flung himself down onto the hard, wooden chair on the deck and sighed with relief. It was just as uncomfortable as he'd left it, and the pain it pushed into his back had only one cure. Beer.

"That's a familiar sound."

"Ayleth, by Fyaldha, it is good to see you!" Papa exclaimed, foraging through his pocket and dropping a handful of coin on the table. "I am in dire need. I've been working up a mighty thirst."

"Working, you say?" Ayleth laughed. "I'll believe that when I see it."

"It's true!" Papa pouted. "Here, fetch me a glass or two—and one for yourself—and join me. I'll tell you all about it!"

Over a few hours, Papa, with increasing enthusiasm and exaggeration, regaled the whole adventure to her. Naturally, he overstated his involvement. Ayleth followed along politely, cutting the perfect shape of an enchanted audience. He began detailing his courageous efforts to save Rosalind, but a loud, obnoxious voice broke his rhythm.

"Roce? Father Roce! There you are!" Peer Darys chirped. "I've been looking all over for you."

Papa rolled his eyes nearly clean out of his head, "Well, lucky for you, your looking is all over. You found me. Now it's my turn to seek, so you should go hide."

"We need your help at the commune. There's been an injury."

"What's that, then?"

"Some farmer fellow," Darys explained. "We found him collapsed on the side of the road, just past the old watchtower. We've set him up in a bed, but he needs a proper looking over."

Papa raised a bemused eyebrow, "What's wrong with him?"

"Kicked by a mule," Darys answered. "He's having trouble breathing and all."

"Cosmic justice," Papa chuckled. "Serves the ass right for being at the ass end."

"Papa…" Ayleth chastised.

Papa let out a dramatic groan and slapped his glass on the table, "Alright, fine."

"Thank you, Father," Darys bowed gratefully.

"Yer, yer," Papa said, staggering down the stairs. "Oi, have you got any coin?"

"Yes…Why?"

"Because mine ran out an hour ago," Papa patted Darys on the shoulder. "Settle my bill, would you?"

Darys sighed and began counting out his coins.

"Fyaldha thanks you for your contribution!" Papa called back after him. "Hurry up, null. There's work to be done!"

Chapter 50

◎

Kjara

True to his word, when Thairis Brast was well enough to travel, he and Loreena joined Kjara on a stagecoach ride to the Chedderheart farm. Mado proudly showed them around, answering endless cheese-based questions from Loreena. Her eagerness to understand all the farm's inner workings put a smile on Kjara's face, but she didn't listen. She already knew all the answers.

When Mado and Calarin questioned Brast about Kjara's eye, he expressed sincere remorse and extreme gratitude.

"She saved my life," he said. "She saved my life and Loreena's life. There is nothing I can offer that will ever make up for what she has done for us. And what it has cost her."

Although they tried their best to hide it, the sadness behind Mado and Calarin's eyes shone through. But equally so did their understanding. When Brast broached the subject of Kjara working for him, Mado and Calarin shared a look of scepticism.

"Our daughter working for the region master, what an idea!" Calarin exclaimed.

"Please, don't consider my ranking, only the job," Brast replied. "I understand if you say no. It is a lot of responsibility. And more time away from your daughter."

"Responsibility?" Calarin laughed. "Kjara?"

"I'll send my wages home," Kjara said. "So you can pay for another farmhand."

Kjara's suggestion silenced Calarin, and all she could do was stare. Mado leant over to her. "And you said my plan wouldn't work. I'd say it's worked all too well; wouldn't you agree?" He took more credit for Kjara's attitude than she perhaps would have agreed with, but she remained silent on the matter. It was nice to see them again, and she didn't want to spoil the mood by arguing.

"If you think you can cope with her," Calarin said to Brast. "Then fortunate you. Consider the offer accepted. Permission granted, Kjara."

Kjara's heart swelled with gratitude.

Being home felt good after all that had happened. It felt safe. After reuniting with Mutton, Kjara played fetch, soaking in the relaxing smells of the farmlands and the warmth of the sun. Loreena joined in and played in silence for a while. Mado, Calarin, and Brast sat together at the rear of the Chedderheart farmhouse. Frequent laughter rolled across the fields. Occasionally, Kjara caught them looking at Loreena and her.

"What do you think they're talking about?" Loreena asked.

Kjara shrugged, "Cheese, wine, weather? Whatever it is that old folks like to chatter about."

"Your farm is fantastic, Kjara, fascinatingly fantastic. This here," Loreena said, holding up Mutton's stick. "It's exactly what I needed."

Kjara smiled, "You don't miss the capital? You don't miss your people?"

Loreena laughed and threw the stick, "How could I? My people are right here."

Your people are right here.

Mutton belted across the grass and slobbered up the stick with a playful growl, before running it back to Kjara. Her turn to throw the stick.

"So…What do you plan to do with Nine Mirrors?"

"She will be sent back to the capital," Loreena answered shortly. "To serve out the remainder of her natural life in prison."

"You're not going to execute her?"

"Why? Do you think I should?" Loreena shook her head. "I'm not going to execute her. There's no point…I mean, it might make me feel better, but not for long." Mutton returned the stick to her. "Execution feels almost petty, small. I don't want to be that kind of leader. I don't want to be that kind of person. For better or worse, she gets to live."

The light in Loreena's eyes dimmed. Kjara had reminded her of the very thing she was trying to forget.

C'mon," Kjara said, collecting the stick. "I'll show you the view from the top."

Kjara took Loreena up the steep hills that bordered the Chedderheart farm. The view from the top was expansive, beautiful, and familiar. Kjara sighed in contentment, taking in the sights and smells. Warm air, with a mixture of cow dander, manure, grass, and the unique tang of intentionally curdling milk. The pastures stretched out before them, dotted with cows, goats, and sheep. The metal roofs of the farmhouse, stables, and the processing and ageing house reflected the sun like beacons. Loreena stepped up beside her, holding up the hem of her ankle-length skirt.

"This is stunning."

"Yer, it is. This is home. The best view of the farm is from this hill. See? There's the ageing house, the farmhouse, the stable."

"Is that blue line the ocean?"

"Yer. And if you look that way," Kjara pointed, "that's the Over-bite. Where Thairis Brast's manor is. If you can see it from here."

Loreena leant forward with a squint but stepped into a soft splotch of manure. She slipped and nearly lost her footing entirely.

"Cow pats. Watch yourself."

Loreena scanned the hilltop, "There's so much of it."

"It's a nice view for haffelins," Kjara shrugged. "But it's a nice view for the cows too. And they are far less shy with their expulsions."

"How do you keep from stepping in it?"

"Practice. A lot of trial and error. One time, I was bringing a basket of fresh-washed sheets back from the river, and I slipped. Fell all the way from the top. Stopped at the bottom, covered in grass stains. And manure. Mum marched me right back to the river and made me re-wash every item. Even the ones that hadn't been soiled."

"There's a river?"

"Yer. Just on the other side of the hill."

"Can I see it?"

"Of course."

Passing through the tall grass and low hanging branches, Kjara led Loreena through the brush and into a gully. It opened up into a long flat sandy stretch of stones with a crystal-blue river passing through it. Tree roots twisted out from the dirt embankment on either side. A few larger rocks and pieces of driftwood peppered the shore.

"Here it is. This is where we come to wash our things. And our-selves."

Loreena gazed in appreciation, "The water is so clear. It's almost invisible!"

"It's rainwater," Kjara explained. "Comes down from the moun-tains just south of here. It gets saltier further north when it hits the ocean. But here it's all fresh."

Loreena wiped the sweat from her forehead and smiled at Kjara, "I'm going in."

Dashing to the bank, Loreena threw off her shoes. She hitched up her skirt and waded out until the water was up to her knees. At the river's edge, Kjara stuffed her socks into her boots and placed them on a nearby rock. She rolled up her trousers to the knee, her sleeves to the elbow, and stepped out into the water.

CODA

Kjara stepped from rock to rock, ducking under tree branches and hopping over vines, careful not to trip. Kneeling, she searched for the narrow passage between the stones that lead into the cave system beneath the Timelong Mountains. Squeezing her way through, she lit a torch and weaved through the dripstone pillars until she found the underground river. She continued along, keeping the torch over her head and her eye on the ground, scanning for the shimmering of metal buttons caught between the rocks. It wasn't far, but it wasn't easy, and you could get lost if you didn't know the way. But she knew the way. She'd memorised every inch of the journey.

The tunnel opened up into a natural limestone cavern with a hidden rockpool, littered with gold coins piled into a small mountain. Kjara's wet footsteps bounced off the cavern walls as she moved across to the pool. She swallowed nervously as the tapered snout and long neck of Azmariliz snaked its way out of the water.

"Hello, Kjara, you have returned. It is good to see you again."

Its warm rumble of a voice sent a shiver down Kjara's spine. Being in its presence instilled a feeling of unease. Not the instinctual sense of fear one might expect, but a lack of it, she should have been afraid but wasn't.

"You were successful."

Kjara nodded, "Your vision was true, the naistinn was attacked. We saved her."

"But there was a cost," Azmariliz said, cocking its head.

"There was," Kjara adjusted her eyepatch. "I tried to do something beyond my reach."

"Nothing is beyond your reach."

Kjara steadied herself, "What am I? Why can I perform calibration with no training?"

Azmariliz let out a soft chuckle, "Calibration, little haffelin, it is just a parlour trick. The last scraps of a long-forgotten gift, taken from those who abused the offering. It is limited. You are not. You are capable of so much more. You can make your desires a reality, no matter what you want."

The spiral patterns on Kjara's hand swirled in the flame light. The hum resonated in her ears as the fire danced around her forearm, synchronising with her markings.

"Show me."

Acknowledgements

Before trying to write a book myself, I'd always thought that they were written by an author. Singular. As in one person.

I was wrong. So, so, so wrong.

There is a literal busload of people who contributed to making this thing in your hand a reality and it would be criminal to take all the credit for myself. The hundreds of storytellers I've encountered in my life notwithstanding, this book could not exist without Rowan and the team at Vulpine Press. They saw something in my work that resonated, and were confident enough to take it on. It's one thing to hear my writing is good, it is another feeling altogether when someone is willing to invest in it financially.

But this story would not be possible at all without the help and feedback of my family, my friends, my students and beta-readers. A big thank you to all the Speculative Fiction Bison in my writing group for being my kind of weird, to Mountain Ash Chapter for your support, and to C.K Malone and Jenny R for your phenomenal feedback. Shout outs also to Joey BS, Zac BS, Mark F, Scott F, Matt W, Adam P, Phil V and Andrew F for being my cheer squad and my inspiration. Mum and Dad, you get a 'thank you' too, for letting me lose myself in the library, and find myself in books.

The biggest 'thank you' I have saved for my wife, Toni, for pushing me beyond ordinary writing. At every turn, she saved me from the trap of mediocrity. She forced me to consider better plot points, stronger character choices, and alternative perspectives. If this story is worth anything as a work of literature, it is because of her refusal to let me get away with 'good enough'. She helped me to create something that I am truly proud of. And thank you to my son, Quinn, for sleeping soundly while she read it aloud to me and pointed out all the problems with it. (Hey Quinn, did you know the first book we ever read to you is technically this one?)

Finally, no book is complete if left unread, so if you have made it to the end...

Thank you, too.

And I'll see you for the next one,

Kel

Kel White is a lifelong lover of story and song, so it seemed natural that after years spent making music he would turn his hand to writing novels. When not hunched over a keyboard, he can be found working as teacher in Melbourne, or out in the wild with his wife and son.

You can follow him on Twitter and Instagram @kelwhitehere or visit his website, www.kelwhite.com